PALE HARVEST

A novel by
Braden Hepner

TORREY HOUSE PRESS, LLC

THp

SALT LAKE CITY · TORREY

First Torrey House Press Edition, September 2014
Copyright © 2014 by Braden Hepner

Published by Torrey House Press, LLC
Salt Lake City, Utah
www.torreyhouse.com

International Standard Book Number: 978-1-937226-39-8
Library of Congress Control Number: 2014939590
Author photo by Ernesto
Cover image by Braden Hepner
Cover and interior design by Jeffrey Fuller, Shelfish.weebly.com

MIX
Paper from
responsible sources
FSC
www.fsc.org   FSC® C011935

To Elizabeth

PALE HARVEST

This star of heaven which descended like a meteor from the sky; which you tried to lift, but found too heavy, when you tried to move it it would not budge, and so you brought it to my feet; I made it for you, a goad and spur, and you were drawn as though to a woman.

— The Epic of Gilgamesh,
translated by N.K. Sandars

1

I N THE EXODUS WEST SOME CAME IN BORROWED WAGONS
and some pulled handcarts. Abandoned by their government,
exiled and driven by their countrymen, these pilgrims trod a
harried trail across the Midwest, seeking asylum and isolation enough to build the kingdom of God. A people proud without
reason, tormented by God, and self-chosen. In winter, mothers lay
infants without names in the frozen soil along the way and these
graves were not marked but for piles of stones placed on the mounds
to deter carrion feeders. They crossed a wild land in search of one
wilder, carrying their peculiar ways, strange doctrines, their faith,
sorrow, and hope. They crossed the mountains and arrived gaunt
and clothed in rags like a sect of vagrant scarecrows wandered from
the fields of the civilized world and come to behold a land of desert
grass and salt, their new promised land. They carried what civilization they knew, and the land, unclaimed by methods of the world
they'd fled from, was deeded according to infant law, and they tilled
the earth and planted seed and claimed it for their own. They dug
ditches and channeled water that flowed from snowbound peaks.
Their prophet foretold glory as Bridger did doom. They multiplied,
and the children of the first generation expanded their holdings.
They moved about between the mountains, uprooting sage and

planting grain, replacing desert grass with crop. They raised industry. They enlarged their borders until all land was accounted for in records they had fashioned. They built kingdom and commerce. They increased faith and wealth. Later generations lost the land, it was deeded again, lost again, most not a hundred years from the time the progenitors broke the first furrow, and it was a portion of this land that John Blair Selvedge worked now, twenty years old, without parents, unknowingly come back to the land of his forbears in the sixth generation, a diesel tractor and a shaftdriven implement with which to work, not an owner of the land, but a daily toiler of it.

The summer solstice had passed and these bright days led him toward the darkness of December. He rarely failed to notice the solstices. When he came into his adolescence and first felt the foreboding the summer solstice brought on, the subtle realization that although the days were as bright and long as they had ever been they would now begin to grow shorter and the dark would come earlier and stay longer, he did not want to go into the darkness alone without the warmth of another beside him, someone with whom to spend the crepuscule of the long evenings and the dark cold nights that would follow. This feeling of apprehension and loneliness recurred each year but had lessened as he fell farther into his solitude and his drawn out days on the farm.

On a summer night when the temperature dropped and the last light drained from the sky, this tractor work was therapeutic, meditative. The field he cut lay between the railroad tracks and the road. He was alone with the beat and hum of the swather and with the dog that followed behind, gulping down freshly killed gophers and mice spewed through the back of the machine until she puked. The machine sang a song that evoked his deeper thoughts and the vibrations beneath him shook some themes loose from others, settling them among their kind. A freight train appeared in the distance, its headlight like a slow comet. It shook by with no whistle, for there were no crossings near, and from his seat he watched the cars glide through the darkness and disappear. In the open field he felt a pull. His lights caught the reflections of feral eyes, carnal creatures slinking under the blanket of night to appease basic appetites. Were it not for the low thrum of the swather he might have held a hand out flat and watched it shake at what chaos could roil inside him, a young man, tried and found wanting, alone in this field under the black sky.

When he had done enough he left the tractor and drove the mile into town. He drove past the small park, through the town square, over the railroad tracks and to the co-op, where he took a Pepsi from the machine. From the town square a man could walk in any direction and be in the open in minutes, the open that surrounded the town and pressed it together into a bleak huddle, that reached in like tongues to the center. There was the concentration of houses on a few fragmented grids set up around the square, but the puny town proper had never warded off the tremendous open, never established itself with any conviction on the landscape, and the open threatened now to overturn what had been done, to restore what had been altered. The town had begun its demise as soon as it was called a town, and sat in its demise now, no running businesses, no fresh paint. No upkeep but the old brick church. Beyond this, fields stretched into the black open of night.

Within sight stood the house he had grown up in before his parents were killed coming back from a temple service in Willow Valley, before his move to his grandparents'. His father was thirty-eight, his mother thirty-seven, and they had left this world together. A run of premature death narrowed his father's line, his father's grandfather dead at thirty-two, his father's uncle at thirty-nine. He'd heard of others up the tree when he'd cared to listen to the old woman tell it. She told it no longer.

At four in the morning he drove his grandfather to the barn and listened to the sloppy sounds of peanut butter smacked around in a soft maw as the old man tongued it off his palate and dug it out from the recesses of his mouth. The smell of it filling the cab of the truck was a thing to hate each morning. The dog met them as they parked, wagging her tail in the darkness. Clotted blood stained her white ear and as Jack bent down and fingered the fresh tears she whined and nipped at him. The two men did their work without enthusiasm. They worked in an open-ended concrete pit with six cows above them on both sides. Stairs at the rear led to the holding pen, and the open end diverted to the tank room and front entrance, the office, and the side entrance. The milking barn was a plain cinderblock structure built into an incline of earth, painted white with red trim, a fading wooden sign announcing Blair Selvedge and Son on the front above the landing. Raccoons lived in its roof. With milking at four in the morning and again at four in the evening Blair had been married to his farm for fifty years, and there was no vow stronger than his devotion to his cows. Five hours a day these animals required, coaxing from them a spare living, and only gathering their milk at that. Everything they did on the farm led to this task, which was as much a part of their lives as eating. Before the milking was through, the faulty front gate on the east side broke open while the last of the cows still had their milkers on and the trundling fools surged forward and around the corner and, goaded on by Blair's angry yells, ran like heathens down the exit alley where they mixed with the others in the corral.

Back at the farmhouse Jack fed the heifers and when he came in Blair told him to say hello to his grandmother. The old woman had long haunted him with her stubborn presence, her waning refusal to submit to the grave. Her dim room near the staircase smelled of death's encroachment. He moved slowly, his left hand outstretched, feeling for the footpost as he sought her shape. He made out the white slits of her eyes, her hair, thin and matted like an ancient pelt, her pale face. He said hello, and when her wrinkled mouth cracked open and issued a cloud of foul breath he said it again. She murmured something. The haze of her breath and the smell of bitter beads of sweat along her hairline caused his mouth to tighten. He took a step back and watched her. Her mouth opened farther, then closed, then opened, as if he had roused some cave creature in its death throes. He left her there gaping.

In the kitchen Blair stood over the stove, a tall man, taller than Jack's six feet by a few inches and thickening from the toes up, his body building to a neck that rose in a straight line up the back of his head, and that line rising farther through the rooster tail that ever shot up from his stiff white hair. His face was gritworn from wind-driven dirt, everlastingly tanned and deeply lined like the palms of his cowhide gloves. That was a face well worn, or badly worn, those great wrinkles. There were men in town who had their occupations in Willow Valley thirty miles away whose hands didn't know callus, whose faces were soft and kindly worn with wrinkles like those found behind a child's knee. Blair's face looked like a gnarled tree at timberline and he seemed one of the last in a long line of something. It had spent the majority of its existence exposed to the elements. Bristly hair crept from his nostrils and spiraled from his ears like coughs of frost.

In the mornings they took bricks of sausage or bacon from the freezer and sawed off thick slices and laid them on the hot skillet where they spat and sizzled, a pig they had raised in the shed behind the house. Jack worked bread in and out of the toaster. He placed a large tub of butter on the table and peeled the lid off to reveal a scarred mess sprinkled with toast crumbs, smears of jam and peanut butter. They settled into their chairs and Blair dished a bit of scrambled egg and sausage onto a plate for the old woman. He took it to her and returned and the two ate slowly and enjoyed it.

Around them hung off-kilter and dusty photos of family, one of father wife and son, Elmer not twenty years old, grinning like a dimwit in a baby blue suit, and one of Jack and his parents when Jack was twelve. There were clothworks stitched by the old woman when she was well that declared maxims too simple for thought. The carpet was littered with food refuse and crumbs, bits of straw and hay from their socks, and was worn bare in the doorways and thinned in their main pathways of travel, thinnest into the living room where sat a broken couch and each man's own chair which would never be used by the other anymore than would the other's soiled underwear. Into these chairs at night they would sink like stones in a bog, hardly moving, dozing, Jack often falling into a hard sleep and waking alone in some odd hour of the night. Horrid smells came from the kitchen sink and lingered even after a thorough dish-doing at Jack's hands. In the small bathroom the toilet sat seat-up, its rim stained with dried urine, long twisted hairs trapped in dark yellow cakings. The tub held a black halo of filth and a gutter of dregs like the tail of something unsightly gone down the drain. The sink and counter were discolored with general use and peppered with whiskers caught in evaporated puddles of anonymous remains, the Lava soap they used to clean their hands lying cracked on the sill. The soap itself was dirty. When women from the church came to clean and saw this primitive hovel in a state of squalor and semi-ruin they wore masks and elbow-length gloves and remarked afterward how all their effort seemed to come to nothing. It had been this way since the old woman became sick, bedridden and blind, some four years before.

The sun already hot on the back of his neck, the muscles in his shoulders and back sore. Jack's damp skin bloomed goose bumps as he pulled his shirt off and shook it out, ridding it of fine hay leaves. The dog got up from where she'd been drowsing near the haystack and trotted after him and he walked the corridor between the west manger and the hayshed and listened to the chewing of the animals as their rough tongues pulled at the hay and gathered it in to be mashed, later to be brought up and chewed on again as cud. So much these cows ate and so much they shit, massive solid animals, nimble as planets, passive as stones.

He stopped at the corner of the hayshed when he saw Elmer come out of his house and sit on the back steps to put his boots on. Elmer made it twenty feet before his sprig-eared boy slipped out the door behind him and trailed him furtively like one of the wild cats of the barnyard. Elmer turned and walked him back to the house and shut him inside. The boy's name was Edward Elmer, named after Blair's father and his own father respectively. Elmer the elder's underslung chin sloped down to his neck in a long curve of soft flesh, giving him that single resemblance to a pigeon, and his stride was uneven across the barnyard as he walked toward Jack, a disarming lope, not carefree, for in forty-one years he had not known a full week of wellness. It was said he suffered from chronic fatigue syndrome, among other things. It was said he also had irritable bowel syndrome. Jack walked across the straw-littered gravel and squatted on his heels.

—What do you got going today? said Elmer.

Jack squinted up at him.

—Scrape the corral, straw the stalls, he said. Then I was going to start on that thirty-acre piece.

—Well, you mind taking them weaned calves up the house and give um their shots fore you swath?

—I won't have time for swathing if I do that. You don't want that field to blossom.

—No, I don't think it will. Them calves need to be taken up the house though. I guess you could do that.

—I guess I could. But that field needs to be cut.

Elmer stared at the ground with a half-smile. Jack picked at the torn sole of his boot.

—Take them calves up and you can start on that field tonight or tomorrow, said Elmer. Thank yuh kindly.

Jack grunted and walked to the tractor. He remembered once when he was a little boy and his mother had taken him out to the fields to find his uncle. Jack had spotted him far off in the field discing the soil and his mother had driven him over the field and Elmer had stopped and lifted him up onto the tractor to ride on the wheel well. This had happened dozens of times, but he remembered this one time, the sight of the tractor pulling the discs slowly in what seemed then to be a large field but what he knew now was not so big.

The work in the corrals took him into the afternoon and not another word nor sign from anyone. When he was done he backed the truck up to the calf pen and threw three calves in the bed and hogtied them and drove to the farmhouse where weaned calves grew until pregnant. The house was a hundred years old and had stood once at the edge of the barnyard. Near the top of the south gable was his bedroom window and above that a small hole into the attic, broken open from the years. The house sagged like an aged face and had bald patches of veneer and leprous paint that bulged, cracked, and fell. Sunburnt aluminum shutters hung beside the windows, one tilting, one gone. Low juniper shrubs claimed ground from the ragged lawn in a low and steady surge from the front and back sides of the house. The whole structure looked blown out at its bottom, as if a jack had given way at the lowering onto this, its second foundation, and the house had fallen.

He was surprised to see the old woman sitting outside in a lawn chair as he rolled by the house and toward the pens out back. When he was finished with the calves he walked up. It was easier to approach her in the out of doors in true light than in her room or as she wandered the house like she haunted it, spectral in her nightgown, feeling her way through familiar doorways and touching walls with outstretched arms that hung and swayed with loose flesh. She turned her wrinkled face toward him and he squatted next to her chair. She asked if it were him and he said it was. Her voice was slow and measured, witnessing her years.

—How do you like being home? he said.

—It's good to be back, she said. Have you been taking your grandfather to church?

—We go to church.

—The church is true, she said solemnly.

He took in her creased hands, splotched and purple-veined, where they lay in her lap. He let his eyes move slowly over her as he would spotting deer on a hillside. Blair had dressed her in a shirt of red gingham and maroon pants. Done up in fresh clothes she nearly looked as she had years ago in his boyhood when she sat at the kitchen table with him and they played Go Fish.

—I been meaning to talk to you about my wages, he said. I wanted to wait till you felt better. Grandpa won't give me a straight answer. Keeps saying he needs to talk to you when you get feeling better.

—These rare days are a blessing, she said. They nearly give me hope.

—Are you afraid of what's coming?

—Not afraid.

A robin chirped in the near tree and she tilted her head toward it. Her suffering seemed to have brought her wisdom, perspective. She suddenly seemed regal to him.

—So what do you think about the wages? he said.

—Since your parents passed on, we've taken care of you, and we always will, she said.

—I don't know what that means.

—I was there the day you were born. Seven pounds, nine ounces. A full head of dark hair. You were a beautiful baby.

—What can you tell me about my wages? he said.

—Lay not up for yourself treasures on earth, where moth and rust doth corrupt, where thieves break through and steal, she said.

He thought a moment and said, An idle soul shall suffer hunger.

She said, Before ye seek riches, seek ye the kingdom of God.

—I've sought the one already, now I'm seeking the other, he said. And I will come near to you with judgment, and I will be a swift witness against those that oppress the hireling in his wages.

—That's enough, she said mildly. The farm is a fickle thing. It doesn't make much money. Riches is the last word to describe it. I would think that by now you'd have learned that this is no way to make a living. Haven't you learned that?

—It's all I know.

—Go to town. Get an education.

—Town and college ain't for everybody.

—Aren't.

Her breath had grown heavy.

—This is no way to make a living, she said.

He picked up an old leaf from the grass, curiously intact from the ravages of seasons past. It was worn thin, threadbare, the veins brittle and the skin transparent. He held it up to the lowering sun and squinted.

—What does the sky look like right now? she said.

He looked around. The land spread out in all directions except farther behind the house where the river took it down into itself, and beyond that the Sisters range built upward like a mammoth fortress of stone and dirt, the massive cliff bands no longer than a little finger from where he viewed them. Crown-lifted cotton-woods grew in stands on the landscape farther down, along small creeks, some of them already dry, and big pines stood as wind-breaks around homesteads. From the panorama he tilted his head skyward and looked into its depths. Dusk was still an hour away, that time when the scratching in the south gable would begin and the nimble bats that caved there would drop one by one into the night. The house had been placed on the edge of the hillside above the river but had no view of the river because of the pens and sheds behind it. The old woman, young then, had requested only a clear view to the east and west when fifty years before they dragged the house there from the barnyard. She believed the Savior would appear in the east when he came, and she loved the smoldering sunsets over the sage plain to the west. A farmer's wife, she'd had an obsessive habit of watching the sky before she lost her sight, anticipating weather patterns sometimes better than the Doppler radar, and like everyone in that dry region she welcomed rain when she could get it. She forecast now by her bones, her eyes like boiled eggs turned to the wind.

—It's blue, he said. It's the deep blue that comes after the solstice. There's jet trails crossing the sky. One's being made, and the others are fading. All of um've caught the sun.

—A jet plane?

—That's it.

—Where is it going?

—Too high for Salt Lake. Looks like it's going straight up, say to the moon.

—My what man has done.

Her voice trembled with age. Gravity had pulled her head low and she spoke these last words into her lap. Her shoulders strained at the weight. She was born before the Great Depression and he guessed she'd seen some things since then, had marked both progress and regression. She was dwindling, but not in unbelief. He remembered her steel will well enough, this righteous fearless matriarch, heard without clamor and powerful without menace, upright before her god but wavering now in the flesh, and this weakness made him ambivalent toward her, a mixture of embarrassment and pity, as if such degeneracy should be hidden away rather than seen, displayed even as she was in her own back yard. What loathing did he possess toward the weak and dying. What latent dread. Yet this woman, even now on her deathbed, old and venerable and immovable, wielded a power that was hard to understand. She was an oracle, a quiet might to be reckoned with, and he was unsure how to approach the battle. She was as good as slain by the diseases that troubled her, yet her control was in place and would outlast her.

He looked back up at the sky, finding the jet again and watching it bloom a dual contrail behind it, watching closer as the vapor shot out the back of the engines, slowed, held, and expanded. Some of the contrails that crossed overhead were sheer wisps like fragmented cirrus clouds. He imagined the tall cities like clustered stands of trees around the curve of the earth in all directions, the places he had never been and would perhaps never see, the places these jets were going. Blair came out of the house and approached them.

—Come on dear, he said. Let's get you back inside.

Adelaide, her head bowed lower now and shaking with bared nerves, the fixed smile of the aged on her lips, tried feebly to raise her arms like a child would as her husband of fifty-two years approached.

He spent the morning of the next day and part of the afternoon with the dog, shirtless, sweating in the sun and repairing the long fence line that edged the hillside above the river bottoms. It was their largest field, sprawled out like a lake, lapping up to the barnyard on one end and the farmhouse on the other. It was from this field that they harvested the bulk of their alfalfa crop each year. He rolled alongside two miles of serpentine fence in his truck. In the back lay a spool of barbwire and what Elmer called the neck stretcher, a pile of steel fence posts and a post driver, tie wire, a sack of fence staples, a hammer, and a shovel. He took a pair of fence pliers from the glovebox and stuck them in his back pocket and worked at tightening and splicing loose or broken sections of wire. It was quiet, careful work, the only sounds his breath around soft execrations and the clatter and tweak of his tools. He mended the fence and enjoyed the solitude of it, the time to work slowly and do something well and completely. There were still many wooden posts on this line. The fence had been built with wooden posts entirely, denuded crowns of trees, as big in girth as a man's shoulder and tapering off toward the top with the nubs of cut branches natural supports for the wire, but each year before sorting the heifers he ran this line and when he found a post rotten or leaning or suspended in the air he dug it up and replaced it with a steel post. He stretched the hours also and finally at the far end climbed through the fence and sat a few minutes with the dog at the edge of the hillside overlooking the slow river. He lifted her ear and looked at the healing tears. She was just past a pup, a Brittany mix, her ears already tattered like the edge of old newspaper, faint lines of gathered scars across her nose. He ran his hand over her soft fur, feeling with his fingertips where bone gave way to muscle, gently kneading while she dozed with her head on her paws.

On the other side of the river and up the hill a vacant dairy operation stood like an emblem of a former time. It had gone under three years before, the cows sold, the barn stripped, the corrals left empty and the manure turned to dust. The place looked sunbleached as cattle bones. It seemed that most dairy barns in the area held corrals of weeds instead of cows anymore. Milk prices had been low that year. Another outfit across town sold its equipment and livestock the year after but was sitting on the land, waiting for the rumored money to show up. Something about that abandoned place across the river made him want to go there, because it would be strange and secret to walk around it, nothing but birds for company, and maybe not even them, since there was no spilled feed for them anymore. His father had foreseen this. He had broken with the farm at eighteen for a college degree, leaving Elmer to sit at their father's feet a lone disciple. Jack's father had not worked another day on that ground because Blair forbade it. When the old man saw his eldest son forsake his birthright he hefted a chip to his shoulder that he'd not shrugged to this day. Jack's view of this schism was more seasoned now, and he suspected that his father's unorthodox views of the church had something to do with Blair's paternal hostility. Jack's father taught him to respect physical labor, to love it even, but not to rely on it, and had disapproved of his slow gravitation toward that lifestyle. His father said that if a man had the option, physical labor was to be more of a balance and a release than a livelihood depended on for basic sustenance. A man should have two sets of practical skills, that which he did with his hands and that which he did with his mind, and Jack felt what would have been his father's disappointment that his only child had never acquired an obvious skill of the mind. Never mind that he knew each cow by her udder, knew her number and the number of her mother, could quote milk records and birth lines. Never mind that he knew how to harvest hay and corn at its highest yield, that at age twenty he was confident he could run this entire farm by himself if he had to. He could hear his father saying that some were meant to be simple men but some chose to be fools, and some were meant to do greater things than pull the teats of another man's cows and wait for an uncertain inheritance whose tacit promise brought ambivalence at best.

In some dead hour of the afternoon he walked through the oppressive sunshine and dragged his feet in the gravel of the barnyard. Elmer called to him from where he rested, post-lunch, in the shade of his trees and told him all four tractors needed greasing. Jack walked on like he hadn't heard. He worked on his back beneath the tractors and by the time he ran out of grease and made a run to the co-op for another box it was nearly time for milking. Looking out from under the biggest tractor he saw dust, and when it settled, an old blue Cutlass Supreme parked alongside the diesel tank, and when its door opened, Roydn Woolums. The farmhand stepped out and walked up the incline on his way to gather the cows. He stopped at the tractor and Jack looked out at his manure-caked boots and kept working. Roydn never washed his boots. He either lacked the perception that this small crumb of dignity might be had in this profession or he didn't care. He stood there for a full minute before he spoke, spitting once in a while on the gravel.

—Hello Selvedge, he said finally. Hot bitch, ain't it?

—Didn't Blair tell you? said Jack. You've been fired.

—What'd you do today, said Roydn. Beat off and sweat over it?

Jack scooted over and saw the kid swiveling his bean-shaped noggin around in the afternoon sun. A large round chin and bulbous forehead made up the balance of weight above bony shoulders and a sunken chest, and they bent toward each other as if they hoped to touch someday. There was a lump in his throat like he'd swallowed a knotted tree branch, a knuckled growth that moved up and down when he spoke or swallowed. He held in his hand a bottle of Pepsi and pulled out a wrinkled package of corn nuts and threw some in his mouth.

—Give me a few of them corn nuts, said Jack. I ain't ate yet.

Roydn handed over the bag and Jack shook some into his mouth and immediately regretted it. He slid beneath the tractor and found another grease zerk.

—So what'd you do today? said Roydn.

—Fixed fence.

—Where abouts?

—This one here that runs to the house.

—That's a long one. Say, is Blair ever going to sell any of that piece? I been looking to buy a little land to start my operation.

—Why don't you talk to him.

—Well ain't you going to get half?

Jack grunted. He was sweating freely and smears of black grease covered his arms and old grease was packed under his fingernails, so he couldn't wipe the sweat from his face nor away from his eyes where it ran in and stung them.

—What's that supposed to mean? said Roydn. I bet you get

half. This place is as good as yours. You was born into it. When you share the place with Elmer you let me buy some of that piece for my operation.

—What operation is this now, Woolums?

Roydn came down on his hands and knees close to Jack, trying to look him in the face, but Jack wouldn't allow it.

—Well you know, he said, when I was in Nebraska I seen hog farms all over. I knew some real well-off hog farmers. So it's a hog farm I got in mind.

—What happened to the turkey farm?

—The turkey farm? He sat back on his haunches and let his head drop and stared at the ground. He rubbed his whelked chin as he considered. Well, that failed about a year ago it must of been. Bout the time I got back. Pa wanted to make um free range, but we lost money that way somehow. We're tending compost piles now, and that ain't going nowhere. And by the way, Pa wants to know if he can come get some manure with his pickup. Wants to know if you got any drier stuff available.

—What'd you do with the bull calves you bought?

—One died, and the other I sold to that halfwit Wrink Poulsen.

—Make any money?

—I made a little.

—How much?

—Enough.

—How much?

—Seventy bucks.

—That after feed?

—Nah.

—So you lost money.

—I don't member how it went.

—That ain't worth the effort, said Jack.

—Would be though, if I was to run a feed lot and made a

small profit on every bull.

—That's a better idea than the pig farm. The town should have a problem with a pig farm.

—I'll get um to change their minds on it then, said Roydn. His eyes squeezed up in hurt and frustration. Guy's got to make a living. I'm a grown-ass man, and what am I going to do with myself, work for Blair the rest of my life? You know that ground behind my house is worthless. It's full of clay. Can't get nothing but a few rows of half-assed raspberries to grow on it.

—There'll be community opposition too, said Jack. That stink carries for miles. It'll become the town's new identity. And you sure as hell can't put it in the field out there.

—Ain't nobody'll give me a good price. And my pa ain't got the money to lend me. He's trying to save for me to go to college. I'll just wait it out for you to get some land and sell it to me. I know you're good for it.

—You better go get the cows, said Jack.

—Hold up. I tell you I'm going to college?

—Somebody let you in?

—I ain't in yet. But my pa thinks I oughta go. He never got the chance to go, and he wants his sons to have the chance. Thinks they got something to teach me, but I ain't so sure. Probly be the other way around.

—No doubt.

—When he gets the money saved up I'll go. Plenty of girls at them colleges, you know.

—So I've heard. But not a one of um'll be interested in an ugly bastard like you.

—Plenty of girls. One for everybody. Sometimes two. He looked up at the tractor. You just greasing or you repairing something?

—Do you see any tools around?

—No.

—There's your answer.

—Two of these tractors are pieces of shit. I ain't got to tell you which ones. They need to get rid of that Thirty-Twenty at least. Jumps like a mule and the smoke pipe's busted.

—They'll drive it into the dirt, said Jack. The Selvedge way.

—My pa told me they about got this place paid off. That true?

—If you heard it, it must be true.

—That's an accomplishment. Takes most guys two generations to start a dairy farm from scratch and pay it off, and Blair'll do it in one.

—That's what shafting your hired help will do.

—Aw, you'll get what's coming to you. And you don't see no brand new toys around neither. All old worn out stuff here. Frugal outfit. Pennywise and niggardly, my pa says. You agree?

—That's one way to put it.

—Hm. This is one big-ass tractor. Wonder will Blair or Elmer ever have me drive it. I'm going to ask one of um if I can drive it in the parade tomorrow.

Jack slid himself under another grease zerk and cleaned around it with his fingers.

—You're going to be in the parade?

—Only if I can get this tractor to drive. I ain't interested in the usual bullshit my ma puts me up to. Wonder which one I should ask. Which one you think I should ask?

—Either one. They're both liable to say no.

Jack looked at Roydn and his eyes were unfeasibly large behind his glasses.

—Now why is that, you suppose?

—Cause you could go into a fit any minute and kill somebody.

—That ain't true. I ain't got it that bad. I got a damn driver's license. That oughta count for something.

—You know how they are about their tractors.

—They shouldn't be. It ain't like they're nice or nothing. Just thought I'd ask. Can't hurt to ask.

—Hand me another tube of grease from that box there, will yuh.

—I think I'd ask Blair. But he's a hard old sumbitch. I'd ask Elmer, but he says no to everything. Took him two years to upgrade me from the four-wheeler to the danged farm truck.

Jack scooted on his back under a set of zerks near the front wheels.

—Why don't you go get the cows in the barn, he said. You're late now. They're dripping milk into their shit.

—Hold up, said Roydn. I tell you I just saw something nice down the lane here?

—What was it, Woolums, a goat stuck headfirst in the fence?

—A girl. Saw her walking down along the lane. You know who it is?

—I don't.

—Rebekah Rainsford. Thought maybe she was coming back from here. Did you talk to her or something?

—What?

—Did you talk to her or something?

—Rebekah Rainsford?

—It's what I said. She's back in town.

—Since when?

—I don't know. But she's back in town with her mother. They're on the run from their old man, holed up at the McKellar place down there. She was about my age. Still is, I guess.

—She was younger than you. Younger than me even. What the hell do you know about anything?

—You don't know nothing about it? All right. I suppose I could tell you. I suppose it wouldn't hurt. Look here, I'll tell you what my pa told me. They're running from trouble. It's her and her mother moved here from Salt Lake cause their old man left um in financial frig all. Left um, flat out. He's gone. And now they're here.

—How'd he go about it?

—Gambling is what I heard. Probly a little whorin on the side. They usually go together.

—Gambling, huh?

—It is what I heard. Over in Wendover. So what do you think of her?

—I never knew her that good. She was always kind of snobby.

—Well I'd like to know her. Like *Isaac* knew Rebekah, you read me?

—You irreverent frigger.

—Well let me know what you think of her once you see her. Should be at church I suppose, and there's a good reason for you to come back. I told you I'd get you back to church someway, and it looks like I got one. Yes sir. She'd make a man a good wife. I'd like her to bear my children and be waiting for me when I got home from milking these whores. That'd make it all worth it. This here's the summer of opportunity.

Jack pulled himself out from under the tractor and stood up. Roydn didn't step back and they were face to face with Jack pinned against the engine of the tractor. The lenses of Roydn's glasses were thick and dense and his black eyes wandered wetly behind them.

—Welp, he said, looking up at the sun again. Guess I'd better go off and gather them cows. They ain't about to milk themselves. He leered ugly over his shoulder as he walked away. And you know, buttwipe, he said. You might put in a word for me about this tractor, huh? This big one here. I don't want to drive nothing else. Cause if so, I got to come tonight and warsh it. Tell him I'll warsh it for him. See what he says.

Roydn tilted his head back to see him rather than push the heavy glasses back up his nose. He grinned and shuffled off through the gravel toward the corral.

—Going to college, he said to nothing in particular, and started to whistle.

When he was gone Jack walked to the far edge of the west haystack where he could get a good look at the lane across the field as it led away from the barnyard. It was empty as far as he could see. After feeding he left the dog on the ground while he climbed up the supports and under the open-sided hayshed. The stack was uneven near the back. They had hand stacked bales in something like a broad staircase on top of what the bale wagon had brought, and the stack was higher there than the bottom of the tin on the sides and dim. It was a good place for respite and hiding. He'd been going up there since he could climb, always careful where to step, because the way the bale wagon stacked several loads side by side in row after row, holes were sometimes created where stacks met that went all the way to the ground. He had taken many naps under the shed, drowsed away afternoon hours, hidden from his grandfather and uncle. He listened to the pigeons cooing their soft dialogue from the rafters. From where he sat in a throne of haybales he could look out over the west field and see the top of the McKellar house where it sat shrouded in a fortress of pines.

That night he took his boots off and trod the footworn path on the carpet into the washroom where he shed his stinking clothes and stepped into the shower stall. The smell from handling cows clung to him like a second skin. Sometimes he bathed twice a day to stave it. Most nights bathing seemed senseless since in a matter of hours he would rise and undo the effort, but he did it daily; it made him feel connected to a greater civilization than what he daily saw. Blair was never without the smell. It lingered on him and moved with him from room to room. It was on him even as he sat in his church pew on those singular occasions of attendance, and if a man couldn't get clean for church he couldn't get clean. For them the smell of cows was like the grease in the knuckle lines of a mechanic or the thick arms of a mason. It was a symbol of identity Jack tried each night to shed, because while his blood cried for the field work he did, milking cows held no dignity. Anything but standing beneath the dumb beasts and gathering milk from their pink, thick-veined udders while their golden spray and heavy excrement fell from above like unwanted boons. Blair had picked the worst kind of farming when he bought the first Holsteins. A man could work his whole existence out upon a small dairy farm and provide this obscure service to humankind and be always near sunk. But the smell was an unpleasant thing, possibly the worst thing, surpassing even the endless burden of twice-a-day milkings. If Jack showered hard and vigorously and scoured every inch of his skin and ran a fingertip through the geography of his ears to check for stray manure, dirt, tractor grease, he came away clean, but he was never certain the smell was gone. Smelling it on his grandfather when he should have been clean made him doubt that anything but a permanent departure from the trade could rid him of it. There was the cramped shower off the laundry room or the tiny bathtub, and he took the shower. Blair chose the tub where he sat in a rank stew of his own molting, and in this way they coexisted at nights when both needed to be clean before bed.

Jack walked into the kitchen and found his grandfather sitting alone at the clothless table eating dinner, which was leftover lunch, fried hamburger molded by hand into crude patties, and buttered potato slices, the way the old woman had made it day in and out in her better days. Blair never looked so weary as at nights in the kitchen, shoving food into his mouth under the fluorescent lighting, when it seemed like he could hardly hold his head up and move his jaw. He was lifelong fatigued in his off time. They said nothing as they ate, the elder sitting, the younger standing, both watching an old Eastwood western play out on the television across the room.

When they were done eating Blair said, Go say hi to your grandma.

—Where is she?

—In the other room.

Jack walked in the living room to see her sitting like a stone on the couch, her blank eyes half open and turned toward the television where black and white static hissed on the screen. He asked her if she wanted him to put something on and she didn't respond. He watched her for a moment, waiting for the rise and fall of her sloped breast, and when he saw movement he turned and left the room. He grabbed a misshapen chunk of hamburger from the plate and walked out the door and jumped in his truck and drove in the long light of the evening to find Heber at the park under the trees. Stars appeared above him like the firmament was being shot at.

He felt the loneliness of being twenty years old on his grandfather's farm, womanless, with but a couple friends to watch what small events befell their moribund town. His father used to tell him that a man made his destiny with whatever he was given and that he should not depend on luck. He said that men wait their entire lives for luck. He promised that opportunity would pass a man by if he didn't learn to act. These days Jack wondered when those opportunities had come, for he had never recognized them as such, and such things seemed as vanished now from this town and from his life as his childhood. On this night he felt nostalgia for things that had never happened, pining for things he could not name, and when these anxieties took him he felt in tune with something larger than himself. They were a sober component of his disposition. In these moments, with voices from the dead murmuring a susurrus through his mind, it seemed nothing less than fate speaking to him, some low piercing voice of vague origin, and he could not understand it. And so he only listened to the strange tongue speak in mutters and went on.

He came to the park. In the soft obscurity between dusk and dark a girl was on the swing set. She made the chains of the swing groan and took them nearly to their horizontal limit. She looked to be his age, too old for the swings, but swung upward, her toes pointing to the sky, then tucked them back as she fell, and each time she reached the apex her dark hair lifted and fell. It startled him, and some strange hunger moved inside him. He slowed. His fingers found the knob to turn the radio off. She looked toward his truck through her flying hair. She was alone, and he didn't dare watch for long, so he drove a little farther and turned into the grass-sprung parking lot and left his truck beneath the denuded basketball rims. The swings were no longer visible because of the pine trees and the pavilion in between.

He found Heber under the trees regarding the evening generously and nursing a bottle of beer. The querulous moaning of the chains floated across the park to them, and when he told Heber what it was Heber rose and they went to find her out, to discover her mystery, to put to rest their slow thudding blood and their mad wonderings. When they rounded the pavilion she was gone. The swing still moved, and as they reached it Jack put a hand out to steady it and felt the seat still warm with the heat of her body. The two of them looked around. Jack gave the seat a push and it swung askew and they turned and walked back to the trees.

Heber rubbed his blond red beard and said, Who was it?

—Might of been Rebekah Rainsford.

—No.

—It's what Woolums said.

—The hell does he know?

—Who else could it be?

—How beautiful was she?

—Hard to say.

—That girl was always beautiful and would be now. Why'd you come to me first? You need someone to show you the way?

—She's too young for you. And she's wholesome. You'd corrupt and defile her. You'd ruin her.

Heber laughed from his belly.

—How do you know she's wholesome? She's been gone a long time.

—She always was. She was untouchable.

—This is good for morale, said Heber.

They sat together under the shivering stars, among the rubbing crickets. Heber sat against the tree and picked up the beer he'd left behind. He wore a strange shirt that fit his broad shoulders and soft gut well. It was garish and outrageous, intricate sketches of tiny pale flowers overlaying the white fabric. Down the middle of the front on both sides of the buttons ran vertical lines, some thin and some thick, of red, brown, yellow, and blue. Down either side of this lay heavily embroidered patterns of large blue flowers with small flowers filling in between.

—You ever wear that shirt when you sold real estate? said Jack.

—I bought it for that.

—That's probly why you never sold anything.

—I wish I could blame it on the shirt. But I'll redeem that failure and you'll see a picture of me on my business card wearing this very shirt.

—Get the picture taken from the neck up then.

—Selvedge, if I die before you I promise you can have this shirt.

—I could probly use it to wipe my butt.

Heber drained the last of his beer and reached into the pack for another. He pried the lid off with his pocket knife and said, How's your grandmother?

—They couldn't do anything else, said Jack. Said she'd be more comfortable at home.

—You know, there are accounts of Eskimos sending their aged out to sea in a canoe. Shoving them off and that's that. There comes a time when they've served their purpose, things get worn out, and death is the best thing for everyone. They've done you wrong to wait this long. What do you think you'll get?

—No idea.

—They haven't said anything?

Jack shook his head.

—And you haven't asked?

—It's a hard thing to ask about.

—How would you feel about taking a drive to town, refill on drinks? said Heber. I'll fill up your tank.

—What've you got there?

Heber shook the box on the ground and five empty bottles rattled against one another. He stuck out a dry warm hand and Jack got up and pulled him to his feet. He walked tenderly to the truck, leaving the bottles beside the tree as if to save his place.

—Feet hurt, he said. I don't know how much longer I can lay brick of a day.

The wind came to them across the desert and through the town like a clean hot exhalation and the trees sighed with it. As they got in a sudden gust rocked the truck on its springs.

—Storm coming, said Heber. From the heat. Could be the real thing, bring us some rain.

—Be only wind, said Jack. Heat lightning.

Jack drove them through the derelict town square, the two of them the only life in it. Heber said, What built this place? And why didn't whatever built it keep it going? My old man was going to set fire to this square. When he found he couldn't resurrect it a little, revive a business or two, he wanted it all gone. Burned to the ground and leveled. Thought it would never be reborn otherwise. I was poking around in the back of his little vet shop the other day and found forty gallons of gasoline under some canvas tarps. The town knows he was a fine mayor, whatever other problems they had with him, but they would've lynched him for that.

—That's all the character the town has left, said Jack. You might see it come back.

—When things leave here they don't come back.

—You did.

—Because I was kicked out of college. And out of the world in general.

—To hear you tell it.

—How does it go. Let's see if I can remember. Had it once… In this town the last house stands as lonely as if it were the last house in the world. The highway, which the tiny town is not able to stop, goes deeper—slowly goes deeper out into the night.

He paused for a moment and thought.

—The tiny town is only a passing-over place, worried and afraid, between two huge spaces—a path running past houses instead of a bridge. And those who leave the town wander a long way off and many perhaps die on the road.

—Have you talked to her lately? said Jack.

—This thing is seven years running, broken and spliced as it is. It's become tradition. She'll be back.

—Who was the other one?

—You don't know her.

—If you've lost her… Things ain't as plentiful as they was once. I don't know how you end up doing it time after time.

—Same as every man before me has done it and every man after me will do it.

Jack knew what Heber would speak before he spoke it, this holy hymn that fell often from his lips.

—But she was a strange woman at first, he pre-empted. And the one before was the familiar.

—Indeed. Heber nodded. That's always been the trouble, and it always will be. There will always be other women. What to do about that stark fact is up to you.

He cracked the quarter glass and produced a cigarette and lighted it.

—They ain't as plentiful as they once were, you say, he said. He squinted through wreaths of smoke and tried to wave them out the window. It is the opposite that's the trouble. My old man knew it. Most men know it. Sometimes it takes a shift in perspective, but we adjust and see new beauty all around. But I'd be lying if I told you this one didn't seem to hold more weight. I do indeed regret it. I think I love that girl.

—She was a good girl, said Jack. She probly just finally wised up. Saw what she was dealing with and lit out.

—Maria is back, too, said Heber. It's just raining girls these days. Our own little Juniper Scrag renaissance. Plenty of things are coming back.

Jack reached forward and turned the large tuning knob and Dwight Yoakam became a murmur in the dashboard. Heber spoke with the energy of alcohol in his blood.

—It's a revival of sorts. And she's got the finest ass I believe I've ever seen.

They rolled along through the dark sage desert, the radio playing quietly, listening to and feeling the smooth growl of the truck beneath them. Driving in the old pickup at night with its rumbling motion on the road and the spacious cab and the dark all around felt right. The truck was comfortable. Jack slumped forward on the big wheel, his foot steady on the gas, and the whore lights he'd put beneath the dash in high school shone soft blue onto the floor.

—Every time I think I've got it, a stranger comes along, said Heber. And lo, there's a stranger. He rolled his window down and let his arm hang out. There will always be other women, he said. My old man knew it. But he was tied up. So he broke the institution like a stick on his knee and started a flame with it that he couldn't manage. Couldn't keep it steady. He suppressed it too long. If you don't pretend it's not there, it can't surprise you.

—I'd like to get tied up with that girl at the park, said Jack.

—Since I was a boy and began to notice the girth and curve of a girl's thigh, or the perspiration on her chest in the summer, or the taint of spent air once it's been in her lungs, I've studied them and loved what I've found. They are marvelous, beautiful creatures. I love them.

—No one questions that.

—I'm weak against beauty, said Heber. And it's everywhere. But you can't tell whether a girl is beautiful until you've watched her for a while and considered on her flaws. Let her grow on you. One of the most amazing girls I was ever with, a Mexican girl, she was a little plump and she had these stretch marks on her thighs where the skin was a lighter color, like tiger stripes. Couldn't get enough of that. He shivered deeply. I wonder where she's at now. When a woman has the native knowledge in her of what she has, that's the true sublime. It's her sex that makes the world go round. Not love, not money. The women who know this rule the earth, and the men that pretend to serve them. Everything men do is to get to the women—and it's what's between their legs that is the nexus of the universe, whether God likes it or not. Think on it a minute.

They did.

Jack's eyes were raw and their lids heavy. He found the lighted liquor store on the close edge of Willow Valley and parked. Inside the store Heber looked haggard under the fluorescent lighting, his sharp blue eyes crowded with blood vessels, his hair thin and tousled, his beard scraggly, his clothes badly wrinkled and spotted with crust and stain. His shirt was outrageous.

—You okay? he said. He ran his finger along a shelf of bottles while Jack followed behind.

—Yeah.

—A beautiful store, this, said Heber. You want some?

Heber browsed the hard liquors and made his way to the refrigerators at the wall. He removed a pack of longnecks and carried it toward the front of the store where a tall balding clerk with a curved back stood behind the counter.

—That's it? said Jack. We came all the way into town for a six pack?

—You've got to moderate your acquisition. That's the difference between me and an alcoholic. An alcoholic takes a bottle to keep in his cupboard. Or his closet. You should know that.

He set the drinks on the counter, leaned back on his heels, and squinted wisely at the man.

—You own this place? he said.

The man shook his head.

Heber nodded.

—I wonder how much money a place like this pulls in of a week. Do you know?

The man shook his head again. Heber chuckled.

—Can you speak?

Heber looked at Jack and flashed his strong teeth. They left the man and walked outside and the hot wind moved around them.

—Summer storms, said Heber. You feel the energy?

—I'm tired. I got to milk in the morning.

—You know how much money I make laying brick?

Jack looked at him.

—Take what you make an hour and times it by four and you're still not there.

Jack grunted.

—I can get you a job any time. Does Blair know the calendar year? Does he know what minimum wage is? He pays Captain Dipshit over minimum, don't he?

—Probly.

—What are you doing?

They climbed in the pickup and shut the doors.

—What are you doing? Heber said again.

—I'm working. What do you want me to say?

—I want you to tell me that you believe something's coming your way, that this is some means to some better end.

—He's only told me that those things'd be decided once the old lady passed on.

—That's vague, said Heber. As if it will take care of itself. If you do not want to lay brick with me there are plenty of jobs here in town.

—Farm work is better than desk work, said Jack. He started the truck and backed into the street.

—You know, you're wasting away the best years of your life.

—No, I don't know that.

—Best advice I ever got was to spend my youth like I'd die at thirty, said Heber. My best years are behind me, and I can't believe how fast it went. You live to maximize the moment, you spend more time doing than considering, than balking, and you'll have fewer regrets. But if you dally, why then you'll spend the rest of your life thinking of what you could've done.

—I haven't lived a dull life.

—But you've become complacent. Stagnant. You've stopped living. All you do is work. Where's the opposition you used to entertain. Where's the excitement. You brood too much lately. Blair's a wily old fucker. I'd just have other options if I were you. Let's do a business together. Once upon a time you wanted to. We could be masons. I can teach you.

Jack grunted.

—I need you, said Heber. I've been saving, but it's taking too long.

—You want to spend a little money to get us something to eat? said Jack.

—Take us there.

They rode in the pickup on clear streets beneath stoplights. On occasion a tumbleweed blew in from the desert and rolled across the road with the wind. They turned in at Beto's and pulled up to a menu of ill-lighted and drab dishes.

—A good choice, said Heber. A good choice, my friend.

The wind hit the truck like a shoulder and whipped it with a few hard raindrops as they ate their food, but that was all, and in the sudden lightning the rolling clouds above them looked like the serried underbelly of a great beast. There was energy in the storm, but no rain.

2

THE MILKING WAS DONE EARLY AND IT WAS DONE THE same, those stark hours of darkness just before dawn the barest of all. But they were changed for his thoughts of the girl. When they were finished he drove them past the McKellar house and was struck with a mood as from a dream, a nostalgic emotion from that same nameless range. Blair began to hum some old love song, supplementing it with fragments of half-remembered lyric.

It was the twenty-fourth of July and they were back at the barnyard just past eight o'clock. The thermometer on the barn neared ninety. They walked to Elmer's lawn where they sat in the shade of the short pine trees and waited for Elmer to come out of his house.

—If you ain't going to the celebration this morning you ought to gather up the pipe from the lower field, said Blair. Bring some up to this field here where we could run it from both ends. If we don't get rain it won't be enough to run water from one end to the other in one line.

—I could. Or I could just take the day off.

—And do what?

—Get the hell out of here.

—You member when I used to clean up a tractor and drive it in the parade, and you'd sit on my lap up there and throw out candy? When's the last time we did that? Must of been when we bought the Thirty-Twenty, and how long ago was that?

—Long time. Cause I was young enough to let you talk me into sitting up there with you.

—Careful, boy. I could still whip you and put you up there with me. Roll through the square now, the two of us.

Blair spat soundlessly and said, You fix that old John Deere yet?

—They're all old.

—The Thirty-Twenty.

—The smoke pipe?

—It's rattling like hell and killing me with diesel fumes.

—Am I supposed to weld it?

—If you can get to it.

—What if I can't?

—Then get to it anyways.

—I'll take it to the co-op.

—No you won't. Milk prices are low. If you can't get to it with the welder use wire.

—Listen, said Jack. Is the farm paid off?

—No, the farm ain't paid off. I wished it was.

—The tractors?

—They're paid off save for the new loader. About time for anothern though, soon as one of these older tractors gives up the ghost. Take your pick from the Thirty-Twenty and the little one there and then we'll be back in the red. It's a never ending cycle, I tell yuh.

—Where do you see it in the next year or two?

—Oh hell. It's hard to make a terrible amount of progress in just a year or two. So much depends on the weather and the crops. We don't have room for much expansion. Land prices've gone up some recently, Lord knows why. And with it, taxes.

Elmer came out and loped toward them with a consternated grin on his face and they watched him approach.

—Hullo Pa, said Elmer when he reached them. He was already sweating. Hullo Jack. Hot enough for yuh?

—Jack'll take the pipe out of that lower field there and bring some up to this one here, said Blair. Run it from both ends.

—That sounds good. That's sandy down there anyways. It gets sandier every year, it seems.

—Farming gets harder every year, said Blair.

—I need you to help me move that welder, Jack, said Elmer. Better yet, why don't you just take it over to that east side where the dry cows are and weld that broken top bar. That way I won't get all sweaty fore the parade. You know which one I'm talking about?

Jack spat.

—I got to get ready, said Elmer. I'm taking Edward Elmer and Carrie. We're staying for the lunch and all. Can I bring you back anything?

—Like what? said Jack.

—Oh, I don't know. A sloppy joe or something. Have Eddie grab some candy for yuh. You want to come with us Pa?

—Maybe I will. It's already too hot for work.

Two hours later Jack was thirsty. He sweated when he stood still and when he moved it poured out of him. He had welded the bar on the fence, dripping sweat into a puddle at the bottom of the welding mask, and then had gone into the cool dim barn where he drank a cup of thick frothy milk cold from the tank and slowed the push of his sweat until it stopped. He got in the truck and drove toward town, and because the main road was closed took a grassy track that ran behind a string of houses. He went to the co-op and bought a Pepsi from the machine and headed back. He parked in the shadow of the big red barn behind his old house and walked toward the parade that was making its way through the square. He stood back at a distance and watched. It was a pathetic parade, a few utility trailers turned ragged floats, boys on bicycles with cards tapping their spokes and trailing crepe paper streamers, tractors pulling implements, some not washed, people proudly leading farm stock along. He could see a swath of streetside folks, but no girl that looked like the one he had seen the night before, indeed no girl anywhere close to her age. But there was Roydn Woolums coming along on an old lawnmower, a rusting sputtering hulk that lurched forward on four bald tires, its seat covered with a pillow taped to the frame. Colorful streamers hung from its handles and completed the spectacle. He pulled a small wagon and in it sat his youngest brother, the one they called Rapscallion, too old to be in a wagon in a parade but throwing homemade hardtack candy to the crowd with strangled enthusiasm. Roydn had given himself space and drove in figure eights and circles, shoving his glasses up and taking his hat off to wipe his brow with a forearm. Sweat climbed upward and outward from the seam of his hat brim and his shirt stuck to his torso. He ran the throttle up harshly in clouds of popping blue smoke and the mower leapt forward in its transition through the gears. His face was a tortured mixture of public humiliation and some small rustic pride.

Jack spent an hour gathering empty grain sacks and blown garbage along the east fence. The wind had run over the barnyard the night before and the close hayshed looked askew on its poles as if it had been pushed by the wind, leaning eastward. Later he was in the lower fields pulling a pipe trailer with his truck and gathering the sunbaked sprinkler pipe onto it. He had forgotten gloves and found those he kept in the glovebox taken, so he took off his shirt and used it as best he could to guard his hands, but still they were burned. He worked alone and it suited his mood.

In the evening when the work was done he drew milk from the tank into an old tin pail he had cleaned with hot water and soap. He balanced it cold between his legs on the seat of his two-stroke three-wheeler and opened the throttle on the lane and looked through the soft light ahead. He smelled the swamp water as it pumped from the pond below the barn and through the sprinkler lines. The sprinklers, drowned out by the whine of his machine and the gravel beneath its tires, turned in stuttered circles with each beat, pounding crops and soil with water. His stomach lightened and his blood surged and not from his speed. If no one answered he didn't know if he would leave the milk on the doorstep or if he would pour it into the wild barley at the side of the lane. But as he rose over the last crest and came down he locked up both brakes and slid out of control toward a heifer standing dumbly in the middle of the lane. The rear end of the three-wheeler swung around and ran parallel with the front wheel, and he slid toward the animal sideways, pushing a spray of gravel ahead of him and bringing with him the roar of dragged stones. The machine grabbed and flipped and in a splash of hurled milk he catapulted onto the road where he slid to a stop and curled into a ball to wait for the pain, his flesh torn and dusty, his breath knocked out somewhere on the road. When the pain came it rolled up and down his body and he could get no air. He tried to swear but sounded like a deaf man croaking out a guttural demand. His three-wheeler was on its top behind him, its wheels standing in the sky like an abstract sculpture. He smelled gasoline in the dust.

When he could get up he rose and limped over to the machine, muscled it onto its side, and flipped it back over. He climbed aboard and kicked the starter. He kicked it again and again and got nothing, and when he was sure it was flooded he pushed it off the road and looked out across the hay field toward the riverbottom fence and saw three more heifers wandering around in the green hay. He looked at his arms and hands, the skin gray and dirty, the blood holding sheens of dust and patches of tiny rocks. He picked at his torn shirt and pants. Blood ran down his left arm, down his fingers, and dripped into milk still puddled in the dust in globular patterns, the blood breaking apart first in smaller spherules and then spreading in trails as it dissolved into pinkness. That image stayed with him. He looked for the pail and found it dented in the late sun near the fence and found its cap upturned on the road behind the wreck with beads of milk still holding to it. He capped the pail and hung it on the handle of the three-wheeler and cursed the animal as he walked toward her. She'd been tame this way since she was a calf. She followed him with her head until he slapped her rump with his good arm, and then she moved to the side of the road and grazed in the grass there. He walked toward the McKellar house.

There was no answer at the front door so he went around back between the lilac bushes. As he stepped into a yard surrounded by a border of tall pines he met the gazes of two women on the porch. A woman he recognized as Martha Rainsford rose from her seat beside her daughter and met him in the middle of the yard. They were surrounded also by the strange playground toys Tom McKellar had built in the heyday of his bizarre creation. As Jack explained how he had rolled his three-wheeler and asked to use her phone, Martha took his left arm and studied it. She instructed Rebekah to call Blair Selvedge and tell him his cows were out, and the girl rose and disappeared into the house. Two glasses of lemonade sweated on a table between chairs. Martha took him inside and sat him at the kitchen table and disappeared around a corner.

—What's the number? said Rebekah from behind him.

He turned and looked at her. The soft fragrance of shampoo and soap lifted from her and floated toward him. She wore shorts and he could see her bare thighs without looking at them. She was tall and full bodied, her skin having taken a healthy color from the sun. Her dark hair was pulled up loosely and her posture listless, unaffected by his plight. He gave her the number and she dialed it and handed him the phone. It took effort to keep from arguing with Blair. The old man was unable to take simple orders. Rebekah stood in the doorway to the kitchen, listening to him talk.

—No, he said. There's at least four. You need to get Elmer to help you.

—I don't know where they got out. I wrecked. I'm at Tom McKellar's house. I'm bleeding.

—I did fix the fence. I don't know how they got out.

—No. I'm telling you, I'm bleeding all over the place.

He looked down at his left arm and saw that blood was dripping off his fingers onto the linoleum in bright, coin-sized droplets. They had splattered, each surrounded by its own series of moons. He hung up the phone. This was a situation the old man would have to see with his own eyes to understand. He had a small imagination. Rebekah came for the phone and after hanging it up brought him a glass of lemonade with a paper towel for his arm and sat down at the table with him. She regarded him with bright limpid eyes and asked him if it hurt. It burns, but it's not too bad, he said. She said she'd never seen so many scrapes, and that he must have been driving too fast. He told her there was no speed limit on this road and she said it was twenty-five unless otherwise posted. He said if he knew there was a heifer standing in the middle of the road he might have slowed down. She asked him if it was the cow's fault and he said it was always the cow's fault.

He was aware of his smell in the kitchen. Martha returned and set gauze, tape, creams, bottles, scissors, and tweezers out in a line on the table. As she did her work he could feel Rebekah's presence beside him like a hot stove. Her eyes clear as running water in the light and burning dark otherwise. She had a shallow cleft in her chin that he did not remember. The kitchen was clean and small. The refrigerator clicked on and hummed in the corner. The house seemed kept with a simple pride, its modesty and tidiness creating a calm, wholesome feeling, something absent at the farmhouse. The farmhouse was a dwelling shades above a cave, the upper room he slept in akin to a child's treehouse. Scab carpet unfastened and without padding covered most of the wooden floor, drab brown, curled and frayed at the edges. His narrow rank bed bent from use and the wallpaper flyspotted and yellowed, wallpaper whose maddening pattern, circles and lines, lines and circles, ran down the wall like strange liquid, wallpaper he had stared at for long periods until it had come to represent the toil of his young life, the convolutions and implications of his existence, his faith, and farther until it traced the wild, entwined history of humankind in its lines, for so many years its presence like an unpleasant friend become tolerable through relentless visitations, the sharp edges of its desperation worn round, a certain acquiescence or submission granted. The whole dim room tilting one way and the delirium of his simple life draining out the window. The place where he now sat was a home, and within it her slow beauty worked on him like liquor.

Martha cleaned and dressed his knee, an abraded area above his hip, and returned to his left elbow, all the while asking questions about the town she and her daughter had left, the people there. He answered her questions and his voice seemed thick and bucolic in the room, a stark and roughhewn contrast to the honey that spilled from the throats of the women. He tried for clearer, more enunciated language and his words came out stilted and foreign.

Rebekah got up and returned with another wet cloth. She set his right arm on the table and began wiping his elbow. She became involved in this task, and underlying the pain that throbbed through the torn skin, shooting along nerve tracks and reaching into strange parts of his body, he was awash in warmth at being touched and cared for by these two women, having their sole attention this way. The pain Rebekah caused was tremendous, her hand not as careful as her mother's, and it traveled to his heart. Her face gathered into a scowl of focus and the pink tip of her tongue stuck out from the corner of her mouth. Once he hissed and she looked up at him from her crouch, dark-eyed and guileless. As he admired the clean line of her neck he noticed what could have been a tattoo on the nape, though from his angle he could not see it well.

Wrapped up, with a stale pain warming under each bandage, he pulled his pungent shirt on. Martha put a good sandwich and a pitcher of lemonade in front of him and left him alone. When he was through he went outside and walked across the lane and looked into the field. It was almost dark and he couldn't see any heifers. Inside Martha's car he smelled dried sweat, cow manure, old sun, all wafting from his skin and clothes and mixing with the scent of antiseptics. As he climbed out at the farmhouse the warm feeling from before was gone and beneath it lay only the pain of his stiffening wounds and the dark knowledge of work the next morning. Blair called out when he entered the house. Jack ignored him and went toward the stairwell. As he rounded the corner he heard a noise in the darkness and was suddenly face to face with the old woman. Her bedroom door was catercorner to the opening for the stairs, and it was from there that she had emerged like a wraith. She staggered forward malodorous, her white eyes open in the dimness, her heavy arms outstretched and feeling, and he sidestepped her and climbed the squealing stairs to his room.

He slept badly that night, no position comfortable and the plea of his wounds breaking any stream of slumber into fragments. When he got up predawn, stiff with surface pain, a few of the bandages had bled through and others were yellow with wound seepage. He tried to rewrap one of them and did a poor job. Blair came into the kitchen and took the jar of peanut butter from the cupboard.

—Happened to you? he said.

—I told you. I wrecked.

—Only a matter of time with one of them.

—Would of happened with anything, said Jack. The hell do you know about it.

—Can you milk?

—I'm up ain't I.

Blair took a spoon from the drawer and probed around in the jar.

—That storm knocked a branch down from the big tree on the corner there, he said. Crushed the fence. They just stepped right over it, pretty as you please. Didn't take um long to find it. We're lucky more didn't get out. We left Elmer's truck there, but you'll need to get to it today and fix it up.

—If you want it done today you can do it yourself, said Jack. I ain't doing it today.

—Well it's got to be done. They'll bully it till they can squeeze between the truck.

—You or Elmer can do it. I ain't doing it today.

They rode to the barn in silence, passing his three-wheeler in the weeds. It was a cool morning with a drizzle of rain. Rain in July was fickle as it was rare and he guessed it would barely dampen the dust and be gone with the sun. The cows were wet, fetid, and kicking, their udders like things that should not be seen. They swung their tails into his face and lathered him with rank rainwater and urine. Some tails were clotted with smooth ovals of manure worn hard with age, and the cows swung these like medieval weapons. He tasted warm shit in his mouth when the cow he was working on lifted her tail and dropped it from above. It hit in sections and shot outward and upward from the waist-high milking deck. He spat and swore, and after sticking the hose in his mouth he washed the hot mess down the grate. He lost the bandages on his palms and his raw hands stung. The bandages on his arms became wet and hung and flapped until they fell off. One cow kicked like a machine set to do so and he tried again to guide the milkers to her swollen teats. Her leg moved mechanically, lifting and kicking at his arm, swiping blindly at the milkers. He had placed all four on her udder when her hoof came up and pulled the apparatus down to the concrete with a clatter. He grabbed the sensitive skin of her udder between his knuckles and twisted hard in a place where she could not reach him with her hoof, and she raised her trembling leg and held it as though it were struck with palsy. He tried to place the milkers again. Her hoof rose and tore his bandage off, opening up part of the wound on his left elbow. His face grew hot and he reached for one of the metal weights they kept on the milk tubes below the splash guard—a cylinder of solid steel five inches long and thicker than a shovel handle, a thing Blair used often to beat at their legs when he wasn't up to employing his fists or the splintered axe handle that leaned against the back wall. But the girl had whetted his spirit and therefore his nature. The memory of her calmness and composure coated his mood and he felt some warm longing in his chest, some fierce hope budding. He set the weight down and tried again. When the cow continued to kick he went up the steps at the rear of the barn and walked down the exit alley to where she stood. He feinted at her and pointed his finger within inches of her enormous head and she flinched and jerked in alarm.

—Not today bitch, he growled. Not today.

He walked down and tried again and she took the milkers. His arm bled and dripped thickly until it congealed to a clotted crust over his elbow and the pain subsided to a hot throb. He worked on the animals with Blair, who used epithets improvised and traditional like only men who work with dairy cows can. The old man didn't embark on his journeys of violence so often anymore, those trips where he methodically grabbed the axe handle, his serenity sticking to him like an odor as he walked up to her level and fleeing as he wielded the stick against her huge head and neck until the other cows were spooked and he was satisfied. He'd once knocked a half-grown heifer over the head so hard with a two-by-four that her eyeball fell out. She lived a long one-eyed life, her milk production among the best in the herd. His booming voice from below was often enough to scare a cow into cooperation. Sometimes he loved these cows with the diligence and duty of a good father tending to his handicapped children. Other times they were only a dirty, stinking living, nearly too brainless to exist within their own mapped hides but producing a white product he could sell.

Then they were through it and the sun was well up, bursting through the dispersing clouds in slanted pillars. The rising sun was the redemption of milking in the morning. As Jack unrolled the hose to wash down, Carrie walked through the side door. She was dressed so far as he could tell in Elmer's clothes. She wore one of the yarn hats she knitted herself. Her large pale face, its skin prone to purpling in the cold and burning in the sun, twisted now into a shallow greeting. He handed her the hose and they exchanged rote words and he got in the truck with Blair and left.

Sunlight fell onto the table and the kitchen was busy with the sounds of the two men eating and the low, unheard mumble of the local news as a third companion. The old woman had not appeared from her bedroom. Blair left and came out with her on his arm. He guided her gently to the table like she was made of blown glass and set dry toast, bacon, and scrambled eggs in front of her. Her wiry hair was matted in some spots and stuck up crazily in others, like a play doll whose specialty was a stiff workable thatch on its pate.

—Do you need me to feed you dear, er… said Blair.

She mumbled something, her lower lip sagging to reveal a collection of narrow, crooked teeth, some twisted, some leaning against another, all yellow and worn, not unlike the teeth of the aging horse they kept. She picked up the fork fist-over and leaned above the eggs. Jack watched her. Her hand trembled so that her first effort at bringing eggs up failed when they fell off the fork and it reached her mouth empty. She did this twice more, slurring words neither man could make out. Blair looked at Jack with a slight smile and a twinkle in his eye, his mouth full, his jaw working. The old woman set her fork down and her fingers descended like spider legs onto the plate and picked up a mess of eggs and brought it to her mouth. She blinked her milky eyes as she chewed. One of them ran. Jack stopped watching her and watched Blair instead, who ate steadily and shared his attention between his wife and Jack's own reaction to the spectacle. She ate her eggs, feeling out the last curds with her fingers, and then ate the toast in methodical bites and took small sips of milk. In all she tried to say she hadn't spoken a clear word and when she finished she sat in silence with her head bowed in fatigue.

Jack gathered the dishes to the sink and climbed into the tiny shower in the wash room and bumped his raw elbows as he cleaned himself, some wounds opening again and bleeding a thinned pink onto the floor. Since he did not have what it took to dress his wounds he put on clothes and searched for his good boots. The scrapes had scabbed over and felt tight and they burned until he was nearly comfortable with it. When he passed the living room the old woman was on the couch in her nightgown. Blair had put Matlock in the VCR and she sat listening to it, perhaps recalling the scenes from memory.

It was past eight o'clock by the time he came to the three-wheeler. He could see deep tracks in the hay where Blair and Elmer had driven through, evidence of their laziness, and Elmer's long Chevrolet parked across the field beneath the big tree. The machine started on the third kick and he killed the engine and sat on the seat awhile looking toward the McKellar house. He drove his truck to the barn to refill the dented milk pail and then returned to the McKellar house and got out with his heartbeat filling his ears. There was no answer at the front door. He walked toward the back yard and found no one there. He knocked on the door, called out. Then he entered the house, called again, and walked into the kitchen, his boots sounding heavily on the floor. He put the milk in the refrigerator. After taking a quick look around, feeling what seemed some kind of reverence for the place, he left.

She was blue water in a yellow land. In the days that followed, she flavored his life. He waited for those times he saw her outside her house, or walking the lane, stepping off into the wild barley that brushed her thighs with heavy heads as he passed. And when he touched a cow, ready to drain the milk from her swollen udder, he touched her more gently, his reckless mind insisting that somehow Rebekah could be connected to this action.

3

H E WATCHED THE OLD WOMAN EXPIRE IN INCREMENTS. It was impossible to say what went on when he left the house to the two of them, but he reasoned that there might be a side to his grandfather he'd never seen, that such a thing must have been there in the beginning even if it had been tempered or diluted by the years. Blair had started writing Jack's paychecks himself in a chaotic back-slanting scrawl. When Jack came upon the aged two together in the living room watching Matlock, her favorite show, or outside on lawn chairs under the tree, or at the kitchen table, Blair serving spoonfuls of soft food into her mouth, it seemed the old man was letting her down slowly to the grave. It was strange to lend any pity to a man who seemed indestructible and who would have none of it outright, so he didn't, but he wondered what toll her death would take on him. This woman was a zombie and as unsightly, the grandmother he'd known all but gone in spirit and the flesh only a failing receptacle waiting to be shed. Her imminent passing meant she would be relieved of her pain here, of her muddled mind and the stupor of her fading mortal existence, but it also meant that the matters of the farm would be decided. He did not know where his heart was on the matter, how much or how little he wanted what seemed to be coming his way. But he had waited and he felt ready for whatever would come. His father had said a man could only fashion his fate with what he was given, and fashion he must, but so far it seemed he had not been given much with which to work.

Early twilight and he drove the loader tractor to the bull pens carrying a one ton bale of hay on the forks. As far back as he could remember they had kept rodeo bulls, incredible beasts even in decline, like stoic gods when dormant, like the demiurge when in the violent throes for which they'd been bred. They were fed by a round metal feeder at the edge of their pen. He dropped the bale into it and cut and pulled the baling twine from around it. Seth McQuarters came across the field from his house and the two leaned on the plank fence and watched the big animals eat. Seth was of medium height with a slight wiry body muscled from a life of farm work. Dirty blond locks of hair curled from beneath his Peterbilt ball cap around his ears and his hair in the back was a little longer than the rest, a thick pad bulging from the band of his hat. His close-set eyes moved over the herd. The muscles of the bulls moved like hard rolls of earth beneath their hides. They looked agile, despite their size. Seth wrestled a hard pack of Reds from the pocket of his jeans, and throwing a glance at his house he wiggled them back in and took out instead a can of Copenhagen and plugged his lip. He held it out in offering and Jack took a pinch and worked it down with his tongue between gum and cheek, minty, rank, and comforting. He told him the can would leave a ring on the pocket and expose his new habit to his mother and Seth said to hell with the frazzled woman, he didn't care. Jack told him about the wreck, about Rebekah, and they spat dark streams into the dust and the evening was wide all around them. Darkness and coolness replaced light and heat and from where they stood, fields of crops spread to the foothills in one direction and toward the smoldering horizon in the other. It was a gentle night, and it felt right to be leaning on this fence, engaged in gentle vice, examining these bulls from a distance.

—Which ones can I ride? said Seth.

—Any you can get in the chute, except the one that killed that guy in Evanston. The old man said he'd need to talk to your dad first.

—No worries. He used to ride broncs.

—Bronc riders are different.

—I already talked to him about it. My mom forbid it, but she ain't approved of a thing I done since I got weaned off her nipple.

—These bulls are dangerous.

—I know it.

Seth tilted his head down in thought. It was only a matter of time with these bulls, a law of probability. Who did Jack know who had ridden bulls for a time and didn't still carry the visible proof in a limp or a vulgar scar or a wandering focus? He felt dread curdle like old milk in his stomach and fear coursed slowly through his veins. He admitted that he was afraid. It wasn't fear as long as they were stock in the pen, but to agitate them, to provoke them and pretend even for a few seconds to dominate them was more, and the consequences could be grim. He guessed that the fear he felt now was similar to when he first started fighting in high school. Once he was hit, the fear left and there was only the thrill of the fight and an abundance of violent energy to be dispensed. It seemed a similar purity that drove Seth, some design of courage, but it wasn't all courage. It took a measure of guts to get on a bull, but also a measure of willful ignorance, and a good amount of recklessness, and this became Seth's brand of originality.

Seth leaned his body against the fence, his arms folded on the top rail and his chin resting on them.

—That one there, he said, and spat into the dirt of the pen. You see the brown one with the dark neck? He's looking at us now.

The bull's bleary eye regarded them indifferently as he chewed hay, his hump massive and solid, his chest the girth of an oak tree.

Great wrinkles hung about his neck. The tips of his horns had been trimmed to blunt points but could no doubt still go through a man with all the greater wreckage. Each bull was monstrous and beautiful, animal gods incarnate, their balls hanging like sacked stones between their legs.

—What's his name? said Seth.

—I'd have to see his tag and check the records.

—How many's he got in there, about twenty?

Jack nodded and spat.

—Why don't he run um no more?

—Don't know. Elmer used to do it. Was his thing. He failed at it and here they sit.

—Which one has killed a man?

—It's the white one there, or is he cream-colored.

—What's his name?

—Little Boy Blue.

—Did they retire him when he killed that cowboy?

—I believe so. I never went with um for that stuff. I had to stay back to milk and feed.

—I watch these bulls from my window, said Seth. It's part of the mental preparation. Eighty percent of the ride is mental, Balls says. You got to find your peaceful center, your spot of balance on his back, right up on the rope, riding on your hand almost. That's the peaceful spot. Stay out of the house of pain and stay off his crown. You got to anticipate what the bull will do. Most guys get out there and it's just a blur, a whirlwind and they're on their ass and scrambling for their lives. But if you can slow time down, then you got it. The bull, he can only do so many things. He can buck, twist, or spin or throw any combination at you. He can throw hisself all four legs up in the air leaping like a frog and bending like a banana. So you got him then. I sit on three stacked bags of rolled barley with a piece of twine wrapped around um in the barn where the old lady can't see, and I grab hold and close my eyes, and then

I just sit there and imagine, lean in and out, back and forth, with what the bull's going to do.

—They give a buckle for that?

—Piss up a rope, said Seth. We got to get a watch. He dug in his mouth with an index finger and flung the wad of chew onto the ground like an animal had shit in his mouth. His tongue worked to gather the fine remnants. Where you figger we can pick one up?

—Town someplace.

Jack looked over the herd. The air cooled further and wild stars began to come out with no moon to dim them. Lights had appeared in Seth's house across the field and he left for dinner. Jack went back to the farmhouse dragging an anxiety he couldn't shed. His thoughts ranged in his head and overran one another. His blood was agitated and roaming.

Talk of drought sounded in murmurs like the rustling of dry corn stalks and it was not new talk. Blair preached about the management of the reservoir above them some hundred miles, told of great and scheming water wars waged silently, methodically, and with evil intent between farmers who sucked the reservoir nearly dry by summer's end to carry water to their crops. He said the field for a farmer was like his child, and the worry and anxiety that overtook him concerning his field was not unlike that of a father striving to provide bread for his little ones, for it usually translated into as much. Smoke from desert fires hung above the horizon and seen through it the distant ranges were blue and thin like ragged fins. Third crop alfalfa was paltry and the general feeling was that fourth would not be worth the diesel required to harvest it. One arid hot morning as they drove back to the barn after breakfast Blair remarked how tenuous a thing was farming in the desert. A livelihood in which everything depends on uncertain rainfall and unstable prices. He said if someone would have put it that way before he started he wouldn't have done it. He just thought people drank milk, and he could give it to them. He licked his chops clean of remaining breakfast juice and stared stoically out the windshield. They raised dust along the dirt lane and it came in through their windows and filled their noses and settled on their clothes. He said who knew what Brigham Young saw when he came through the canyon and viewed the Salt Lake Valley below him, but it couldn't have been much. People likened him to Moses, but he led his people out of the Promised Land instead of into it. Brought them to the desert where they now claim not to wander. He said it was worth wondering if the old boy stuck his cane there in that patch of dirt for no other reason than it looked like the most godless land he'd come to yet. A means for proving his people, and his people shriven. Raise something out of nothing. Turn the devil out of his playground and make the wilderness as Eden, her desert as a garden, and comfort all her waste places. He said it was a testament to human will, whatever else. It couldn't have been a trivial thing to turn this region into productive farmland and the same could be said for the keeping of it now. So much depended on the precarious turn of the seasons. Time was a man couldn't make it here without the Lord's help, he said, and that's the way he'd have it yet.

He rubbed a rough hand across the stubble on his face and it made a rasping sound.

—But now look at us, he said. Don't you ever forget, boy, that the Lord give us this land as a stewardship, and we can lose it in a blink, same way others did, this whole damn nation.

They picked Elmer up and Jack sat between them. They drove back down the lane past the McKellar house and across the paved road to where the corn grew. They talked of the pond as they unloaded from the truck, how it would be too low to pump from in a week or two, and the river was low too, the flow of the ditches drying up. Jack only listened while the two men discussed whether they would have to harvest the corn sooner than usual or whether they could wait and gamble for rain. They sent him into the tall crop and he walked the narrow trench between rows, from the front end of the field where the stalks were tall and deep green to the end some quarter mile distant where less water reached and the crop was short and thin and yellowing. He examined the ears and shucked some along the way. They didn't look as bad as he had feared. They had a month left to grow.

Down in the riverbottoms there was a fire going within a ring of stones. The dog came panting along the dirt track, happy with the result of her effort and wagging her tail, and he scratched her behind the ears and told her she was a good dog. Her breath was hot and foul in the air, her tongue stretched out like pink taffy. She tried to lick his shrinking scabs and he pushed her away. Heber peered into a tackle box on the tailgate of his Bronco. They were on Blair's land, below the farmhouse. In most spots a man could throw a stone across the river. The water flowed between sheer and crumbling dirt walls in places, its water brown from manure pollution and from the shifting sand beneath and the dirt it ate with its ever-expanding width. It ran clean and swift in the steeper land to the north, in Idaho, but slowed and muddied through this plain. Sandbars surfaced and disappeared as the river chose to build and destroy them. It wound an inefficient, tortuous course through the land, kissing the town of Juniper Scrag briefly and passing one clustered settlement after another before it spread out in an alluvial plane like the veins from arm to hand on its way to the dead sea that was the Great Salt Lake. A furtive dumping ground, it contained various refuse. Downriver, the arm of a disc-plow stood, rising stark and black above the water. Farther down the hood of a car could be seen when the river was low. Below him on the sandbank lay a rotting sack of dead puppies, washed unaccountably upon the shore and still tied to another torn sack that had held the stones. The corpses were decomposing in their slicked down muddy fur, their tiny white teeth bright in contrast, their dull skulls shown through in spots and their bodies picked at by scavengers. There was always wondering what else was under these muddy waters.

—Forgot the chairs, said Heber.

—That's all right, said Jack. It's good to stand and fish.

They searched the deep spots where the surface curled and eddied and where small whirlpools appeared and disappeared at random, Heber's hook perhaps fishing also for the ghost of his drowned father. Jack remembered the time they'd sat around an evening fire like this and Heber's father had placed a beer in the hands of both his sons and offered Jack one as well. When Jack turned him down Heber's father asked him if he was a man or a pussy and kept on until he had stirred up enough confusion and emotion that Jack felt tears sting his eyes. Heber, eight years older, sat at the fire smiling, and his little brother Henry took forceful drinks from his own outsized can. Jack and Henry had been young, maybe eleven or ten. Heber's father had been a true son of a bitch at his core, that was the bald truth of it. And even though Jack later began drinking in a way that made refusing a single beer seem silly, he didn't regret refusing it, because it had been a clear choice. And after Jack's parents died and Heber's mother had taken Henry and absconded, leaving Heber alone with his father, and Jack started drinking with Heber, and then began drinking more alone—that surging, muddled time when he hid bottles of whiskey in his closet even though neither Adelaide nor Blair would ever climb the stairs to his room, had sat on his narrow bed every night he was not still sick from drinking the night before, pulling long from the bottle's bitter mouth or taking shots from a plastic cup until he was reeling, alone, once or twice waking in cold urine to having pissed the bed blindly—that had been a choice, and it had been his, not because some bigmouth in a red checked flannel jacket, mayor of this puny town, said it was time, and he had made the choice on his own timetable. No one but Heber seemed sorry when the elder Rafuse was found in the river, not far from this spot, not a stone's throw, but it had worked a dark spell over the town and transfixed them all for some time. A ragged and frayed man he had been, unable to exist in his own skin. Heber put it that he couldn't manage the flame and it had spread forth and burned him up. He was always talking about that flame like he was always saying there were other women. Jack had seen Heber's father slap him once, soon after they'd been left. The man had slapped him, openhanded, like a woman would. And somehow that, the sound of it, was worse than if he would have struck him outright with a closed fist. Sometime after that Heber had set fire to the old paintless barn behind the Rafuse house. It was said that he would be shipped off, but there wasn't enough money. Jack had not witnessed that blaze, but it must have been something to see the barn burn. He had always wanted to see a barn burn.

Heber's pole dipped and his taut line swam in the water. He watched its movement carefully, his cigarette spent and forgotten, his eyes probing the river, sounding its depths and contents. He reeled in, let off, reeled, tested the weight of his catch, and finally the dirty snout of a carp broke the water. He reached out and grabbed the line, dropped his pole, and used both hands to haul the fish to shore where it flopped heavily in the grass. Then he wet his hands in the river and returned to the fish and spoke to it softly. He grunted as he pushed the hook, reversing it out of the flesh with an audible tear that echoed in the fish's open mouth. It was nearly two feet long and its yellow brown scales writhed and shone in the late sun. Its gills worked slowly. He walked to the edge of the river and tossed it in like a stone, then he dropped down to the sandy shore and bent over the moving water.

—This damned river, he was saying. It don't always make sense where it's going but it always gets to the right place, ain't it?

Jack lay in the grass, staring up at the deep sky, the smell of cooking hamburger and onions coming from the fire. Heber came to sit crosslegged, smoking a cigarette thoughtfully, as if it were a new thing, smiling faintly and watching the river like he was contemplating its age and creation. He said, You remember that time Dad brought me, you, and Henry down here to fish? He loved this river. He'd go up and down it in his motorboat, trolling, ruin the engine on the hidden sandbars. It's good to have a river running through your town. This town wouldn't be here, would it, without the river.

When Jack didn't answer, Heber said, I miss drinking with you. I never thought you'd stop like you did. It's not much fun getting drunk alone. He paused. Are you happy with your life?

—Not everyone wants to be happy, said Jack.

—Not everyone wants to be happy, said Heber. But you strive for it, don't you? And feel it come close at times? Tell me, are we meant to eat in sorrow all the days of our lives, or do we exist that we might have joy? And is that joy found in righteousness or in sin? Is it a balance between the two? I would that every person did according to his own conscience, sought his own joy, whatever that is to him, so long as it doesn't harm others or himself. Who is anyone to take my brand of joy away from me, to tell me it is a false joy, when my experience shows otherwise? Some of us don't want safety and peace, which is born from willful ignorance anyway, or we find a wiser peace in natural courses and from experience refuse to believe that there is no peace to the wicked, such as they are defined. A balance, then, an opposition in all things, a perpetual cycle. Each force needs the other, and each man needs both forces to work upon his life if he is to be satisfied. The ancient Greeks used to have pools of hot and cold water. They'd jump into the hot to open their pores, then into the cold to close them, and do it again and again, but it was the shock of the contrast that was invigorating. God bless the culture of morality. Without it, the primitive instinctual life would become common. It wouldn't hold the mystery and satisfaction it does. It's only when we resist it that sin becomes so delicious. But if you believe happiness lies only through some traditional brand of righteousness then you must sacrifice the full enjoyment of what that brand calls sin and in its place experience perpetual guilt at perpetual failure. Is that happiness?

—Only fools and the simpleminded are happy, said Jack. But even a good man does wrong throughout his life. He doesn't have to seek it out.

—But it's not enough to be always resisting, said Heber. That's an imbalance. He must give in once in a while. Let it go. Pick one urge, a good one, and yield. The man who is faithful to one woman despite the allure of another will not allow himself the thrill of falling in love with the other, of taking her as a lover, of having her for a time, of freshening his soul that way. He won't feel the burden of an unreasonable task leave his shoulders, even for a season, but will toil beneath it for whatever reward he envisions in some life to come. He will not be happy so long as he holds himself to the standards humankind has given him in the name of God. He must redraw those lines once in a while, and he does. He must keep a little vice in his life if he is to be healthy in body and spirit. If he doesn't find a balance his ability and desire to rejoice and live free will always be impeded by a heavy heart because he knows he's never truly beaten his own nature, wretched man that he is. God's path to happiness often stands in its own way. It is a snake eating its own tail.

—If God exists, then he'd know best, said Jack.

—A man can believe in God and still not know what he's up to, said Heber. Who he is. Read the scriptures. This is a god of a thousand faces, and an intelligent and good man can't agree with what this god's done while wearing some of them. We can't begin to know even ourselves, how can we pretend to know God? I suppose we all face our own times of crisis, but you're a grown man. A man needs things beyond farm work and loose promises.

—You mean a wife? said Jack.

—I mean a woman. A man needs a woman, or he might go to

cows and work unseemly things. How long's it been since you had a girl around?

—A few months, said Jack.

—It's been over a year, said Heber.

—What am I supposed to do about that? This place ain't a capital for eligible women.

—Then search elsewhere. You never go with me to town anymore.

—I got tired of it. There was no substance to it.

—And that's the cycle, said Heber. You needed a change, sure. But the cycle must continue, like a boy climbing all his father's trees, swinging back down, and his father's trees are endless. You want to live a life of no regrets and you're setting yourself up for a glut of them. You're missing a large part of what it means to be a young man in this rich world. Nearly all the things I regret are things I never did. Experience teaches me this, against the empty rhetoric that is its fabricated counter. It's rarely what I've done that brings remorse, it's what I've failed to do.

—It depends on how you define regrets, said Jack. One man's satisfaction is another man's regret.

—Well said, said Heber. That is well said, damn it.

—What about Geneva?

—If she comes back it's a temporary remedy. I haven't met the woman yet who can be the end of everything and I doubt she exists. Monogamy is a compromise on both parts, a paradox acceptable to most. But until I get there I must take what each woman gives as I encounter each and build myself that way, live that way.

—You've given up living any commandments but those you've wrote yourself, said Jack.

—You're goddamn right! said Heber, and his body went rigid and stiffened forward and his face suffused with blood. He settled back again in a slouch and smiled and said, You've got a good heart, John. A very good heart.

—I used to have a good heart, said Jack.

—This change happens to most men, said Heber. But you've evolved is all. Like an animal in a circus, you were taught the tricks. But at some point you lost the show. You kept performing for a crowd that wasn't there, and though your tricks lost their fine edge and you blundered the steps here and there in an ever loosening ritual, you still retained the basic shape of things. The only thing left for you to do was fall, and that was the natural step to your evolution. After the fall you remake yourself.

Jack said he wasn't sure what had happened.

Heber said, As a boy you cursed God, and as a man you wait in the lee.

—I don't know what that means, said Jack, but I like the way it sounds. Write that down, I'll put it on my gravestone.

Heber said, What happens when a man abandons the religion of his upbringing when he was so close to it, when he asks: Is what I've been taught my whole life of God, or is it the contrivance of man? and finds an unfavorable answer? There's a vacuum to fill, and you have nothing to fill it with. Where do you look for a moral compass? Not society. Only a fool lets the shifting fashions of society teach him how to live. A man must look within himself in order to see beyond himself, and he must look beyond himself in order to see within himself. You're still holding on to remnants, even if you can't see them.

—The death of my parents, bad as it was, was not the beginning of my situation now, said Jack. I've lost some things and I don't know where or when I lost them. But I haven't lost everything.

—A man has nothing to lose but his chains, said Heber. They say peace with God requires strict servitude. But why must we be slaves? God frees his people only to enslave them to himself. One slavemaster is traded for another. Who is this despot we give our devotion to? Are we not the progeny of deity? What end does it serve to receive the greatest gift only to give it right back?

—Belief in religion and belief in God can be two different

things, said Jack. It's hard to say sometimes.

—You've still got a good heart, said Heber. You've only buried it, let it shrivel a little. Let it expand with new blood and you'll be reborn. Your entire life could pass this way if you're not careful. You know what the Lord said about being lukewarm. He will spue thee out of his mouth.

—Am I lukewarm? said Jack.

—Weeds overrun a garden left untended, said Heber. I've heard you say you'd like to get back to the way things were before your parents died, and just after. It seems like it was a good place to be, you say. But the past nearly always seems that way. You had a measure of innocence then, but some questions, when asked, cannot be unasked. You have asked those questions. You seem to be encountering the same doubts as your father, those you read penned in his journal after his death, the ones that shook you to the core, the ones that have never left you.

—Don't worry about that, said Jack. You didn't read them. I did.

—His wonderings were not uncommon, said Heber, and the answers that used to trip off our tongues are insufficient. We had those answers ready once, but they broke down, as they will for anyone once he gives them serious thought. Sunday school answers cannot abide this weight. This plan, this organization of religion, replete with the confusion of a tradeshow with each huckster calling out his brand of ware, in a world of billions of inhabitants, God's children all—are we to believe that God's one true way will be known by so few? That this is the plan of a generous and loving God? Look at the world. Things aren't going well for God, so why does he stay hidden? If he has the ability to manifest himself, why does he allow the world to remain in confusion? He should show himself from time to time in better ways than vague impressions, reward us for our faith. Show your gospel, Friend, don't puff at it like a poisoned dandelion and watch its dead seeds scatter.

—Faith, said Jack. There's something you can think on your

whole life and not understand. It's an abstraction. I guess it has something to do with it, if it's anything at all. But damned if anyone can say exactly what. They start talking about faith in church and you might as well be listening to a lunatic talk about his pecker.

He stirred the coals, readjusted the dinners. Heber stared at him, his eyes wide and sober, worried, his expression one of utmost gravity and earnestness. Jack burst out laughing. Heber's visage softened and he smiled, though his eyes remained wide and his voice intense and prophetic.

—There are no answers, he said. The more you probe the more elusive the answers become. The more you know the more you realize you don't know. We'll just have to wait till we die to see what the big show was all about, and even then we might not know.

—That ought to be something, said Jack. I'd give my dad's silver dollar to find out what's going on over there.

—Look at me, said Heber. Where have I gone? You remember when I used to be good, don't you? Who knows what happiness is? Who can define it? But I guess I'm comfortable and content, and there's a legitimate brand of happiness in that. I'm happy right now, in this moment. I have the river, the grass, the hillside throwing good shade. I have good food cooking and a good drink in my callused hand. I look at you and I only want you to be happy, whatever that is to you. You are the most important person to me. Did you know that? Dad's gone. That bitch of a mother… You're it, brother. All right. We'll find new blood for you, and it will change your life.

—Already found it, said Jack. It's up over that hill there.

—You don't think I can do that for you? said Heber.

—It's not too much to ask, is it? said Jack.

—No it's not, said Heber. We'll get you there, buddy. We'll get you there. She's got the blood you need.

—You going to work some spell that makes a proud city girl fall in love with a stinking dairy farmer? said Jack. I'd owe you. I'd owe anything that made that happen.

—All good things come at some price, said Heber.

—I need something, said Jack. I feel like I'm about to go buckwild. If nothing comes, it'll be buckwild for me.

—Buckwild's a good place to go, said Heber. Be the wild man of the woods for a while. I've been there a few times myself. You need something. Some expansion, some catalyst for revival.

—Right now I'm just hungry, said Jack. I need food.

Heber regarded him evenly from across the fire, looking wise in his tattered clothing, his beard, his holey shirt and frayed pants, like some river guru in the wilderness, ready to take him down to the river for baptism.

—I am the bread of life, he said.

—You are a blasphemer.

—Let's partake.

The river moved by. They burned their fingers opening their dinners.

The dry days passed into late August and what little grain they had was harvested by a hired combine and the stalks spewed out in straight rows. Then the baler did its own work behind the tractor, its rolling teeth gathering the rows, the auger and claw carrying the straw to the press chamber where the plunger shook the whole machine with its motion and created a rectangular bale that was bound with two lengths of orange twine and dropped neatly into the field. The hit of the plunger rocked the tractor and swayed him in his seat in a steady rhythm and his eyes were red and worn from the diesel smoke that escaped prematurely from the broken muffler. He thought he would get a spell from either Blair or Elmer, and he thought one would bring him food and water, for he'd been on the tractor since morning and had broken down twice and had repaired the baler both times with tools and bolts found in the baler's toolbox, but so far no one had come and he now believed no one would. By evening he still baled golden rows on golden stubble and watched his shadow grow longer before him when he moved away from the sun. His vision was filled with the rows shining on the field. He thought he would get most of this field done and quit, but as the long solitary hours grew longer he worked like he needed it and knew he would finish the field. He baled straw in the soft gloaming and was finished when the light was a wash of pale blue in the west. As he drove away pulling the dusty implement he looked back at the clean field and the yellow bales studding it.

Down the darkening lane his lights caught a figure walking ahead and a jolt coursed through his tired body and ebbed away slowly. She swung the empty milk pail as she walked and turned back once to see him approaching. He rolled up next to her and nodded to the wheel well and she climbed up. The night was dry and warm and she was strange on his tractor, a craved apparition appeared to fulfill his longing.

—Coming to steal some milk? he said. I should charge you.

—What will it cost me? she said.

They were close enough that his dusty arm brushed her knee as he ran up the throttle on the tractor, and he rolled the big machine forward. She wore shorts and after setting the milk pail down on top of a piled chain put her feet on the armrest of his seat and scratched at her shins with both hands, providing a good angle of her full thigh. She scratched indulgently, hissing breath between her teeth and grimacing. He looked at her.

—Eczema, she said.

At the barn he led her through the front doors and into the tank room. The last pale light of the day gleamed dully off the silver surface of the big oval tank. He bent at its base to unscrew the drain cap and she stood close.

—Have you done this before? he said.

She shook her head.

—I'll show you how, so next time you don't spill milk all over.

He set the cap and its center on the concrete floor with the inside facing up to keep it clean. He tilted the pail under the mouth of the drain and turned the lever a little. White milk gushed out in a twisted stream and made the pail ring. Exhaustion settled over him and he relaxed with a sigh.

—Don't ever turn it more than this, he said. He looked up the length of her body to her face. This is like a fire hydrant. Much more than this and you'd have a hell of a mess. Knock the pail right out of your hand. Knock you over maybe.

When the frothy head reached the top he closed the lever and set the pail down and screwed the cap back on the drain.

—There you go.

She thanked him and bent for the pail and turned to leave.

—I haven't seen anybody come get milk in a while, he said. Tom used to.

She looked down at the dented milk can.

—This is the milk you got from your cows this morning?

—Yes, he said, standing. And tonight. But they aren't my cows.

—Why not?

—I work here. They aren't mine.

—Well don't ever sell one for a handful of magic beans, she said. Or maybe you should. She gave a soft laugh, barely smiling, and its oddness was fetching. She was a consistent series of pleasant surprises and he watched her like she was something new and wholly unusual.

—Come in here for a minute, he said.

He moved across the room and opened the door to the milking parlor and waited for her to come through. The barn was dark and cool and blue light fell from high windows that dimmed farther with each minute gone. Their movements echoed. He didn't bother with the lights.

—Is this where the cows come? she said.

—Twice a day. They never stop coming. Sit up there.

She inspected the milking deck to see if it was clean and jumped up.

—It's cool in here, she said. Feels good.

He came to her with a small tin box.

—This is a salve medicine we use on the udders when they get dry and cracked, he said. I've heard women use it sometimes too, on their fingernails. But it might help your legs. Where does it itch?

She pointed to several areas on both shins, and as he bent and examined them he saw patches of troubled skin, irritated from the assault of her fingernails. Her bare thighs had flattened on the ledge. How tender the skin was where they pressed together he could only guess.

—Stop swinging your legs, he said.

She stopped. Her eyes were like dark teardrops on her face and when he looked up at her he saw in them the reflection of the windows. He wiped the yellow clear balm on each spot and after setting the tin down began to rub it in with his thumbs. His fingers pressed into the limp flesh of her calves. He waited for her to speak, to object, or to say it was enough, but she only watched him with that calm stare that heated his blood so slowly, and her legs shone faintly in the failing light.

4

WITH THE MURMURING APPROACH OF AUTUMN came the corn harvest. Elmer pulled the chopper through the distant field and Jack and Seth ground the gears of the old woodsided dump trucks and made them belch black diesel smoke to make the switches in time. The trucks groaned up the lane full of crop and rattled back down empty. They dumped their loads under the rapacious gaze of Roydn Woolums, who worked the three-sided earthen silage pit with the loader tractor and with a newborn pride barely contained. He pushed and leveled his self-made mountain of kernel cob and leaf and tromped it down with the heavy wheels. Throughout the day the chopper rarely stopped. As the roaring tandem took the corn several rows at a time small groups of deer bolted from what had been summer protection, bounding across the field as if on springs. Full days of Jack and Seth driving back and forth, Roydn tromping, Elmer chopping, and Blair spelling his son during the hottest part of the day and in the evening after milking to allow him rest. The work went on late into the night every night, headlights moving up and down the dusty lane and the lights of the tractor scouring the black field. Upwards of forty times a day Jack drove back and forth past her house while rusted springs poked through the mouse-eaten seat and into his thighs. He dumped chopped corn at the mouth of the silage pit, drove back down the lane, and clattered and bounced his truck along the trenches of leveled corn rows toward the creeping green tractor and its hungry implement. It was this kind of field that spoke to him, that he had always loved for its desolation. And loved the entire landscape this way, in autumn, the trees stark and skin-stripped, a land laid waste and all things barren. The ground breaking down annual life to humus and skeleton. A land of ferment and sweet odorous decay. The land spoke a truth in autumn.

On the third day Roydn leapt out of his tractor and walked to the dump truck and said, Let me take that truck for a round, Selvedge. I'm getting bored here.

—You ever been in it before?

—It don't take an idiot to drive one.

Jack got out and Roydn climbed in. He shut the door and gave Jack a salute and Jack stood watching him. Roydn looked around for instructions on which gears were where. Finding nothing he pushed the clutch in and revved the engine and jammed the gear shifter down into the wrong gear and the truck lurched forward and stalled. He started it up again and ground the gears. Jack watched him push the stick around, a terrible sound coming whenever he pulled down or pushed up, unable to find a gear. Finally he studied the bald knob that topped the gear shifter as though an answer might be found there. He cursed and looked at Jack.

—Get your ass out of there, said Jack.

Roydn climbed out, got back on his tractor, and ran the throttle up.

It was past dark when the last stalk fell. Jack dumped a load at the pit and gave Roydn the finger and as he drove back down the lane he saw Seth coming, who flashed his lights and honked the truck's horn to signal they were finished. The corn gone, its shorn stalks standing like a field of tombstones, marked the end of one season and the beginning of another. The field stood open again and would till next spring, its fortress reduced to rubble and stocked away for feed. As he pulled into the McKellar driveway to turn around it seemed like the last chance for something, that she might be in there to hear the truck's engine rattling the cups in the cupboard. He had not seen her since that day he drew her milk.

At the barnyard they gathered on Elmer's parched lawn and waited for Blair to roll up with the chopper. They could hear his tractor coming in the distance. Carrie came out with reheated pizza, bought earlier that day in anticipation of ending the task, and an iceless cooler of some generic cola, and Jack was not too tired to curse their frugality in a low voice. They lay themselves out on the lawn in a ragged picnic, suns and planets wheeling brightly overhead. Seth stretched out on his back and fed himself from above. Roydn sat cross legged and hunched over, his back curved in the moonlight. He sniffed a few times, his head bending farther toward his open crotch to determine if it was indeed from there that the dark stench came. No one spoke. There were sounds of guzzling throats and stifled burps, long tired sighs, and then a noise atop the front step of the house and Jack turned to see the boy, Edward Elmer, crouching in front of the door in his pajamas like a misplaced lawn gnome. Carrie turned and said, Go back to bed, Edward. Go tell Daddy to put you back to bed.

The boy rose and went inside without a sound. Blair chugged up, bringing dust with him, and killed the tractor. He left the tractor in the middle of the lane and walked over stiffly. His face was haggard and dusty. He managed a foolish smile for them all and said something foolish, but had no appetite for the pizza. They all parted in a feeling of silent congratulations at the job done, and as the two men entered the farmhouse they found it empty. Jack sat down at the kitchen table to wait. When Blair did not return he walked into the hallway and through the darkness saw the shape of his grandfather standing by the bed with his back toward him, staring downward, his arms hanging at his sides.

Despite the hopeful whispers he heard, the body of the deceased did not look good, it did not look peaceful. It was a corpse, less alive than the dirt it would be buried under. The force that had made it something more was fled, drawn from its nostrils by the perpetual breeze. The eyelids were the colors of bruises, the cheeks sunken, the skin waxy and pale, the lipstick, applied by the hand of a dark artist, flawless. Blair stood alone at the coffin, staring into it as he had into the bed a few nights before, studying its contents. He reached his hand inside and rested it on the remains and before Jack could turn his head for what he saw coming he bent and kissed them. When Jack looked back Blair's shoulders were buckling, a physical change taking place like a mountain shaken by earth tremors and sliding. The wail that came from the old man's throat made the joints of the wooden pews buzz and the silence that followed as he pulled in wind was stricken and terrible. He sobbed, his body heaving with the force, and then it was over. He stabbed his eyes with a blunt finger and thumb and turned them red-rimmed upon the gathered. Bleary of face and small-eyed like an aggrieved beast, those two points of red misery searching the congregation for what, Jack?

The day was bright and blustery and ringing with autumnal tones as they carried the body out of the chapel after the service and the procession made its way out of town, west across the tracks, past the co-op. For the number of deaths visited upon the town its cemetery was meager, a small rectangle, not seventy yards long and not fifty across. It sat on a high knoll, the town beneath and the river beyond, and for the sharp curve of the earth you could not see the whole of it anywhere you stood. It had been planted with oaks, which had been watered well and were grand trees. They seemed larger than the cemetery itself and stretched their arms over the ground. Their limbs moved in the wind and the noise rushed around the group. Windbeaten gravestones stuck up like crooked teeth in the grass, some old and thin from when the first settlers had perished as they coaxed crops from the land. There were more attendant than were buried here.

Heber and Seth left after the burial service, seeming uncomfortable in their suits among the woeful tenor, and Jack walked away from the departing group to his parents' graves. He looked down at their single gravestone and turned and leaned against it. He watched the people and listened to the trees sigh. He had not been to a funeral since his parents'. Even at age fourteen it had seemed a sick thing to display a corpse, or a pair of them, in front of a congregation. There was nothing wrong with the service then, or the one this day, nothing wrong but the corpse at the front of the chapel. It was a dread thing that drew the eye repeatedly to it like a dark smudge in a photograph.

Rebekah stood at the open grave and now she left her mother's side and walked toward him. Not a few heads turned to watch her walk. She wore a black dress just past her knees with a black shawl over her shoulders and she stepped across the yellowing grass with her feet arched in spiked heels and her slim calves flexing with each step. Her dress moved in the breeze. Her beauty fit the day, raw with sincerity, cold with solemnity. Dark strands of hair blew across her face and she brushed them away. Her large eyes were lightened like shallow puddles in sunlight.

—I'm sorry for your loss, she said.

—We knew it was coming.

His tie lifted in the breeze. She reached to tuck it into his suit coat and her hand moved up to his neck for a warm moment before it fell to pull her shawl tighter around her shoulders. It was a quick, sure action, done naturally and without thought. The licking wind stole the warmth of her hand from his neck, and as she turned and leaned against the gravestone with him he looked to the layout of his small world, fields of harvested crops, the little cluster of his town, the simple homes. Autumn had come on fully, turning the leaves before felling them, and the land itself was bright with death. The leaves on the oaks would soon be yellow. Stripes of cottonwoods already yellowed in the small creek beds that led down from the mountains. The scrub oak in the foothills would become red and were also turning. Vast fields of wheat stubble lay ready to be burned, some fields already scorched black and plowed under. Oblique light slanted across the land. Balls Murphy's old backhoe, which he ran on the side as the town's gravedigger, sat in the bordering grass and sagebrush, covered in faded yellow paint bubbled and chipped and revealing spots of dark rusted metal. The landscape, the cemetery, and the girl lent a strange beauty to this death. He felt little emotion, no urge to weep. He had braced himself for a wind and received a breeze. Though he had certainly loved the woman in her time, that love had cleared like smoke, and there had been time since to prepare for this and it was no surprise. It occurred to him that things might come out, even that evening. He imagined that those things had been settled firmly and cleanly sometime in the past and that this day when the old woman was put in the ground would be the day his future at the farm would be revealed. It would be momentous if it came out in the immediate wake of the burial, it would seem his mantle, magnifying the drama of the passing, honoring it even, and he did not know how he would respond. He did not know if he would be able to think clearly should it come that way. The emotion of the moment might suade him in a direction he was not sure he wanted to go. Did he want the farm? To stay here alone in this town and work a lonesome and obscure life out in the same fields, gathering milk twice a day, beating his life out upon this ground—this was the natural course of things, the path that would unroll before him in some laissez-faire of fate were he only not to interfere. Was this the future he had envisioned for himself? This farm was both a boon and a curse, then. The boon was the curse. But the dignity of having that option should not be denied him. He should be given it if only to reject it, if that was what he chose, a small matter of human dignity and a symbol of gratitude. Human dignity among the eternal and ubiquitous odor of cow shit and fermenting corn silage. If he were given his right share this would be his living, his life, and how long could he last at that. With this girl could he do it? Even with her here now he viewed the world differently, even this death. The town was changed for the presence of her spirit and this change beat in his blood. He tried to envision her as a dairyfarmer's wife and could not. He tried to picture her living out her life in this town and could not. These unwelcome revelations crossed him like shadows as she leaned beside him on the gravestone. He saw Blair sitting him down at the kitchen table after milking and feeding were done, telling him, Son, you've worked hard for this farm. Here you go. He placed Rebekah in this future and it was a dream. He blinked his stinging eyes, his mind full of the vision, and Rebekah turned him away from the departing group. With an arm around his waist she walked with him toward the back edge of the cemetery where the wild yellow grass grew.

Heber wore a red and black checked flannel jacket over his broad shoulders and huddled himself down to ward off the cold of the night. When any one of them shifted, the dead brown grass crackled and rasped beneath them. Heber let fall an unopened pack of cigarettes on his palm and the steady tap was a drumbeat as they sat under the trees at the park and looked out at the leveled field adjoining. Heber and Seth smoked and held bottles in their laps and were enjoying themselves and being redblooded and vulgar. They were comfortable.

—Good beer, Seth? said Heber.

—Good beer.

—You wouldn't know good beer if it bit you on the ass.

—This is good beer.

—What makes it good?

—It's just good beer, Rafuse. I know good beer.

—You're a few years shy of twenty-one and you know good beer.

—Am I drinking a beer right now Heber? Do I got a beer in my goddamn hand?

—Better than what you usually have in your hand, said Heber. And don't forget where you got it. And don't drink it so damn fast. Enjoy it.

—I'll drink it as damn fast as I feel like it, said Seth.

—In this town a boy picks up his habits of vice and mayhem early, said Heber, like embracing new friends decreed by fate. But you, Seth, you've collected them late and desperately. You defy the relaxing manner these habits naturally inspire. If you're not meant to be together you'll couple by force, won't you. These vices are supposed to bring a measure of peace, but you haven't found it. You've done it wrong. You've gone from one frenzied consciousness to another. Traded each for each. Poor fella.

—Piss up a rope, said Seth.

—And now I hear you're riding bulls. And your mother will feel new ulcers bloom in her stomach as she drops more often to her knees in what must be as fervent prayer as there ever was.

—You want her prayers, you can have um, said Seth.

—There is no peace, saith the Lord, unto the wicked, said Heber. What of the wicked then? Are they not at peace? Do they not peacefully enjoy their lives? We do. Compare us.

—Just let me enjoy my smoke, said Seth.

Heber looked at him for a moment, then at Jack.

—Here's to the late and dear Adelaide Selvedge, he said, holding up his bottle. Here's to her, John.

Jack raised his Pepsi and they all touched bottles.

—She was a fine lady, said Heber. That we'd all be lucky

enough to find someone like her.

—You didn't hardly know her, said Seth.

—I knew her enough to say we'd all do well to find someone like her. A bit younger maybe.

—You'd take it from her corpse on the right weekend.

—Hey now, that's off limits. Tell him that's off limits, John.

—Where's Geneva? said Seth. I ain't seen her in a while.

—Welcome to the present hour, Seth. Where the hell have you been? I quit with her before summer.

—Hm. I liked her.

—So did I.

—Did she leave yuh?

—It was mutual.

—So she left yuh.

—I said it was mutual.

—She left him, he said to Jack. No shit. She still in Salt Lake?

—Finishing law school. She'll be done in the spring.

—Maybe I'll go look her up. Marry me a lawyer.

—You want my sloppy seconds?

—That's what you get with most girls, said Seth. Or fifths and sevenths and so on. Can't be too choosy. If she's a lawyer, that'll do.

—Will it?

—She was all right. I thought she could be pretty sexy once in a while.

—Once in a while, he says. Ignoramus.

—Why'd she end it?

—She wanted what I couldn't provide, said Heber. She wanted to get married and get back to the church, after we were through sinning. Wanted me to move to the city too. Can't practice law in Juniper Scrag, can you.

—What's wrong with moving to the city?

—Nothing. I can't go back to church.

—You should of done it for her.

—That ain't it, said Heber. He leaned forward, close to Seth. Do you realize the damage that is done, the rending, the tumult, the casualty of soul in hoping for obedience or progress, knowing a thing is required of you and knowing at the same time that you cannot do it?

These words were low and passionate and he leaned back against the tree.

—The atonement is rhetorical labyrinth and riddlecraft. Why must we be ritually cleansed of the natures God gave us? Do you beat a dog for being a dog? It's a fable designed to create guilt and the power that relies on it. Church government. Moral authority. Hierarchies of power. We are commanded to be good, yet destined to fail. We are told that we have sufficient within us to withstand evil, but we do not withstand evil. By some inexplicable justice we are held accountable for a fall we had no part in. And we seem to believe there is a line beyond which grace can come no farther. What is grace then? What of all the counsel and the guilt? Sermon and scripture alike bring it on like a shitstorm. We are made to feel interminably guilty when we can't leave natural behavior behind, something God put in us like a vital organ and asked us to wrench free and discard. What man seeking the joy he is meant for can break the restraint of everlasting guilt? *This* man, he said, thrusting both thumbs into his chest. We are creatures subject to our natures, like all creatures. This is what God and the world show us. We possess reason and conscience, which should give us an adequate measure of restraint, but when we spend our control on petty fabrications that confuse and supplant the conscience, which fabrications are beyond the basics of conscience and reason, we build ourselves a cage of falsehood, within which we reside like dreaming halfwits. This false construct creates its own brand of fear, anxiety, behavior, work, and counterfeit guilt.

—A lot of people seem happy in it though, said Seth. It ain't for me, but why tell another man how to live?

—If I tell you something that isn't true, said Heber, and this false knowledge brings you joy, the joy you feel is true. And if you never discover the deceit, the true joy remains, and so does the deceit. Whatever joy is created is true whether the thing that created it is true or not. This is the system, and the system is flawed, unnecessary, and not of God. If a man can be as good a man without the belief system, of what necessity is the system, and of what necessity is belief? If you can answer that question satisfactorily, I'll step down. There are two alternate scenarios, then. There is the man who has learned to be good without a church, and there is the man whom religion has shaped into being good, and believing in this goodness per se, he no longer needs his religion. This is common sense, though mostly we fail to see it. We somehow blind ourselves to sense in favor of its opposite, and when having faith in something ceases to be reasonable, which does a rational being abandon, faith or reason? What would a rational god expect his subjects to choose? The god we claim to know is a god who would be obeyed, with those who will not obey cast off. The problem is, no one can be certain of the rules. Where is he now? He's distant from us. Any town that's not on fire looks peaceful from a distance. But walk the streets, know the people, listen to the talk, read the local paper, and you'll see the poverty of soul, the disorder, the horror. Our god will let things get worse as we move toward the end, withholding his intervention, although you can be sure the chaos and destruction are indeed his doing, his passive vengeance—guilty by way of indifference. Where are the miracles, the intercession? Where is the peace from the Prince himself? They are withheld, and for good reason. The more degenerate the world, the more welcome the salvation and the more heroic the carrier. The stage must be set in the end for high drama. Bedlam. Carnage. Depravity. The devil's reign of blood and horror at its zenith. And then, in the middle of it all, who is that coming from the clouds, heralded by trumpets and carried on a sunbeam, coming to us across the bloodsoaked sand of the desert? And does he carry in his hand salvation or doom?

—Evil, said Heber. It makes us gladder for his arrival. There is a plan, no doubt, but does this plan win your approval? And yet God keeps sending them down where they struggle and moan and gnash their teeth and fester toward their horrific end. That he may do his work, his strange work. Everything is part of the plan simply by virtue of the existence of God. It's just a poor plan. Perhaps God is subject to some higher, natural law and is merely waiting for the terrible day of accounting over which he must preside. People pretend that such a god would not be worthy of worship, but God is God, and we have no other option. We'll take what we can get, I suppose, in the end. He may be a god of order, but the world he's created is not in order. He has set things in motion and has let them go on to what pandemonium must follow such a sophisticated and dangerous thing left to itself, and perhaps this is the way it must be. Perhaps he can only watch with great futility and some regret what we will do with ourselves. What we have done.

Heber paused to shake a cigarette out of the pack and put it in his lips. He lit the cigarette and inhaled and let smoke trail slowly from his nostrils.

—Jack knows, he said. He knows it's best to keep away from the fire that would purify us as gold. We don't need to be reminded. I give my demons rein. I give them rein. Most say too much rein, but if they only knew how I pull back. If I could change one thing about my life it would be to unshoulder this burden of truth. I weep sometimes when I'm alone and get to thinking about it. It's when I can no longer believe that I need belief the most, but I cannot undo my unbelief, and I did not seek it out. And for this we pretend to want truth, but when truth comes to us we would murder it, would crush its terrible beauty under our heel like a purple flowered thistle. Truth kills mystery and requires action—two things that don't agree with us. We want mystery, and we don't want to be required to act, to change. When truth is realized it leads a man either to his salvation or his damnation, both terrifying prospects. We've all got demons, and it takes something marvelous to tame them, if they're ever to be tamed at all. Jack may have found his remedy. The god he has shunned has not shunned him. You've got something special there and I hope you get what might as well be yours. It's not good for man to be alone. What are you without a woman? I wash my sheets. Do you wash your sheets?

Jack thought of his holey gray sheets that used to be white and realized that he had not once washed them. It struck him like an idea newly given to humankind. His bedding was a set of torn, stained, fetid, ragged, grease-shined pieces of a fabric. He had bought sheets some years back in a weird splurge at Kmart and it was probably time for another set now.

—I wash my sheets, Heber went on. It's proof of a civilized nature, of at least occasional female company through my days and nights. What would you be if you were alone in a house, either one of you? You'd get crazy. You'd wonder what you could get away with in whatever crude dwelling you called home. Your meager collection of dishes would clog the kitchen sink and counters because it could, and you'd half-assedly wash one at a time as you needed it, only to deposit it back in the sink dirty. The bathroom would fill with whiskers, nail clippings, little tumbleweeds of pubic hair. You'd start smelling the crotch of your pants crumpled in the corner to see if they were clean enough to wear. What couldn't you do alone in that place? Satisfy any perverse craving, entertain any bizarre impulse. You might have something, John. How lucky you'd be to have something to lift you up. At the funeral we were waiting for you in my truck when she came up to you, and we watched while you both walked away. She took you to the wild grass and that was a beginning. But you shouldn't talk to her about your feelings, if that's what you're thinking.

—I'm not thinking that.

—There was a serenity about her at the funeral that would lure a wretched man like you to spill everything, but it's only rocks there and if you go in she will break you.

—How often do you see her? said Seth.

—She comes to get milk sometimes.

—I'll bet she's got some good milk, said Heber.

—Think she's a virgin? said Seth.

—A question for all times and peoples, that one, said Heber. He settled down against the tree and said, But she's not.

—The hell do you know about it? said Jack.

—None of us know her history. She's a slow river. Who knows what's beneath the surface? But clever girls are perceived how they wish to be perceived. I know it ain't what you want to hear, but if she's that type—then my god man, you've got your hands full.

—And that proves it, does it? said Jack.

—You get a feeling from girls, whether they are or not. They behave in certain ways that betray the state of their virtue. This is a girl with some experience. I watched her grow up. She had a slow-burning beauty, a grace you can't teach, even then, and I said watch out. Watch out for that one. Girls like her can't stay pure.

—Maybe you see what you want to see, said Jack.

—Maybe you do too, said Heber.

—I used to want a virgin, said Seth. Hell yes, I did.

—This purity, it's not the only road of value. There's reason to value also a girl with experience. To two virgins it's a mystery—the kind you don't want—and without drawing on the accumulated knowledge of millennia of collective effort, it may forever remain so. They are children smashing a hotdog and bun together. Imagine spending those precious first months, years, not having figured it out, this thing that drives the very will of mankind, this reckless thing that God has inserted within each of us and told us to use with care, but which he uses just as recklessly to populate his worlds. It's no detriment to find a girl who has screwed around a little. Give me a warm tart over a frigid virgin any day.

—Is anyone even listening to this? said Seth. He raised his bottle to his face and examined its dregs.

—Regardless of all your theory and speculation, that doesn't mean she ain't, said Jack.

—Some part of us all wishes for that, said Heber. But have you ever considered that this virtue takes its very meaning from its loss?

—That sounds ass-backwards, said Seth.

—Some believe it can last in its rooted form indefinitely, but the greater tragedy than seeing it plucked is to see it wilt, to see its value fade until it is a nonfactor, nothing at all like it was and worst of all, forgotten. Tell me, Seth, do you feel the same for any girl's virtue? Do you pine and mourn over every rushed undoing, or is it only for the beautiful ones? It seems that some girls are so desirable that there ought to be a national monument erected when they are deflowered, said Heber. And the fellow that did it properly ought to have a parade. And yet we'd gladly murder the fool who takes it from one of these selected before it is proper. But when it happens this latter way we are absolutely mystified. We brood about it, obsess over it. What is this element, this virtue, and can it replenish? Put it on the Periodic Table. What is this deep mystery that stirs both our loins and our spirits so profoundly? It is God at his most mysterious and abstruse. And when God is crucified afresh with each spoiled flower, we are deeply shaken. But we also lust with a regret deeper than our sorrow that we had been the spoiler.

—Hey, you all know a girl by the name of Erica Birch? said Seth. From Hansel?

—I knew her from school, said Jack.

—Not that I ultimately give a damn, but what do you think?

—Good looking, said Jack. Definitely no virgin.

—That's just it. Girls that smoke are easy. She works at the Horseman. I see her there when I go in.

—Well, said Heber. That's something else. It's not every day. You wet your wick yet?

—My wick? At least I ain't hung like a grease zerk.

—That's me, is it? said Heber.

—I need some advice, said Seth, and since I can't get any around here but from a assclown like you, tell me what you know.

—What do you want? said Heber.

—Give it all to me.

For a moment Jack felt the sadness Seth's mother must have felt every time her son deliberately burned another moral bridge under her stern vigil. It was the glee with which he watched the flames, as if they alone were the pursuit. Heber was comfortable tonight playing the sage, if they cared to listen. Seth was drawn down to humility and innocence as he asked Heber questions about basic female anatomy. Heber began explaining, folding his legs beneath him and shaking two cigarettes out for them to smoke.

Jack wanted to take her down to the river to watch it move its brown mirth past the banks. There was something raw about the river, something primal and ancient. There was a duckblind down there, a shack like a lone, derelict temple, sitting on what was almost an island for the river's curve. When it came to getting a woman the farm was a fetter, though Elmer had done it. Blair once called that event an act of God. Divine intervention. Carrie worked hard at a man's labor when they needed her, washing the barn, milking some mornings, driving tractor, feeding, moving pipe, and Jack felt pity for her, was softened toward her, even though he felt he hardly knew her and her demeanor toward him was civil at best. And their boy, there was their boy to consider.

—What's up, John? said Heber. You look like you got your peter knocked in the dirt. I tell you I saw her the other night, right before the funeral?

—Where at?

—I walked here to the park to sit under this tree, and directly I heard the chains of the swings going. So I got up and wandered over and there she was. She seemed distrustful of me at first.

—You seen yourself lately?

—I learned a little about her. She's studying botany.

—All right.

—They left a bad husband and father. Abusive, probably, though she was reluctant to spell it out.

—Yes.

—She's active in the church. She's trying to live righteously.

—Yes. I know all this.

—She told you?

—No.

—Who told you?

—Woolums.

—Woolums told you? What does that asswipe know about anything?

—All of what you just told me, and a lot sooner.

—Did he tell you if she's a virgin?

—Dumbass, said Jack.

—Who? Me or him?

—I'd put you both on that train and wave goodbye.

Heber said, Tell me with a straight face that you expect her to be a virgin and I'll tell you you're seeking something that no longer exists, and that you can't demand it. Tell me you're ready to throw that worn out scruple to the wind.

—If there are no girls like that around anymore then God himself has also left us, said Jack.

—He hasn't left us. He's as bent over his work as he's ever been. But what you see around you is his work.

—I guess there's nothing wrong with looking for it, if you want it.

—Do you think you deserve it?

Jack looked at him.

—You're marooned on a remote set of standards that you're neither close to nor willing to forsake, said Heber. How long will you keep it up?

—In my estimation she's got what I'm looking for.

—Spoiled goods, said Heber. You don't want spoiled goods.

—I didn't say that.

—Be that as it is, in my opinion there is great glory in either possibility. You might try it. She might give you her kingdom. You're still in the market for kingdoms, aren't you? She has pearls, does she not? Indeed.

Heber resettled himself on the ground and let out a guttural grunt of satisfaction. He chuckled to himself and said, Would it change your view of her if you found out she'd fucked a score of men through high school and college, that she tasted it at fourteen and hasn't gotten enough since?

—You make a passable dipshit, said Jack.

—My guess is somewhere close to but under fifteen. She's got the attention for it, no doubt. Question is, how'd she respond to it.

—She's a good girl, said Jack. There ain't many like her.

—My estimate is only so conservative because she's the kind that will stick with one partner for a while. But I'll bet she's been fucked hundreds of times.

Jack laughed out loud.

—Who can find a virtuous woman? said Heber. For her price is far above rubies. Don't confuse beauty with purity. I understand a man's wish for girls to stay chaste and wholesome, however he defines it. But they don't. It ain't that type of world no more, if it ever was. All a guy can do is get his hand in the jar before all the damn cookies are gone.

—I'd take some cookies right now, said Seth.

—You're right that there aren't many like her, said Heber. She's that rare kind you could do anything with and never feel ashamed. Anything. Never regret a thing. It's a rare kind, that.

—She blew my mind at the funeral, said Seth. Looked so damn good.

—Got one of those fresh faces, said Heber. Could eat her with a spoon.

—She looks clean, said Seth. Clean as hell.

—Lick her like a lollipop and taste candy, said Heber. Get you some R and R. Some registered taffy. Take a ride on the Rebekah Railroad. If it ain't owned you can buy it.

—Rafuse, said Jack.

—Come on, Selvedge. I'm just messing around. It's not just how she looks. It's her energy. God, she's like a force of gravity. She's a juggernaut. A man needs to solve the enigma, examine her soft corolla, pull her apart, peer into that mystery a little, touch it, taste it, see whether it's the same as all the rest. And her writhing like a backbroken snake.

—Say one more thing, said Jack.

Heber shifted and grunted low in his throat and said, I'll bet she grips like a new sock.

Jack lunged at him. They collided and Heber accepted him into his open arms like a lover. They scuffled on the ground and Jack hit him in the face before Heber got his hands up. He struck at him as he would a stubborn cow, two more blows glancing off his arms. Heber pulled him down in a hug and Jack swung away at his exposed sides. His fists hit the ground, his knuckles burning on the dry grass. He tried to push himself up with his hands. Heber held him close and awkward with the dire arms of a brick mason, waiting beneath him, not letting him up.

—Let go of me, said Jack.

—Are you done? If you're done I'll let go.

—Let me up.

Heber loosened his arms and Jack got up and stood over him, breathing heavily. His heart pounded dully in his chest. A knot was forming at the corner of Heber's eye. Heber touched the spot gently, a sincere hurt and confusion haunting his eyes as he looked at Jack. Jack knew he would not come for him. He didn't know if he could take him if he did, but Heber never would come for him. Heber touched the bump again. It was over and Jack felt it drain out of him, that familiar release that brought with it a deep remorse and compassion. He stepped forward and extended a hand, and Heber's grip was strong and dry as he pulled him to his feet.

—My mouth got away from me, said Heber. Should've hit me in the mouth.

—I'm sorry for hitting you.

—I deserved it.

They were silent for a minute as they sat back down and Jack tried to think of an easy way to leave.

—You won't get it until you show you don't want it, said Heber. You know that though.

—Maybe.

—She makes you a little depressed, don't she? said Seth. I can understand that. Hell yes, I can.

—He ain't sad, said Heber. He's sober is all. He has always been. He is aware, and this has sobered him. He feels the way all good men feel when they are let down by something they trusted, something they loved and still love. But good friend, he said, you've found a new object for your ardent love.

Jack breathed out and let his shoulders slouch. Heber shook his head and watched Jack's face as if reading something there, and Jack stared at the earth he sat on and kept what he could away from that probing gaze.

5

I T WAS A GOOD BREEZE THAT CAME THROUGH HIS WINDOW
as he drove to the co-op the next morning. He walked into
the small store and up to the counter and said hello to Noreen.
She filled out an invoice as he recited the list of feed to her
and then read it back to him. She was a middle-aged woman, fine
wrinkles on the fair skin of her face, which had begun to sag gently.
She had dark brooding eyes, and had seen two daughters and a son
leave her and her husband for other places. Rumor was she had
been wild in her younger days. In certain moments she emanated
a mood of some missed thing, some alternate life she might have
lived in some other place. Other times she seemed as though she
belonged, a stitch in this common fabric, as if her essential fate had
always been moving her toward standing behind the counter of this
feed co-op and going home to her husband at night.

—I'm sorry about your grandma, she said.

—It was coming for a while.

—She was a good woman. She'll be missed.

—There wasn't much to miss by the end.

—Did the cows behave this morning?

—No.

She clucked her tongue and shook her head, eyeing him in

mock seriousness.

—Are you coming to church on Sunday? she said.

—Maybe I'll be there.

She laughed and covered her mouth.

—Should I save you a seat?

—We preciate the food you brought over the other day.

—That was several months ago, she said. Can I get my dish back?

—I didn't know we still had it.

—My last name's on the side on a piece of tape. Bring it to church, if you can find it. I'll save you a seat next to Bruce and me.

He folded the copy of the invoice she had written up and put it in his back pocket and said, Don't guard it with your life.

He walked out to the truck and drove across the broken pavement to the mill and backed up to the loading dock. He jumped up and handed the slip to Dirt Claude Simmons, who nodded to him and took the list into the dark, chugging mill. Claude returned a minute later pushing a dolly stacked high with white sacks of rolled barley. He took one end of a sack with his lanky arms while Jack took the other and together they swung the eighty pound bags into the bed where they bounced the truck on its springs.

—Heard about your grandma, said Claude. My condolences.

—Thanks.

—Nice day though.

—Nice day. How's Murphy?

—Good as a homo like him can be I guess.

The corners of Claude's mouth collected a dark brown residue from the Copenhagen he chewed, and his breath was rich with it.

—He's gone on a load up to Hansel. You know he picked up a night shift at Spackman's?

—I didn't. So now he's slaughtering beef along with this and the other? The crop dusting? When does he sleep?

—He's saving up. Wants to move down to Texas. He's scarce these days.

—Who moves to Texas?

—Him I guess. I don't know why he wants to go there. He's part sane, part insane. Claude grinned.

Wrink Poulsen walked out, his thin mullet curled over the collar of his shirt. He hunched a little and showed a smalltoothed sneer and his teeth were glazed with a brown veneer. His teeth were impossibly small. He spat tobacco juice in an arcing stream out over the edge of the concrete dock and nodded to Jack.

—How's it going Wrink?

—Fuck all, Wrink drawled, and spat again. He watched them unload the dolly without saying anything else and Claude went in for more. Wrink spat and put his hands in his pockets and leaned back against the wall of the mill.

—How's old Blair Selvedge these days? he said.

—Ornery. Belligerent.

—You know I worked for him for one day.

—I remember that day.

—I didn't quit. Ruther he fired me.

—That's because he thought you were lazy.

—Cocksucker. No offense.

—None taken.

—He was always a tightwad. Couldn't squeeze a penny out of his ass if you ran him over with a steam roller.

Claude came out of the mill with the dolly stacked full.

—He was a boxer at some point, ain't it? said Wrink.

—So he says.

—Who's this, Blair? said Claude. I ever tell you the time he busted Jim Goody's nose?

—Yeah you told me, said Wrink. You damn near of told everybody on the planet.

—I wasn't talking to you, Dink. He turned to Jack. Milk in the bucket, but wasn't that a punch. There's a man's got a violent streak. You could see that it was a natural part of him. Golly but he's a hard old boy. One of the old ones. Just stand in a ring and punch each other in the head.

—Can't be worse than rough stock rodeo, said Jack. There is a vicious sport. It takes a type.

—A type I ain't no longer, I tell yuh what. Guy can't last long in that game. Not long at all. And look what it did to the old Dink Wrinkle there. When that bull came down on his head it knocked the shit out of him and now he ain't got nothing left.

—Fuck it, said Wrink, and spat. He gripped his large buckle with both hands and thrust his hips forward, unrepentant, displaying a worn prize from days foregone and unrepeatable.

—A man of immense vocabulary, said Claude.

He sniggered at Jack as they bent for another sack and Jack could smell the tobacco. They threw the last bag into the bed. Jack jumped down from the dock.

—Hey hold up, Selvedge, said Claude. You oughta talk young Seth there out of riding bulls. He's been coming over to Murphy's place and begging him to teach him.

—Yeah, said Jack. I'll talk him out of it.

Jack waved to Wrink as he got in the truck and Wrink nodded and spat and Claude hit him in the testicles as he walked by, bringing Wrink's hands out of his pockets and doubling him over. Wrink spat his whole wad of chew at Claude's boots and swore darkly as the other walked inside the mill.

Jack rode back over the tracks and between the old buildings in the despondent square, and turning, went north toward the farm. The back end was low, the front end light, and he made quarter turns on the wheel to keep the pickup on the road. He drove slowly, feeling no hurry. He pulled in to the farmhouse and rolled back to the pens and killed the truck and sat for a minute. The truck smelled pleasantly of hay and old manure and he took a deep breath of it. After a while he forced himself out, stood, and stretched, raising his arms skyward. Elmer would have work lined out for him back at the barnyard, and he saw it would be one of those slow sunny days when he worked on the farm and lost track of his place in the universe.

Blair found a dead raccoon near the grain bin and Jack matched it a few days later with a mangled cat by the diesel tank. The dog had blood on her coat and a wound on her neck that oozed into her fur. Jack wrapped it with gauze left over from his wreck. That afternoon he called her but she didn't come. He and Blair found her behind the east haystack between the horse stable and a stretch of defunct farm machinery, lying down with a fresh puddle of vomit near her head. Her eyes were fevered and glazed and she drooled steadily into the dirt. He called her and patted his leg as he walked toward her. She lifted her head. He tried to get her up with the excitement in his voice but she wouldn't stand. After bending to pet her head he left her there and walked toward Blair.

—Can you do it or do you want me to? said Blair.

Jack scowled and looked away.

—I can do it if you don't care to, said Blair.

—I'll do it, said Jack.

—Got to do it soon, said Blair. Before she turns.

—I *will*, said Jack.

He told Blair he wanted two mornings off, and Carrie would milk in his place. Blair asked him what for and Jack said he could take a couple mornings off for whatever he wanted. That evening when the work was done he parked his three-wheeler at the crude temple that was the duckblind on the edge of the river, below and east of the barnyard, well beyond the small pond they pumped from. It resembled an outhouse in shape, built of wood, weatherbeaten, with a gabled roof. It was tall and narrow with a square base and room inside for a cot, a stove made out of a small steel barrel, and a spot of standing room. Grass and river surrounded it on all sides, making it secluded. Holes had been bored through the walls for gun access, and can tops, now rusted, nailed over them. He asked why the river didn't push that much farther and save itself a long senseless loop and produced no answers.

He unfolded the cot inside and unrolled his sleeping bag and walked to a stand of trees to find wood. He fried hamburger in a pan on the stove, quartered an onion, and watched it all cook. It tasted far better than it did at the house because Blair liked his hamburger plain and that's how it was made. When he had eaten he lay on his cot and watched the red sun sieve through the boards.

The hut was gray and dim when he woke. He walked outside to see if it was night or morning and finding it was night went back to his cot and fell into a broken sleep. He had tried again and failed to get the dog to follow him and became spooked several times during the night. When he woke to things splashing in the river and moving loudly in the grass his breath clouded the air and he burrowed deeper into his bag, divining what kind of creatures crept and swam around him but second guessing his conclusions. He dreamed strange dreams and when he woke at dawn he was possessed with obscure longing.

The sun came over the top of the mountains and shone through the gaps and knotholes of the boards and lit up the structure like a shrine. He walked into sunlight and through the shining frost-covered grass and urinated off the bank, his sparkling stream spiraling out cleanly until it broke form and thudded into the river.

He worked that morning at winterizing several implements, and before he finished he coaxed the dog behind the west haystack with a strip of bacon. At first he stood above her, looking down the sights of the rifle to the spot between her eyes. She looked back at him like she had done something wrong. He lay the gun on the ground. He knelt and gathered her into his arms and held her and said that she was a good girl. He petted her fur and kissed the top of her head and squeezed her as hard as he dared. She trembled slightly in his arms. Standing above her again with the rifle he judged that it was too great a distance to be sure of a clean shot, so he took her drooling chin in his hand and set the edge of the barrel between her eyes and pulled the trigger. He felt when the life left her, would have seen it leave her eyes had he not blinked at the shot, and now watched it drain from her body through her twitching legs and a few last beats of her tail. He had cried the last time his dog had been killed, but that was years ago. It was the last time he could remember crying. When she stopped moving he scooped her up, the wound in her head dripping blood to the soil in a broken line, and carried her to a corner of the near field overlooking the river. He buried her with a shovel. She was his fourth dog, all of them earning premature deaths and not one by his hand until now.

He worked sullenly and felt a winding down of things as he finished with the equipment. Some tug from a nameless direction. It seemed rooted in the burial of his dog, but sharpened as a skein of wild geese flew over his head in a loose wedge, honking and wandering south through the sky. When Elmer trespassed into his melancholy and told him they needed to haul manure he went and climbed onto the tractor. The afternoon was crisp and the sun fell with increasing weakness in its season. By the time he had the spreader hooked up and pulled over behind the west hayshed Elmer was already in the pit pushing manure around with the front-end loader, looking like a simpleton aboard the machine. After being loaded he drove down the lane, took a left at the end, and dripped manure down the paved road.

Once he got to the corn field he was in full view of the tree fortress that marked the back yard of the McKellar place. His daydreams settled into a new intensity with the rhythm of the driveshaft that ran the spreader, the rumble of the machinery, and he let this lovesickness wash over him with no restraint. He could let the energy she had brought to his life run through him freely. Her body was ineffable, her particles inscrutable. Her tenement was the medium through which she lived, a corpus of dust and flesh between her imponderable spirit and the world, that which touched the earth, almost as protectorate, a marvelous shell, keeping the spirit insular. Whether by evolution or God's hand or both, it was here in this town and she moved it upon the round earth. Her heart, by schemes he did not understand, beat regularly without compulsory means, fine, inexhaustible valves at work, an electric pulse at the center, drawing blood through her veins like milk through pipes. In her wanderings her skin collected the smells and textures of the earth and produced its own, and with his tongue he could taste these, could make her skin clean and original. That she could command her limbs seemed a marvel, fine limbs, or that her skeleton should be so straight and limber. When he thought carefully and tried to reason himself out of it he did not understand why he loved her breasts, why their form produced a yearning in him with which he could hardly reckon. Two pouches of flesh, slung lovely in skin, sitting up high on her chest in a way that dizzied him, each crowned with a featured nipple, a softly fleshed circle culminating in a salient tip. Her body as well curved in ways that stirred him deeply. Why was this? How could it be? Biology alone seemed insufficient to account for it. Hips, thighs, navel, breasts, fingers, wristbone, calves, jaw, ankle, and cheek. He could discourse on any part of her body, for this was how he had imagined her, but he could not reckon with her soul. He only knew that her soul moved him, that she drew him to her spiritually, and that this attraction was the more powerful, for it was the most refined. As he built things in his mind a surge of light-spiritedness ran through him and he sang loudly above the roar of the tractor and over the open field. He was proud of who he was and reasoned that she would be drawn to a young man like him.

It was simple work. The spreader's conveyor belt carried the manure to the rear where big twine-laden beaters spun and flipped excrement into the air. Occasionally a wet chunk would catch him in the back of the head. He would curse his superiors, their cabbed tractors, and wait until the manure was dry before picking at it. Sometimes he spoke aloud to himself and the noise of the tractor swallowed his babblings. He returned trip after trip, finding his stolid uncle waiting on the tractor with his bucket full each time. There would be no music in his cab, despite a good radio system. Elmer was the simplest man Jack knew, his life little more than a plain method of modest survival, mere shades above the sophistication of the very beasts that provided his means. Once when Jack was a boy and they'd been walking across the barnyard together, they experienced a small earthquake. They both stopped and watched the hayshed sway on its supports. After it ended Jack asked him what caused earthquakes and Elmer said it was when the earth got stuck in its rotation and then unstuck itself. The glory of God, the glory of man.

When the spreader was full again Jack ran the throttle up and eased out the left pedal and the tractor leapt forward a little as it always did with its shoddy clutch. He called it a whore and its tires spun on the slick ramp before grabbing and pulling the load upward. He rolled down the lane again, which was shellacked brown now by the uncontained drippings of the spreader.

Elmer called lunch around two. Jack wasn't hungry but was glad to get off the yellow seat of the tractor and walk through the barnyard. His high mood was spent, and in its place, apathy. Elmer walked ahead of him with a loping step. He turned and invited Jack in for some supper, but Jack declined. Elmer gave a strained grin and walked on.

That evening at early dusk Seth was on the chute platform above a dark brown bull identified in the records as Billy-Be-Damned. He and Jack had arranged the gates so that there was an empty pen to ride into, and the two stood on the platform looking down at the dusty broad back of the bull. Seth had on a vest, glove, a pair of old chaps he had bought from Balls Murphy—handsome red and black leather chaps bordered with full tassels—and thick metal spurs turned inward.

—No helmet? said Jack.

—That's for pussies.

—Is your mom coming to watch?

—She'll be hightailing it across that field if she takes a look out the window yonder.

In a minute he had eased himself onto the bull's back. Jack helped him get the bull rope around the animal's massive chest, then stood above him and pulled it tight. He watched Seth wrap his hand and listened to him recall the method Balls had taught him and speak it aloud. A low fear lurched up his throat like acid.

—Don't wrap it too tight, he said. You should give yourself a way out on your first ride.

Because Jack said this Seth wrapped it tighter than he would have. He wrapped it three times before he was satisfied and pounded his fist closed with his free hand and the leather creaked and the bull sat more or less calmly beneath him in the chute.

—I meant for my sake, said Jack.

Seth forced a grin.

—Don't worry. If I get hung up you just come in there and give this loose end a yank.

—Just come in, said Jack.

—You say you got that bucking strap cinched down tight? said Seth. His face sobered. His close-set eyes were burning and wet. Ain't no atheists in the bull chute, he said. Lord, I could use a little something here.

Jack climbed over the chute and into the pen and picked up the pull rope. When Seth nodded he yanked the gate open and the bull stood for a moment, two-thousand pounds of potential energy, Seth atop him, rigid as bronze, his muscles pulled tense as rigor mortis. Then with a hellish groan the bull was out. Jack felt the thud of the hooves on the earth from his boots to his crown. The deep grunting of the animal vibrated in his chest like a primal impulse. He stood to the side and watched as the bull threw its body into the air, its tail flinging up, its legs twisting to the side. The power of it inspired awe in him, and this replaced his fear. The bull leapt and bucked athletically, sure on its hooves, controlling that huge mass and moving like hell itself was on its back. It sprang into the air, all four hooves leaving the ground, and twisted its long thick body beautifully. Seth didn't last three seconds. He was tossed clear and Jack felt a surge within him as he readied to throw himself in front of the bull for distraction, but the bull trotted away, its head held high and its muzzle dripping, and the heavy cowbell pulled the rope to the dirt. Seth was up and yelling. He looked good in his chaps and vest, his hat in his hand, his whole self dusted over from his fall. He arched his back and screamed, showing his molars to the sky.

—Shit you picked a mean one, said Jack.

—I'll ride him through fore long. You watch me.

At the co-op they sat on the curb in front of the soda machine and pulled from their drinks. The sun was gone. The temperature dropped and the gray town lay docile around them.

—You want to go to the park and find Heber? said Seth.

—He ain't there every night.

—Where do you think he's at now?

—I don't know.

—Well you want to go find him?

—I hadn't thought to.

—What else you want to do?

Jack shrugged.

—You think he's at the park? said Seth. We could go look for him there.

—I said I don't know where he is.

They got up and drove over a few blocks, beneath the dark

church and around to the old parking lot and found no Heber. They drove to the shed and he wasn't there. When they came to his doublewide the porch light was on. Behind his tilted and bumperless vehicle a late model Impala was parked.

—What do you think he's doing in there? said Seth.

—I don't know.

—Think he's got a girl?

—If he didn't, he'd tell you tomorrow that he did.

—He gets girls, said Seth.

—What do you know about it?

—I know enough about it. You think he's in there?

—Son of a bitch, McQuarters, it looks like he is.

—Well if he ain't in there let's get out of here, said Seth. Go somewhere else.

Jack looked at him evenly, and when he got out of the truck, Seth followed.

Before they could knock Heber opened the door shirtless, his slight paunch held toward them like a greeting and a hand absently scratching his chest. He looked at them plainly for a moment before speaking.

—Seth McQuarters, he said. That you again? We were just about to come find you both. I'm looking for a shirt. Come in and see Maria and Penelope.

Two girls sat on the love seat. The one Jack did not recognize had a tongue piercing she played with and her eyes were black and heavily lined. Her applesized breasts strained against her shirt. She was taller and slimmer than Maria, who smiled at him and said hello as he sat down. Both girls were sloe-eyed and sultry and gave an energy that made him feel anxious and interested. Heber returned with a vintage high school T-shirt and pulled it on and said, What's going on tonight?

—Seth rode a bull just now.

—What bull?

—One of Blair's, said Seth. His chest expanded and a proud smile filled his face. Billy-Be-Damned. Mean as hell.

—Did you stay on him for eight seconds? said Penelope.

—How long was I on him, Jack? Felt like a week.

—Well, said Heber. What do you say we head over to the bull pen, have a fire? I'd like to see that bull Seth rode. He winked at Jack and turned to the girls.

—Too close to my house, said Seth. Let's go to the river.

—To the river then.

Jack was tired and wanted to go home and sleep, but already his blood began to awaken him, and as he stepped outside into the frosty night and took a breath of cold air, his fatigue fled.

Heber took the girls with him to Willow Valley for alcohol and Jack and Seth loaded the bed with four pallets they scavenged from the grounds of the co-op. They rolled in the truck over silent dark roads, down below the farmhouse to the gate Jack and Heber had gone through to fish. They drove through a corridor of star-limned branches and night shadows, and when they broke into the open they backed up to the fire pit where many fires had been built, many nights spent. They used to camp here as boys, scaring themselves sleepless and speculating about the mysteries of the world—God, Satan, sex, the liaison between the three. Back then they had discussed how God was. In these later days Jack only wondered how God might be. They unloaded the pallets and stretched out in the bed of the pickup and looked up at the Milky Way, a bucket of white froth spilled across the ink sky.

—I'm still buzzing from it, said Seth. Sitting on him like that in the chute, and then I got to tell you when to open up the gate, and then it's on. Mean bastard.

Jack felt weariness drift toward him again from out of the black night. The sky was enormous and cold above him, and from the river a trickle of current sounded.

—Hey, what do you think about Erica Birch? said Seth.

—What about her?

—What do you think about me going for her?

—I'd say good luck.

—Heber says to get on as many girls as you can, while you still can.

—That's what he said to you?

—You see those girls in there? How does he do it? He says it ain't that big a thing. Just happens and then you're onto it. It becomes a recreation, he says.

—The mysteries of life and sex, courtesy of Heber Rafuse, said Jack. Not the gold standard, is it. He couldn't keep it in his pants and now he's lost a good girl. He don't know when to stop. His god's a transient and he won't be able to catch it. Not around here will he be able to catch it.

—Yeah, but he's getting some.

—That's never been in doubt.

A screech owl called from the hillside like a girl being murdered in the trees.

—Listen, said Seth. You member the time we found that magazine in the ditch walking home from church? That was my first time seeing a naked woman. Member how surprised we was they looked like horses?

—I remember.

—Anymore I'm craving something I don't got. Birch's face keeps coming up. And her ass. He shuddered. I wish she was here now, right here with us right now in the back of this truck. You feel it?

—The older I get the more it seems like I messed up somewhere, said Jack.

—You sound like a old man.

—We'll be old men before we know it. I used to have lines and now they're gone. It's all a wash. I need some kind of lines again, some goals even, but I don't think I can redraw them. Everybody's gone. I feel like I've peaked already, but I look back and damned if I can see when it happened.

—I think I can get her, said Seth. I don't think she's out of my reach. Heber's educated me on a few things. I feel readier now.

As if summoned, Heber's holey mufflers sounded behind them as the Bronco rodded its way through the trees, and when he broke through his one headlight lit up the bottoms around them. Like the missing headlight, the rear bumper, back seat, a quarter glass, and other things were gone, transplanted onto Heber's project—his father's Ford Bronco of the same year, which sat in his father's shed at the edge of town. Jack saw the faces of the girls through the windshield when Heber killed the headlight and in his stomach settled something like a warm ball of wax against the cool night.

—Hello fellas, called Heber. A burning cigarette led his way out of the Bronco. Got—what do we got? Got beer. Got a bottle of Schnapps. Got smokes.

He was large with the evening and pulled out a case of beer and lugged it over to the tailgate of Jack's truck. Maria carried a six pack of longnecks and Penelope cradled a tall bottle across her stomach like a suckling infant. The girls whispered and giggled as they came. For the moment they were all in darkness, plumes of breath lit up by the stars.

—You get enough? said Jack. Hell sakes.

—What, you say you got some wood there? Heber called roughly. And matches?

Jack pulled a can of gas from the bed of his truck and poured it on the pallets. When he threw a match there was a soft explosion that sent him backward and had him touching his eyebrows to see if they were still there.

—Goddamn, said Heber. He spread his arms behind the fire's glow and spoke around his cigarette. I said let there be light, and it was done.

The box of beer was torn open and the cap of the liquor unscrewed. Jack was glad he wasn't milking in the morning. It was a terrible thing to do after a late night even though he would not be getting drunk. But the others would. The fire was hot and it warmed the metal of the truck. Soon they shed their jackets and sweaters and the girls danced around the fire to a song on the radio coming from the open rear of Heber's Bronco, which had lost its tailgate also. Heber said, Maria, darling, I can't give you downtown, but I can give you the bridge. Let's go.

Jack watched them. It was true that Maria had an astonishing backside. It was bigger than he liked to see them but it drew his attention simply because it was extraordinary in its form, and every time she turned her back to him some inner working clicked and he looked that way. And whenever Penelope lifted her arms into the air and swiveled her hips, long inches of firelit skin showed above her jeans. Lifted higher, her shirt revealed the perfect naked curve of the hourglass, which was hardly broken by the snug waistline of her jeans. Her navel jewelry glinted and trembled as she danced and moved her body. Heber corrupted the scene by hobbling over and dancing with them, all of them laughing. He raised his arms and stomped around spread-legged like he had crotchrot, a sourceless petroglyph come to life. Conversation spawned and lingered around the tailgate—fragments of introductions, stories, common plights, and always Heber's voice, subtle in its persuasion and powerful in its resonance. He came over to Jack and turned him away and pulled him close.

—There she is buddy, he whispered harshly. She's all yours. She thinks you're cute, she said so. *God*, she's beautiful!

He sauntered to the river and back, dragging deeply on his cigarette. Jack watched Penelope, who stood by the fire with her arms folded. She placed a cigarette to her lips and drew and he thought he heard the crackling of the burning tobacco, the slight pop of her lips as they released their grip, and the rush of her lungs. She caught him looking and held his gaze. She turned her back on him and walked around the fire and he saw a long, narrow slit in her jeans just beneath the right rear pocket that revealed a slice of skin where her buttock finished its curve. It made his adrenaline run. He saw that many things were unfair.

He looked at Maria and thought of her mother, who had always seemed like a good woman. She was mostly housebound these days for some reason he couldn't remember. She'd been his Sunday school teacher when he was a child, not spinning the web, but teaching the web, innocent in her virgin belief. Thinking of Maria's mother made him think of Seth's mother, who scrambled to keep up with her son's latest defiance, who laid down stricter rules which he only broke with greater energy. He thought of Rebekah's mother. She seemed a good woman. He remembered her sure hands as she bandaged him up, her wholesomeness and warmth, her soothing voice. Her beautiful daughter. That girl was up there, just up that hill not a mile away and across the field. He could walk the distance in twenty-five minutes. Though the memory works a subtle scheme of alteration and mended remembrance, he believed in the imago of his own mother, that she had been as good a woman as the one he now knew in his mind. She had been a pure woman, and why such a thing should be taken from this earth was a question he struggled with yet. She had warned him against iniquitous girls like this one he watched dance, her bare stomach smooth and flawless in the firelight.

The pickup's bed was clean save for some deposit of hay in its corners and soon a pile of empties began to collect at the front. Seth slugged his finger against a can of chew and offered it to him. Jack took a small pinch of the fine moist mess and put it in his lip. Penelope wound her way back to the truck and sought the bottle. This close he saw the lines of her makeup, her own careful artwork around her dark eyes. The black lines thick and turned up at the ends, the glittering smears of flesh-colored paste on her eyelids. She smelled good. He held a bottle of beer not half gone in his hand.

—If you keep going like that you'll be ready for another one by morning, said Penelope.

—He'll only have the one, sweetheart, said Heber from the fire. He keeps a hand on it so it doesn't overwhelm him.

—What else does he keep his hands on? she said.

—It's like you'd do with an unpredictable dog sniffing around your heels, said Heber. Something that could be dangerous. He keeps a hand on its head, lets him know where it is at all times. That way it can't surprise him.

Jack spat on the ground.

—You got it all figgered out, don't you.

Heber and Maria climbed into the cab of Jack's truck and soon rendered the windows opaque with their breathing. Penelope leaned languidly on the tailgate near Seth, who was acting as hard as Jack had ever seen him.

—They've got their own little privacy in there, she said.

Her face was open and full in the firelight. The darkness around her made it look like a marvelous sculpture, shadows and fire playing on it, shading her full lips and embellishing the texture of her skin. The exaggeration of firelight upon a woman's beauty, it will do for now. She watched the fire and began singing softly along with the radio. Seth drank beer slowly and steadily, accepted the bottle of liquor from Penelope when she held it out, and chain-smoked a pack of Reds. Jack moved to the far side of the fire, nothing finer than its warmth on a cold night. It felt strange to be down there, gathered around the flames. The moon was just rising and was large above the mountain ridge. The energy in the air made his teeth buzz and his blood rush. His mind wandered and fixed.

—What's wrong?

She had walked near him and now stood very close. He looked at her.

—You seem like the only one not having fun here, she said.

—I had to shoot my dog today.

—Oh, she said. Why?

—She got bit by something. Got the rabies.

—I'm sorry.

—It's the way it goes.

She stepped up quickly and kissed him on the cheek, and the spot tingled afterward.

—You poor thing, she said.

The physical contact changed something. He became aware of her there and she reacted to it. Her eyes smoldered like coals under wind and there was a sudden heavy heat in his chest that draped over him and spread through his body, numbing and tingling as it went until he felt weak with it, and she wouldn't look away. Her perfume worked all the way down to his loins. He could smell the cigarettes she'd taken, the scent of her hair, the liquor on her breath, a pleasant odor, and the rawness of her young skin. He considered her firm body. He stepped back from the fire, into cooler air, and she turned to him.

—Do you want me to get you another drink?

He shook his head and held up his bottle.

—This is good.

—Don't go anywhere, she said. I'll be right back.

She went away and he waited for her to come back. He wanted her to come back. He wanted two things, but he couldn't have both. He walked to the water's edge. The river looked ominous, as feral water does at night. Glancing downstream past the Bronco he saw her near the river also, a crouching figure half in, half out of the quavering light, squatting on the ground near the tall grass, her smooth haunches bared and the orange light dancing on them. The stream of urine falling from her caught firelight. Her face was turned calmly toward the moving water. She hunched over farther and groped at herself. He turned and walked back to the tailgate. Heber climbed out of the pickup laughing, followed by Maria pinching her nose, and they crossed behind the fire and got into the Bronco. It started up and drove off, lumbering away like a wounded bear. Seth composed a surly look on his face and said, The hell they going.

When Penelope returned she leaned against the tailgate. Her black hair splayed over her shoulders and one lock snaked into her shirt between her breasts. Jack looked at Seth, who was trying to blow smoke rings. Seth grinned at him and his eyes were swimming.

—What's up buddy, he said.

He threw his cigarette into the bed, leapt over the side, and disappeared into the black line of foliage, snapping branches as he went. When Jack turned she was beside him, close, puckish, ripe. She pressed her hip into his leg and laid a hand on his arm and her hair tickled his face and her smell was around him. He felt the light, soft touch of her breast pressing on his arm and her hot breath in his ear as she whispered words that burned him violet to the marrow. Her other hand fell on his leg in a hot grip and he had the notion that if he turned his body to her, allowed her a way into him, it would be as good as over. His want for the one was different from his want for the other. This one he wanted only to plunder and take, to leave her smirking and languished. The breeze came and he caught the odor of her spilled urine in the soil and he was off the tailgate and stepping to the fire. He laughed loudly and she stared at him. She walked over and grabbed his shoulders with her thin hands and looked into his face. She was nearly a full head shorter than he. He watched the trees where Seth had disappeared and she reached up and tilted his chin down with her fingers. Her eyes were dark and wanting.

—I'm serious, she said.

He let her move close to him and press her body against him and he let her kiss him, a trace of her tongue breaking the threshold of his mouth, that one taste of her, and then he was away from the fire, tilting his bottle upward and walking through shadows from the hung moon. He belched and tossed the bottle into the river. He turned, half expecting her to be right behind him, following him into the privacy of the darkness, and what would he do then. But she was not there. She stood at the tailgate alone. When he turned back his bottle was ahead of him bobbing in the current. He dug in the grass for a stone and missed with the first throw. He saw the splash and heard the gulp, and the disrupted water moved on a little before sealing itself back up, whole. The river absorbed the rock and seemed no different, but that rock was at the bottom and would be pushed across the sand at the slow insistence of the river indefinitely. He kept pace with the bottle as the river turned, and looked for another stone. He shivered because he had left his jacket on the tailgate. The black cold settled into him and his feet were wet with freezing dew. There was something white on the bottom of his shoe. He looked down and smeared the tissue she had wiped herself with on the ground and walked on. As he rounded the bend he looked back upriver to where the bridge lay like stacked bones in the darkness. He threw again and missed. He threw stones until he found one that fit well in his fist and zinged it and got for his effort the water-dulled break of glass and the bottle sunk.

The far riverbank looked more wooded and tangled than this side. Wilder. More so a place for wild animals than this one that had been tamed by man's hand and trod by man's stock. Its willows and dark recesses begged exploration because it had always been there, so close, and he had never gone to that side. Someone else's land. Upriver the fire shattered its image on the surface of the water and played its light on the trees of the hillside. From the trees above the river he had seen men dragging the water for the body of Heber's father using dragnets and hooks, men in diving gear complaining that they couldn't see the bottom until it was a foot away, complaining that they couldn't find the bottom in some spots, that they got turned around with the currents, thought they were going deeper and they'd surface, not allowing for fear but fear lacing their voices as they protested the futility of going back down. Then a hook brought it up. They had been men at work, scattered up and down the banks until they all gathered in one spot to view the thing they had searched for. He remembered feeling some peace when he saw them drag the limp wet corpse ashore, as though some good was done, some thing finalized to his satisfaction. Watching the men had been his own work the day they started searching, and the day after that they found the body. He thought of Heber's father waiting on the cold sandy bottom of the river, waiting for the hook. Huge blind carp swimming around him. The rasp of the hook dragging through sand, coming nearer, touching him, hooking him, lifting him, dragging him toward the shore.

Jack looked at the black water beside him and the heavens trembling in it. When a man drowns himself, does he swim for a while, thinking it through, extending his final moments, or does he sink right away. Does the river pull him under, and does he let himself go under, or does he fight some. When does he release the last breath he has taken and held, or does he take and hold one at all.

By the time he returned to the fire Heber was back and had brought with him a boon. Rebekah stood near the tailgate with the others. Jack squatted without a word at the fire to warm himself. Penelope was near him, holding the bottle of liquor. She took a drink from its mouth.

—It warms all the way down, she said.

—I know it does.

Rebekah kicked his foot lightly on the other side and he looked up at her.

—How did he talk you into this? he said.

—He knocked on my window. He's lucky he guessed right or he would've gotten my mom.

Penelope had moved closer and now her hand was on his leg. She looked up at Rebekah and Rebekah walked away. Seth dropped another pallet on the fire and a flurry of sparks pulled upward in an ephemeral ascent into the darkness. Heber was telling a story about a bricklayer who had fallen thirty feet off scaffolding straight into a tub of mortar, not a scratch or dent on him.

—Some men are marked, he said. I think Seth is marked. He's got that light in him. You just know he's one who's untouchable.

Seth swelled under the attention.

—Jack and I on the other hand, we've got the darkness, don't we Jack. Ours is to struggle and lurch through this existence, and we make our way slowly.

—Penelope's got the darkness, said Maria, and she and Penelope laughed.

—And what do you have, said Heber. The light?

He turned his attention to Rebekah and looked her over and said, And what about Rebekah?

—There's a girl's got a dark cloud following her, said Maria. You can tell just by looking at her.

Rebekah looked up from the fire.

—It's in your countenance, said Maria. You have a dark beauty, honey.

—Where does this darkness come from? said Heber.

—It doesn't come from anywhere, said Maria. It just is. Some people are born with certain things, like gifts and talents. But dark things, too. Bad luck is just another inheritance.

—Fate, said Heber. It's not luck. It's fate.

—Same thing, said Maria.

—Do you have the darkness? said Heber.

—It's been bad for us lately, that's all, said Rebekah. Things will turn up, I guess.

—I believe they will, said Heber.

The bottle was passed around and was over half gone, and when it left Penelope's lips and came to Rebekah she shook her head.

—Sounds like you need it more than the rest of us, said Penelope.

—I don't drink.

—We're in Mormon country, aren't we? said Penelope. She

passed it back the other way to Seth, who drank and passed it to Heber, who drank and gave it to Maria, the viscous liquid thrown against the sides of the bottle with each swing upward.

—Why are we so serious tonight? said Penelope. She spoke to no one and everyone but she looked at Jack. Isn't this a party?

—No California party, honey, said Heber. No such celebration of good life in general. Our times here in the riverbottoms are solemn and thoughtful. We're profound drunks if we're drunks at all. But we've all got our addictions. I'm an alcoholic, and Jack there is a melancholic. We're all slaves to something. The wicked are slaves to their vices while the righteous are slaves to God, but the strictness of God's commandments has little on the austerity of greed, the demands of lust, the rigors of various iniquity.

He opened a can and took a drink.

—Look at mean old Seth there. Pride of Juniper Scrag. He thinks he's found freedom in rebellion, but he's bound by those choices and to his newborn impulses just as Jack is to his moods, his indifference, and to a want the strength and depth of which, the power of which, he can hardly conceive, couldn't have three months ago, would've called the man a liar who spoke of it in the very ways he's now tortured with.

—Go piss up a rope, said Seth.

—Thanks for the sermon, said Penelope. You should be a psychiatrist.

—I liked it, said Maria, and she warmed next to him.

Penelope laughed loudly and wiggled the bottle in the air and laughed again. She looked from Heber to Rebekah to Jack and smirked.

—He's a talker, she said. What is it that you want so bad?

—I don't know what he's talking about, said Jack.

—What kind of a name is Juniper Scrag? said Penelope.

—It was supposed to be Juniper's Crag, said Seth, because of the junipers and crags in the mountains. But the map guy heard it wrong.

—Yes, said Heber. But it was specifically because of a huge nine-hunnerd-year-old juniper that grows out of a cliff face up near the treeline. It's still there. Guy who first climbed the mountain saw it and got them to rename the town from—are you ready for this? Heberville. Named after Heber C. Kimball, settled by his kin. How'd that've been?

—How do they know it was that old, said Penelope. Guessed?

—One ring for every year, said Heber. Science. How's that for a guess?

—Science is a bunch of guessing anyway, said Penelope.

—But with enough evidence the guess becomes law, said Heber. There is nothing surer than sound science. Nothing.

The fire popped loudly and shot coals out into the grass and one girl screamed shortly and the others laughed. Before another hour was up Rebekah said she had to leave. Heber offered to drive her back and she declined on account of him being drunk. Jack said he would do it, but there was large objection to taking away the warm tailgate, which was their center of operation. So he told her he would walk her home and they started off through the riverbottoms, leaving the fire behind and walking past shallow ponds of singing frogs, cattails standing like unlit torches. When he looked down he saw that her pants were wet below the knees and shining in the moonlight.

—Do you wish you hadn't come? he said.

—I wanted to come. I've been bored out of my mind. And it's kind of nice out here this late. It's unusual. It makes me feel better to get out at all.

—You should come out more often then.

—I've never been invited.

—I thought you'd left. I haven't seen you since the funeral.

—I come and go.

—I would of, he said. But I didn't know if you'd like it. I didn't know what kind of girl you were for sure.

—And what do you know now?

—I know you weren't comfortable at the fire back there. It's just what we do, these fires and things.

—What else do you know about me?

—Why don't you tell me something.

—Nothing to tell, she said. What you see is what you get. If my dear old dad taught me anything, it was that a person can't be held in the light of his past, good or bad, because it might be over, no matter how recent it is. Everything is changing, and I'm changing with it.

—Changing how?

—I've been sobered, for one thing. And I don't mean from drink.

She paused.

—I guess I would tell you about all of that sometime, not tonight.

—Can I see your tattoo? he said.

She stopped and smirked at him, then lifted her hair. He moved behind her and peered down at an elegant character of some kind stenciled on the back of her pale neck, its uncovered presence at once sinister and stirring in the moonlight. She let her hair drop.

—Do you have any others? he said.

—No.

—What does it mean?

—Hope, she said.

—Hope? he said. That's it?

—It doesn't just say hope, she said. It expresses the idea.

They reached the hillside and began climbing. It was steep and twice she slipped on the wet grass and he gave her his hand and pulled her up. When they reached the top, both were breathing heavily. He parted the barbwire in the middle, pressing one wire down with his foot and pulling another up with his hands, and she bent to go through. Her hair caught on the top strand and she froze, crying out and reaching behind her. He bent and his fingers followed the taut line to where it was tangled on the barb and worked it loose. Then he climbed through. The hair of many animals, mostly cows who rubbed their thick hides on the wire to satisfy an itch, remained on the barbs of this fence. Now her hair was caught there too, a mark of her passage.

She looked across the field to the lights of her house and sighed and he wanted to hear it again. She thanked him and they parted, she to walk over the low field in the scant light and he to skirt the hillside along the fence. He stopped when he was above the fire. Through the trees he watched it burn in the night and heard the drunken laughter and discourse, and Heber's voice overrode them all. He saw the shadows they cast like worshippers moving in ritual. He walked on. When he got to the farmhouse and into his bed, his clothes shed, his warmth returning, he tried to shuck off recent memories as easily as corn husks, but they stayed.

6

HE WAS ON THE GROUND TANGLED UP IN THE DISC plow, replacing bent discs and thinking about the long acres of soil he would work with them. Discing and plowing were the best tractor work of all, to feel the earth pull back as he took the heavy implement over it and laid its soil open. None but the disc and the plow provided that satisfaction and none but they produced such dramatic results. The sunlight was thin and the day windy and she walked up so quietly that when she said his name his head rose sharply and cracked against the steel frame of the implement. He despised the pain until she bent by his side, her warm hands on his head like a blessing and her dulcet voice cooing soft words of apology. Then she laughed long and full, cycling through tracks of laughter between breaths. The sound loosened him inside like fingers, and he rubbed at the rising goose egg on his head.

When she was finished laughing she looked over his work.

—Will the seagulls come? she said.

—Seagulls?

—Will they fly to the field to look for worms when you plow?

—I guess.

—My mother used to tell me the story about the crickets.

—Tell it to me.

—When the pioneers settled the Salt Lake Valley they planted their fields, and when it was almost harvest time a hoard of crickets came in on a wind and fell on the crops. They were eating everything up. It was all the people had, so they prayed, and thousands of seagulls came and ate up all the crickets. The crops were spared. There's a monument.

—Sounds like a good story.

—It's why the seagull is the state bird. And it's why that kind of cricket is called a Mormon Cricket.

—Except the crop was still mostly wasted, said Jack. And the seagulls showed up for other infestations, too. That's what seagulls do. It's been spun into miracle in order to promote faith. But deception is okay if it promotes faith.

—That's not the way I heard it.

—We prefer the miracle.

—I like seeing the field when someone's plowing, the seagulls. They're pretty on the dark fields.

—Yes, they're nice, he said.

She breathed deeply. Her eyes in the natural light were the color of stones under a sunny stream. He paused in his work, straightening his back and taking her in with a long look. She was dressed in blue jeans and a hooded sweatshirt, her hair gathered quickly into a ponytail and loose strands of it blowing around her. Only below her waist could her figure be seen. Her sweater muted the shapes of her breasts, but her hips filled out her jeans and her legs were long and full. This youth that made her body firm, that maintained this beauty in its prime—not by effort, but by simple biology in its full flowering, as though by leaving something untended and untouched it could reach its zenith—this youth that gave her strength, that made her skin glow, that lent her confidence and power, was surely a provisional thing. This beauty, the cant of her hips, the rolling of them, the long curves natural as hills, the high monument of her breasts, these things he could worship. What would it take then to bring it down, to abolish the idol and throw it to the moles and the bats? He could only wonder at the profundities of her body, only guess at her inscrutable mind. In his farthest ranging dreams he possessed her soul like a demon and her body like a tenant, her body like land, to inhabit, lay hands on, and requisition. She moved around and rocked in front of the late sun and became a silhouetted figure with roving hair and red glowing ears surrounded by an aura of golden light, and he squinted to see her. He pulled his hands back and untangled his arms. A strand of hair had caught in the corner of her mouth. She rose up and down, rolling and straightening an ankle beneath her. A natural flush bloomed in her cheeks, spreading over her face and uncovering her eyes, mystery of the body and blood.

—What? she said.

She was subdued in nature and leaked something somber into the air that he could taste. The barn hummed across the way and Roydn's shrill cries floated toward them as he pushed cows in to be milked. She set her eyes on Jack and he felt a great load leave his shoulders. She sat down on one of the wheels and crossed her legs and leaned forward and sideways with her arms in her lap and her hands pulled inside her sleeves.

—Can I sit here and watch you work? she said.

—I guess so, he said. He worked himself farther beneath the implement, lying on his back beneath the suspended discs.

—How come you have holes in your one pant leg but not the other? she said.

He raised his head and looked at his right thigh where the denim had been worn away and his thigh bore light crimson scratches.

—Carrying bales, he said. I should use chaps.

—Is it dangerous, lying under those things?

—The chance of the hydraulic pressure failing is basically impossible.

—Why don't you stick something under the corners?

—Cause it won't fall on me.

—That's stupid.

—You think so?

—If that thing came down on you, you'd be dead.

—I won't argue with you.

—I'm going to leave unless you put something under it.

When he didn't move she got up, he thought to leave until she drifted in the direction of the other farm equipment. The idea of her wandering around his barnyard and walking where his feet had worn the seams out of so many pairs of boots was pleasant and intimate, but he called to her and climbed out from beneath the discs. He carried a bale of hay over and dropped it under one corner of the frame. She sat down and watched as he did the same for the other corner. Holding out a dirty hand for her to take, he lifted her off the wheel and pointed to a spot and told her to stand there. He started the tractor and lowered the discs until the frame sank into the haybales. Then he went back to the discs, worn shiny and bright around their perimeters from turning the soil, but a blackened iris of aging metal spreading from their centers.

—Thank you, she said. Death comes in threes.

—That's a superstition.

—It happens more than you'd think. Like with my granddad and your parents.

—Is that it? Just the one time?

—There've been others.

—Give me another.

—I know there have been.

She watched him work until he was finished. She followed him to the haystack where he pulled down a tower of bales and picked one up by the strings and hefted it down to the end of the manger. His blood pumped an audible rhythm against his eardrums and his skin was cold on the outside against the air, but he sweated from the labor. He broke the bale in the manger, slightly winded and glad to have the effort of the work to structure his face as she watched him. Then he was done and the cows were eating with their heads through the bars in a long line. He threw a few leafs of hay to the horse and then motioned for her to follow him and led her behind the hayshed to where a bale of hay lay weathered and shrunken, hunched like an aged and fallen widow. They were out of sight now of the whole of the barnyard and they listened to the noise of the wind humming through the hayshed that could have been the rushing sound of the sun as it retreated behind the curve of the earth.

—I like the field, he said, gesturing outward with his whole arm. And the riverbottoms there. This is the best spot of the barnyard, so I buried my dog right down there yesterday.

He pointed to the spot.

—The white one?

—That was her.

—How did she die?

—I had to shoot her. She was sick. She might of attacked you when you came to get milk, or turned on anybody. She would of died of it anyway.

—I'm sorry.

—It's all right. There are worse things.

The sounds of pneumatic pumps and surging milk hoses and tinny AM country music converged in a familiar symphony as they walked into the milking parlor. Roydn raised his head from the udder he was washing and did a sharp double take. He stared at Rebekah while Jack looked up at both sides of cows, searching for a tame one she could touch.

—Blair here? said Jack.

Roydn's Adam's apple jerked up and down and he appeared to be trying to wet his throat.

—He was, he croaked.

Jack walked to the rear of the barn and turned to face Rebekah, who had stayed near the front and wrinkled up her nose at the smell. He held his arms out, showcasing the milking pit.

—I don't know where he's gone off to, Jack, called Roydn over the din, looking at him earnestly. You need me to find him?

Jack shook his head. Rebekah covered her nose and stepped toward him. Roydn's eyes were on her again, his sinewy neck twisting until it seemed it could snap. Then his head whipped around and he caught her from the other side. She walked to where Jack stood.

—It smells worse in here, she said. Why are some dirty and some clean?

She pointed to a younger cow that had large oval chunks of dry manure clinging to her legs like some kind of self-made armor. Roydn looked like he wanted to come over and join them but didn't know how. He removed the two-by-four they'd been using to brace the faulty gate and jerked the lever and the cows on his side began walking out.

—Do you ever wash them? she said.

He shook his head and felt the udder of a tame cow and took a teat in his hand. He bent slightly and, pointing the teat toward him, squeezed a line of milk straight into his mouth. She grimaced.

—This kind of thing puts old women to sleep at night, he said.

He moved out of the way and motioned for her to grab the udder. She took a teat in her hand and produced no milk. He stepped close to her. He touched her hand over the teat and she moved it and he showed her how again. She tried a second time. She pulled her hand back and sniffed her palm.

—It's an art, said Jack.

He grabbed the teat again and brought a thick stream of milk onto the milking deck with enough force that it splashed upward from the concrete. He motioned toward the front of the barn, and while Roydn brought the next cows in with boisterous yells and epithets to spare, an overwrought performance for his company, they walked outside.

She followed him as he carried a bucket of milk from the barn to the calf pens and began filling bottles. He showed her how it was done, feeding two calves at a time. The pen held seven calves, and any calf without a nipple in its mouth was a nuisance, pushing its head forward and reaching for the nipple with its cold wet nose. She asked questions about the farm and he answered them. She squealed when a calf without a bottle kept troubling the animal she was feeding and then licked her hand with its slimy rough tongue. In the pen next to the calves a bellyswollen cow lay calmly in the straw, gazing out and chewing her cud. Jack looked at the cow and then at Rebekah. He asked her if he could come see her around seven the next evening.

—Are you going to tap on my window? She laughed. Come to the door. That way my mother will believe they still raise gentlemen here.

—They don't, but I bet we can fool her.

Squeaking noises came from her bottle and he reached over and pulled the nipple out of the calf's mouth.

—That's it, he said.

—He doesn't think so.

The calf strained its neck through the bars of the fence, reaching for the empty bottle. Rebekah set the bottle down. She said she needed to be going and he watched her walk away. Roydn appeared outside before she had rounded the corner of the barn and he took a long look until she was out of sight. He came toward Jack wearing his filthy chore boots. On his head a neon green hat advertising a boyscout camp sat offkilter and he wore a manure-stained black sweater with wolves on the front, its collar separating itself from the main.

—Jacky boy, he said, grinning. He did a quick jig or a dance, something that looked like a mistake. A fresh batch of red acne spread under the corner of his mouth, raw wet and aggravated.

—Last sides are in, he said. I put Blair on um. I heard you guys are riding bulls out there at the pen. I think I might come join you.

—Have you been invited?

—Here, you want me to help you out?

He popped one of the reaching calves hard on the nose with his fist and laughed. The calf jumped back, stunned, its tongue sticking out and its mouth working. After a moment it was back reaching for the nipple. Jack pushed it away. Roydn sucked on one of his filthy knuckles. Lazy aureoles of cow shit like grains of pine spread down his hand.

—Little son of a bitch, he said. Cut my knuckle on his teeth.

He sucked the knuckle again and held it up for Jack to see: a bald clean knob, a small slice across its serried derm, raw white flesh revealed and welling blood like water through stone.

—Jack, he said.

—What.

Noises of squeaking air came from the bottle in Jack's left hand. He dropped it and stuck four fingers in its place.

—Fill that bottle for the last one, will yuh? he said.

—Jack.

—Yeah, I said. What is it.

—What in the almighty hell was she doing here just now, that fine specimen?

—You forget her name?

—I know her name. Rebekah Rainsford, he said, sucking on his knuckle again. Soon to be Rebekah Woolums. He looked at the ground and smiled at how it sounded.

Jack laughed hard enough to cause Roydn to look up sharply.

—That's good, Woolums. And you'd deserve it. Every bit of it.

Roydn handed the bottle back full.

—What was she doing here, buddy?

—Just seeing about things.

—She taken?

—What do you mean?

—Does she got a boyfriend?

—Doubt it.

—You going to take her?

—She came to see about the farm is all.

—You going to make a move?

—I guess I have already.

—Well you're taking too long, said Roydn. And I saw her first, remember. I'm going to show you how it's done next time. Give her the real tour of the place. I'll take the blanket from off the seat of that old John Deere. Take her up in the west hayshed, up in those rafters where it's nice and cozy. Spread that blanket out. Or if she's in a hurry, I'd take her into that office you're pulling your pudding in all the time, shut the door and get private with her.

—You talk pretty filthy for a kid that's just served a mission.

—I'm lonely is all. I need a girl bad. You know I'm all talk anyways.

—You want it so bad it hurts, said Jack.

—I want it so bad it hurts, said Roydn.

—She's too tall for you.

—Shit. I like them long, full bodies.

—She'd eat you alive, Woolums.

—That sounds good to me.

—You better go wash down the barn before Blair starts yelling.

—What base have you got with her?

—What?

—What base?

—You damn fool.

—Hey, she looks like she's grown into a real nice girl. I don't member if she's got a sister.

—I ain't seen one.

—What about Seth's little sister? Can you get me started with her?

—She's too young, you damn pedophile.

—Hey, if there's grass on the field, play ball.

The last bottle began to squeak and Jack pulled it from the calf's mouth.

—Don't leave without me, said Roydn. Tonight I want to ride a bull.

He walked away with a springing step and a loud monotone whistle.

An hour later they were at the bull pens with pale light spreading out of the west in a vast wash of color. Heber rolled up in his Bronco and got out stiffly and waved Jack over.

—The hell did you go last night? he said.

—Home.

—Why didn't you get it going with Penelope? She was ripe for it.

—Why didn't I?

—Listen, said Heber. I understand if it's about Rebekah. It's why I went and got her. Everything worked out well enough in the end anyway.

Jack grunted.

—Here's the best part, said Heber. He put his hand on Jack's shoulder and pulled him closer. Seth did her last night.

—Did who?

—What do you mean, who? Penelope. Three times.

Heber beamed like a proud father. Soon Roydn Woolums was set with the stop watch and instructions to press the button only when the bull broke the threshold, and to press it again when Seth hit the ground. He argued about being in the pen, complaining it wasn't safe to run the watch and be aware of the bull at the same time, but Heber told him if he wanted to be there with them he must do it. The bull was Buck Finn—jet black, smaller than the others, lean and well-muscled. He had been ridden three of fifteen outs his last year in the circuit, with a note of a dislocated shoulder a cowboy had received some years before. Seth sat astride the bull bold and sure. He pounded his fist closed with his free hand and jammed his cowboy hat down on his head and nodded quickly and Jack pulled the gate open. The bull burst out like an explosion.

Roydn had misjudged his distance. He backpedaled and fell and the watch flew into the air. The bull spun a tight bucking circle in front of the chute, flinging snot and foam and low grunts around it. Dirt from its hooves hit like birdshot against the chute. Seth leaned into the spin, his legs tight around the bull, his spurs gripping beneath, and rode until the bull shifted out of the spin and he lost his balance and was thrown hard to the dirt. The bull lowered its head and feinted toward Seth and Jack darted in and waved at it and it lost interest in the fallen rider. Roydn Woolums was on his feet but without his glasses. When the bull looked his way it was like he was jerked from the spot by a rope. He scrambled half blind for the fence, scampered up and over, and fell to the ground on the other side, clutching his ribs. Jack worked to get the bull back into the chute and removed its bucking strap and turned it into its pen.

—What was the time, Woolums? called Heber.

—Mean son of a whore, Roydn marveled. He slipped back through the fence and walked to the spot where he figured his glasses to be, rubbing his ribs as he went. What?

—The time on the watch.

—Yeah, it'll be around here somewheres.

He dropped to his knees and squinted into the dirt and raked his fingers through it. Heber went over and picked the glasses up and started laughing, bringing it up from his belly and letting it roll out into the frosty air. He handed the glasses over.

—No worry of these breaking, is there? he said. They're industrial strength.

—I busted um before, said Roydn, taking the glasses and examining them. I busted um plenty of times. See the residue of some tape here.

—Just what can you see without those stuck on your face? said Heber.

Seth found the watch and held up its running numbers. Heber looked at it and said, Woolums, you shithead.

—How long you think I was on him, Jack?

—You were close. You had him on the spin for a good bit. Five seconds maybe.

—Well that's the last time Woolums keeps the watch, said Heber. He has a hard enough time keeping the shit out of his pants when the bull comes out.

Seth was watching Jack. He had hardly stopped looking at him all night.

—Hell of a good ride, said Heber. He patted Seth on the back of his vest. Let's say you nailed it. Let's say eight seconds. Eight seconds! And this vest looks damn good on you.

Seth laughed loudly, ridding himself of leftover nerves.

—What do you say, Woolums, said Heber. You next?

Roydn took his glasses off and worked on the lenses with the sleeve of his dirty sweater. Jack could smell the raw stink of the dairy barn on him at a distance.

—I ain't— he mumbled. I ain't got the stuff. I ain't got any of that.

—Well you'd borrow mine, said Seth.

—Naw, I don't think so. Not tonight anyways. I don't got my nerve up.

—He's right about that, said Heber.

—Longer you think about it, the worse it is, said Seth. Just got to get on one.

—Naw. I don't think so. Not for tonight anyways.

—It ain't for everybody, said Seth. It ain't for chickenshits. He took a can of chew from his back pocket and slung his finger against it.

—I'll do it, said Roydn loudly. He shoved his glasses on and faced everyone. Just not for tonight. I don't got my nerve up. I got to get my nerve up.

Three of them squeezed between the rails of the fence while Seth gathered the last of his equipment and shoved it into a duffel bag. The rear of Heber's Bronco stood open without its tailgate, a cargo net strung across the back, and inside a plundered case of beer was cold from the air. Heber passed a can to Seth and held one out to Roydn.

—No thanks, said Roydn.

Heber held the can toward him and waited.

—No thanks, I said. I don't drink, you know.

—Woolums, you old miscreant. Heber looked at him and shook his head. Where did you come from and where are you going?

—I can only have one, said Seth. The old lady's been checking my breath lately.

—Is that right? said Heber.

—She does it, but she don't think I know she's doing it. When I come in late I have to tell her I'm home or she'll come in my room and check. And she makes me go in and kiss her goodnight. That's when she tries to smell my breath.

Heber laughed. He turned to Roydn.

—How bout you, Woolums? Your sweet mother make you kiss her when you come in at night?

—No, she don't, said Roydn. She trusts me. And I ain't never done nothing to break that trust.

Heber appeared to be struggling with what he wanted to say. His eyes held a hard blue twinkle.

—Good Lord, Woolums, but she is the ugliest woman I have ever seen.

Roydn looked at Seth and then at Jack and there was a thick pause.

—Kidding with you, Woolums, said Heber.

—Well I'm done, said Jack. I'm going to take off.

Roydn got into his Cutlass and raised dust as he left.

Seth looked at Jack.

—You going home?

—I guess.

—Let's get a drink at the co-op.

—You guys want to come over to my place? said Heber. We could maybe get a few girls over there.

—No, said Seth. I just thought about getting a soda, but it's fine.

—Well let's go get one, said Heber. Or come over if you want.

—It's fine, said Seth.

He turned to walk across the field to his house. Heber watched him and then waved to Jack and got into his Bronco. Jack started his truck. Glass-packed mufflers let out a snapping roar.

—Seth, he called. Let me give you a ride.

Seth started back. Heber rolled slowly out of the dirt and onto the pavement. He moved down the road, the only thing on it, his headlight illuminating the way toward town. Seth got in the other side of Jack's truck and they sat there. Jack turned the heater on and waited.

—Aw hell, said Seth. He hit the dashboard lightly with his open hand. Well. That girl last night. Penelope? I did her.

—Heber told me.

—She was… whispered Seth. It was…*wild*. But I've gone up and down about it today. Don't tell nobody about this, but I woke up feeling crazy this morning. I didn't know what to do. I wanted to come find you, but you weren't at the barn. I wanted to talk to somebody about it. Just strange. Feels like a huge thing I done. I keep asking myself, how was it? How'd it go? And I can't really say.

—Well you got what you wanted, and she gave it to you.

—It was kind of a blur, kind of hazy and quick. You know what I mean? I don't know how to tell it. It was like I had no choice with her coming onto me like that. But I kept thinking, just a little more, so I can see. And then it was all over. I don't know who she even is. It was like I left myself and watched it happen. I been thinking over it ever since. I just don't know what to make of it. We done it twice.

He laughed shrilly.

—I don't blame you, said Jack. She was aggressive.

Jack balled up his fists and set them on the steering wheel and rested his head on them.

—You never came back, said Seth. And Heber and Maria was in his truck with the doors and windows shut. And it was Penelope standing at the fire. She kept giving me the eye and talking with me. *Lord*, she was sweet. Then she told me to come here, and we went to the side of your truck and she pushed me against it and came at me hard. You want to hear it?

—That's all right.

—Are you pissed with me?

—Why would I be?

—She was something else.

—She still around?

—I don't know. I think she was leaving. I want to do it again, but I want to pay attention this time. She dragged me into your truck and we didn't worry about nobody else. Holy hell, I tell you. That was something incredible. Just us down there in the wild, alone, firelight coming in the truck, and the whole night ahead of us. What's left to do but screw her brains out? It was like we was the last two people alive or something. Nothing could of stopped us then. That was it, right here where we sit now.

Jack raised his head and looked down at the seat between them.

—At least you remembered to take the condom with you, he said. You give it to your mom to put in your scrapbook?

—We didn't use one. We was like animals in here. *Animals.* The things she did… She was purely wicked.

He sprayed uneven laughter and as it rang in the cab of the truck his eyes revealed some new awareness. Already he was looking forward, whatever inborn need for penance he had was satisfied in this confession. Jack leaned into the corner with his head against the window and folded his arms. The heat in the cab was putting him to sleep. He felt a great love for Seth. The warm bitch. She was Seth's opening into the world.

—Let's go to Heber's, said Seth.

—I'll drop you off, but I don't want to go.

—Nah. I'll go home.

—You all right?

Seth nodded.

—I'm fine.

—You're still a good man.

—No I ain't. But I don't give a shit no more. Haven't for a long time.

They sat in the truck awhile. Jack felt a sadness he couldn't explain. He pressed the stiff tuner buttons below the radio and watched the needle leap back and forth. Later on he moved the shifter forward and turned on his lights and rolled down the road in a low gear.

7

JACK WAS ELBOW DEEP IN THE WOMB OF A HEAVING COW, a pair of calf pullers lying next to him on the straw. For an hour she had been on her side, her great ribs pushing in and out, and Jack knelt behind her, feeling within her for the calf. Blair stood watching, an unnecessary coach. Roydn had finished the milking alone and now stood in the exit alley beside the pen. His hands dangled over the top bar and he chewed a toothpick he had produced from somewhere on his person, and he too offered advice. The cords in Jack's arm stood out like hard rope and the veins bulged. His breath came heavy between grunts. The air was filled with the raw smell of things inside now outside. He felt along the leg, searching for the second hoof or the soft snout of the calf, but instead felt a thin, hair-covered bone.

—She's breech, he said. Backward. Only one hoof pointed down.

—She's going to suffocate, said Blair.

—What else you want me to do about it?

—Wonder should I get the tractor.

—I'll get the tractor, Roydn offered.

—It's been too long already. It'll be gone by the time we get it hooked up.

—What's that? said Roydn. You want me to grab the loader?

They did not work as men excited nor affected by what they did. Jack wrapped one hand firmly on the leg, the other gripping his forearm, and pulled, his neck straining, his mouth turned down in a grimace. His arm moved out in centimeters and then came out suddenly, but without the calf, and he fell into the straw. Blair came forward with the pullers. Jack knelt again and pushed his hands in to attach the chain to the leg and then both men were pulling. They groaned and cursed with effort, Blair on his knees and leaning his entire weight backward, Jack sitting with his feet against the big animal. They heaved together. On the fourth pull there came out the tip of a pale, translucent hoof, on the fifth the calf to its hips, and then they repositioned and pulled again and there was a slick rush and a warm weight in Jack's lap. Blair yelled and was on his back in the straw. Roydn cackled. Jack got out from beneath the calf and knelt by its head and stuck his fingers into its mouth.

—Ah damn, said Blair. Damn.

Jack rubbed its slimy side vigorously and probed his fingers deeper. The calf's nose was purple and its eyes covered in a filmy fluid. It lay still. He lifted a leg and saw a small penis, the forehair curled to a wet point.

—There's one bull I won't be tempted to buy, said Roydn.

Jack dragged the calf through the straw to the gate and returned to the cow and pulled at the knotted afterbirth trailing from her womb.

—That's it, said Roydn. Get it out of there. That's going to be your supper tonight.

—You feed like I told you? said Jack.

—You know I ain't, cause I ain't moved from this spot since you told me.

—Go do it.

—Fine. I got to get home anyways. Less a course we're riding bulls tonight.

—We ain't.

Roydn walked off toward the west hayshed. When Jack had the afterbirth out in a tangled, clotted pile on the ground he turned to see Blair standing over the calf, the pullers dangling from his grimy fist. The old man was a picture standing there like that, his face open, betraying his mind. It was death at his feet, reconsidered.

A figure stepped around the outside corner of the pen. Jack patted the cow's firm black neck and climbed through the gate and bent at the spigot to wash the afterbirth off his hands and arms. The water was cold. Rebekah stepped over to him.

—How long've you been here? he said.

—A while.

—What time is it?

—You're late.

—I lost track of time when she started.

She shrugged.

—What happened?

—Came breech. But it was only a bull.

—Well hullo there, beautiful, called Blair. Aren't you a sight for sore eyes.

—I'm sorry about the calf, she said.

—It's okay dear. It was only a bull.

A hillside above the river at the far edge of the lower field held the bones of wasted stock. Jack wrapped the calf in a grain sack and carried it limp and heavy in his arms to the bucket of the tractor. He drove the tractor to the lower field and she sat next to him on the wheel well, the bucket of the tractor holding the dead calf before them like an offering. Hay grew poorly in this sandy loam. Over the barbwire fence on the gentle hillside bones stood from the sand and yellow grass like ruins, the white architecture of death. She grew quiet when she saw them. He raised the bucket over the fence and tilted it forward and the calf slid out and tumbled down amid leg bones and pelvises, skulls and rib cages, most skeletons incomplete and scattered. How to describe what flowers grew from those bones in the springtime. Of deep purple and yellow, blue and red and white. Each one a marvel worth contemplation. Fragile, delicate. How many times had he stopped to watch them tremble in the wind among the white bones. There were no flowers this time of year.

When they returned, five gaunt cats had assembled around the mess of afterbirth like old women quilting, their bony shoulders tent poles for unsightly fabric. They hunched over the pile as over a puddle of spilled milk and feasted, and there were more making their way straight there all the while, slipping over the barnyard as if along spokes to the hub of a wheel.

He showered hard and fast but was careful to clean his whole body, needing to be rid of the smell of his work and of the dead calf. He picked her up on his three-wheeler from where she sat on the small bench in front of her house, as if she had waited there for him the whole time. Their ride was cold and the headlight shook a pool of yellow onto the ground in front of them. He pointed at an open field where a few deer had begun their evening feeding, their attentive shapes and large ears silhouetted against the slash of muted blue in the west. He drove by a line of huge dead white trees that kept scores of sandhill cranes in the summer. The nests of their seasonal colony filled the branches.

He had come from a different way and at first didn't realize the duckblind for what it was. As he entered he felt emboldened, as if the tiny structure gave off some kind of power. She laughed when she saw the cot inside. He reached above and pulled down broken sticks from the attic. He walked outside and gathered grass for kindling. One match burned and the fire took. It turned cozy inside the blind. As he leaned back against the wall she sat close to him and stared at the warming stove. Yellow light shone around the edges of the little door and from holes in the rusted metal. The wind picked up outside and whistled around the structure. The heat was immediate and filled the small shack and he shed his jacket and shoved it in the corner and lay back against it.

—I would have never guessed this is where you'd take me, she said.

When he looked over her darkened eyes were on him.

—Guess we could have gone to dinner.

—This is fine.

—Are you all right here? he said.

—Here in this shack or here in this town?

—Both.

—I was in my grandmother's closet today trying on her old earrings and shawls. She was a fancy dresser for this town. People used to say she was eccentric. They've left her clothes in the closet all these years. My father thought it was a bad idea. He said it was unhealthy to leave everything like it was. But who cares what he thinks. We'll leave it that way until we can't any longer.

The fire popped in the stove. She pulled her hands out of her vest pockets. They were lovely hands.

—Where is your father?

—How much do you want to know?

—Whatever you want to tell me.

She laughed in a way he didn't care for.

—You should think about that before you answer. Once you know things you can't unknow them.

—I'm not afraid of it.

She looked straight at him and held his gaze.

—He did things that a father should never do, she said.

—So he's back in Salt Lake, I guess, he said.

He stood and took down more wood and fed it into the stove and shut the door. Then he sat down beside her and watched the glowing barrel. She shrugged her shoulders hard and sighed and her breasts lifted and her posture loosened with the exhale. But there was energy in this uncivilized temple, wild grass growing through the boards, dirt floor, hot red fire. When she turned to him her eyes were intense, the light of the stove trembling in each pupil. Her first kiss was dry but then moistened with her tongue. Her lips were warm and supple, her mouth soft, and what she did with her tongue brought him to a rare threshold of life. She was slow and deliberate, not hungry. She paused between kisses, as if deciding whether to go on. They kissed this way, and then it was over as suddenly as it had begun. Her chest rose and fell with her breathing. He moved toward her and kissed her unresponsive mouth. She pushed him away gently.

—What is it? he said. Do I still smell?

She watched him so oddly he couldn't imagine what she was thinking. She straightened up on the cot. A sharp crack came from the river like a rifle shot and she jumped like she'd been caught at something.

—What was that? she said.

—I'll show you, he said.

They stepped outside and moved to the grassy edge where the river rimmed the earth and there was nothing around. The river was pale silver, its mirror surface throwing back the sky above it and the burgeoning stars.

—Come here, he said.

He led her downriver around the curve and jumped off the bank onto a narrow strip of sand, against which the slow water pushed. She let him help her down and he pointed to a dark pile of mud and sticks where it sat under the eroded bank.

—A beaver, he said. Slapping its tail. It's a warning.

—This river's so quiet, she said.

She shivered. She stood at the edge, level with the water. A breeze moved through the dry grass around them and he chose not to tell her that she was too close.

—Do you ever swim here? she said.

—Never.

—Why not?

—It's dangerous. This river has shifting sand and bad undercurrents.

—So you're afraid.

—I don't know how much is true or not, because I've never swum in it, but I was told enough stories to keep me out of it for the rest of my life. I don't believe it all, but it's like Judgment Day. You'd hate to be wrong about a thing like that. Besides, you never know what might be under the river.

—Does that bother you? Not knowing what's under the river?

—A little.

—That's why people fear water. They can't see what's beneath the surface.

—I once saw a cow disappear completely. One second she was standing on a sand bar, knee deep in the water, and the next she was gone. She never came up.

—I almost don't believe that, she said.

She dipped the toe of her shoe in and looked back at him. Then she crouched and put her hand in the water and came up with a handful of dark dripping sand.

—It makes you want to go out in it, and maybe never come back, she said.

—It does.

She took another handful up, let it go, and ran her hand around in the water, staring out across its dark plane.

—What stories?

—Drownings. Suicides. My grandma used to rattle off a pretty good death toll. She'd try to scare us away from it. The strongest man with the strongest horse... You know. But she was always waving around the newspaper clippings to back up her warnings, so some of it must have been true. People would try to swim in it and drown, or cross it on horseback and drown. Didn't you get warned away when you were a kid?

She shook her head.

—I never came down. It's not that far to the other side.

—That's what they thought. She put this plaque at the old bridge below the house that told when the last death was. She updated it every time someone was killed. Last I checked it was gone. Probly thrown in the river. I've seen plenty of kids jump off that bridge, so it doesn't get everyone. Heber's father committed suicide in it, at the same bridge below my house.

—I know that.

—He doesn't talk about it. He thought his father was the greatest man to ever live. And he doesn't believe it was suicide.

—What then?

—Murder.

—That's incredible.

—One day his old man went into the desert and wandered out half naked and delirious and was almost hit by a grain truck from the co-op. People thought he was getting better, and then he was found in the river. Heber thinks three men threw him in. Said he dreamt it. Ever since he feels like it's been up to him to redeem him by being a good son, doing something big. Thinks the town feels that way too.

—That's sad. How far did he make it?

—Who?

—His father. Did he float this far?

—Oh, no. They took him out pretty close to the bridge.

—It's so strange in the dark. It's so quiet you might not even know it was here.

She searched around for something to throw in and found nothing. When she moved closer he grabbed her waist and she jumped.

—Don't do that, she said. You scared me.

—What are you afraid of?

He left his hands on her waist and pulled her to him and she let him. She put her hands on his chest and looked at him. He bent and kissed her again and she pushed against him, but he held her.

—Jack, she said.

He dropped his hands.

—I don't have any regrets except for things I didn't do, he said.

—I won't sleep with you, she said.

—Where the hell did that come from?

—If you want me, you'll have to marry me.

—I'd marry you.

—You are the most serious boy I've ever met, she said. Sometimes I think you'll break from sincerity.

—I'd marry you tomorrow.

—Stop it. You can't say things like that.

—I'd swim across this river right now for you, he said, and bent as if to unlace his boots.

—I would never ask you to.

He let her off at her house and she told him she would be back from Salt Lake by Friday, if he wanted try again at some kind of date.

—And no more excuses, she said with a girlish simper. Don't be late or you'll lose me.

Her casual words drove him into reckless dreams as he rode home and climbed the stairs to his bedroom. When he took his shirt over his head and threw it to the floor he smelled her. He picked the shirt up and pressed it to his face, turned it and pressed it again, searching for her. What marvelous bottles she must have on her bedroom dresser, what cunning potions. Drams of perfume, philters, long tried alchemies for the torture of man, the science that brought them forth nothing short of sorcery. He breathed in what little she'd left him and remembered the taste and feel of her mouth, their time spent in the duckblind. He thought about her father and her obscure history, the things he did not know about her and may never know, no matter how close he let her get. He was troubled by it and felt the rising of some barrier whelm him as he drifted off into an agitated sleep.

Evenings he found Blair watching Matlock instead of picking from his collection of westerns. Adelaide had recorded them from a local channel and labeled them and stacked them in boxes. The old man had pulled the boxes out and they sat against the far wall. Often Jack returned for lunch to find him gone and ate what he could with what time he had. He asked him once where he went and Blair said for a drive in his truck—something the three of them had done often when Jack was young but that they didn't do anymore or did alone. There was a day he came home from work, shed his jacket and boots, and called out to no answer but the flicker of the television in the living room. He walked through the doorway and found Blair facing the screen, Matlock on and turned down to a murmur, the old man's eyes brimming with tears like two rough diamonds in a rock.

These days the sunlight fell delicately through the air and the trees clung to dead leaves despite the persistent wind that moved through, a wind that smelled of winter. They sat watching television in their respective chairs after work one evening when Blair got up and limped out of the room. He came back carrying a paper plate and a pair of grimy toenail clippers. Without a word he dropped the plate in Jack's lap and tried twice before swinging his gnarled, bony foot up onto it. The nails were grossly overgrown, well thicker than the paper plate they scratched against, yellowed and corneous and beginning to curl around the toes like claws. They were serrated and split along the edges, long rifts reaching their length and black from some dark junk, and more crud collected beneath the nails in clumps, and all of it stank. His foot was white as heaven. There was a burdened moment when the two only looked at each other.

—The cramps are bad, said Blair.

Jack picked up the clippers in one hand and with the other handled the long crooked toes. He worked at the nails and cut them back, and three times before he was through Blair jerked his foot away suddenly, staving off a leg cramp and nearly losing his balance, causing the thick crescents to scatter onto Jack's lap and to catapult onto the carpet. When the deed was finished Blair collapsed into his chair, done in by the effort.

—Now that that's over, said Jack, have you got anything to tell me?

—You want a thank you card?

—At least tell me how long you plan on making me wait before I know anything about the farm.

—Let's don't talk about it tonight. We'll go over it tomorrow after the morning chores.

So it was as the two men sat together at the breakfast table after milking the next morning, their hair sticking up wildly from wearing their stocking caps, their hands scrubbed nearly to the bone and still smelling of the barn, yet reaching regardless over a table of bacon and eggs and toast, that Blair stiffened in his breakfast movements and started in with his grim manifesto, laying out his reasoning in a hard line.

—I want you to know that everything your grandmother did she did for you and Elmer, he said, looking down his crooked nose at the toast he buttered. But you know Elmer, and you know his unfortunate situation. And there's the boy. There's the boy to consider. She was mostly concerned about the boy. Elmer's got heart murmurs now, with him and Carrie talking about going for better doctors. And it's the boy, the damned boy. You've seen him. What's a boy like that got to do in this world? Now you must be about twenty-one by now, so we want to give you a share, some land for all you've done over the years. And it goes without saying that we'd like to further your career interests here.

—What land? said Jack.

—The north field and the mountain.

Blair looked falsely pleased with the gift. He took a bite of toast and offered a smile like a miscarried fetus. Jack thought it over. The north field and the mountain. Certainly the mountain was the most worthless piece they owned, and perhaps the pair made the two most worthless pieces, and he told Blair this.

—I never made any promises, said Blair. This thing's got to keep running.

—So that's it? said Jack.

—I was afraid you'd take it the wrong way.

Blair's eyes raged with the cheater's gleam and he said nothing.

Jack walked out of the kitchen amid Blair's petitions to hold up and threw on his boots and jacket and headed out. He got as far as his truck before he turned around and burst with his shoulder back through the door. Blair's face remained expressionless as Jack came up to him. He said, Choose your words carefully.

—Do you realize you're just pissing it away? said Jack. Everything you've built and worked for. Pissing the whole thing away on a man who can't run it and a grandson who wouldn't know what to do with it if they taught it in school. Looks like you finally lost your goddamn mind. You've gone pure batshit crazy.

Blair took a second to stand up from the table. He swung his fist, a long methodical hook, true still to whatever form he'd learned in those early days, and Jack ducked it and stepped back, looking at the old man where he stood heaving and furious. Jack left him standing there and walked back outside and drove to the co-op. After looking over the pathetic food display he grabbed as much as he could hold in one hand and cradled more in the crook of his arm and spilled it all upon the counter. He went back and rummaged through the clothing section, looking for something he might want. He found nothing, but took an insulated cap with foldable earflaps anyway. He asked Noreen to get him an Old Timer pocketknife out of the display case on the counter and told her charge it along with everything else to Blair's account.

At the loading dock Balls Murphy strolled out of the mill into the cold morning and greeted him with a crude epithet. He still wore the large championship rodeo buckle he won in the local circuit some seven years before. Its metal date was smudged and its high spots worn shiny and smooth, and various digs were scattered over its surface. A mature and flaming-red Fu Manchu mustache crept down both sides of his mouth, accented by a blond puff under his lower lip, which bulged with chewing tobacco.

—What you been up to? he said.

—Same old shit, different day, said Jack.

—Why don't you bring yourself out to my place and I'll show the plane to you. You need to come out and feel her up.

—I need something.

Wrink Poulsen came out of the mill and nodded to them and leaned against the wall. He took a can of tobacco from his pocket and slung his finger against it slowly, like shaking out a match. Balls turned and looked at him.

—You all finished in there? he said.

—Not yet, said Wrink. Will be directly.

—What you doing out here then? You come out to make sure the road's still here?

—I just come out to get some air.

—If you don't get them bags moved I'll shove your head up your ass, and then you'll be in the need for some air.

Wrink spat a long dark stream on the landing but didn't move otherwise.

—Damn it, Poulsen, I ain't joking around. You can't get away with this no more. Get them bags moved over and take your break when it's scheduled.

The two looked at each other and Wrink lowered his eyes and spat again. He pushed himself away from the wall, and muttering obscenities, moved through the door.

Balls watched him disappear into the dark and looked at Jack.

—That dumb bastard, he said. Thinks he can get away with anything now that I was made foreman. I'll ride him all day long,

I tell you what. Boss at work, friend everywhere else, is what I told him.

—Where's Dirt?

—Took the day off. Claims he had a dentist appointment. You take a look at them teeth and tell me that man has ever been to the dentist. They've both turned into a couple of pantywaists since I was promoted.

—What do you make now?

—It's all right, he said. It's all right enough to make these boys jealous.

—What do they make?

—They start you at a dollar or two above minimum. And then you climb slow if you're reliable. I make two dollars more than them and it's like they'd slit my throat for it.

Balls went into the mill to fill the order and Jack walked back to the store. He picked up a PBR Finals collection from a small assortment of videos and took it to the front and had Noreen write up a new receipt. When he returned the truck was loaded and Balls handed him the slip and said, You come over and look at that plane, Selvedge, you hear? Just like a woman, you got to feel her up before you buy. But unlike a woman she won't let you down.

—I don't want to go up in it. I ain't ready for that.

—It's fine. I taught my dog to swim by throwing him in the river.

—Yeah but I don't want to go up with you. I'll come over and look, that's all.

—It's fine, said Balls. Come on over. I'll let you take a close up look at her. How's Seth on them bulls, anyway? He kilt himself yet?

—Not yet. He rides um pretty well.

—How bout you? You the bullfighter?

—Yeah, but I ain't had to do anything yet.

—Good. Hopefully it stays that way. You know your job is every bit as dangerous. Sometimes more so.

—You still spraying this time of year?

—A little winter wheat.

—Anything out north of town?

—Sure. You want to come up?

Jack shook his head.

—I'm taking this girl out in a couple days. Just had an idea.

Balls smiled wryly.

—She grew up like I thought she would, he said. Enough to make a man leave the church.

—Neither of us go to church.

—Enough to make a man leave just about anything.

—Enough to make you go back to church maybe, said Jack.

—Damn near, said Balls. Not quite.

At the house he dropped off the grain and headed slowly for the barn, where he hoped to avoid Elmer. But Elmer was there scooping corn silage from the pit and dumping it in the auger feeder. The silage had turned brown and steamed as it was exposed to cold air. It smelled fermented and bitter and was in his mind an odor synonymous with farm life and inseparable. Some preferred the smell of manure to the smell of silage, but he believed both could be pleasant given the right circumstance. He caught a glance from his anemic uncle through the tractor windshield when he looked up, and as Elmer gave a dopey smile and waved he diverted his eyes and drove up near the east hayshed. He avoided him for twenty minutes before he was caught slipping through the manger bars into the corral to cross to the other side unseen. Elmer called three times before Jack turned to see him approaching in his crooked gait. His uncle wore coveralls with worn holes that showed red lining and white insulation in half a dozen places and a blue bull semen hat on his head with the ear flaps pulled down. His hands were gloveless, red and raw.

—Hullo Jack.

—Hello Uncle Elmer.

—Are you going to do something right now?

—Sure.

—Oh. Well I won't bother you then, but when you get a minute can you come in the barn?

—For what?

—Just to go over a few things is all.

—Let's do it now.

Elmer smiled like a fool.

Blair sat behind the desk in the small office, his face resolute and without emotion. Jack leaned against the edge of the desk, Blair to his right. Elmer stood in the doorway to his left, boisterous as the moon. Jack folded his arms and fixed his eyes on the opposite wall.

—I had more to say at the table before you provoked me, said Blair. Stay with us and we'll take care of yuh.

—That it? That's what I missed?

—Love to have you stay on the farm, said Elmer.

—I don't doubt it.

—Don't be proud, said Blair.

—We'd raise your pay, said Elmer. Settle on something better. Could be a salary.

—You got the farmhouse, said Blair. You always got that. That's as good as yours.

—Elmer, if your salary is anything like your hourly wage, I'll tell you what you can do with it. I could make better money picking up cans on the side of the road.

Jack alternated his gaze between them as he spoke.

—The games we've played up to this point have been interesting, but I don't plan to be stuck here on this farm for some salary wage that puts me under the poverty line.

—What about them bulls? said Elmer. I know you've took an interest in them bulls. You want um, you can have um.

—The bulls? said Jack. Why don't you go milk the bulls, Elmer, and put it in your cereal.

—Now show some respect, said Blair with heat in his voice. Don't talk that way to your uncle. We want you here, but don't think for a minute that this farm sinks or swims at your bidding. It existed before you and it can exist after you.

—You might find out soon enough what'll happen without me here, said Jack.

—Threaten me boy and I'll put you through that wall. You think you're the only person alive can run a farm?

—If you step up from that chair, old man, I'll show you what else I can do.

Blair didn't rise. His hand flashed up from the desk, and Jack, against the wall, couldn't dodge the reach. Blair's hand clamped onto his throat. He realized his mistake too late and as Blair's grip tightened Jack began to choke and his eyes ran water. He raised a boot and kicked Blair in the chest, enough to break the hold. Blair was up from his chair. Jack struck first. His fist pistoned out in a vicious jab, and there was a pop, and Blair's already crooked nose slid cleanly to the right before the blood had a chance to run. Blair seemed not to know he'd been hit. His straight left caught Jack's cheekbone and rocked his head against the cinderblock wall. It was a dull thud, and there was time for Jack to admire the old man's speed before his brain registered a temporary shutdown and his body crumpled into the corner.

He was on the road to the farmhouse with a rising headache, the dull throb building as if it would split his skull. He had regained consciousness in the corner of the office and heard Elmer's murmurs in the washroom as he tended to his father. At the farmhouse he took a green bottle of Excedrin from the bathroom cupboard and shook a few into his palm. His neck and jaw were sore. A shiner swelled beneath his eye.

High clouds covered the world in thin light. He drove over

the river and along a series of dirt roads before he found the one that led to the north field he was to be given. This field was a semi-level platform atop the first rise of foothills, perched above the plain and puddled at the base of the larger mountains. It was roughly a fifty acre finger. When he reached it he drove its length over native yellow grass, rodding the engine and making the truck fishtail. He spun the wheel to the left and whipped the back end around, tearing up damp soil and throwing chunks of dirt and grass behind him in double rooster tails. He cut several deep donuts into the earth with a grim smile on his face and his teeth grinding against the throb of his head, and when he could smell the truck's response in burning oil and coolant he drove easily to the end and killed the engine. He looked north where the black desert spread its jagged basalt and sage desolation. He made out the irregularity that was the road to Hansel. To the west the world was open and vast, a long plain that stretched to distant mountains and the curve of the earth, cut by the silver river. There were towns like his own that he couldn't see out there, scabs on the land lacking promise, claiming civilization enough to justify their presence, grouped together against the loud sky in a few grid streets and spread out in sprawling farms. Dull streets, sunblanched, sluggish, static. To the east the Sister Range swept upward in long, steep slopes, drawn up like a sheet held by invisible hands, its ridges taut with slack folds in between. Just behind him was the best penetration into the mountain, the only access that led into its deepest parts. Blair owned the lower reaches of that canyon and it was the other piece of land he would give Jack. There was no road there but a spoor-riddled game trail.

This land was nearly perfect, not as a matter of opinion or preference but perfect in fact, as only natural, unaltered earth is perfect, having been formed in some primordial epoch and left alone to the geological whims that continued to shape it. What did they fight against, those early settlers, in the wilderness? What projections did it harbor for them? What did they see in it that they saw also in themselves, that they wanted to subdue? He wasn't sure this field had ever been planted. If so, the mountain had reclaimed it, and except for the black ruts his tires had made it looked like any of the hillside around it, only naturally more level. He pictured the lower foothills covered with houses like blown litter and refused to believe it could happen. The land out there in the black desert was as the land had evolved to be by natural forces—plates moving, lava spewing, sage spreading, single junipers coming up from the dung of the Bohemian waxwing or the red fox—all this without human intervention, and it seemed all right to leave it that way. He felt most comfortable and inspired in the natural land, be it riverbottoms, mountain, or desert. Had gone there with his free time as a child, went there now as a man. If God lived then he lived there, not in the ramshackle home nor in churches and temples built, for none of these could match the peace and freedom of what God had put down and thrust up. This was the truth as he knew it. He could verify nothing more. He looked at the town, so small, and then beyond it. The entire landscape testified of a simple existence. Here it seemed a man could live a good life in simplicity and purity, where his considerations held meaning and substance each and were therefore fewer and less wearisome, and a man sought to stay rather than to leave. Life as it had once been, when men worked for modest survival instead of enterprise and acquisition, where people made livings, not fortunes. This nation had lost something as it grew rich, had forgotten things worth remembering in its pursuit of gain. Heber often wondered aloud about development, the bench spotted with gaudy homes, the area humming with what some would call progress. As yet this town didn't know a clear division between the wealthy and the common. Heber believed a dead town could be razed and changed, that a version of progress could take place that way, that Juniper Scrag veritably breathed with this potential, but that if it were restored to its former simplistic prosperity it could better resist that kind of change, or at least that the change it underwent could be controlled, its antecedent firmly in place to guide it. But in ruins it could be flicked off like a dead flea and forgotten. Jack thought of building her a simple house up here, of running electricity and laying a good gravel road. There would be children and the balance of their lives to be spent looking down on the sage plain. They would see the rumored progress the town was prone to or they would flee before it to more remote lands.

Surveying the desert below him he saw movement. He squinted and couldn't make it out. He pulled binoculars from the glovebox of his truck and found it again, but he couldn't get the focus right. He closed one eye and focused one lens and made out four or five animals in a pack, wild dogs or coyotes moving between the road and the mountains, moving toward him. He watched them pick their way through the sage until he could better divine their color among the colors of the desert. The lead dog looked black. But they didn't move like dogs. If they were wild dogs they wouldn't last long. There had been organized slaughters in the desert for lesser offenders. He had once come upon a heap of dead rabbits stacked on an abandoned rectangle of crumbling concrete. The pile had been taller than he was. He'd always meant to go back, to see what was left, whether it was now only a pile of bones and sinew or whether scavenging creatures had scattered them, but he had never been able to find it again. He watched the dogs with his naked eyes and then raised the binoculars again. He was tempted to call them wolves and said so aloud, but wolves had been extirpated from this region the century before and there were no wolves from the reintroductions down this far. The pack changed its direction and headed north, away from him, and he watched them until they disappeared.

8

THE SIDE DOOR TO THE BARN OPENED AND ROYDN Woolums walked in and unleashed a tremendous belch that made the walls of the empty barn ring. Jack stayed quiet in the office until the farmhand had taken a noisy drink from the hose, cursed the entire farm from boss to beast in one breath, and was gone to gather the top herd for milking. Jack got up and walked into a lingering miasma of digesting Pepsi and corn nuts, the hovering stench of the belch already a full minute old. He had showered long and hard after milking that morning and had avoided reacquiring the smell of cows again, and so did not want to be in the barn when the animals entered. He would go home and take another shower and then he would pick her up. He found Roydn gathering cows and told him to feed before he left. Roydn shrugged as though he could choose not to.

—Say, did you really break the old man's nose? he said. Is he pulling my chain?

—He's telling the truth.

—That's crazy. He shook his head and laughed out loud. Give the old boy what for, huh?

—You've got shit on your glasses, said Jack. Don't follow um so close.

Within the hour she was beside him on the seat and he realized how dirty his truck was. They rolled along the edge of the north field, the truck whispering through dry grass, and drove out a little where the round foothill fell away steeply. The sun dropped into a brown-red autumn haze on the horizon and cast a surreal light on the stony beauty of the peaks above them. She sat on the tailgate and swung her legs, and below an immense field of winter wheat was pulled with the light toward the sun. He took wood from the bed of the truck, made a small ring from gathered stones, and knelt to build a fire.

—Is this where you've always brought your girls? she said.

—Never.

—Then where?

—People go anywhere remote. Which is anywhere around here. Into the desert. A lot of babies made out there. The desert is just big and empty. People go there to fool around, drive around, shoot guns.

The sun flared out in what looked like great flames but were sparse clouds torn apart by the violence inherent in its beauty, and the world to the west was set afire. They were quiet as they took in the view of the plain below. The river of molten slag seared their eyes in its fiery twist through the desert. Indeed the land was on fire somewhere west of them, and as the sun fell farther into the smoke it enlarged and became a red orb, a wizard's glass that could be looked at straight on. It sat enormous and trembling on the rim of the earth and then dropped quickly, and with it the temperature. A dark spot appeared within its upper corona and moved toward them. She pointed at it and asked what it was and they watched it take the shape of a double-winged airplane. It lowered and ran parallel to the flatness of the field and disappeared for the curve of the hill. Suddenly it roared up from beneath them in a long groan. The fire grew agitated and danced under the push of air. Rebekah jumped backward and fell in the grass. The plane's red belly seemed close enough to touch. It made a sharp turn high above them only to fall toward the earth again and straighten itself out for the next line.

They watched the plane work a ballet in the air. It flew about twenty feet above the young wheat blades, its proximity to the ground accenting its speed, then pulled up sharply when it reached the edge in the distance and turned a long arc in the air before straightening out and coming down again. With each pass fertilizer sprayed from the apparatus beneath the wings and floated down and the pilot seemed not to miss an inch. The plane worked a progression along the foothills away from them. They watched it take the field one strip at a time, and on the last turn it came back and dove at them like a hornet, clipping through the air above their heads. Rebekah screamed and crouched into Jack, and Jack looked up to see the pilot's head sticking out, goggled eyes, a long scarf blowing behind, a madman's leer on his face, and then the plane was gone, back into the dusky haze at the edge of the world.

He looked around at the mountain grass and out where the sky changed its color every minute, fuchsias, purples, blues, growing paler each shade upward to where it was washed of all color. The torn clouds left behind by the sun were still emblazoned around their edges as if they'd been charged with its energy and left to light the world in its absence. They faded like the cooling embers of a fire. It was an uninhabited world down there on the sage plain, nothing but rolling desert and an old lava flow. It was the same view the ancients would have seen, that land that had been taken from them, that they had taken from each other, the land that had perhaps been taken from peoples throughout all human time and not only that recent time written in history books. That land sat empty as it always had, unchanged but for the human imprints of illegal dumping and random litter, anonymous cans and broken bottles, vehicle tracks in the dirt which would heal given time left alone. Had he not reached her on the phone earlier he would have been here alone, watching all of this from his field.

He looked at her as she crouched by the fire like some primitive and beautiful squaw, her face curtained by her dark hair, her pants stretched tight around her haunches, her palms and fingers splayed out over the flames. Her jaw colored by the light of the gone sun. In a moment like this she moved him deeply. He walked to the edge of the hill where he saw a good rock to bolster the fire ring. He bent for it and leapt backward and felt his heart skip a beat, startled to see a snake there, fat and coiled not a foot from the rock. It watched him with a mad glare.

—What is it? she said.

—Rattlesnake.

—Did it rattle? She walked to him and he held an arm out to keep her back. She pressed her midsection into his arm and said, I can't see it.

—Right there.

When she finally saw it she jumped back a little.

—Why doesn't it rattle?

—They don't always rattle. It's a little cold for it to act right. Stay back.

He walked downslope to a juniper tree and took a withered branch from beneath it. He pushed it forward and the snake came to life and hissed and began to rattle. Then it struck and she stifled a scream but didn't move. He dropped the stick and walked to his truck and opened the door. He came back carrying an unsheathed machete and before she could realize what he was about to do he stepped to the snake and brought the blade down, severing its head a few inches down its body. It started buzzing and its three-foot body writhed in the grass, turning the white, scuted underbelly over and curling around itself. He bent and picked it up near the cut neck and let it curl around his arm in reflex, the hard tail still buzzing at his elbow. Its skin was dry in his hand. She gasped.

—Why did you do that?

He looked up, surprised.

—I don't know.

—Because it was poisonous?

—No. Maybe. Well, it is poisonous. If I'd put my hand on that rock it would of bit me without warning. It could of bit either one of us.

—So this is the second time you've saved me from danger by killing something.

—What was the other?

—Your dog.

He unwrapped the body from his arm with some difficulty and threw it sidearmed over the edge of the hill. The headless snake straightened with the force of the spin, a black line against the lurid sunset, then curled into a bundle and dropped from their sight like a dark stone. Its head sat in the grass, its eyes open and glaring, glazed over, its black tongue flicking out yet to taste the air. Back at the tailgate her face was clear and cold in its possession.

—Did I tell you this is my field? he said.

She shook her head.

—It's what I was given for a lifetime's work.

—Your inheritance?

—Sure.

She shrugged and threw a glance over her shoulder at the field.

—It's nice.

—Worthless, he said. What do you think I could do with this field?

—I don't know. I don't know what farmers do with their fields, except plant them.

—Too hard to irrigate, so it would be dry farm, like those below. It wouldn't produce enough crop to justify driving our equipment this far up. Plus it's rocky. Take years to clear out the stones.

She was looking off to the west where the lower sky glowed like a dull red hell placed at Earth's edge.

—Is something wrong? he said.

—My mom's worried about me right now. Because I'm with you.

—What's wrong with that?

—She's asked around, and what she's heard hasn't been good.

—That's nice of them. What'd she hear?

—That you left the church and turned wild.

—Cause and effect, no doubt, he said. Maybe she should get a second opinion. From me.

—Drinking. Fighting. Jail time. Girls.

—I never went to jail.

—You don't go to church, you hang out with Heber Rafuse, and you don't have a solid future.

—Is that right. These are her concerns or yours?

—She loves me. She wants me to be happy. I thought you used to be a good kid.

He didn't answer and she looked at him.

—She thinks it's because you lost your parents.

—Why are you with me right now?

She shrugged.

—I wanted to be.

—Tell your mother to ease up a little.

—She's seen what's happened in the past. She's a good mother.

—What's happened in the past?

—What my father has done to my mother and me has created an emptiness inside that I've never been able to fill. Nothing has ever made it go away.

She stared straight into the coals, her body turned rigid in its crouch. Her jaw clenched and loosened, its taut muscles working in the fading light.

—What can be done? said Jack.

—There's nothing that can be done. And as for my father, it's only a matter of time before he comes here. Mom feels protected in this town, but I don't. It's a fantasy. It's like she believes the magic of her childhood here will save us. She brought us back because things were good here once.

She looked out across the plain as though her father might materialize there.

—He could drive right up the lane and there would be no one around.

—I'm around, he said.

She smirked.

—You are that way.

—What way?

—You'd try protect me from my dad if he found us.

—Try? I wouldn't just sit around and let it happen. If the son of a bitch showed up in this town I'd come down and do something about it.

—Don't call him that, she said. You don't have the right.

—He doesn't sound like a sweetheart, said Jack.

—I heard you like to fight.

—I have. But not anymore.

—Good, she said. When he shows up I'll call you. You can come save me.

—Listen, he said. Do you want me to tell you I'd beat the hell out of him if he came around? How does that make you feel?

—He's a pretty big guy.

—I know some tricks.

They were quiet.

—My mother just wants me to find a good man, she said.

—I'm a good man.

—Why don't you go to church anymore?

—Just don't, he said. I could go once in a while. That would be good for me. But it *is* boring as hell, if you need a quick reason.

—People deal with grief differently.

—You know, he said, Roydn Woolums is active in the church. He went to Nebraska on a mission. How does your mother feel about him?

—You don't think I could be with a man like Roydn?

—No.

She watched the fire sway and flare in the breeze, and her face glowed in all that dark hair.

—Rebekah, he said. She looked up at him with eyes that bore through him. He couldn't speak.

—It's best not to talk about it, she said.

—About what?

—What you're about to say.

—What am I about to say?

—I don't know how long I'll be here. There's not enough time anyway, even if it was right.

She turned her face to the fire and something inside him backtracked and began shutting itself down, starting with the most recent developments and clicking backward to the time he first saw her on the swing and she had altered his world. His perception had been off.

—Are you hungry? she said, looking up at him. You must be hungry. We haven't had any food. Do you want to go back to my house and I'll cook something? Mom's on a night shift.

—Fine, he said. Let me get this fire out.

She put together a hearty meal. He lounged numbly in the living room while she cooked, the low lamps on, the chair he sat in her granddad's favorite, she told him. The chair offered torpidity and a repose in mute agony. I am from a dead town and work on a stinking dairy farm and stink myself all but permanently and my hands are rough and callused and I still wear flannel shirts and my ways are not her ways. I am no longer my father's son. I am Blair's grandson.

She called to him that the food was ready. This girl had cooked dinner. She stood at the table, each thing set there by her hands, and he would sit with her and eat this food she had prepared. He would take this nourishment into his body, this food she had made and touched with her hands. She poured water for them and said, I'll bless it.

She bowed her head and he watched her face as she uttered a prayer on the food. Those sweet lips offering up a small petition to God, as if God would stir in order to sanctify the food she had prepared. Then he fell to his plate like he hadn't eaten in a week. He ate lustily, like he'd been starving his whole life. Sensual eating, gluttonous. He stabbed at his plate and loaded his fork with potatoes. They held too much heat and he breathed around them to cool his mouth. Before they were gone he added a second piece of chicken to the mash and worked his jaw. He reached for a third roll, buttered it, and took half of it in one bite. He stuffed the remaining piece in and swallowed and reached immediately for his glass of water lest he choke. He chewed rapidly, his clicking jaw the only sound he made, and took great gulps of water and refilled his glass. It surprised him how he ate, how he wanted to consume her also, how that would be the only satisfying ending to the night, the only filling thing and what he needed to be whole. To feast on her thighs, to relish her plump flesh and wipe his chin clean of the juice. When he looked up he saw that she picked delicately and consciously at her food, chewing slowly and watching him.

—Is it good? she said.

He nodded.

—The quickest way to a man's heart is through his stomach, she said. My mom used to say that. She'd say it to my dad all the time. She said she tamed him with a plate of cookies. But it turned out he wasn't tame after all.

She forced a laugh. On his plate lay what was left of his last strip of chicken and a few chunks of potatoes.

—I find the asparagus growing on the ditch bank between here and your barn, she said. It's still growing.

—Well, he said flatly. I didn't know it grew there.

He was finished and was still hungry. He stared down at his empty plate, fork in hand, uncertain what to do next. There was a butter glaze on the plate, a few fibers of meat. He touched one of these fibers with his index finger and put it on his tongue.

—Do you want more? she said. There's a little more of everything.

He reached out and dished things onto his plate and kept eating. She picked up a drooping piece of asparagus between her forefinger and thumb and watched him. He grunted and hunched over his plate like a protectorate, forking up food with a slowly blooming anger like smoke from a growing fire and as unstoppable, and soon he was finished for the second time. And still he was hungry. But there was no more food. He started like something kicked him in the side, and he was up with the plate and gathering pans and used dishes into piles.

—Don't do that, she said. She stood and came to him. She had left food on her plate and he eyed it. She touched his wrist.

—I'm doing it, he said. I know how to do dishes.

He began filling the sink with soap and water and she turned back to the table to gather the dishes. They worked side by side, he washing and she rinsing and drying. She handed dishes back to him when he hadn't cleaned them well enough.

Later she walked him out into the chilled darkness. He gulped the cold air down deeply like a drink. She followed a few steps behind until he reached his door and opened it and stood looking out across the fields.

—Jack.

Her voice was soft. He turned all the way around and she was close to him, her arms folded for warmth. She stepped forward and hugged him. When she pulled away her eyes sparkled from the blue sodium light on the shed.

—I had a nice time, she said. Thank you. She tugged his jacket over to cover him better.

He climbed into his truck and reached for the door and she was in the way. In that moment he wanted to force her back into the house and shut the door against the night. He wanted to pluck her beautiful petals and gnash them in his teeth and swallow them. She placed a hand on his arm and baffled him by kissing him on the cheek.

He lay in his dark bedroom beneath the attic where buzzing, squeaking bats dropped one by one from a hole at the gable's peak like translucent tears. He listened to them scratching through the ceiling above him, and then he heard a noise coming up the stairway, a creak, and another. He knew it was impossible to climb those stairs without sound. The thought of Blair creeping up the stairs rang so wild in his head it seemed like a vibration. He was about to leap from his bed, his nerves still spitting and zinging from being with Rebekah, when he heard his name whispered in the dark. His heart doubled its speed as his thoughts of her played into the genderless whisper, and then Seth was in his room, tripping blindly over piles of clothes.

—Jack, he whispered. I saw your truck go by and walked down.

Jack shut the door and turned on the light. Seth looked feral, his eyes glossy and shot through with veins.

—You been drinking?

—Yeah, said Seth, still whispering. From my stash on top of the haystack. That's where I was when I saw you go by. You want to go out?

—Out where?

—Let's go ride bulls.

—It's too late.

—We can ride um still, said Seth. There's a light on that pole. Why couldn't we?

—Stop whispering, said Jack. I don't feel like it.

—Let's go to Heber's house then. See what he's doing.

Seth would go with or without him, so Jack pulled his clothes back on and they left in his truck.

———

—When a man sees beauty, he
admires it. The bloody dusk,
the moving storm,
the alpine flower, so close.
He considers the stamen—
the pistil where the hummingbird's
tongue sinks deep to tickle the plump round ovary.
He sees in these things a natural symmetry,
a beauty, a rightness.
A woman.
With a cold eye he must view her physical construction
as he would a craggy mountain peak
as it tears the clouds and harbors glacial tarns—
with appreciation, awe, and reverence.
And love.
A deep love,
as if he has understood his god for the first time.

Maria sat on the couch beside Heber, slinking against him, a shape congruent to his. She scoffed and looked up at him.

—It's simply another facet to a blue diamond, said Heber, folding the paper and tucking it in his shirt pocket. Since when did the beauty of a woman become an unmentionable, something not to be praised or worshipped? This is the privilege of beauty, a thing that has exalted common women to thrones, started wars and inspired tragedies. Since the invention of feminism is when.

—Since the invention of you, said Maria.

—Beauty is nature's coin, said Heber. Spend it.

—How many times has that line gotten you into a girl's pants? said Maria.

—Unto the pure all things are pure, said Heber. Don't pigeonhole me.

Jack and Seth had dropped themselves into surrounding chairs. Heber put his arm around Maria's shoulders and drooped a hand above her breast. His other hand now held an unlit cigarette and a drink sat tucked between his legs. Seth drew regularly from a pack on the end table, and with the lights low the living room was comfortable.

—Where's Rebekah? said Heber.

—Home, probably, said Jack.

—No Woolums tonight either?

No one answered.

—What a family, those Woolumses, said Heber cheerily. What a family they make. Ronald, Roydn, Roland, Randolph, Rodney, Rapscallion, and their dear wife and mother Josephine. The last four boys in five years, followed by two stillborns in two, both girls. And that was the end of the effort. You'd think his wife was so gorgeous he couldn't stay off her. But no. His seed was just potent, and his aim sure. She is a woman, but not a beautiful woman. And what does a woman who is not beautiful do in this world so full of beautiful women? She has a rough go of it.

Seth laughed as if it were a great joke.

—You know, said Heber. Ronald's not a bad-looking man in his old age. I can't imagine what the hell happened, and he must be asking himself the same thing.

—Why are you cruel to someone because of the way she looks? said Maria. She can't help how she looks.

—That's not necessarily true, said Heber, holding up a finger. Granted, there's a woman who was born with whiskers, but she has some control over it. Perhaps the hump formed from—well, I don't know what forms them—and maybe the cross eyes can't be fixed, but there's something to be said about daily care and appearance. I saw her down at the co-op the other day shopping the aisles. Sort of bent over and stooping, looking at cans of some homely victual, and she wore these stained pink sweat pants and a flannel work shirt, probably Ronald's shirt. Her hair was a rat's nest. She gave me this kind look, like she had control over everything that matters and she was blessing me with this kind look, like she had something on me.

—Maybe she does have something on you, said Maria. Besides, she was at the co-op. Give her a break. It's not like she was going to visit the president.

—Public appearance, said Heber. Public appearance. It can be the difference between a sucky town and a charming one. Care a little.

—All their kids are ugly, said Seth.

—Hell yes! cried Heber.

—People used to say I was ugly, said Maria. When I was little I had crooked teeth.

She grabbed the neck of the bottle between Heber's legs and loosed it and took a drink.

—You got good teeth, said Seth.

—Braces, said Maria.

—Well you hide the scars well, dear, said Heber. Because I haven't seen them.

—Give her a break, she said. Give them all a break. They're nice people and you're an ass.

—Very nice people, said Heber. Saints. Ronald's a good old boy. He works that land out there like it owes him something, worries it, supplicates it, and doesn't get a damn thing for it. Even their apple trees are wormy. The sight of that family out there bent over and tilling a haggard patch of raspberries or building a new tin shed for chickens or minks or what-the-fuck is as natural to this town as the slow push of the river. There's a family who'll survive the Apocalypse on scrap and sweat alone, living on boot-tongue soup and malformed carrots. They're like a family of dark-eyed mice waiting to inherit the earth. Never getting, always giving. Never asking, always giving. It's something, John.

Jack looked up.

—You all right? said Heber.

Jack cleared his throat and felt a pulse of irritation.

—What is it?

—What's with you tonight? You all right?

—I wasn't paying attention.

—Where are you, brother?

—Is Penelope still around? said Seth, looking at Maria.

—She went back to California, she said in mock sweetness. Didn't she give you her number?

—I don't remember. Seth scowled. I think so. I probly got it somewhere. I was drunk as hell.

He took a sulky swig from his bottle.

—Hell of a thing, said Heber. Only once. It's amazing something like that can happen only once to a man. Sometimes not at all. Old Elmer Fudd about didn't make it, did he John. And when he did he got—well…

Maria got up from the couch and turned her back on them as she walked to the hallway, her prodigious backside gripped in tight jeans. Her shirt had hitched up, revealing plump love handles that pushed at the waistline. Heber watched her rump move and sway as she walked and then he turned and looked frankly at the other two. He drew a deep breath. When she came back she stood in front of him, a strip of bare midriff in his face, and her denim-slung bottom poised into shape not three feet away from where Jack sat. It was a reckless thing in front of him, that close and suspended in form like that. Not a single thread of fabric in those pants but what was stretched taut as a fiddle string. There was an allure to it that begged the grip of the hand if only to better comprehend the shape and confirm the malleability the eyes conveyed, to employ another sense to take in the wonder of it. As if reading his thoughts Heber reached his hand around and lifted one ponderous cheek with an upward clutch and let it fall. It settled with a bounce and his hand continued on to cradle her soft hip.

—How you doing, baby? he said.

He pulled her down to the couch and kissed her sloppily and when Seth lit another cigarette Jack was tired of the smoke.

—I'm going to sit on the porch a minute, he said. Get some air.

The others watched him get up and walk to the door. Outside he breathed deeply. The cold air filled him and countered the restless muttering of his blood. He sat down on the steps and looked out at the dark street. Through the field on the other side he could see the park: the tall church house with its lofty steeple, the barren basketball rims, the trees under which he had spent so many evenings with Heber. This town more so now than ever seemed small and stagnant, void of hope and opportunity. The farm had driven him, but the farm was thrown into chaos, its promise confused. He had found another reason, brief and bright and unexpected, and now it was turned cold.

He walked a couple blocks to the town square. It was a little square, ill-lit by streetlamps and lifeless. Two-story buildings lined the far side of the streets with a square of grass and benches and trees in the middle. The whole thing was dilapidated, gaunt and eerie, looming over him in its vague history and emptiness. He imagined the buildings with all the windows whole and lighted, people moving back and forth between shops. For the first time he tried to read the weatherworn names on the storefronts. Some had vanished completely, their identification now a mystery to him. Wriglesworth's, the old general store on the close corner, was the most legible. Moving west from that there was a barbershop and a bar with cardboard in the windows. A small yellowbrick library sat on the far street, boarded up and scrawled with faded graffiti. There was a mechanic's shop, a cafe, a gas station on another corner, the station's antediluvian pumps rusting and showing prices that were absurd now. It was impossible to divine the past function of some of these places. Imagining all of them open for business on a Saturday morning it wasn't hard to picture the town with bustle and life. If he could resurrect anything it would be the general store. Wriglesworth's had been the last business in the square open, surviving the others by a decade or so, and had closed when he was young. He remembered his favorite candy bars running out, and what a crime that had seemed, to bring the money only to find the box empty on an afternoon, and the cool, crooked eye of Mrs. Wriglesworth regarding him without pity from above the counter like a strabismal buzzard on its perch. Old Mrs. Wriglesworth. He wondered if she was buried in the cemetery. If he could get his hands on that old place and start it up again that would be something to do. That might be all it took to liven up the town, some center of daily commerce and sociality, a place for idlers to sit and pass time. A good store did that. He sat on a bench and welcomed the distraction. He viewed the defunct square like some ruins from which could be discerned a valuable lesson. The town was so static that the second floor living spaces of the buildings were also vacant and without realtor signs. The destiny of this town and the destiny of the men and women who lived there seemed intertwined. Was it that men were destined for a certain fate or that they created their fate because they believed they were destined for it. How much of the future was destiny and how much effort and hope. Did a man fashion his fate with what he was given, his situation, his ability, or was there a measure of luck involved. Could the two elements shackle as well as propel. That anyone could do or be anything he wanted was utter foolishness, he believed. He did not believe in even endowment. But he was uncertain whether God knew his future, or whether it could be made known that way at all. If God knew his future, how could he turn to the right or left of that knowledge, independent agent that he seemed to be? At times he felt he would be great someday, and he wondered how many men felt the same way. He had that hope and it drove him. His father said that hope is what drives the world. He said that a man could learn to control his hope, but that he could not self-vanquish it, and that was good, because without it he would cease to be. That is why we dream, he said. In our dreams our hope is unrestrained. Take away a man's hope and you take away his will to live. Hope for anything desirable to that human being. He said that a man must manage his hope, so as not to despair. He must manage his hope, purify it, and work toward it. After the death of his parents the way people spoke of his father made him wonder if he had been a great man in the eyes of their diminutive world, as if greatness could be realized in such a place as this. Somehow he had done it. He wondered if a smalltown store owner could be great in his own right if he were content, if he did his job well and with respect. A man's signature of integrity seemed not based necessarily on his chosen career. This old store could be built into a better store than what had been. This town could use a good store. He had a vision of himself running the counter, shooting the breeze with some idling farmer while Rebekah sat in a white skirt in the corner rocking a damn baby to sleep. And the late afternoon sun coming in through the windows and the aisles lit in gold. And peanuts in his soda pop, like he used to take it.

9

WHIPPING CREAM, FIDDLEBACK, THE HOOKER, and Sky Pilot; Lilliputian, Grave Digger, Pussytoe, and The Preacher; Caboose, Million Bucks, and The Lover. Seth was riding two bulls a night. They were fine days, frost-tinged days when the sky was cloudless and open and held a profound autumnal blue, the best color to encase the yellow land. Seth's was the clear and certain danger, although each man in the pen faced the recklessness, the unbridled mass, the mighty aggression ungovernable. Nights were dark by the time they started and the pole light near the chute cast a pale blue value over the pen. Each time the gate was pulled the bull burst from the chute like black wind, twisting and groaning its way to throwing Seth from its back. All were unchecked force, terrific power. Seth picked bulls at will, rode whichever came into the chute, and hadn't yet received a bruise in all the bulls he had feigned to conquer. Jack kept the files of each bull in his truck and checked them after the animal was in and the ear tag could be read. Each time Seth was through for the night he walked to where he could see the white bull, Little Boy Blue, well set hump above its shoulders, sturdy curving horns like cornucopias, chipped and ragged at their ends, lying like a ghost in the starlight. The bull wasn't white, but being the color of curdled milk it was called white.

This bull in the chute now was brown, and under the dust of its coat dark stripes ran down its hide. Its eyes were muddy and passive. Rebekah usually followed him to the truck, leaning over the records with him, getting close enough he could smell her hair like the sweet decay of apples. But this time she remained by the fence with Maria. A loud clanging came from the chute and Jack looked up to see Seth, who sat on the bull, gripping the gate with one arm, the other entwined in Heber's, who stood on the platform. Heber called out to hurry. Jack went back to the papers and found the number. This was Tigger. It had rendered a severe concussion, two cases of broken ribs, a broken wrist, a half dozen dislocated shoulders, a compressed spine, a damaged spleen, a ruptured kidney, a broken femur, and three lesser concussions, shared out between riders and bullfighters alike. It had done all of this before Blair had acquired it, and had not been employed by the Selvedges.

—Hold up, called Jack. He walked over and climbed up to the platform. This one's bad, Seth. Let's turn him out and get another.

Seth looked spooked from the bull's restlessness. Roydn goggled up from the inside of the pen, his hands on the pull rope.

—Ain't this the one I rode the first time? said Seth. I was telling these guys I think this is the one I rode that first time.

—No. This one's the worst yet.

Seth looked at Heber and back to Jack.

—I got him, he said.

Jack read the injuries aloud and said, In thirty-one outs he was ridden once.

—Well let's make it twice, said Heber.

—I guess you could make it twice, Jack said to Heber, if you want.

Seth hesitated. The bull shifted its bulk in the chute. Hooves and horns clanging off the wood and metal, the animal started a series of small leaps forward, only moving a foot or so back and forth each time but with wound muscle and great force. Heber braced the rider and Jack dropped the paper and stepped forward, readying to lift him out. Rebekah and Maria had walked around behind the platform and Rebekah asked what the matter was.

—Did Blair ever mention him? said Seth.

—What the hell does he know? He's an ignorant old man. He ain't looked over these records in years.

—I don't know, Seth… said Heber.

Maria was coaxing Seth to come off the bull, and Seth looked of three minds, his close-set eyes mean and raging. The bull rose up beneath him like a ground swell and stuck its enormous head over the chute, grunting gutturally and blowing snot in arcing strings. Its gnarled horn gouged the chute, revealing bright wood like a new plowed furrow as it fell to four hooves again. Seth unwrapped his hand and said, Hell with it. Lift me out. I'll take him another night.

Jack walked to his truck and Rebekah followed. He could feel her standing just behind him as he replaced the record. When he turned toward the pen, sure she was watching him, she stood gazing over the dark expanse of the country. She faced him and gave him an even stare. Roydn cursed loudly as he and Heber pushed another bull into the chute, and Jack walked over to help them. This bull was dirty white with wild black spots on its hide that traveled like a galaxy from head to rump. It smelled of sweat and bull piss and filth and put off a hostile air. Roydn used oaths like preachers use scripture. According to some strange arithmetic in his head, a self-devised equation that solved what the girl must value, he had begun a habit of letting loose a string of profanity and immediately looking to see its effect upon Rebekah. If Jack cared to follow his gaze he saw indifference, a face turned elsewhere as though she hadn't heard a word. He called for the bull's number and pulled the record.

—Uncle Buck, he said to himself. Only used in one rodeo and threw the guy off. So he's a hunnerd percent unridable so far.

The bull hesitated a moment before coming out, as if trying to remember what was expected of it, and then leapt from the chute and tried a few spotty bucks and a low bellow before settling into a predictable spin. Once Seth leaned into the spin he had it until Heber hollered out the time. Seth freed his hand and floated away from the bull, landing on his feet and tossing his hat in the air. He let out a whoop and turned to Jack. Jack met him and they slapped hands.

—That oughta about do it, said Seth. Did you see me spurring him on the outside? Judges give points if you spur um on the outside when they spin.

Roydn stood behind them and said in a voice barely audible, Hell, I could of rode that one.

Heber paused with his hand on the bucking strap.

—What's that, Woolums?

Roydn started and looked up. He took his hat off and scratched his greasy noggin.

—I said, hell. I could of rode that one.

—What, you got your nerve up? said Heber.

Roydn looked at the ground and kicked the dirt with an old leather boot.

—Aw hell, he said.

—That's a decent bull for a first ride, said Jack.

—Aw hell, said Roydn.

He kicked the dirt again and hooked his thumbs in his belt loops. He was digging a row to plant beans in. He jerked his head up toward where the girls stood outside the fence and it tottered there on his thin neck. Rebekah looked straight at him and his jaw trembled and he stared at the ground again.

—Aw hell, he said, his voice unsteady. You sure you don't mind letting me use your rope, McQuarters? What if I bust it?

—Take it, said Seth. He held it out. You can use the spurs too if they'll fit on those bent up clodhoppers.

—Let's go, Woolums, called Heber. Do you want him or should I turn him out?

—Aw hell, he said. Aw hell, lemme have at him.

He walked stiffly toward Seth with his thumbs still in his belt loops and took the bull rope with sudden authority. Then he just stood there looking at them all.

He changed his mind once he'd settled onto the bull's back for the hard muscle, the restrained power beneath him, the pure savageness of the animal and that close, but Heber refused to let him up and kept one hand on his gaunt shoulder. Seth climbed onto the gate to help him and Heber slapped the would-be rider hard on the back, spouting words of encouragement.

—Come on, Woolums! he cried. If only your momma could see you. You ain't shown this much courage since you suckled on her hairy nipple!

Roydn glanced up a dozen times, looking futilely for the two girls who were hidden around the side of the platform.

—There, said Seth. Now what I do is give her a twist in the palm there.

—Like this? said Roydn. His throat bone bobbed up and down like he was struggling to swallow a dried turd. He emitted strange clicks and wore the look of one trying to understand how things had gotten so far out of his control. His thin bony frame aboard the bull looked wanting in strength and ability. He did what he was told and Jack picked up the pull rope and stood back.

—Get your ass set firmly there and you're ready, said Seth. You just tell old Jack when to pull that rope.

—Naw, naw, I can't do it, said Roydn. He looked up at Heber and his voice was strained. If I get knocked wrong I could go into a seizure.

—You can't get out of there now, Woolums, said Heber.

—Naw, I can't do it. I don't want to no more.

He swung his head around looking for relief, some help, and found nothing.

—You got it, said Seth. And you can always throw yourself off if you get uncomfortable.

—I'm uncomfortable now, said Roydn.

—Girls love a goddamn bullrider, said Seth.

Roydn resigned and settled himself into his seat. He looked at Jack and then down at his fastened hand.

—I guess I'm ready, he said.

He held up his arm crookedly.

—I'm ready, I'm ready! he yelled.

—Do you want someone to hold your glasses? said Jack.

Roydn visibly deflated and handed the heavy glasses to Heber.

—Ready? said Jack.

—Naw, hell. Lemme the hell off this thing.

He began to jerk his hand loose from the bull rope and Jack pulled the gate. He came bouncing out completely uncommitted to staying on the bull. The first buck unsettled him and the second threw him into the air askew. The third met him coming down and he flopped over the back of the bull like a wet rag. There was an audible rush of breath from his lungs and he collapsed in the dirt. The bull trotted away and Roydn lay on the ground, curled up like an injured worm. Soft moans escaped his throat. From the chute Jack heard a rasping noise and saw Heber redfaced, in need of breath, doubled up and shaking with laughter.

—You all right? said Jack.

He knelt on one knee beside Roydn. Roydn shook his head slowly.

—Bout seven more seconds and you got it, called Seth.

Roydn got to his hands and knees and made moaning sounds as he tried to pull air in. Jack went for the glasses. When Roydn was breathing again he gathered himself and took the glasses and fixed them on his face.

—I done it, he said weakly.

—Are you all finished? called Rebekah from the fence.

Roydn stood up and took his glasses off and rubbed their

lenses with his sleeve. He chuckled like stew boiling.

—I can't believe it, he said.

—Is the bull out? said Rebekah. Can we come in now?

—It's done, called Roydn. I done it. Come here, Rebekah. The bull's out. Get in here.

He let out a strange screeching howl. The girls squeezed between the planks of the fence and walked over.

—Did you hurt yourself, Roydn? said Rebekah.

Roydn shrugged his shoulders, settled the glasses on his face, and turned to shock her with a grin.

—Naw, he said. Call me Roy. Bull bucked me off was about it. What about was it, fellers? Five or six seconds? Maybe seven? But I about had him. It's the way it goes. Pretty good for a first ride.

—I'd say you were airborne at a full second, said Heber. But the watch stopped when you hit the ground, which was three-point-one.

—Aw, hell, said Roydn, grinning. I know I was on him longer than that. But don't it go by in a rush.

He looked to Seth for support and Seth nodded. He went to jamming his shirt back into his pants all around.

—Careful, said Seth. He nodded to Heber's shoe. You stepped in a pie.

Heber lifted his foot up and swore softly.

—When did he do this?

They made their way out of the pen and Heber limped toward the water pipe like his foot was wounded.

It was cold inside the trailer and all the windows were open. Maria had left the pen for a night shift at a gas station in Willow Valley, where she worked two jobs to save in the hope of school, and Heber had asked Rebekah to ride with him in his Bronco so he didn't have to go alone on his birthday, swearing it was safe despite its appearance and holding the passenger door open where the window had been replaced by a piece of cardboard. He now announced that he had quit smoking and went around closing windows. When he was done he crouched with a box of matches near the wood stove.

—Woolums, he said. What's that sticking out the back of your pants?

Roydn twisted around to look at himself and his hand moved back to discover that he had tucked his shirt into his white underwear. There was a surge of laughter and his face flushed red. He yanked his shirt out, and after tucking part of it back into his pants he pulled it out again and let it hang.

Rebekah walked over to him and stood close and her hands worked deftly at tucking his shirt in. Facing the rest of them while she did it she said, It's okay, Roy. It's part of your charm.

Roydn's face was empurpled. She pulled a little of the shirt back out with her thin fingers and from the waist down he could have been a model for Rustler jeans.

Jack sat down first so that the decision to sit near her would not be his. He had taken the loveseat, and in a moment she sat next to him. Seth and Roydn sprawled themselves open-legged on opposite ends of the long couch. Heber disappeared down the hall and returned barefoot with a pair of socks in his hand. He tried to put them on standing and as he stood on one leg to fit the second sock he lost his balance and came hopping at incredible speed sideways, where he crashed into the wall and shook the trailer. He asked Rebekah for help in the kitchen and the two disappeared. The stove's warmth spread through the room. Jack felt it on his hands first and then in his knees. His face felt tight, as if it needed to be stretched.

—Hey old Seth, said Roydn. That was a good ride tonight.

—He got in that spin, Woolums, said Seth, and I was able to hold on.

—Yuh. He tried the same thing on me, cept I couldn't yet handle it like you done. But I'd get me one in a spin again, and I'd lean with him like you done and just let him spin, all eight seconds.

—And I was spurring him. Did you see me doing that? You spur him on the outside on a spin and the judges'll score you better.

—Yuh, I'd spur him, said Roydn. He left a hand in his lap gripping an imaginary bull rope and raised the other. He looked over at Jack, his dark eyes floating enormous behind the lenses of his glasses, and lifted a leg and tapped a heel into the couch. On his feet two socks that had given up. He reached into his pocket and pulled out a wrinkled bag of corn nuts a quarter full. He opened it with difficulty—the top kept curling back down—and held them toward Jack. His head was tilted back as it so often was when he tried to look through the heavy glasses where they had slid to the bottom of his nose.

—Hell no, said Jack. You been holding onto those all night?

—No, just since before milking.

He threw some in his mouth and started to crunch and soon the bag was gone, wadded up and shoved back into his pocket.

Jack heard Rebekah's laughter from the kitchen. She came out carrying a bowl of salsa and one of tortilla chips. She bent to set them down and he was in a swirl of her scent. Roydn scooted himself over to the bowl and began eating chips.

—Jeez, Roy, said Seth. Sounds like a house falling down. Close your mug.

Rebekah reappeared, followed by Heber. Heber worked at opening a bottle of champagne and said, Thanks for being here, everyone. Even old Bumgardener there. Rebekah, he said. He released the cork with a hollow pop, caught the foam with a dishcloth, and poured into a common glass. This one's yours.

—No thank you, she said.

—Not even a sip for a toast?

—Do you have anything else?

—I do.

Seth came from the kitchen with a beer he had pilfered from

the fridge and he drained Rebekah's glass in a few gulps and cracked open the can.

—Here we are, said Heber as he walked back into the room. He took another glass and filled it with sparkling cider and handed it to Rebekah. He filled his own with champagne and raised the glass.

—To the lovely Rebekah Rainsford, he said. May she be repaid a hundred fold for the graciousness she's shown to our humble town. We are very glad to have her.

She colored and touched glasses with him. Seth raised the can of beer and Jack and Roydn had nothing to toast with.

—To her and her mother, said Heber. May they find safety, peace, and a new start—here, or anywhere else they go. But I hope it's here.

He raised his glass again and drank. Rebekah stood, her hips canted at an angle and her eyes glittering like a fast moving stream in sunlight. She was near enough that Jack could have reached out and touched her leg, caressed it as one lover caresses another, or as two people familiar with each other's touch would touch.

—I think I'll ride me another bull soon, said Roydn.

—It's getting cold, said Seth. Might have to wait till spring. We'll start riding again in the spring.

—Aw hell, I suppose we could keep riding into the winter if we had a mind to.

—Break bones that way.

—You only live once, McQuarters, said Roydn.

—Who brought the cake? said Heber.

Everyone looked around.

Roydn Woolums seemed to be enjoying some new status among them. Seth had never treated him so well. Heber and Rebekah talked about college. Heber ran through his professors to see if they'd had any of the same. Jack listened to it all and felt himself being whelmed by a dark mood he had no control over. Heber seemed a self-aggrandized fool. Roydn seemed an imbecile for that leer on his face and for his simpleminded elation. Rebekah was so clean and untamed and so beautiful, aware of her body, proud of her sex, unwilling to restrain its natural power yet withholding it as something forbidden. The nubile wench. The attention of each man in the room was centered on her, the onslaught of their unbridled desire and lust and madness nearly palpable. Roydn let his large wet eyes roam over that full corpus thoroughly. Heber behaved as if there were no one around but her. Even Seth stared as if seeing her for the first time, and for it all she seemed emboldened, impassioned with something rare and unrefined, and the men in the room sensed it and reacted as if to heed some atavistic impulse. These were not games they were playing. There would be no end to it, and so she must leave. If she stayed she would be ruined. She would develop an unabashed want for what the men would bring upon her, a burning counterlust, and she would seek this fate out and make it her own. Or if she could avoid it she would still be worn down like a stone in weather and she would be spotted before middle age as one who stayed and was worn down. She knew this, and for it all she kept herself aloof. It seemed that she could have been anyone's that night, and no one's, and Jack was made to take deep breaths often.

—John, said Heber. Are you getting the farm soon?

Jack shook his head.

—Here's to John getting the farm! roared Heber. He drained what was left in his glass and refilled it just as quickly. Old Blair, he said. A shrewd business man if there ever was one. He owns what, seven-hundred acres?

—Five.

—That piece up next to the mountains. What's that, about seventy?

—Fifty.

—That's a nice little piece. It's the kind of piece a guy could build a house on. Money's coming to this town.

—Is it?

—Did you know Willow Valley is passing development restrictions? Wease told me there'll be an indefinite moratorium on land development. That means places like this catch the spillover. They're full up over there and looking for satellite communities to build up. We're only thirty miles away. What would you say to that?

—Nothing.

—If you inherit your half of the farm you might have a say over that piece up there.

—If I inherit my half of the farm, said Jack dully, I'll give it to you.

—With your father gone you fall into place as the rightful heir, said Heber. The laws of primogeniture. It's time you stopped fretting and faced that fact.

—Believe what you want, but don't be ignorant.

—You should be thinking about the future. This town could become greater than it is now. You have a role to play here.

—What's wrong with it now?

—Well it could grow. Give people like Woolums here something to do besides pick his bum all day. Give Rebekah a reason to stay. All it takes is the interest of people. People come and infrastructure follows. More people and more money and therefore more people.

—Who wants more people? Why does our measure of progress have to involve development and wealth?

—Easy buddy, said Heber. We are evolved and evolving. Dad had the vision. When he was mayor he had things on the upswing. He may have been misguided in other areas, but he was right in what he saw as this town's destiny.

—Destiny? said Jack.

Heber stared at him strangely.

—Your father was the mayor of five hundred people. Willard

Smelley was his successor. Sexy Rex Randall is the mayor now.

—Oh, said Heber. I see.

—I'll go get something to put candles in, said Rebekah. Do you have something like that?

Heber was still looking at Jack and without breaking his gaze he said, In the fridge, sweetheart, there's some leftover cornbread. I don't have any candles.

She brought three-quarters of a pan of cornbread in and they all sang. The cornbread was served and the room broke into leaping conversation. When Roydn came back from a long recess in the bathroom, Heber said, Good Lord, Woolums, you got any skin left on your pecker?

Roydn turned red.

—Or were you laying cable. You damn well better have closed the door behind you. There's a can of fragrance on the back of the toilet.

Roydn returned to the bathroom. Jack received the warmth from the stove and listened to the wood burn inside. He could enjoy the heat from the stove and the warmth of the girl beside him both as objects in the room. She had taken her place on the couch with him and had not fought the way the cushions sank in the middle and pulled them together. He caught the scent of her hair when she tossed it and it went straight to his groin where it glowed warmly. Some striving chemist had figured it out. He could admire that level of knowledge and skill. Rebekah laughed beside him, along with everyone else in the room, at Heber. She leaned into him, and when she placed a hand on his thigh he turned and whispered into her ear and asked what she was doing. She removed her hand as if it had been burned. A moment later she got up to use the bathroom and when she came back she sat between Roydn and Seth. They were surprised and delighted. He watched her and marveled at how generous she was with her hands, how careless with her steamy smirks, but she had not been that way with him. He had been made to work for everything as if milking a dry cow, gathering mere drops into his hands that he might saturate his tongue, and every drop was a voluntary touch, a rare caress, or the irretrievable deluge that had been their one holy kiss.

Heber was telling a story and she watched him, rapt. He made her burst into laughter and then extracted that laughter from her like a fisherman pulling a line from the water with his hands. She laughed until her composure was gone. Her nostrils pulled back in an unbecoming way. Her mouth was agape, every tooth and filling seen, her red throat open and pulpy and glistening. She wiped tears from her cheeks with the greater part of her thumb. Her face was blood red and a Y-shaped vein stood out in her forehead. Then Heber was finished and the room was drunk with mirth. In the vacuum of silence afterward Jack felt a sudden clairvoyance for the small group gathered there, a heavy portent even among all this laughter, as if they might leave this place and go their ways to separate dooms.

—What about you, Rebekah? said Heber. What's your history?

—I'm beginning a fresh history now, she said.

—Careful. Somebody here might see that as an invitation to participate. He laughed. I mean, he said, leaning forward, showing teeth, his face reddening, what's your *history*?

She blushed and Heber's eyes held a hard gleam as he stared across the room at her, waiting. She didn't answer until she understood that they were all listening for it.

—I've known bad men, she said. And some boys who wished they were men. So you tell me, where are the good ones?

—Now that's an invitation! said Heber. He grinned like a fool.

Roydn, a good man, looked helpless. Her words had struck him like a club. As she spoke she had stared at Jack with smoldering eyes, and he imagined the lovers she'd had and every man that had taken her. He saw her face as it would have been beneath them, listless, as if in compromise that if this were all the world held she might as well indulge, her cleft chin raised in defiance toward, or triumph over, God, and the men would bite her chin. The vision wrecked and ruined him, but even so he warmed and ached as it seared his mind. He had the need to take her away, to rush her to the farmhouse and up to his small bedroom and to ravish her on the unwashed sheets. To take what other men had taken before him and to do so in a compensation of furious plunder. It was a great distance between his spirit and his body, and it had always been.

10

HE PLOWED THE FIELD AND THE SEAGULLS CAME. They rose pure white in the sun with wings fixed rigid in the breeze, a stark contrast against the purple storm that moved to the north beyond them. Inside the cab of their most powerful tractor he turned the old corn stubble from spent gold to scallops of deep brown one narrow strip at a time. The plow dug deeper than the disc and churned the roots and soil upward. He was an alchemist working in reverse, preparing the soil for the spring, and he imposed his will upon the field. He was alone with the birds in the midst of the open field and a worn out opera tape Blair had left in the deck played over and over. The music was strangely suited to his work, an accompaniment to the high growl of the diesel engine. The gulls fell behind him on the black field. When he got out to remove a stone uprooted by the plow he did not question its age nor origin. He was small in the field beside the tractor. A man is always small in his field among the big machinery and the long round earth. He is smaller yet when he has to walk across the earth carrying a stone. When he must he moves miniature and slow across the expanse and all he does is small.

He remembered the time Blair taught him to plow. He was very young. He sat on Blair's lap and Blair told him to keep his eyes fixed on a faraway point instead of on the field in front of him—a farmhouse beyond the riverbottoms, the peak of a distant mountain, a gnarled fencepost he could distinguish from the others. He taught him to work the wheel in continual small turns back and forth instead of trying to hold it straight and steady. This produced straight plow lines, straight planting lines. He used this method still with the plow and planter, but he had failed to keep his life steady this way. He had failed to swing his wheel back and forth, but had held it steady, and had veered from the unseen course.

The steady rumble of the tractor and the heavy pull of the earth against the plow as the plowshares cut the soil worked to quiet him and prepare him for winter. From the tractor he could see the field before him that was his future and as he rolled forward he felt older than he was, looking back on the torn furrows of his life through black diesel smoke, and it was all the same. He entertained thoughts that at first she'd been too pure for, too fresh, but which came late anyway, and these thoughts were a welcome balm as they writhed across his inner eye. In these dreams he wanted merely to possess her, to usurp her will and requisition her desires. She had brought with her an essence that was even now strange and obscure. It was like some experience, some knowledge she had carried with her from a place that imparted such a thing, something that this town, this hub of both transience and stagnancy, could neither fathom nor offer. It was a sullen thing she carried, in some ways frightening and in some ways appealing and in all ways maddening. It was something he needed but could never get in the remote and meager collection of houses like some future museum of how men used to live. He believed in the living God and in good and evil but he believed also in her, in her warm and ample body, in her mind— her body because of its power and beauty, and her mind because only it could be kept until she wished to give it. She could give him of her spirit, her body, her life. She could give him of her substance.

The flank of the storm moved in as he finished. He stepped

out of the tractor and felt the cold drops of autumn rain on his neck. Now that the crops were in and the fields bare it rained steadily all evening and night. He woke to rain at his window and wished like a boy throwing a coin into a well that he didn't have to get out of his bed and milk the cows. The rain was gentle on the pane, the right sound for the dark room at early morning. When he fed the cows after milking the rain was gone. He looked to the east and saw that the clouds had drawn up the mountains like a lifted skirt revealing the rugged peaks white with fallen snow, fresh as anything first seen.

He was never alone with her except in his thoughts, and those rare early times they had spent together seemed unrepeatable. When they gathered at Heber's in the dark evenings they did so without Roydn. One night they drove through the desert, following endless roads through the basalt fields and sage for no reason that was ever spoken. She had not gone with him that time but had gone with Heber and Maria. Seth had gone with him, the two following the taillights of the Bronco sullen and womanless, Heber parading in front like some polygamist of the desert. With them all she grew larger, the center of all things, the lifeblood of the group. And when he worked balm into the udder of a cow he remembered the warmth of her legs under his fingers, the flex of the muscles in her calves. And on many cruel mornings, black with the strengthening cold, he reached his hand for a warm, milk-stiffened teat, and as his fingers closed around it he thought of her.

Sunday morning he sat in his pickup at the far edge of the church parking lot and watched the windy day. The meeting had started inside. Beside him lay the glassware he had brought with him, on it an ovenburnt piece of tape scrawled with Noreen's last name. His white shirt was threadbare and fit too tightly and he had undone the top button. His tie was bungled at the neck in some invented knot. It was a great old building in front of him, circular stained glass windows high in the solid walls, intricate brick masonry of the kind rarely lain anymore. Ancient trees spread limbs toward the structure. This old building was the best kept in town, scrupulously maintained and venerable, the only building of worship.

A stiff wind blew when he stepped from the truck and walked toward the church with the dish tucked under his arm. He shoved his hands in his pockets and flexed his muscles. The shadow God's building threw was cold, but it protected him from the wind. He walked to the doors and paused. There was a sign there in marble with the name of the church and beneath that the stone-chiseled message that visitors were welcome. He stopped and looked around. He lay the dish down on the steps and turned to leave and there was Rebekah walking toward him on the sidewalk. She was underdressed for the weather and her arms were folded tightly over her chest.

—What are you doing here? she said.

—Getting ready to leave.

—What have you got there?

—I brought it back. She'll get it when she comes out, or someone'll get it to her.

Her skirt revealed the long shapes of her thighs and stopped just past her knees. She wore a thin buttonup sweater and her hair was loosely curled and fell around her shoulders. He had not seen her in these clothes, this heightened care rendered to her body.

—It's cold, she said. Are you coming in?

—I'm going home.

—You put on a shirt and tie to drop this dish off at the door?

How could he tell her that it was better for him to be in the rank living room in his collapsed chair watching television with Blair?

—Come sit by me, she said. I'm alone today.

She stepped up to him and threaded her arm through his and her perfume was around him.

—Get the door, she said.

He opened the door and she preceded him through and the dish was left sitting on the step.

The hymns warmed him, bled into his heart and filled him with something he'd forgotten. The heft of organ music recalled a younger lifetime in those pews. He looked around and met so many eyes looking back that he eventually kept his eyes on the speaker. After the first meeting they were intercepted by a warm-handed multitude. People waited in line to speak to him. He got not a few sly grins from the men and was surprised at how warm Rebekah was toward everyone, how well she knew them all. She had changed the membership, given it amperage. She had become the center. As the host moved toward Sunday school he and Rebekah escaped to the parking lot and his truck, where he ran the heater.

—Did you see Roy in there? she said. He's usually there.

—I didn't look.

—Why don't you guys ever invite him to come out?

—Because Heber does the inviting, and he doesn't like him.

—Why not?

—Because he's ugly and righteous.

—That's not nice.

Jack rubbed his palm over the worn shifting knob and listened to the heater.

—He acts shy when I see him here at church, she said. He doesn't seem shy when he's around you guys.

—It's because he's in love with you.

—Don't say that.

—It's true. He's got you to himself in there.

—He's not in love with me, she said. But I think I know why he's not here today. He came to my house last night. He was dressed up with clean pants and a polo shirt and was wearing cologne. He'd combed his hair. He had a single red rose in his hand. I wonder where he got it. He was so embarrassed his face was redder than the rose. I went outside with him and we sat on that little bench by the lane and he gave me the rose. It was all very sweet. He said that if I was free he wanted to date me.

—What did you say?

—I told him now's not a good time.

—Why isn't it?

—We're leaving tonight for Salt Lake. For Thanksgiving. But I'm staying longer.

—Is that here already?

—Mm-hmm.

—How long will you be gone this time?

—Maybe a month.

—Why so long?

She shrugged.

—Just visiting people. Watching kids.

—How'd he take it?

—He said he understood.

—I'll bet he did. And I'm going to kick his scrawny ass.

—Why?

—You know how these things go.

—But I'm not your girl.

—That's true.

She trailed her finger along the cracked dashboard and turned up the pad to see what dust it had collected.

—My dad called a few days ago.

—It's got to happen sooner or later, he said. I'll help you out. We'll get rid of him.

He spoke these words but his heart was not in them.

—You're sweet, she said. I wish it were that easy.

—Don't leave.

—Why not?

—If you leave you'll miss the other deaths.

—That's not a good thing to say. No one else will die. It's been too long. They have to come together.

—Don't leave, he said. Have Thanksgiving here and have me over for dinner. You're a great cook.

—I need to go.

—Don't you like it here?

—I like it here fine.

—But you like Salt Lake better. If it wasn't for your old man you'd go back in a second.

—I'm going back because of him. He knows where we are now.

—Are you even going to come back at all?

She pulled him to her and kissed him quickly on the mouth.

—Yes, she said. We're attached to this place. Then she smiled and put her hand on the door lever. Bye, she said. I've got to go back in.

She left him, and drawing farther away from her as he drove down the road he knew he had squandered the late time.

That afternoon he sat in the office in askance light as Roydn and Blair milked the cows and their yells sounded through the doorway. He opened the green fridge that stood in the corner and filled a paper cup with milk he had drawn from the tank. It was cold and thick and delicious. A calendar of Case tractors hung in front of him, speckled with brown dots from flies long dead in the season. The vibrations of the compressor engines thrummed in the wall behind him and he listened to the chugging and popping of the machines as they coursed milk through hoses and pipes and into the cooling tank. The old radio played country music to the cows and he tapped his foot along with Baby's Got Her Blue Jeans On.

Roydn came through the door and swore loudly. He took his glasses off and rubbed them with his sleeve and his eyes were minuscule and beady without them.

—What is it? said Jack. He pointed to the empty chair and reached behind him to the fridge and tossed a Pepsi over and leaned back.

—Selvedge, said Roydn. He popped the tab partway and slurped at the hissing fizz, then opened it and took a deeper drink and burped. You need to get another employee.

—You quitting?

—No but I oughta. I'm real close. I'm tired of being on the bottom rung.

—What bottom rung?

—I've worked here a long time. And you know I ain't even taken one step up.

—It's a dairy farm, Woolums. Where did you hope to go?

—Well you ain't hired anybody else since I been here. Shit.

—That's because you're good. You're all we need.

—Well hell, it's about time you thought of getting somebody underneath me. Just hire somebody from town here. Plenty of fools'd come milk evenings. Hell, you could hire Duncan Fitz. He's retarded, but he could help milk at least.

—And put you over him?

—Well, sure, I guess I could do that.

Jack leaned forward.

—Woolums, he said. Do you see me sitting here?

—Yeah.

—Well here I am. Consider what I've put into this place and consider what I've got out of it. Now that things have settled and the dust has cleared, see what I've got.

Roydn squinted his eyes wisely and nodded.

—You got shafted. Just like you always said you would.

Jack looked at him.

—If you're looking for fairness at the Selvedge Dairy, you might as well shit in one hand and wish in the other and see which gets you there sooner.

Roydn brooded.

—That ain't good, he said. That ain't good to treat you like that. He paused to consider. You know, cow shit is the cleanest shit

I have ever encountered, but it's still shit.

—Well said. Now I've got to go feed.

—Hey hold up. Roydn picked at his face. We riding bulls again soon? I can't get that out of my head. My little brothers don't believe I done it, and I want to show um I done it and would do it again.

—It's too cold and dark. You get hurt easier that way.

Roydn puffed his chest out.

—Fine with me. The more dangerous the better.

—Okay, we'll put you on Little Boy Blue next time.

—That the man killer? I'd ride him. I think I would. Only the good die young, you hear me? You can't live forever. Got to grab it while you can. I rode me a bull and now I got to find me a girl to marry. You know any?

—The same ones you do.

—What's up with Rainsford?

—What do you mean?

—Gosh, she's something. She's goshdamn blown my mind and changed the way I look at things. She's the kind of girl you look at and have hope for humanity.

—That's profound, Woolums.

—Listen. Roydn's face turned serious and the muscles of his throat worked. You can clobber me if you want for what I'm about to tell you, but that girl has got under my skin. I think about her when I go to bed and I think about her when I wake up and all the time in between. It's half killing me.

Jack felt a surge of grief run through him at knowing the truth of what Roydn said, at sensing its hopelessness, and it unsettled him to where he wanted to beat the kid, pound his well-meaning and unsightly face in for no sensible reason.

—I went to see her last night, said Roydn.

—I know, said Jack. She told me.

Roydn blushed.

—Well, shoot. You wasn't doing anything. I figgered I'd better get me a chance.

—It doesn't matter, Woolums.

—You don't got a problem with it?

—I never had a hold on her. She told me so herself.

—It makes me sad to hear you say that, buddy.

—It's just the way things are right now.

—And how's that?

—I got work to do every day so I do it.

—Yeah, well, we all got to work, I suppose.

Jack nodded.

—You know, buddy, said Roydn. The problem with girls like her is they show a guy what's possible. How's he supposed to operate after that?

—You said it.

—May the best man win when she gets back from the holidays, then, said Roydn.

He stuck out a rough hand stained with manure and udder dip. Jack grabbed it and they shook.

—All right then, said Roydn. You know, my pa's saving up some money for me to take a few classes at the college. Maybe next fall, he says. Thinks they got something to teach me, but I don't believe it. Probly be the other way around.

—You told me already, said Jack. You're bleeding.

Roydn's hand went to the spot on his face he'd been picking at and his fingers came away smeared with blood. He made a series of fierce grunting noises that could have been restrained curses.

—I'm twenty-two years old! he cried. I'm a grown-ass man. What about you?

—I don't know what to tell you, Woolums. It ain't as bad as it once was.

—Whorebait! said Roydn.

—You better get out there before Blair loses it. And I've got to feed.

—Well you come find me fore I leave. We'll talk bull riding and women. Sound good?

—Sounds good.

Roydn got up and turned to leave, then turned back.

—Hey, Selvedge, he said. You know it's my birthday in a couple days. Let's celebrate the damn thing.

Jack followed him out of the office and walked up the rear steps, down the alley, and under the hanging lime sacks that dusted each cow's back as she left the barn. Cold light was pulled westward from the sky as he yanked bales of hay down from the stack, loving the thud they made as he ran from beneath the falling towers and they tumbled behind him and pounded the ground. His body heated up as he carried them to the manger, broke them, and spread them. As he crossed through the corral to feed the other side a hollering came from the barn. There was always hollering in the barn. A line of six cows came running down the exit alley, their vulgar udders swinging beneath them, and he guessed the gate had broken open again. He went for a bale, lugged it to the manger, broke it, spread it. In a minute he saw Blair hustling toward him, and he realized watching him come that he'd never seen the old man run before.

—Hey! yelled Blair. I need your help in here.

In the barn Roydn lay sprawled out on the empty milking deck in fresh manure, his glasses lying beside him. His head hit the floor irregularly and he made spit bubbles. Jack knelt and held his head, which was bleeding and filthy with shit. Blair came with a sweater and shoved it beneath, and Roydn began to breathe raggedly, gurgling in phlegm, his convulsions becoming weaker.

—How'd he get up here? said Jack.

—Aw, he was beating the hell out of one of um, and they got spooked and the damn gate busted open again.

—He get run over?

—Not as far as I could tell. They came around and the last one caught him off the bars and he just fell. His mother said five minutes. If he don't come out of it in five minutes we call the paramedics. She's on her way. He'll be all right yet. Just give me a scare is all.

Jack dialed Rebekah's house for Martha and got no answer. He left to bring the cows back and saw the axe handle broken in two pieces and lying on the milking deck a few feet away.

—Broke the damn beating stick, he said.

When Jack returned from gathering the fugitive cows Roydn sat on a chair holding an ice pack to his head.

—Let me alone, he muttered, scowling at anyone who touched him or asked him a question. I ain't dying. Just let me alone.

Josephine Woolums knelt beside him in her great bulk, and Elmer, Carrie, and Edward Elmer, the boy, stood off a ways. Roydn went home with his mother, still bleeding into the sweater. Jack and Blair turned their attention to the cows that had been waiting in dumb generosity, their udders bursting with milk. Jack shook off the bizarre event and lost himself in milkgorged teats and the throb and pound of the barn.

Roydn came to work the next day in the passenger's seat of the blue Cutlass next to his mother. He got out and waved to Jack, though the familiar lewd grin did not hang from his face and he did not come over to talk. The evening presaged snow. Roydn went about his work morosely and when Jack found him gathering cows and asked him how he was he shrugged and said he'd had worse seizures.

—You don't seem yourself, said Jack.

—I'm all right. Hell.

—Why don't you take a few days off?

—Need the money, Roydn grunted. His voice was hoarse and cracked and it broke and turned into a whisper when he spoke.

—Badass, said Jack.

Roydn smiled faintly.

—Hey, he croaked. She's coming back to town after the holidays, ain't she?

—That's what she said.

Roydn shook his head and muttered something and went into the barn to milk. He moved about his work, an unfortunate looking fellow, a good member of his church and community. He played a role in their town, their small world. Heber was a failed promise, a talented squanderer, and why people were more interested in the likes of him who trampled under his feet the very virtues they stood for than in a pure, thoroughly good man like Roydn Woolums was an enigma of human nature. Whatever principalities and powers of darkness he wrestled against, he seemed to more or less whip them soundly. He was good. This was a truth. He would find a good, homely wife and marry her and love her and he would never stray from his faith and would raise his own uncomely family within it. He would rear simple, hardworking children, teach them to want little, and they would therefore be content. He would stay in town and farm some scratch of land, build various operations and so forth, and he would be happy. He would prove that he and his had some claim on a measure of happiness. It was this simplicity that kept so many in their town whole.

Roydn milked that evening with Blair and when he went out to gather the low herd he locked them in the holding pen and didn't come in. Blair let him alone and Jack helped finish. When they were nearly done Blair walked out and hollered Roydn's name.

—The hell is he? he said.

—You don't think he could of walked home, said Jack.

—It's hell of a long way and it's going to storm, but he's thick-headed.

Jack milked the last cows alone and Blair went off in the truck to search along the lane and farther. He drove all the way to the Woolumses and came back as Jack was washing down.

—Nothing, he said. Now what in *the* hell?

Jack rolled up the hose and turned off the lights. They walked outside and it was snowing, big flakes that floated down through the light on the east hayshed. Blair hollered again but the falling snow dulled his voice and kept it close. He pulled Elmer from his house and the three of them split up and searched the barnyard. When they were confounded they called the Woolumses and within a few minutes the entire family was present in two vehicles, crawling over the barnyard. Church membership and the community were summoned by phone and soon there were scores of people there in scattered automobiles, lights and lanterns probing through the falling snow and people pooling together to talk in loose groups in solemn stimulation. The barnyard looked like some game of hide-and-seek gone awry. Search parties on foot tramped through the tree-covered hillsides above the river and four-wheelers moved over the bottoms. Trucks ran the roads and their spotlights combed the blank white fields. There was much debate on whether tracks would stay visible in this new snow, should he be walking around somewhere, how fast they would fill with it still falling and the wind rising. There was concern that it was getting cold. All night they turned the barnyard upside down, triple checking every known inch, and vehicles and people were still pouring over the country-side when Jack reunited with Blair to milk the cows again at four. They had run the propane space heaters all night in the barn and people came in yet to get warm as the dawn approached in its vague grayness and Jack and Blair gathered milk. Jack stood by the roaring heater near Tim Smelley and heard him tell how the iced river was being searched for holes. Roydn's father returned once more at five o'clock, speaking softly with Blair, letting him know that Roydn was not at the house. This had been a last hope. By the time the milking was finished the wind blew horizontal snow and the search was suspended, and when Jack walked out of the barn after milking snowdrifts covered the land like frozen waves.

11

BLAIR HIRED ROYDN'S YOUNGEST BROTHERS, RODNEY and the one they called Rapscallion, whose real name no one could remember, and gave them better pay than their brother had received, which meant significantly better pay than Jack. The two boys worked silently and acted spooked as he taught them the routine. He could spark no relationship with either one, social introverts that they were. They watched him with solemn eyes and never spoke, only nodding when he asked if they understood. The cows responded with more emotion. The brothers didn't even speak to each other while working. During one of their first nights milking, with the boys still nervous around the big udders and fast legs of the cows, one ornery animal caught Rapscallion's elbow well with her hoof. He cradled it and looked hurt and confused and for a minute it seemed he would cry. Blair laughed long and slow from where he sat on a small folding chair at the head of the parlor, bruises fading around his eyes and nose, and it sounded like a cold tractor trying to start. He went into a fit of coughing and spat a wad of phlegm on the floor. Jack motioned for the boys to follow him. They walked up to where the cow stood big-eyed and smug.

—You have to tame these cows to you, he said. They know

what's going on down there, and the way you tame um to you is by teaching um about consequences.

He punched the cow rapidly in the side of the face three times. On the third hit his fist glanced off the animal's soft rearing nose and into a steel bar and broke in a boxer's fracture, that old wound he had first received in high school from the hard head of Bobby Sue. The two boys could not have known it and might have taken his red face to be one of vengeance rather than pain. At Jack's insistence Rapscallion placed the milkers on all four of her ripe teats and Jack left to drag haybales to the cows one-handed and spitting dark oaths.

Mornings Blair spent most of his time sitting on the folding chair near the space heater at the head of the parlor while Jack milked and stained his cast with iodine and manure, rendering a stinking husk he wanted only to be rid of. Blair stayed in the house after milking. Jack returned for lunch to find him in the living room with the drapes pulled, the room smelling of despondence, flatulence, and old man creams, watching Matlock. It was embarrassing when Jack had to coax him out of bed in the morning. Blair was awake before Jack stepped into the room, but two or three trips back were necessary before he got up and shuffled in his long underwear to the bathroom and from there to his work clothes at the back of the house. Always a stout, thick man, the flesh beneath his chin had begun to deflate and loosen, swinging pendulously with his movement, wrinkled and unsightly as a turkey's wattle. He revealed his forearms one night and Jack noticed how pale and thin they had become, their blue veins prominent beneath the mottled skin. His right eye grew rheumy and leaked down the coarse skin of his cheek without his notice. More than once Jack was struck with the notion that he could take the old man's death without blinking. He grew comfortable in the gloom that surrounded them and it soon became his. His upstairs bedroom was unkempt and malodorous. He bought new clothes rather than wash the soiled ones and it felt good to spend money. There were moments when it seemed best to sit down and do nothing and he would find a bale of hay or a cold tractor cab and be surprised when he discovered that a half hour had passed.

The dynamic of the group had shifted. One night in the doublewide Heber suggested that Roydn might have gone to Salt Lake to see about Rebekah and gave Jack a look of wild speculation that was nearly comical. Sometimes Maria was there. Seth brought Erica Birch. He threw an arm around her and she leaned into him but their contact seemed tense, his grin overdone, Erica's eyes darting around the room like a wild thing caged. She did not exude the sensual confidence of Maria or the comeliness and quiet dignity of Rebekah. She appeared used up, spiritually bankrupt, her bleak emotional insides bared to view. And so their time together as three friends was strained and their sessions grown few.

He was in the barn office one evening going through records when he looked at the calendar and realized it was his birthday. He drove to the co-op to get something to celebrate, as he had the past few years, but he was too late and it was closed. That evening he sat at the kitchen table with Blair eating a bad casserole someone had brought over a few days before. The food smelled of fish but there was no fish in it. Blair in his undershirt, his aged and loose body shown in pitiful form, hard round gut pushing against the table, emaciated arms, redskinned chest with coarse silver hair sprouting above his low scooped collar. Was this his grandfather? When had it happened? Jack was listening to the smacking sounds of Blair eating and thinking about his own new age against the age of the other when there was a knock at the front door. He answered in a weary stupor like a troglodyte at the mouth of a cave and was embarrassed to see Martha Rainsford standing there, smiling, holding a plate covered with foil. He led her into the kitchen and turned off the television and began picking things up, but finding no place to put them he set them down again into the clutter. Blair came out of his bedroom buttoning a shirt and looking displaced in his own house. Both men were still dirty from the day's work and both smelled of it. Martha lit the cake with matches she had brought and she and Blair sang, the performance inelegant, a bad harmony, yet by the end inspiring a surprising swell of gratitude in Jack. As they ate cake at the table they discussed Jack's hand, Rebekah's wellbeing, and speculated about the disappearance of Roydn Woolums. Martha, sitting in this slovenly room with two soiled men who stank of the animals they kept, appeared comfortable, a credit to her pretense or her soul. It was a whirlwind event with her there, a strange thing to have her in the house. She wasn't there and then she was and then she wasn't again, and the two men were left looking at each other over the remains of the cake. Jack was left unsettled. He turned the television back on and Blair muttered that he was sorry for forgetting his birthday. He seemed to be calculating in his head, trying to recall how long it had been since he'd remembered, marveling that the thing did indeed come around this time every year. He found a pen and scrawled a note on the calendar day, as if the same calendar would be hanging there next year. They couldn't seem to settle back down at the table, and soon made their separate ways to their bedrooms.

Jack lay awake aching for her. He thought about his situation, releasing slowly the feelings seeing Martha had brought him. It had done his heart good because she was the girl's mother. The winter to this point had lacked focus, or rather its grim regularity had become jumbled up with the girl and with the inheritance, so he looked to spring and saw how it would go. He could only fill his future with the certainty of work—the same work, the same cycle, putting seed in the ground, raising crop, taking the harvest, and milking, ceaselessly milking—and he wondered with some astonishment whether a man's life could be stacked up and predicted this way a year ahead of time, ten years, thirty, longer. He wondered if he had become as Blair, wholly consumed by the necessity and perpetuation of his work, rendered cheerless and without humor, utterly stoic and without imagination. None of it seemed worth doing anymore without her. He pressed his mind forward but his heart brought it back. He was fettered to her, however unwillingly, and he could not make it otherwise. As he searched into the future as if with a seer stone for some alternative, the vision was not clear, and no revelation filled his mind.

On a night in the last raw week of November he drove into Willow Valley alone and exhausted. It was dark when he reached the liquor store. His truck was the only vehicle in the parking lot and he sat awhile waiting as if he could change his mind and knowing he wouldn't. The same man was working as had been the night he'd come with Heber. He thought about browsing the aisles, seeing this world again with a neophyte's eye, an enthusiast's vigor, but went straight to the wall of hard liquor and took a fifth of Jack Daniel's from where it sat gleaming dully on the shelf. He paid without a word and left.

In his bedroom he uncovered the bottle from its sack like his firstborn child sleeping. The weight and beauty of the bottle in his hand lifted his heart and gave him this small thing to hope for. He cracked the cap and salivated as the smell came up, remembering the bitter heavy taste of the whiskey, remembering that he hated it. In an instant the smell recalled the heartburn and the vomiting, the halfdrunken mornings milking cows, the sweats, the headaches, the spinning in his sleep. He had done it then despite all this and he would do it now, and he would seek moderation. He went to the closet and rummaged for the small plastic cup he used to drink from years before when he used a cup at all. He found it beneath a pile of clothes. When he poured a drink and brought it to his lips his stomach turned. He took three drinks and sat back to wait, and soon he was haunted by an old sensation. As he felt his sobriety fading he missed it and felt sorry to see it go, to embrace the new reality that supplanted it, the objective itself, which was not as welcome as he had hoped until it became all he knew, and only then was he sure he wanted it, that it was the better way to be. He took another three and began to feel good. Felt the warmth coming on heavy. He turned on his dusty radio and found a clear station. He missed her. He convinced himself that she would not be coming back, or worse, that if she did, she would not be his. In his heightened sentimentality he wondered what he wouldn't give to have her there beside him even for that night and the answer was nothing.

A phrase from scripture came to mind, and he read through the vast works on the shelf above his bed searching for it, but his eyes went on without his mind and he came up with nothing and closed the book. Maher-shalal-hash-baz, he muttered finally. He had another drink and went downstairs. Before he would always drink in odds. Putting on a thick coat and boots he wandered outside and trod off through the snowy field toward the riverbottoms. The child of the earth was nearly full, a pale and skewbald bulb in the sky, almost offensive in its brightness, and when he stopped at the fence and put his hand on the frosty barbwire he looked up and fancied a man and his spacecraft on its marred face. He looked down the fenceline in the direction of the lane. He reeled and sat down hard. He found a wooden post with his back and leaned against it and let his head drift to his shoulder and listened only to his breath as it went in and out. He watched it plume into the air. The coldness seemed a friend to him and he considered that he couldn't feel it in his numbness. He laughed a few times and fell silent. His thoughts went toward the terrible questions and he considered their titles like books on a shelf. Some stood as bright and immutable as they had when he first formed them. Others had morphed into complexities that threatened to undo their own logic; they were phantoms this way, though nonetheless real. Some he could discourse on, others confused him with their elusiveness and labyrinth of paradox. All disturbed the remnants of his faith.

There was something coming through the riverbottoms. The sound came from behind him and as he heard it he lifted his head and positioned his ear. A squabbling barking rose from somewhere in the land below and carried up the hill to him. Yips and broken howls. Coyotes, he thought, and mad. They sounded frantic, bloodthirsty, roaming through the bottoms in search of whatever pandemonium might be found there. He'd never heard coyotes sound like that, so wild and bold, so strong, and he wondered if he was imagining it. They sounded and faded out, running the river toward the desert. After a while he decided he was freezing and staggered back to the house, drunk and weaving. He clattered through the back door and pulled himself up the stairs, where he fell to bed in his coat with one boot still on.

If the sun showed on a late afternoon with its angled rays, casting shadows surrounded by thinned light, there was never better clarity with which to view the earth. In the early evenings the western sky glowed like a coal furnace and bathed the white landscape in shades of pink and red. There was an early cold spell and the temperature did not rise above single digits. The alternative to working outside was to stay inside the stale house, just the two of them, so Jack moved around out of doors in layers and insulated coveralls, his head topped with a MoorMan's stocking cap and its silly bobble. He climbed stiffly onto tractors and turned their engines over in stubborn revolutions to no avail, coaxed them with soft maledictions and a spray of ether. If the engine took he got off and huddled near it for warmth and windblock. He found the simplest pleasure in running the space heater into the small office of the barn, taking his boots and socks off and holding his bare feet up in the hot current. Below zero mornings he dragged Blair to the barn where they kept heaters blazing at both ends and handled the mysteriously warm udders of the cows. They went through tins of udder balm and watched for frozen teat. They split teats with new razors that brought gouts of blood and clotted milk when it could not be helped. When the cast on his hand was darkened and stank to keep him awake at night he took a hacksaw from the empty pig shed behind the house and cut it off and regarded his wrist and hand, how thin and pale they had become. On afternoons when he saw the blue Cutlass pull next to the diesel tank, it seemed that he could expect Roydn Woolums to step out of the driver's door and sidle up to him like a friendly bedlamite, a vulgar grin on his face, his eyes wet and magnified inhumanly.

Lord, she was larger than she'd ever been. He grabbed his rifle and saddled the horse and went north when the cold spell broke to see about the land he'd been given. He trotted the horse for a long mile beside the pavement until he was at the edge of the wind-scrubbed desert and then rode a track as far as he could, an hour in and out of drifts until the track ran out of itself and simply vanished into the sagebrush and left him to look at nothing. He took the horse forward through the snow until he reached the perimeter of the ancient lava flow and weaved in a makeshift path, staying below the thrusts of basalt when he could, between jutting rises of hardened black stone with its jagged cracks and fractured ledges. Snow had blown and collected irregularly over the rugged land. It was deep in spots where it had been deposited and at times the mare sunk to her belly. There was life even on the stone in winter, green and orange lichen like smears of tiny blind eyes. Winds over centuries had carried silt and dirt from the surrounding earth and dropped it in shallow piles and crevasses, and from this, sage and bunchgrass and bitter brush had grown, along with the sporadic juniper tree. In this way the desert was a great craggy stretch of black stone and white snow and drab winter foliage, with junipers popping up like single green flames on the plain. It was so cold and lonesome he could only curse the land with every foul word he knew. But because he felt captivated by the desert he rode on.

There were vertical cliffs with talus slides at their bottoms where the rock had fallen off in large sheer-angled shapes, and he believed he could sit and wait for the next to fall. One year. Two. A hundred. He could see how the lava had flowed over the desert floor, how it had slid down inclines and puddled at their bottoms and hardened there, but the cliffs and platforms were a mystery. There it had piled curiously into blunt crags and hardened and broke with the earth's movements. Pillars rose upward and some of these split apart in four mammoth pieces like the Holy Spirit had blown them open. Huge sinkholes where the cooled lava formed giant cracked bowls. Three hundred square miles of this beauty, and this flow preceding Christ by a thousand years.

The remoteness of the desert pulled at him with a dispassionate force that stirred his spirit. Any man who found himself alone and pensive in the desert knew this force and reckoned with it. The desert was a place that could lure a wretched man to wander in with his miseries, where he then wandered within the miseries of the desert, and their miseries became one barren song, whispered through dry grass and fragrant sage, whistled over hard stone and lichen. It had pulled Heber's father in and spit him out mad. The first settlers must have felt it, those builders of the high desert, pilgrims and strangers, dispossessed and driven from their incipient nation into this primordial and unbroken desert, a lonesome and solemn people, wanderers in an empty land, their lives passing away as it were unto them a dream. How loud the sky must have been as they broke the first furrow and raised the first timber, how large the wildness of the desert. The land back then had been bigger than humankind itself, something to entreat and supplicate like a god, to learn its ways and moods at the calamitous repercussions of hazard and death until inured.

He rode past misshapen juniper trees with gnarled peeling trunks that leaned east from ages of wind, gaping and crooked crevasses like dry mouths, empty game trails that wound and fringed along basalt acreage and small box canyons, between heaving swells of broken black stone, its edges dulled by windborne grit. The desert here provided complete and bizarre solitude. He came to be beyond the sound and sight of civilization. He might as well have been in any epoch in the history of humankind, utterly alone with the horse. It was this kind of gargantuan isolation and obscurity he sensed that must have evoked and reinforced in those first ragged saints the need of faith in God—faith in something larger than the individual, the group, larger than humankind, for the desert and its emptiness were something larger.

The only sounds were the horse's breathing and her hooves on the earth and the ring of wind over the cold plain. He made for a small rise to get his bearings. The horse's shoes clanked brittle on the hard dark stone and once or twice she slipped in climbing. He dismounted and led her, careful to navigate the fissures that could swallow and break her legs, the larger ones that could swallow them both. At the top of the rise he could see the white mountains rising above the plain. He could not see the town for the undulating hills and broken terrain like an immense bed sheet being shaken. The Sisters threw back a sheen of sunlight that caused him to squint, but he made out the north field and the geography that surrounded it. And beside it the cleft that was his canyon. What could he do with a canyon? But he was a land owner now. In the context of human history the idea that he, John Blair Selvedge, owned a small patch of earth grew within him. It was the same earth the ancients worked, that God had seen created and was his to apportion. And so it was given, taken away, given again, taken, and ended up now in a system that allowed Blair Young Selvedge to claim ownership that others would honor and that he might then give to Jack. This idea seemed absurd in the scope of the earth's age and history and man's ephemeral presence within. Blair always said it was a stewardship, never an ownership, because it could be taken away as it had been before by superior forces, whatever they may be. That the land spue not you out also, when ye defile it, as it spued out the nations that were before you. As the steward pleased the Giver so he might retain his stewardship, a fragile contingency at best. And an entire nation unaware, dragging itself toward what awesome doom awaits it.

He rode for the canyon. It was a two-hour ride to its mouth where an old gate stood between railroad ties upended, and where barbwire in need of mending stretched to the canyon walls on both sides in a loose grin. Clouds had formed above him and hushed the world in soft whiteness. He did not have the key to the padlock, so he took from his saddlebag a pair of fence pliers and went to work near the closest canyon wall. He pried at the old wooden post until he had the nails out and after some work the top two strands broke and he was able to hold the others down and lead the horse through. The snow was untroubled and deep. He mounted the horse and broke a trail, keeping to the bottom next to the dry creek bed. On the south-facing canyon wall the snow was thin and yellow grass stood from its crust. Game trails were visible like fine scars. Scrub oak climbed the hills at both sides and at times formed a passageway around him. He rode through this corridor of gnarled trunks and branches, snowy knobs and brindled wood, until the canyon turned south and opened in a broad expansion of gentle hills and thick sage. Given the deep basin shape of this land it was called the Cauldron. The three tall peaks that surrounded it were called the Hooded Sisters, and they each had names. He had last been here with his father, and the canyon had seemed much longer. It had been summer, and when they reached this spot they had sat among the sage and his father had produced bread and cheese and a thermos of cold lemonade. His father had named the peaks for him, but he could not remember the names now. Their north-facing slopes held dark pines and these pines thickened upward toward their summits in long pinnacles of blackgreen, though the crowns of the Sisters were above treeline and therefore barren and snowbound. At the top of this glen the canyon ended for all but game, diffusing into several steep draws that swept their way upward toward the saddles and summits. He broke through to the bottom edge and looked about him. The land was tall and solitary, starkly hued and completely silent. The place seemed secret. There could be a simple cabin built in any of several patches of the scrub oak that covered the rolling land in wayward stripes. He had thought cattle, but now it seemed cattle would compromise things. He would keep the shit and the flies down below.

He stayed to the west side and stopped once he had gained a vantage point over the glen. He tied the horse and dismounted, made golden slush, and as he turned and swung into the saddle movement from below caught his eye. He squinted to see but the cold air caused his eyes to water. He made out a small pack of coyotes, three at least, coming out of the copse of trees where the walls converged, following his trail. Two stood upright watching him and another slinked along to the side of them. He felt for the brass bullets in his coat pocket and brought the rifle to his shoulder and looked through its scope. By the time he sighted the spot where the coyotes had been they were gone. He scanned the next patch of trees, looking for movement beneath their bare branches. Four of the animals emerged into his clearing and they were larger than he had thought. They disappeared into a depression and broke over the next rise, trotting where snow covered the bald crowns thinly. He had never seen coyotes so bold, not in daylight. Elijah Warren, sheep farmer along the highway to Hansel, used to pay three dollars a carcass. He took a brass shell out of his pocket. It was long and shiny, heavy, with a slug that tapered off to a sharp gray point. It bespoke death. He put it in the chamber and set the rifle across his lap. The horse jittered back and forth in the trampled snow and her breath came in plumes. She lifted her tail and shat great steaming loafs of dung. A shell fell through his cold fingers and he was on his way to swinging off to look for it when the horse whinnied and stamped. He could see the animals well enough now unaided, and what he saw gave him pause. The pack moved closer, picking its way up a shallow rise, led by a black animal he had not seen before. He knew then the source of those wild, broken howls from the riverbottoms the night he had sat against the fencepost drunk. These were wolves, not coyotes, and their sporadic lopes slowed as they encountered drifted snow and made their way up the brushy terrain toward him. He caught his breath at knowingly seeing this species for the first time. He waited to see how close they would come and grew nervous as they approached. He raised the gun to the sky and fired, the report loud in the glen and caroming off the peaks. The black wolf stopped and put his head to the air and looked up to where Jack had him crosshaired in the scope. He led the pack sideways and down and out of view. Jack watched the landscape until he saw them again. They had gone east across the glen and were approaching at a new angle and splitting up, sending two high and three low, four hundred yards off. He was run through with a sudden primal fear that thrilled him. He turned the horse and took her down the slope to the windblown snow and pushed her into a lope up to the top of another rise. He scanned the base of the east wall for a break in the tree line until he saw one, and above it, the lines of game trails under snow. He dropped into a quiet depression and the horse broke snow and breathed heavily coming up the other side. There was no sign of either contingent when he turned back to look, and then the black wolf broke the crest of a deadgrass hill and came rushing through the sagebrush two hundred yards off, coming now at a broken run. Jack worked forward and upward toward the east wall, urging the horse on with his voice and the pressure of his legs. When he reached the edge of the slope and the horse had climbed the game trail with a few lunging jumps he reined her in and turned and looked down at the gathering wolves, rifle in hand. The five came together not fifty yards below, and there they stopped and looked up at him. Some of them sat, all of them large and grinning openmouthed, their pink tongues pushing in and out. They guarded the easy way down but now seemed to be reconsidering their prey, curious how the fight might go with a two-headed creature. They stood in the snow and panted, glancing around, up at him, back down over the trails they had broken, waiting for Jack to speak to them from his hillside pulpit. He studied the black wolf, its yellowgreen eyes, a purely wild thing, lupine and strange. Beautiful, strange creatures they all were, warm in thick winter coats, their tired grins reminding him of his old dog. He did not fear them. He did not see the beast in him in them. As he coaxed the horse up the game trail which traversed the south wall and led toward the copse that stood at the canyon's debouche the wolves trickled away. He circumnavigated the scrub oak below and made his way down the canyon wall until he reached the broken fence and crossed through to behold what civilization they had come from.

12

I N THE DAYS THAT FOLLOWED HE DROVE SLOW TRACTORS and felt a lessening of hope, and in its place something the same hue and flavor as the pale winter sky over his shabby town spread. Some cold late December evening he lay in his room and stared at the cracked ceiling. He had put the whiskey away and was focused on the onset of warmth. The house was dark and quiet, a pall settled over it as over his heart. He heard a knock on the front door and heard Blair leave his chair in the room beneath him. Then he heard a sound like the distant music of bells and his heart twisted in his chest. She entered their lowly abode and filled the rooms one by one with light ahead of her until he felt that light pulse up the stairs, turn the corner to his room, and lap like warm breath against his skin. In a moment the creaking floorboards moved to the hallway at the bottom of the stairs and Blair called up to him, and again, and he remained dead still in his bed. He heard Blair say she could check if she wanted, and then her mellisonant voice like slow sweet thunder in the morning, and her climbing footsteps, and he was out of his bed shirtless with the window open. He climbed onto the sill and ducked through the window, his feet gripping the cold ledge with desiccated fly carcasses crumbling beneath them. He swayed and steadied himself with a hand on the eaves of the gable. He shut the window with his foot and dropped to the ground in the snow and hit hard and rolled and was up, making long spread footsteps out back to the shed where they kept pigs when they did. She might examine his bed with its gray sheets and fouled pillow. She would certainly smell the defilement in the room and if she looked she would see the dark stain where he lay his head. But she would not find him lying in this squalor drunk. If she went to the window she would see his tracks. If she were determined she would follow them. He could run farther. His adrenaline wore off and his feet stung and ached from the snow. He found a corner in the dark where a heap of burlap gunnysacks lay and sat down on these and held his bare feet in his hands and shivered. He started to titter, then laugh, and the sound died in the dark shed. He brought one dusty, thicksmelling sack around his shoulders for warmth. When he heard her car leave he rose freezing with his teeth chattering and his body spasming and stepped quickly back to the house. He entered through the back door and climbed the stairs. He could smell her in the room. Lord, he could smell her. He walked around and breathed deeply through his nose and would have drunk her smell if he could.

In the morning he was at the co-op with a headache and a small grocery list Blair had scrawled on a napkin. He got what canned goods he could find and walked to the back to pick up a new axe handle to replace the one Roydn Woolums had broken. Balls Murphy met him walking out and insisted on buying him a Pepsi even though he already had one in his hand. Balls was dusty from working in the mill and when Jack looked toward the loading dock he saw Wrink Poulsen standing outside the big door, leaning against the building with his hands in his pockets.

—You don't look so good, said Balls, his words tangible in

the cold air.

Jack put his elbows on the hood of the truck.

—I don't feel it neither.

—It's been cold.

—It has, said Jack. He unscrewed the lid to his bottle and took a drink. His eyes watered and he burped. Your real name, he said. Is it Balls?

—Arnie.

—Arnold?

—Just Arnie.

Jack looked at him like he wanted more.

—Well, because no one likes the name Arnie. And since I had red hair that was two strikes against me right off the line.

—Where does Balls come from?

—It's cause I got big brass ones.

—You'd have to, to fly that plane like you do.

—They call me the Red Baron, too.

—That's what you wished they called you. Either one's better than Wrink, though.

—Anything's better than Wrink. But he ain't any smarter than a dink wrinkle, so he's earned it. Look at him up there, the lunatic.

—I thought you two were close.

—We're close, but I'm his boss. At the end of the day we can always sit down for a beer, but I'd be lying if I said he didn't put a strain on our friendship that time he pulled the stiff one-eye on Maria. In my own home, no less. I had to bust him in the mouth, make those little teeth of his bleed. Kid like that needs to keep it in his pants whatever he does. We don't need no more halfwits walking around. That poor bastard had no say in his parents being cousins, but there he stands anyway. It's the way they do it up in Clark. Why roam when you can get it at home, they say. God loves him, but I'll be the first to take him down and out if need be. You know he never even lost his baby teeth?

—I didn't know that.

—He didn't lose a one. What do you make of that?

—I don't know what to make of it, said Jack.

—Well, that ain't true, said Balls. One of um rotted out and he put a piece of silver in its place. I told him I'd pry it out of his skull if I ever found his corpse laying in a gutter somewhere, which will happen like as not.

—Tell me, said Jack. How'd you get into crop dusting in the first place?

—That's a long story, but the short version is I won some money riding bulls. I saved it all and bought out old Eli Warren's operation before he went strictly to sheep. Only had but the one plane, and I picked it up summers.

—Sounds like a good job.

—Well I tell you what. I'd sell you that plane for a better price than I told you last time. They ain't too many crop dusters around, and it's becoming more fashionable to use one. A guy could do well if he was ambitious.

—I'd be lying if I said I wasn't considering it.

—Tell you what I'd do if I wasn't leaving. I'd work a loan up and buy two more planes—not expensive ones nor brand new, just like this one I got. I'd hire a couple pilots and all three of us'd stay busy all season. I turn down so much work it'd make your head spin. They get a guy from Willow Valley to come over, but he only has a few planes. If a guy got ambitious…

—Then why not quit this job and do that full time?

—What would I do in the winter?

—Go to Mexico.

—Shit, said Balls. Sounds like you got the right head for it. I could take you up and teach you a few things. You could get your license. I aim to make my way to Texas soon, so consider a little harder on it.

—What you going to Texas for?

—I'll take Maria with me, if she'll go, and we'll start our lives down there.

—A little late to be starting your lives, ain't it?

—We believe in second chances.

—What if she don't go?

He shrugged.

—Then she don't. Can't force her. I'd have to find me another'n down there. Plenty of dark-skinned beauties down that way.

—You're crazy for that type I guess.

—I love her. But she's wild. This town does it to um. I know why she left this place and I don't know why she came back. They never do stick around. Probly just as well. This place'll ruin um. She's already picked up a wild streak a man couldn't beat out of her.

Jack took another drink of his soda and Balls watched him.

—Look here, said Balls, lowering his voice. What do you know about her and Heber Rafuse?

—What about um?

—I'm asking what about um.

—They get along pretty well.

—I know they do. I know they get along real well. That's what concerns me.

—What's it to you?

—She's made promises. He put his hand on Jack's shoulder and gripped firmly and leaned in, his voice lowering. You know we're still engaged to be married, friend.

—I did not know that.

—Well, truth is things has been shaky between us, but we never did officially call it off. She still wears my ring, and I got some suspicions that our main troubles start with that sly dickhead friend of yours. Guy like Heber's a menace. He's a threat to the balance of society. But what can you do? Can't just go off and shoot him like some fevered pup. You got to live with it and take the right precautions.

—What's he done?

—He ain't ever been an angel, that's for certain. But it's as much what he's liable to do as anything. You don't wait for the rabid dog to bite, do you? You recognize the signs and take preventative measures. Seen him the other day slouching around looking desperate like a cornered coon. He's a wildcard. He messes around in stuff he ought not and destroys it. Just like his old man was. Guy's got to take preventative measures once in a while, is all I'm saying. You might tell him I say to watch out what the hell he's up to.

—I'm not hearing you clearly, said Jack.

—You keep your nose clean. I know you're friends with him, and it ain't my place to damage that sort of thing. Keep your eye on him is all. And tell Seth hello for me. Tell him to stay on them grain bags.

Balls grinned.

Lunch was beans, potatoes, and a pork shoulder Jack had dropped in the slow cooker after milking that morning. It was on days like this when the farm played a minor role that the simple constitution of Blair's life was laid bare. Jack looked across the table as they ate and saw that the old man was really putting it down. Blair mumbled half a dozen times through his food how good it was. This was his grandfather after all.

After Jack cleared the dishes Blair sat at the table looking out the window and running his tongue around in his mouth. Jack hadn't told him about the wolves on his land, and he wouldn't. He went to the old closet in the hallway, the one Adelaide had stored games and puzzles in, the one she had shuffled to innumerable times as he had sat at the kitchen table as a boy. He took the worn deck of Go Fish cards from the middle shelf and dealt them out.

—Do you got any fours? he said.

—Go fish, said Blair.

He found Heber in the shed on the edge of town as night fell, nursing a bottle of beer and reconstructing the passenger's door on his father's Bronco. The door was detached and lay on a worktable. An old singledeck radio sat on the workbench, spilling out the slow twang of a steel guitar like liquor. The shed was an old veterinarian shop. It was small with a stainless steel workbench and sinks on one side. The project sat where the vet truck had sat. The space in the rear was cluttered with dismantled shelving units, piles of old canvas tarps, pieces of engine and body, and a stack of split firewood. A small stove sputtered warmth from the corner and threw slight shadows on the hulking project. On the wall above the workbench hung strange tools from the days when the elder Rafuse had been in business. Cabinets above the sink held old medicines with rubber caps.

They made various small talk, beginning and ending matters, and then Jack told of the inheritance. When he was through Heber didn't speak and Jack worked at picking thick pieces of broken glass out of the base of the door. This Bronco was worn by age, but most of Heber's work had been to fix the damage done by vandals just before his father's death. Broken windows, slashed tires, shattered head and taillights, and sundry dents in the body. Crowbars and baseball bats. Their marks were gone now. Heber brought over two beers from a small fridge and fell into a canvas chair. The caps hit the concrete floor with light clinks and when Jack sat down the two regarded each other.

—It's an amazing thing, said Heber. It confounds me to see him bend you over like that.

—It don't make any sense, said Jack. He's all but written the death certificate to his own farm. I thought it meant more to him than that. He's spent a lifetime building it.

—Even if it did make sense, where are his principles? Why didn't you tell me when it happened?

—It wasn't good news.

—No, it's not something to brag about, said Heber. Damn. Well, forget it. You're not made for the farm anyway. Take what you've learned and go. You were never meant to be some hermetic dairyfarmer in this spent up place. There's no glory in it. Go out and do something. Come lay brick with me. We'll start our own company. Get big, get rich.

Jack said nothing.

—The canyon, said Heber. That goes back a ways.

—It goes up and leads to a little valley. That's where I saw the wolves.

—That's something we hadn't figured on. What if I was to tell you there's been a company out of Park City that's taken interest in that mountain there.

—For what?

—A ski resort.

—They want to make a ski resort in these mountains?

—Their exact plans are little more than rumor, but I know of some true interest. They've tested our snow and they like it. And I know for a fact they've been looking from here all the way up near Jackson Hole. But they favor these areas closer to Salt Lake. Think the Olympics might come here someday. And guess what, buddy. You now own the best access to the only spot feasible for a ski resort.

—A big resort?

—It'll be a little smaller.

—Where are you hearing this?

—Weasel, mostly.

—What does he know about it?

—He's in the market.

—What's he say it's worth?

—I could ask him.

—Why not the Green Rock or the Wasatch?

—Not sure. But we've got steep slopes and plenty of snow.

—What kind of bone did the old man throw me exactly, mused Jack.

—Could be a good one, said Heber. Could be one with some meat on it.

Jack laughed and took a drink and Heber warmed up to it.

—Yes sir, Selvedge. You ain't going anywhere. The Scrag raised you, and the Scrag needs you. It's guys like you and me give the town hope, he beamed. Guys like you and me.

He took a long drink from his bottle and drew a low belch.

—So Rebekah. She said she came by your place first but you weren't there. She said it was late. Where was yuh?

—I don't know what happened there.

—Well, she looked great. Full of color and good blood. But she didn't seem to know it. Platinum confidence. Lord.

—When did you see her?

—She called me up to ask if I knew where you were, and so I took her to town to get some food.

—With Maria?

—We've been on thin ice lately. She's going through some personal crisis. She needs to get her shit together. I don't want the baggage.

—That's because she's still engaged to Balls. Did you know this?

Heber shook his head.

—That's what he says, the dumb bastard. Guys like him... It's hard for women to get them out of their system. They mess them up for life. They're like black holes, pulling the girls they've ruined toward them all the time, never letting them up.

Jack looked at Heber, who was smiling slightly and gazing into the darkness of the shop, and said, You trying to move in on her?

Heber's smile increased and he looked at his bottle and rolled it in his hands. His father's wedding ring clinked against the glass.

—We get along, he said. We have a little chemistry. We've forged a good friendship. But that's all. He looked up and met Jack's eyes. But let me talk straight with you as a friend, he said. Anybody could have her, and there'd be nothing you could do about it. This is a world of natural selection. Anybody back in Salt Lake, or anybody else in this town. Did you think about that?

—I do all the time. But what's your part in it?

—If I were you and you were me, wouldn't you feel you had to act? Wouldn't you move if you thought you had even the slightest chance of getting a girl like that, even if it was to displace me? You're damned right you would.

—There are unwritten rules, said Jack.

—The only rules are the ones you impose upon yourself, and in the end you'll be immobile and defeated, wrapped up in the restraints of your own peculiar gospel and baffled that everyone has moved on without you because they understood something you didn't.

—You're setting yourself up for an asskicking, talking this way.

—Am I? Is it against your rules for me to bring the girl to town for some food when she can't find you and she's hungry? Wild times! Wild times out here in the country, Selvedge! Would I make tender love with the girl? Yes. What man wouldn't? But I won't. That's the difference between me and everyone else. This is the hand we've been dealt and it falls in your favor. I respect that. But some won't, and you need to move on this.

—Son of a bitch, Rafuse, do you think I haven't tried?

Heber drained his bottle, lobbed it into the back corner where it shattered, and leaned forward in his chair.

—Listen to me, he said. You've built her up in your mind until she's become a goddess, and you can never have her that way. She'll never take you on unequal grounds. You need to make love with her, get naked with her, and then all this mystique that's got you spinning, all this overblown infatuation will disappear, and the only thing left will be the reality. You pull it all down. There's something about getting naked with someone, letting down all your guards to grunt and fuck and yelp, working together in that shameful, bewildering way, that levels things out. You'll never look at her the same again, but will move to higher planes now that the physical is known. She'll cease to be a goddess and will become real to you, accessible, common. This is what you need. Pull down the power.

Break the mystery. I'm not moving in on her, but you're a fool if you think you've got time. You insult both of us with your ditherings.

Heber stroked his beard and looked intensely at Jack.

—I'll tell you this. I don't do anything but when I have you in mind.

—Horseshit.

—I'm working for you like I said I would. Just the right amount of persuasion. This is a fine, subtle work. My own strange work. I work so hard for you, John, because I promised you I would. Someday you'll thank me. You'll look back and thank me for all I've done.

—Everything you say is horseshit, said Jack.

Heber shook his head.

—Just watch yourself, said Jack. You damn well better watch yourself.

Heber got up and shuffled to the fridge for another beer. He came back and set the bottle on the supine door and turned his back to Jack as he resumed his work. Jack stood to leave.

—Don't be selfish, said Heber without turning.

—What?

—This girl is a blessing to all of us, not just you.

If Heber wanted to say more, Jack wouldn't hear it. He left for the barnyard to finish his chores.

In the frigid cold he reached up and tugged on a bale of hay, leaning and rocking his body backward, pulling the bale out from the bind of the other bales by inches, and when he pulled it loose and the stack started to fall he turned and ran and the bales tumbled down behind him. He carried the bales from the diminished west haystack through the supports of the shed in the dry cold night. Returning for a bale he bent to lift it and jumped backward. A crack of fear and confusion rode through him like lightning. When he had gathered himself and stared into the dark stack he let out a string of profanity and paced, biting his fist.

One summer some years back Shiners Griffith left his dog in the cab of the tractor while he got down to pull loose a haybale he'd been dragging. The dog knocked the tractor into gear, and the big machine pushed Griffith down and ran over his head and then somehow went round and round, pirouetting its big rear wheel on his head, and the whole time the dog sitting up there on the seat, wagging his tail and grinning. Griffith was found by a neighbor who was driving by and saw the tractor turning circles. Robert Glenn was dragged through the field by his harrows a few springs later. He had left the tractor running and climbed down. They said the gearbox was bad. The harrows caught Glenn by the pant leg and took him for a ride. It would have seemed harmless for a while, him cursing softly while trying to get free, maybe laughing as the tractor took him straight through the field on parade as though helmed by a mischievous ancestor. But when it reached the hillside and he still hadn't gotten loose the tractor climbed up and over-turned and landed on him, crushing him dead. Another man was crushed, a father of three, when a gale wind toppled the old wooden barn he walked beneath on the lee side. The window that may have saved him fell three feet away. The entire thing, leaning leeward for decades, blown over in the span of time it took the man to walk its length, and the man survived by a widow and three young children. The summer Heber's father drowned, Ross Apgood was strangled by his baler. He stopped on a slope so subtle it was nearly imperceptible. He either didn't set the brake or it failed and the baler crept forward and caught him underneath. When the rolling teeth grabbed his shirt and pulled it in he was jerked upright into sitting position and choked with his own collar. His leg twisted beneath him and made a late chock for the wheel and kept the baler from going farther forward, and the shear pin finally broke from the pressure. When his son came out to spell him he saw his father there, black as a berry and strangled. There were others. When a farmer was hurt or maimed or killed in the harvest of his fields people would say the wolf got him. It was why Blair exhorted more about disengaging the Power Take-Off and killing the tractor than he did about the Holy Gospel.

Joining this ill-fated line of farm violence, the figure of Roydn Woolums now stood over the fallen bales, propped like a hideous mannequin against the stack. The loop attached to the stems of his glasses held them on and they reflected a pale blue light, making it seem like the corpse was looking straight at Jack with care and intelligence. But for the marks of the mice that had eaten the remains inside and out, it might have looked alive from the distance he stood. The cadaver's arms were raised above its head, elbows pointed south and west, caught in some act of lament or frustration. Straight to the bottom he'd fallen, where he must have bellowed his hoarse voice gone and tried for days to move and gain purchase, the haystack binding him like a straitjacket as he waited in vain and volleyed his silent screams upward.

Jack stared, marveling. He studied the clear outline of the body, the bizarre position of its arms, its apparent woodenness and shrunken visage. The skull's teeth showed beneath its eaten lips. He went into the barn and waved Blair off his chair to follow him, and together they walked to the hayshed. When Blair got close enough to see what Jack was pointing at he leapt in his boots and swore hard. They determined to let the two boys milk the last of the cows, and Blair called the Woolumses. He drove to the other side of town and brought Josephine back and they arrived just as the two boys were finishing in the barn. Together the small family moved toward the haystack, their living breath clouding the air. It was hard to tell if the brothers knew what they walked toward, but they came to it calmly, and the three of them loosened the wooden body from the bales and laid it out on the frozen ground. They handled it carefully. Josephine knelt, her large shapeless body bending over the remains of her son, her moonlike face full of kind grief. She brushed at the forehead, sweeping the hair backward. She removed the glasses to get a better look at the face and wept calmly.

The ambulance arrived and its flashing lights seemed egregious as they splashed the cows with alien colors and threw their hue deep into the white field. Jack slipped through the manger bars to make his way to the barn unnoticed but stopped when headlights shone around the corner and haunted the sky as they climbed the rise. A spray of gravel and the cough of a dying engine, and a thin old man with deep concern on his face sprang from the pickup. It was clear to Jack as he stood amidst the warm bodies of the cows that Ronald Woolums had possessed hope. Then came his slow, grieved wail as he pulled the sheet down and viewed his dead son with his own eyes, a vocal recognition of the end. He grabbed his wife in one arm and an ugly son in the other and pulled them to him and spoke words to them that Jack couldn't hear. Jack watched for a minute longer and then moved through the cows that stood as witnesses.

He left the farmhouse that night and drove the desert with a bottle of whiskey beside him on the seat. There was no learning these roads because there were too many of them. All a man could do was keep the mountains in sight and eventually he would find his way out again. But on a night dark as this there was no telling. He found a low hill and rolled to the top of it and in the mirror he could see the town, a small cluster of twinkling lights. He sat with the engine running, the blue glow from the whore lights illuminating the floor, the radio playing, and drank slowly. He killed the engine, rolled down his window, and faced the empty desert, not a single light within. The air held the weight of snow not yet fallen. He felt the immense dark around him, the empty silence, and listened to the wind. Thick broken clouds above him moved beneath the obscured moon. The sky looked like the vast floor of something rifted and sliding. He watched the moon until it came through. It was meniscate and he could see the whole of it in shadow. Clouds now moved across it, now a sailing moon, the refuse fingernail of a massive god flicked over to light the earth in darkness. As its light shone and darkened so did the desert floor around him, its detail brightening and dimming as quickly as the clouds above it moved. The wind came over the jagged stone and hummed through the trembling grass and sage and moved past his window and he sipped the whiskey from the mouth of the bottle. The moon vanished and didn't return. He started the truck and kept driving.

He wandered out to the Hansel road and turned to head back to town. When he got there he was alone in the square. He pulled over and stepped out of the truck and fancied he could do anything. He got back in his truck and turned down the road to the farmhouse, driving slowly, and as he passed the lane to the barn he looked a long time at her shadowed house where she must be sleeping and went off the road and into a snowbank and hit his head on the steering wheel.

In reverse, the truck only spun its wheels. He dug through the snow with his bare hands and locked the hubs on the front wheels to no avail. He got out and looked down the road toward the farmhouse and up the lane to her house. He had no idea what time it was. To wake Blair with whiskey on his breath was not something he wanted to do. He walked up the lane and circled the house until he had talked himself into which window would be hers, then stood on his toes but still could not see in. His angle through the white gauze curtain revealed nothing. He walked to a tree and tried to tear off a branch, cursing that he'd been found without his new pocketknife and falling backwards into the snow when the branch finally came free. He tapped on her window with it. He tapped again, and when he saw a figure through the transparent curtain his heart jumped because he was sure it was Martha.

—Jack, she said. What are you doing?

—I went off the road.

—Where?

—Just down there. I need your help.

—Let me put some clothes on.

—Bring a coat, he whispered. It's going to snow.

But she had already shut the window and was gone. In a few minutes she appeared at the corner of the house dressed warmly with a stocking cap on. Her eyes were large and dark. He walked up and stood in front of her.

—Did you hear about Roydn? she said.

—Did I hear? I found him.

—It's the saddest thing I've ever heard of.

—Damn near. I wish you could of seen him the way his arms were, like he was caught frozen in the middle of something.

—What a tragedy, she said. It's hard to believe.

—Believe it, honey.

—What happened?

—You didn't hear?

—No, what happened with your truck? Did you wreck?

—I wanted to see you, he said.

—Are you lying to me? Where's your truck?

—We have to walk down and get a tractor.

—Are you drunk? she said.

—Yellow sweatpants, he said.

—I didn't know you were taking me to the ballet. I can smell it on you.

They started their walk down the lane.

—Can you tell me about Roydn?

—I can't talk about that right now.

—Why did you run away from me the other night?

—When?

—When I came to your house to visit.

—Oh, I didn't.

—You didn't jump out the window and run away?

—You saw that?

—I still don't know what to make of it. I thought you might've hurt yourself.

—It didn't hurt.

—Why would you do something like that?

He shrugged.

—I hope we aren't going to start with all that foolishness again.

—I'd rather die, he said, than start with that again. That's dead and gone as Roydn Woolums.

—That's not funny.

—Did your dad find you while you were back in the city?

—No.

—I didn't see him around here anywhere either. Unless his name's Wrink Poulsen.

She looked at him with no expression. He took her mittened hand with his bare hand and she let him. They walked in silence and he brought her hand up and took the mitten off and kissed her delicate knuckles. She looked at him evenly and said nothing and he did it again.

—I'm cold, she said.

He stopped and pulled her to him and kissed her. She was not as warm in her response, but she kissed back until he started getting sloppy, and then she pushed him away.

—Your mouth tastes horrible, she said.

—Yours ain't much better. You got morning breath in the middle of the night.

He kissed her again and this time his hand found her soft backside through the thin fabric of her pants and he grabbed a full cheek to pull her closer. She broke away from him.

—Knock it off, she said. She started walking. You shouldn't drink.

—Sure, he said.

It began to snow and they walked on. When they reached the barnyard there was no dog to warn them off nor to greet them. The snow came down thickly, falling through the lights on the hayshed stanchions and subduing an already quiet world. A billion snowflakes dropping slowly from untold heights.

—What do cows do at night? she said.

—They sleep, he said.

When they neared the corral a few cows got up from their stalls and approached the manger as though they expected the hay to be kicked up. They stood looking at the midnight visitors, chewing their cuds like elderesses of a devolved race, as if they would hold council with Jack on what he had found in their feed stack.

—I love these cows, she said.

—Come here, he said. He led her to the haystack. This is it. Where I found him. Fell all the way down and no one heard a peep.

—What a tragedy, she said. I can hardly believe it happened that way. I guess we all knew he was gone, but not this way. It's unbelievable.

—He didn't have to go this way, said Jack. And I'm the one that checked the stack.

—No one could've heard him, she said. They said his voice was already gone the night he disappeared, and that the sound wouldn't have traveled out of the stack anyway.

—And how many times— said Jack. How many times did I walk past that stack while he was alive inside, took hay from that stack while he was alive in there and fed them?

—That's strange to think about, she said. You shouldn't think that way.

—I'll talk about it with you if you want, he said. But I don't want to.

—We don't have to.

—What killed him? said Jack. What killed him?

She returned his gaze, her eyes wide with fear. He surveyed

the barnyard for the farthest flung tractor and it was the loader. He walked to it and climbed into its cab. She followed and got in with him.

—Do you think you should be driving this? she said.

—Shhhh. He put a finger to his lips. It's got a heater. We need to get out of here as easy as we can. Elmer'll think his damn tractor's being stolen.

He bent and started the tractor and looked toward Elmer's dark house. He smiled at her. He reached for her coat and pulled her onto him. He tried to kiss her mouth but got her hard jaw instead as she struggled to get off him and regain her perch on the wheel well.

—Stop it, she said. You made me hurt my hand. Don't be so rough.

—I want to kiss the back of your neck, he said. Right under your hair.

He took them around the west hayshed and straight out to the fence line. They rode without lights along the fence and then left that path to traverse the snowy field for the middle gate on the lane. She said something to him about tracks but he was too tired to hear it. He drove on in a daze across the field. For a few minutes he lost his focus and his thoughts went completely elsewhere, and when he came back he was startled to find himself still in the field, surprised to turn and see her on the wheel well watching him, beautiful and rousing.

—I love you, he said.

—Don't say that, she said. You don't mean it.

—The hell if I don't. I want to marry you and give you a family and take good care of you. I'll build you a house above the sage plain and give you children.

He let the tractor drive itself across the field and looked straight at her. His words were low and sober.

—I'll take good care of you.

She said nothing, but her eyes turned dark and warm.

—I just wanted to be with you, he said. That's all.

—Shhh, she said.

He felt deflated, collapsed, as though the words he spoke had been his structure, and now they had fallen out before he could think to keep them.

Blair, in an attempt to make up for years of forgotten birthdays, had pestered as much as a man like him could to know what Jack wanted for Christmas. He tried to shove a fifty dollar bill into his hand, but Jack wouldn't take it. Rebekah was gone again and Jack went to the town Christmas party alone. Heber and Seth did not show up. Maria was there. She sat with him and made all manner of comforting small talk. Some of Rebekah, of him, of some possible future for them together, though Jack did not partake of her hope and was not made a believer. She went on about Heber and Balls and as she opened up he discovered that he genuinely liked her. She filled a void for him that night. He enjoyed her female companionship, her conversation, her sincerity. She was warm and lovely and an energy blossomed between them.

Every year at Christmas Blair gave out hundred-dollar bills as a bonus to each employee but Jack, and every year Roydn had worked for them Josephine Woolums had sent him with something to give the Selvedges, which Blair in turn handed off to Elmer and his family. On Christmas Eve Rodney and Rapscallion walked up to Blair before milking and gave him a small basket, handing it over almost reluctantly, shamefully, and while they milked Jack got in the truck to see what was in it. Josephine Woolums had arranged a jar of raspberry jam and another of applesauce and a few pieces of peanut brittle, all of it homemade and composing a humbling sight. But there was a small frame too, and when he took it out he was looking at a photograph of Roydn Woolums. It could have been his mission photograph, the last need for anything so formal. Roydn in a tie and a jacket, his hair slicked fiercely against his bulbous skull, his skin pasty white and his grinning mouth troubled by acne.

After work he spent a few minutes at Heber's house giving him a gift—a gold hits collection of The Eagles—and they had a drink together and talked about Roydn Woolums. But something stained the mood there, and when Heber invited him to stay awhile Jack told him he needed to get to Seth's to drop off a gift. Juniper Scrag had colored bulbs strung zigzag across the streets of the square, and they invoked memories of his childhood as he drove beneath them, of driving under them with his parents, enchanted. He got no answer at Seth's and so returned to Heber's because he was not ready to settle down on this eve in the farmhouse with Blair. They talked as the gifted album played softly. They drank hot cider and spiced rum and they talked more about the inheritance, about prospects. They were able to generate some hope this way. The unease gave way to the stench of loneliness and it lingered on Jack's clothes as he left. He drove home warmly drunk. At the farmhouse Blair had left a note in his backslanting hand that said he'd gone to Elmer's house to visit and for Jack to come over, but Jack settled down in his chair and put in a John Wayne western and fell immediately to sleep.

Christmas morning it snowed while they milked. It had snowed all night and when the two drove to the barn, they made the first tracks in five inches of new powder on the road. The snow crunched and squeaked beneath their tires. Large flakes dashed in front of the headlights. The cows dripped stinking snowmelt from their hides as they came in and filled the barn with a humid reek. As Jack washed down Blair began to sing I'm Dreaming of a White Christmas in a loud reverberating voice that echoed off the walls.

—You know, he said as they sat at the kitchen table eating a slow breakfast. It's the first Christmas in fifty-three years I've spent without her. He looked down at the table and tapped his split and broken nails on its surface, his nails wavy and thick and torn, rifted like the earth after trauma, his blunt, workhardened fingertips drumming the wood also. The sting of love never changes, he said, and I've been stung anew. We are dying the day we're born and each step we take brings us closer to death. The more I see it, the more I understand it. Death is the pursuer. A man can only run through life ahead of it and wonder when it'll catch him. A man gets older, he can only run so fast. Youth, with a little fortune and smarts, will keep him ahead of it. But even then he can only run till fatigued. It's like getting chased by the sun. I am fatigued, my boy. I feel it catching up to me.

They looked at each other for a moment and fell again to eating.

13

EVERYTHING WAS SOFT-TONED AND WHITE FROM NEW snow, and the sun, buried behind solid clouds, pushed just enough light through so that the world seemed viewed through the painter's eye. The river was broken up and heavy with ice floes and they ran together and sounded loud pliant cracks across the bottoms. Jack took a cigarette and allowed Seth to set a flame to its end. He smoked it thoughtfully. They smoked together in the truck and blew their exhalations out the windows and talked about Roydn Woolums.

—It's one I'll be telling my kids about, said Seth.

—You got any yet?

—That's real funny. You coming to Heber's tonight for the bonfire? Cause Rebekah's coming.

Jack grunted.

—It'll probly be one of the last shindigs for me, said Seth.

—Why's that?

—I'm moving to Amarillo soon.

—Amarillo?

—Amarillo, Texas. Like the song. It's in the neck. I'm getting out of here. Away from my mom. Going to move down there with Balls.

—What the hell for?

Smoke spilled out of Seth's mouth as he spoke.

—The rodeo scene is big down there. It'll be a good way in. Good money to be made.

—You know this?

—I don't know it, but all those songs about Texas can't be wrong.

—When?

—Could be any day now. You want to go? There's lots of Rebekahs in Texas.

—There are no more Rebekahs in the world.

—A lot a beautiful girls in Texas.

—You've seen um?

—Balls told me. He says they're the number one state for girls.

—Balls told you. Who's ranking?

—And we're number two. So what about it. You got anything keeping you here?

—I don't know. These chains of the farm, I feel um slipping off my shoulders. I can do anything now.

—Like Amarillo.

—Amarillo, or something.

—So you'll be there tonight?

—You're damn right.

—That's the idea. It's probly better that way. You don't worry about her being with him alone like they do sometimes?

—I don't know that I can do much about it. I don't think she sees him that way.

—Still. It'd drive me batshit, I think.

—If you got something to tell me then tell me.

—There ain't nothing to tell that I know of. I know he wants her, but he'll throw a stick at anything on two legs. When he's got her there in his trailer I'm surprised he don't go to the bathroom right after her so he can lick the damn toilet seat. I'll say this. She's one of those girls likes to touch people, so it's hard for a guy not to react. Don't take this the wrong way, but she's put her hands on me plenty. She just lets um fall all over sometimes. I'd just go a little batshit if I knew they was spending time alone.

Jack smoked and listened to the ice cracking in the river.

—Got to get out of here, said Seth. Go to Amarillo. This place ain't what it used to be.

Heber found him that evening feeding in the west manger. He leaned against a shed support and smoked and watched him finish.

—This haystack here, was it?

—Thought you quit.

—You coming tonight?

Jack nodded.

—You and Rebekah, said Heber. How are you?

—We get along. We have a little chemistry.

Heber smiled.

—Tonight's your night. She's ready.

—Ready.

—Listen, said Heber. I spoke to the Weasel. He's got his ear to the ground, and he has an idea about how much they're willing to offer for your land.

—How much?

—Wease believes you can hope for around a quarter million.

—That it?

—Are you kidding?

—If they're big money and they want to make a resort out of it, that don't sound like much.

—A small resort, keep in mind. Not that big.

—It's a mountain we're talking about here.

—Not a whole mountain. Access to it. Government owns most of the mountain.

They stood next to each other and the huffing and grinding of the feeding cows filled the silence.

—This range isn't their only option, said Heber. They can get something else. And they don't have to buy up a lot. They can lease most of it.

—Well do they want it or not?

Heber looked at him.

—A *quarter million* is the idea, he said. What you need to give your careful focus and consideration. What could you do with that? What could we do with it? Pardon my nerve, but you and I have been talking about going to work together for some time. That's investment capital. That's your part, and with it backing us I'll do mine. I could teach you the trade. My boss'll sell us good used equipment. That's all we need. I'll get my license and we're off. There'd be no worries with that kind of money backing us. We couldn't fail.

—The number ain't that impressive. If they're going to go up there and ruin things they better be willing to pay for it.

—Ruin things?

—Have you been up there?

—Sure.

—I've been up there.

—Well. Heber shook his head. You think it over. Think it over hard. Wease said he'd like to talk with you about it if you're interested. He'd be happy to represent you. But do it quick. They're looking around.

—There's no hurry, Rafuse. I don't even have the title yet.

—If you think there's no hurry, you ain't cut out for that world.

—There's a lot of things I ain't cut out for. That's why I'm still here.

Heber looked around. He patted his pockets for cigarettes. He shook his head again.

—Thought I'd catch you in a better mood. When you get done with work pick her up and come over. Everything's ready. Just get clean and pick up the girl and come over. Hell. I can't believe this. He grinned over his frustration. Buy that damn plane, buy a fleet of planes. Start any kind of honest work you want. Get off the farm. In the name of all that is holy, get off this farm.

When he got to her house in the evening and stepped from his truck the front door opened and she came down the steps and fell into arms he didn't know were open. He felt her body breathe against him. They got into the truck and she slid to the middle. She took hold of the gear shifter and pulled it back into reverse and they drove to Heber's. She was very close to him and in a fine mood and she smelled wonderful. It seemed clear to him that she had missed him and he felt it could be a good night. Heber had taken pallets from the alleyways of the co-op and three sat burning furiously in a stacked pile with two more waiting on the side. Seth showed up with a girl on his arm none of them had seen before, a dyed blonde with dark makeup around her eyes. She had a shrill giggle that she let loose suddenly and unprovoked to shatter what passed for peace there. She was Jane from Hansel, a lone town twenty miles north. They all stood together just inside the invisible ring of heat and Seth shifted from foot to foot before volunteering to visit a collection of partially empty beer cases on the back porch. Heber stood alone across the fire. He carried a beer and turned from side to side, talking to himself with feeling and moving his hands in the air as if working some difficult thing out in his head. He threw his can in the fire and began to saunter over to where Jack and Rebekah stood, but changed his mind and walked to the beer cases instead. He brought back a can and opened it and called in a loud voice, This is for Woolums!

He gestured around with the can and guzzled it down. Halfway through everyone fell silent as they watched beer spill down the outside of his working throat. Seth waved Jack over.

—What do you think buddy?

—He's already drunker than a shithouse rat.

—No, said Seth. Let's go around front.

In the front yard he pulled out his cigarettes. He offered the pack and Jack took one and lighted it.

—What do you think about Jane? said Seth.

—What's her story?

—She just moved to Hansel with her family. She's seventeen. He paused. Sixteen, actually. Seventeen in three more months.

—That's grounds for statutory rape.

—So you think she's all right?

—I don't know her.

—All right. Well you'll get to know her. This is a pretty strange party, ain't it.

—Sure.

—We have strange times here, don't we.

—We do.

—It's cause there's no moon, said Seth. See how bright the stars are?

They watched the sky while they smoked, each searching for what few constellations he knew, speculating some, inventing some and passing them for official. When they were finished smoking they went back to the fire and Jack chewed a piece of gum and stood beside Rebekah. Heber walked over to them and wiped his mouth with the back of his hand.

—Do you want a drink, John? he said. Your hand is empty.

—I'll take a drink.

—What do you feel like tonight?

—You got Pepsi?

—Of course. It's in the fridge, Rebekah.

She hesitated, and when she walked toward the house he watched her go, not hiding at all his stare at her backside.

—One of the most beautiful natural movements in the world,

he said, is the movement of a woman's rear pockets. It can fix a man on a course and lead him to salvation.

After the door closed behind her he turned to Jack and said, Tell me about Roydn.

—Tell you what?

—Tell me how no one thought of the damned haystack.

—If you'd shown up to help search, maybe you could of thought of it.

Heber chuckled.

—I must not be on the bishop's call list. That poor son of a bitch. How he must've suffered down there in that hole, and for how long? Was it thirst? Was it exposure? No one knows. Ain't many fates—ain't many fates worse than that one. Did anybody even check the haystack?

—I climbed up and looked around.

—And didn't you hear him?

—Yeah, Rafuse, I heard him hollering down in that hole, so I took a piss on his head.

Rebekah was back and she slid the cold drink into his hand. Heber smiled, his eyes gleaming, his actions and tongue sluggish.

—Don't be spiteful, John. This is a young man's tragic death we're talking about here.

—Don't be an idiot.

—You're hostile tonight. You still got that bad cloud hanging over you. Rebekah, if you want more peaceful company, Maria is working tonight, and I am lonely, and would appreciate some companionship.

He took her hand and bent to kiss it and she pulled it away.

—Well it's the way of the farm, he said, standing. It's a rough occupation. But not one that you can't handle, right Johnnycakes?

When Jack didn't answer Heber smiled at them both and stroked his stomach through his jacket.

—Got to act fast on these things, he said. He swayed on his

feet and his eyes twinkled coldly. Got to *act*. Got to quit playing with the pud and do something to change things. We'd both regret it if we didn't act. You'd be a fool not to sell that land.

Jack gave him a hard stare.

—Leave it alone, he said.

—*Act*, so as not to be acted *upon*.

—Maybe we could talk about something else, said Rebekah. She smiled sweetly at Heber.

—Honey, do you know what we're even talking about?

—Selling land.

—Then please shut up about it.

—You talk to her like that again, you're going to have a problem on your hands, said Jack.

Heber leaned back and regarded them both with a twisted smile on his face. He chuckled low and long.

—One man's satisfactions is another man's satisfactions, right John? One man's regrets is… Jack the Violent. Jack the Ripper. Jack jumped over the goddamn candlestick. Well, he said. All right then. This is how it's going to be then. Let me just ask you one thing.

—I don't want to talk about it now, said Jack. If you bring it up again we're out of here.

—Speak for yourself. She might want to stay here while you go back to your cows. Come here, Rebekah. Just for a minute.

—I'm fine, she said.

—So you know it then.

—Know what?

—I'm doing the best I can! he roared. I would think you'd have the nobility in you to reach down and drag a man from the gutter, even if it be by the hair. You don't give a damn about this town and it's full of the very people who raised you.

Jack turned to go.

—Don't go, John, said Heber. He lowered his head and held up a hand. Please don't go.

—Are you through?

—Yes. I am, said Heber. And then with something like awe in his voice he said, You ungrateful, greedy, selfish son of a whore. He leaned back and smiled. Rebekah, don't leave with him. He hasn't been himself lately. He's desperately in love with you and this has made him mad. Stay here with us.

—If he leaves, I'm leaving, she said. Let's talk about something else. Let's all say what we liked about Roydn. Let's have a memorial for him.

—Fuck Roydn, said Heber. The ugly bastard.

The pallets burned with a soft roar. Seth and Jane kept their distance near the back step. Heber sniffed a few times.

—Smells like cowshit, he said. He looked at Jack. You smell it?

—You're an ass, said Rebekah.

—Well then. Why don't you go off somewhere. Why don't you go park somewhere and he can get three fingers in your pussy. I guess they'll fit all right.

Heber fell backward over the edge of the fire pit as Jack hit him. He missed the fire and rolled away from its heat. He was tough and strong, and even as Jack felt the residual strain in the healing bone of his hand he was ready as his old friend stood upright and showed a bloody grin. But Heber's attention was solely on Rebekah. He took his front teeth between his fingers and wiggled them. He looked at Rebekah and licked the blood from his lip and said, Honey, I could do such obscene wonders with your mouth.

Jack moved in and hit him again and his hand bone fractured. A sudden rage took him and this man, his friend, was an other, one deserving of hatred and anger and violence. He dropped himself knees first onto Heber's abdomen. He held him with his broken hand and rained down on him with his good fist and felt Heber's head sinking deeper into the thawing earth with each connection. Heber protected his face and head and threw him off and Jack landed crouched on his feet and stood and put the tongue of his boot in Heber's ribs and sent him sprawling. He moved quickly, hovering over the downed man, his broken fist pulled back, until she grabbed his elbow and tugged at him.

—Stop it! she said. He's drunk!

Heber grinned up at him from the ground with blood-lustered teeth that glowed red in the firelight, his nose bleeding over his lips and through his beard. He dabbed at the blood with the back of his hand and looked at it.

—You've made me bleed, John.

—I can bring it faster.

Rebekah crouched near Heber and murmured something and as she reached a hand out to touch his face he grabbed her wrist and pulled her on top of him and held her tightly, laughing and grunting as she struggled against him. When he released her she twisted away and fell onto her backside. This began a scramble, she crawling away on hands and knees and Heber following in like manner. The three bystanders watched them scuttle like animals in mad frolic across the wet, muddy lawn, and then onto the snow, Heber troubling her from behind like some shabby sire bull. Jack made three long steps and dropped him facedown to the ground with a boot to the jaw and Heber lay still.

Worlds and galaxies above the desert shone brilliant, and with no moon they dizzied the man who looked up and made so much below seem at once inconsequent and extraordinary. The light of suns burned out still coursed through the universe and new suns that had come into existence did not yet shine their inchoate light upon them as they walked to the truck. The engine fired up and rumbled through the cab.

—I broke my hand again, he said.

She reached for it and he gave it to her tenderly. A visible lump stood up from the skin, hard and tumid. She brought air through her teeth in a hiss and said, Let me drive you to the hospital.

—I don't want to go to the hospital right now.

He put his broken hand in his lap and pressed down on it with his left thumb and growled. He felt a shift. White stars exploded in his head and his breath was taken. He took a minute and revved the engine and backed out onto the empty street.

—Go to my house, she said. I can find something for the pain.

The town looked modest with its handful of lights as they drove through it and on into the blackness of the country. She had such long dark hair, dark and ambrosial, and he followed it from the truck. Inside she shed her coat and turned to him timidly. He looked at her soiled jeans.

—That was terrible, she said. I feel sick about it. Absolutely sick.

She made a small noise, a sound of small suffering.

—I'm going to change my pants, she said. She clapped her hands to her rump to feel the dampness there.

—Don't change them, he said. Just set here with me a minute.

He sat at the kitchen table and put his broken hand on it and observed the swelling. She opened the fridge and his eyes moved to the seat of her jeans, twin oval marks of wetness. She took an ice pack from the freezer and wrapped it in a clean dish towel and set it in front of him. His pain was tremendous. She read the instructions on a prescription bottle, shook out a pill, and brought it over with a glass of water. He motioned to her face and said, You've got something there.

She touched her face.

—Where?

—Got a wet towel?

She brought him a washcloth.

—Come down here, he said. It's Heber's blood.

She squatted at the base of his chair and he leaned toward her and she shuffled closer. Her pretty face so near, so alive, a smear of darkened blood on her jaw. He wiped it away gently and they looked at the cloth where the blood had turned a brighter red.

She rose and sat down and her fingers touched her white

throat. The muscles there strained and worked under the shadow of her chin. He watched her and felt a heaviness in the room, a viscous weight in his blood. Its inception had been at the park that first night when he saw her on the swings and it had grown like an embryo until now when its weight threatened to split the stomach that carried it and birth itself tremendously on the floor.

—I hated seeing you like that, she said. Hitting him. I can't believe you hit him like that.

Jack looked at her.

—You kicked him.

—He wouldn't go down.

—I hated it.

—What's your relationship to him?

—What do you mean?

—Are you interested in him?

—Of course not. Why would you ask that?

—You know why.

She took a deep breath. They sat there for a few minutes in silence. He looked at her eyes and they were dark. He knew what kind of light played in her eyes like he knew sunlight in water but they were now only limpid pools of darkness. Even so she had become enlivened, her face animated, her personage glowing.

—Did you miss me? she said.

—I barely knew you were gone.

—Liar.

There was energy in the room born from the violence and emotion. There was a new bond in place between them, fragile and tense, with power to create new fortune. She stood up and raised her chest with a deep breath and walked into the living room. He got up and followed and stopped to lean in the doorway. She lit a single lamp and backed into the couch and he watched her from across the room.

—You can come over here, she said.

She sat down and lifted her hand in offering and he moved toward her as if drawn by a current. Her pupils were wide and dark and her face flushed. Her tongue was like spiced liquor. He touched her knee with his good hand and the denim was damp and gritty. His fingers came away with soil on them, the grains of which he rubbed with his thumb and let fall. His good hand slid up the outside of her thigh with a slow rushing sound and felt the contained firmness of it, the tightness and the youth, and he was possessed with such a furious need he was frightened. She leaned back into the cushion. She was as fresh as an aspen tree after rain. He could peel the white bark away and beneath would be the bright wet pith. This girl was not for him. She was not for this town. He tasted the alcohol of her perfume on her neck and smelled her apple-scented hair and her breath came fast and her whole body responded. Her lips were hot and supple from her emotion. Her watertight certainty had disappeared, her composure gone, and she was lain bare. In its place now was some new spirit, some thriving power more awesome than what had been. He bumped his bad hand and the pain centered there like a stone in water and sent its signals out in dull, centrifugal circles. When her hands caressed his face they smelled of damp soil, and he felt he would clean her sullied hands with his mouth. She pulled back a moment and said, You taste like smoke. She searched his eyes. She reached again and kissed him. He understood that these were the best moments of his life. Soft sounds came from her throat. He opened his eyes and saw the blurred crescents that were the lines of her closed eyelashes and then her dark eyes opened and beaded within each pupil was the trembling lamp light and she shifted and leaned back against the armrest and he followed her. He took her ample thigh in his good hand and felt its heft. His hand found her hip, which was uncovered from where her shirt had pulled up. His hand followed her skin until it rested on her ribcage.

—Oh, she said, drawing in a quick breath. Your hand is rough.

He kept it where it was, feeling her breathe. He could feel its roughness against the softness of her skin. Her lips and tongue were marvels of this world. He kissed the fragrant hollow of her throat as it deepened with her breath.

He would think back to this moment not a year from now. He would study it and wonder about it. He would remember how sweet was her working mouth, how it felt to hold her, how long they kissed, how his hand slid farther of its own accord, up her ribs one by one, until it encountered the underside of her brassiere, and this it moved over. He would remember the weight of her silk clad breast beneath his hand, and how his hand moved that weight. How her fingers touched the elbow of his deviant arm, and how her touch might have been succor, her consent, how it seemed not to mean restraint. He would remember how his hand of its own accord pulled back and slipped under the cup and displaced it like one plate of the earth displaces another, until it rested on the hot flesh of her breast. How she stiffened. How she arched her back to fill his hand. And within her breath, short and hot in his ear, she had whispered a word to him, or a noise that meant a word. A time-altered image of her father had stolen into his mind. Not a year from now he would dwell on this, the power of her father's image lost and impotent, and second guess her meaning. He would envision where his hands would have taken him had he ignored her whisper and the sudden, unwelcome image, bizarre and nearly grotesque in that context. He would wonder whether he might have gotten there first, the brash, incipient dreams of his adolescence fulfilled, and how that might have changed things. He would regret not continuing, because he would know then, in that way one can never be certain of because it is colored by late and futile hopes, that she would have let him continue, that the light barrier she threw up in the form of that whisper was her only barrier, and that he would not have been met by others. Lead then, she would have said, and he would have led. He would realize how her virtue was a holy thing, but that her loss of it had not stopped the world as he had thought and that her loss of its renewal would likewise not. He observed the fragile nature of the situation and considered the doing of things that could not be undone. He considered them whole and he considered them broken. He would regret not taking control of his destiny then. The stiffening, the short draw of breath, the rush of whisper in his ear—even in the madness of his new dominion, as his blood thudded through his body with a murmur audible in his ears, he slowed and withdrew his hand. He hovered over her and his kisses shortened until they were simple warm pecks against the tender, spiced skin of her neck, her clear forehead, her cheek warm with blood, her still lips. He buried his face in her neck and groaned.

She pressed her hands lightly against his chest and he rose away. They sat up and she adjusted her clothing, pulled the hem of her shirt down around her hips. She lowered her face and he tried to lift her chin with his fingers but she was stubborn and would not lift it. He leaned over and saw that her eyes were glazed and defiant. She stared down at the carpet as though at some far off thing. He stood and stepped backward to the other side of the room and sat down in a chair.

He breathed deeply and lay his head back and looked up at the ceiling and spoke.

—What are you looking for?

He waited and she didn't answer.

—Whatever it is, I can give it to you.

They left the house and drove toward the mountains. In the truck she sat near him as his kingdom and town shrunk in the mirror. He locked the hubs and took them as far as he could up the road toward the north field, gaining elevation above the town, and when the snow allowed him to go no farther he shut the truck off and they were in a darkness made white from the starlight on the snow. They climbed into the back and wrapped themselves in old blankets and sat in the cold air, and in a hard-lit cluster beneath them the town lay huddled together.

—It's cold, she said.

—Come closer.

Above the town in the cold night he thought of Heber and a surge of uncommon love washed over him. He was gripped with sadness for Heber and its heft fell over him. Below them the ribbon of the river took its eternities to crawl through the land, the pale body of a serpent whose head had passed how long ago and whose tail would come when. He was uncertain, but he pulled her to him and kissed her warm mouth and the cold point of her nose pressed into his cheek. He held her tighter. In the wake of the sadness he felt something else. It was happiness he supposed, something bright and true and whelming, but it also held the undertones of his despair. These low dark whisperings made known that such a thing could not last, that it was not in the fixed course of things. He pulled her against him as if he could make them one, so that where she would go he would go. Somewhere within the dark mountain he could hear the howling of the wolves. He pressed his face into her hair and felt the delicate shape of her ear against his lips, but had nothing to whisper into it.

14

FEBRUARY THAW SHRUNK THE SNOW BANKS AND IN the fields the snow drew back like gums in an aging head. Their mornings together had long been silent events, the solemnity of the early hour causing each man to draw within himself and brood on his own thoughts, but these days they no longer spoke of farm matters beyond immediate tasks, did not bring large ideas into small talk with plans for the future. No man can look forward to milking cows early mornings, but the sun approached from post-breakfast, working backward toward that black-cold three hour session, rising earlier each day. Blair began to bitch about the roughness of the lane. They shared it with a man named Scab Oswald, a resident of Hansel and a middling business owner who had several small operations filling his books. He owned the land south of the lower fields, mostly the wide riverbottoms there, and it was his turn to grade the easement.

The morning wind smelled of melting snow as Jack fed and combed the horse. He heard a helicopter and looked up. He climbed out of the pen and walked to the edge of the barnyard and saw it moving along the flank of the mountains. It disappeared up the mouth of the big canyon, heading toward the Cauldron.

—Goddamn, he whispered.

He walked through the barnyard and looked over to see the pallid boy perched at the top of the pile of grain in the grain shed, his eyes dark-ringed and a hard sediment of snot on his upper lip. The boy's tongue flicked out to touch the crust of mucous, speckled with stuff that could have been only masticated rolled barley. His left ear had sprigs on its rim like a sprocket. He sat with his legs pulled into his chest and chewed on the yellow mash. He was alone, which was something Jack had not seen before, and they eyed each other. Jack took a few steps toward him and the boy stopped chewing. He had been sick with pneumonia that winter and had not been leaving the house since before Christmas. He was growing. The cuffs of his green corduroy pants rode up his calves and revealed smears of cow manure on his ankles above a loose pair of Velcro shoes also smeared in manure.

—Taste good? said Jack.

He expected no answer and got none. He watched the boy awhile and then said, Don't eat the bird droppings, Ed.

He took her into Willow Valley for Valentine's Day and they ate at the Blue Bird—cloth napkins, heavy silverware, waiters in black ties and white shirts. Jack felt confident, romantic, taking dinner in that place with a beautiful woman. He had scrubbed his cast with soap and hot water and a stiff bristled brush and he kept it hidden under the table and ate with his left hand because it still stank. She had dressed for Salt Lake because he had meant to take her there, but Elmer intruded near the end of the day with a measure of work that kept him late. She wore a long overcoat and knee-high leather boots with spiked heels that clicked thinly on the sidewalk. He guessed she had been in her grandmother's closet from the gaudy outdated earrings that dangled from her ears and the antiquated green shawl she wore. Glittering green shadow on her eyelids. Yellow calfskin gloves. This sophisticated dress and manner became her. She emitted a hungry energy which her perfume accented. There was a common word to describe the effect she had on him, the way she looked, the force she emanated. It was a word that could be used for other things, that held power if used right but could be overused. The word came to him at the table after searching for it for an hour or more. She was *stunning*. He rolled it around in his mouth, and as he tasted it, it fell out in a whisper and she looked up from her plate.

Their chemistry was upset somehow from the start and was made worse when on the way home she reached down to her feet to pull at the corner of something under the seat. She took up a Penthouse magazine and turned to give him a long stare.

—I swear that's not mine and I don't know where it came from, he said.

She looked from him to the cover and opened the magazine and flipped through it.

—Boys, she said with a little contempt, and put it back where she found it.

He meandered over uncommon roads to get home, unwilling to let the night go so easily. She dozed against his shoulder and once woke and in a sleepy voice asked where they were. Her breath was fermented and lingered in the air in front of his face. He made something up because he didn't know and she readjusted her position farther away from him against the door.

When he came home Blair was still awake, clad in his sagging long underwear and watching television in the living room. Jack fell into his own chair still dressed, and the old man disappeared and came back and tossed a tube of hemorrhoid cream onto his lap. Blair turned his back and let loose the rear flap of his underwear to reveal buttocks so scrawny and white and marred with age they could only evoke pity. Seventy years of gravity's ceaseless work had pulled the flesh down until it sagged on piles of wrinkles, wrinkles like the rings of trees, showing increments of Blair's life in years, a wrinkle for every decade. Blair said nothing, and it wasn't until Jack read the instructions on the tube and examined the nozzle that he realized what was wanted. He read the instructions again, looking for alternative applications. In the end his good hand shook as he did what needed to be done. He guessed this could go on until the old man was put up, creased and mindless as a newborn, Jack taking care of him as he would a baby. If this was the chiasmus of human life, what had been the vital center that Blair had moved toward for so long and was moving away from now?

The next afternoon Jack and Seth drove to the co-op. They bought cellophane-wrapped sandwiches from the cooler. Sitting near the basketball hoops at the park they could see over small fields Maria's house to the left and Heber's to the right. Jack rolled his window down to air that carried hints of warmth. He felt the stirring that was the season's first hint that spring might come.

—These sandwiches taste like wrapped goat shit, said Seth.

—What's the date on um? said Jack.

Seth examined the wrapper.

—What's the date today?

Jack shrugged.

—About five days ago, said Seth.

Jack took a bland bite and got cellophane in it.

—Well old buddy, I'm afraid I got to leave this place, said Seth.

—Already?

—My mom ransacked my clothes and found some condoms and a can of chew and a pack of smokes in my pockets. That's the godhead of evil to her. She's pissed and tearing my room apart, looking for the devil knows what else. She screamed for a while and tried to ground me, then sent my dad in. I didn't tell him I was going, but it's him I'll miss.

—Do you think she's this way because she loves you or because her pride is hurt when you cross her?

Seth shrugged.

—It's hard to say with mothers.

—You still going to Amarillo?

—I guess.

—Why don't you just move out? Stick around?

—Where would I stay?

Jack lifted his chin in the direction of Maria's house.

—That basement's been for rent for as long as I can remember. You can see the sign from here.

—I thought that was a For Sale sign.

—It's faded out.

—Would you want to split rent?

—I worry about the old man.

—What's the matter with him?

—Not sure, but he ain't doing so good.

—Ah. Well I guess I could afford it on my own easy enough. I just got to work more. When you figger we could start riding bulls again?

—Soon.

—Have you seen Heber since the bonfire?

Jack shook his head.

—He got all sentimental after you left and went on this long preach to me and Jane about friendship and brotherhood. It was stupid, but kind of touching. She wanted to take off, but I knew we couldn't leave him alone like that.

—How long did you stay?

—Until Maria came. She tried to clean the blood off his face and looked at his ribs inside the house. She was trying to take him to the hospital, but he wouldn't go. His jaw swole up. His tongue was messed up. I think he bit it. Made him talk funny. You did a number on him. I can't believe you kicked him in the face.

—He wouldn't of bit his tongue if it hadn't been hanging out of his mouth.

—You kicked him pretty hard. Hard enough to knock him out, anyway. That was a badass beating. He shouldn't of said those things. It was strange, seeing you hit him like that. That first hit, it made me proud of you. I don't know why. But then it just got ugly.

—Yeah, it did, said Jack. And I broke my hand again.

—Might as well keep that smelly cast on forever. You'll probly break it again anyway.

—Tell me something. Do you think people'd shop at a good store if we had one? Sell stuff like a few groceries and things? There's five hundred people in town, and other places like Hansel that come through all the time.

—Sure, people'd shop there. I know it.

—Yeah. I think so.

—You know if you did start a store you could have a deli maybe, with chicken and tater babies and all that sort of thing. A good hot lunch. I'd pay for that.

They reached the ends of their sandwiches and Jack watched Heber's house across the field and nursed his soda. Nothing pressed them for time. They only let the fresh air push through one window and out the other, let it stir them and fill them both with the reawakened yearnings of young men near winter's end. Seth smoked. There was farm work that could be done, but Jack was despondent with the idea of another season starting. The load of work ahead was overwhelming as it was every spring and he wanted none of it. As they sat there Heber turned onto his street and pulled into his driveway. He got out of the Bronco, a torn flannel jacket hanging off his broad frame. He threw a fast look over his shoulder to where they were parked and climbed the steps to his trailer and was gone.

That night Jack got drunk in his bedroom and listened to the bats scratch and squeak through the attic above him. He heard their buzzing queries to one another and saw their quick shapes move past the window. When he slept it was a broken sleep and he woke to find Adelaide beside his bed. She sat with her eyes closed and her hands in her lap and she rocked on a chair that hadn't been there when he'd gone to sleep. She told him number 379 had mastitis. He asked her how she knew. She said, He started a flame with it that he couldn't manage, and the flame can't keep. Who? said Jack. She asked him if he had seen his brother lately. He was suddenly aware that he had a brother, and felt desperate to find him. In repose her face looked at peace. It was not the haggard, tortured thing he'd become familiar with before she died, nor the ashen wax deathmask he'd seen in her coffin. She rocked for a while longer beside his bed with her eyes closed and when his alarm went off he was surprised to find that it was time to get up to milk. It took him several minutes to convince himself that he had no brother.

March was gusting rain storms and rioting temperatures. It rained below and snowed in the mountains, and the rain that fell on the town took the remaining snow with it and deposited it into an engorged river. Even bloated with runoff the river did not appear to move swifter nor ripple more. It simply enlarged, eating away its dirt sides farther and engulfing the dormant grass that lined its edges. When it poured out of its banks and created new ponds filled with carp it was a time for pitchforks and rifles with which to chase the big fish through the shallow pools. A carp was a speeding bump on the surface of the water and a pitchfork could be thrown with accuracy to pin those ripples still. Those left alone died slowly in the sun when the river fell again and the ponds dried up, carrion feeders falling on them even while the fish struggled to die.

He moved with Seth into the basement beneath Maria's house but only slept there on occasion, taking the same cot he had used in the duckblind and unfolding it in the living room. Seth took the bedroom where he slept in a mephitic confusion of soiled bedding and sweating dreams.

Jack grabbed his jacket one evening when he saw the Bronco

across the field and the lights in the house on. He knocked on the door and got no answer. There was cardboard in one of the front windows that hadn't been there before and the screen door hung crooked and broken. He let himself in, carefully opening the screen door and stepping inside and pulling it to and lifting it back up onto the threshold. He walked into the living room where he sat down and listened to the shower running through the open door. A few minutes after it stopped the sound of shuffling bare feet came from the kitchen. The fridge door opened and closed. The tab of a canned beverage popped. Heber hummed the melody of a song that might have been Desperado. As he rounded the corner holding a can of beer his voice broke into a surprised squeak and he jumped at the sight of Jack on the couch. He sloshed beer onto his chest and it ran down through his hair and over his gut and into the towel.

—You son of a bitch, he said.

He set the beer down on a book and pulled the towel from his waist to wipe away the spill. His member hung wrinkled and small from a tangle of unkempt hair like a compressed caterpillar. His testicles hung low and unequal. Naked he was like some sculpture of antiquity—bearded, wide framed, cut lines running beneath his gut, powerful arms and shoulders.

—Scared the hell out of me, he said glumly.

He wrapped the towel around himself and sat down on the leather love seat and took a long drink. He was sullen, his eyes moody and without light and his manner subdued.

—I come over to talk about what happened the other day, said Jack.

—That was two months ago.

Jack held Heber's gaze and waited.

—It's all right, said Heber. You have my sincere apologies.

—Likewise.

Neither spoke for a moment, and then Jack said, What've you been up to?

—I've been going out to the desert.

—What for?

—I've just been going out there.

—Did you see any wolves?

—I've been writing a letter to Rebekah. Do you think she'll forgive me?

—Probly.

—She's very special, John.

They stared at each other.

—I know she is, said Jack.

—I miss Geneva, said Heber. I tried to go see her. Ah, Jack, buddy. My temper's coming loose. I feel run out. I fill my days with what emotions I can contrive. Two days ago I put my fist through the bedroom wall in an argument with Maria. Then I kicked the closet door off its hinges. So then I pushed my dresser over and threw my boots at her through the front window when she tried to leave. Threw them like tomahawks. He reached behind him and rapped on the cardboard with his knuckles.

—I see, said Jack.

—I felt like a fool for it all. I ain't acted like that since Dad was alive. Thought I'd quelled that streak in me for good. I got home from work last night and went into the desert and drove like hell all around it. Nearly wrecked a few times. He shook his head slowly. God Almighty, I'm battling demons of amazing strength. I wish I could tell you.

He let out a slow moan and looked like some savage thing half naked on the couch.

—What's the problem? said Jack.

—It's good to be friends again. You don't know how much I've missed this. Give me a hug.

—Put some damn clothes on and maybe I'll give you a hug.

Heber laughed loud and hard. When he was finished his eyes had tears in them. He laughed again and his body was taken in some resurrection. His muscles tensed and his pectorals hardened and strained against his skin.

—Do you want to go out there? he said. His eyes smoldered to life. Let's go out there. Let me put some clothes on. We'll talk it through.

He left the room and came back wearing a worn pair of jeans, his Tony Lamas, and the red and black checked flannel jacket. They got into his Bronco and the interior smelled of gasoline, but it was lessened by the cold air that came in around a piece of plywood fastened across the back in place of the tailgate. As Heber drove them west and north he was silent. When they had left town and neared the black desert he began to speak.

—I have so much love for Maria, but not for her alone. I still feel it for Geneva too. I feel it for all women. How does a guy make a go of it in this world with all of them walking around, moving so recklessly over the earth, presenting their lovely flesh to the world in all its trembling wonder? Emanating their sex and their spirit to the world like a maddening smell? How can you take it? How can you take it all in? How can you manage these deep needs ungovernable? I wish I were a king, and all of this was my kingdom.

He paused as he slowed the Bronco. They left pavement and entered the sage on a small track of dirt. The land in front of them was wet and renewed in the evening light, the sage a green that came only after rain. The evening sky was fresh and the remnant clouds peach-colored and dreamlike. The beauty of this land filled Jack with a swell of joy and confidence and he thought of Rebekah and believed everything would work out. In the near distance the basalt heaves began, a broken horizon against the paling light.

—It's too much love and not enough girl, said Heber. I can never get a good drink of it. It's like a flame. I've got this flame, and now I've got to hold it steady or it'll burn me. You understand?

Jack nodded.

—Say something then.

—Take it easy, said Jack. Slow down. The flame can't keep. It's not sustainable. This is a simple town. You're a bricklayer. That's all there is to it.

—Good Maria, said Heber. God, she's a good woman.

He looked simple then, the way Jack had described him. This was Heber. Just Heber.

—I've wronged her in many ways, he said.

—What ways? said Jack.

—I've wronged her and continue to do so.

They diverged from their path and headed north again, skirting the edge of the lava flow.

Heber was smiling slightly, adrift in some reverie.

—I envy you, he said. You are on the verge while I am well past it. I've sampled the many emotions this world has to offer with only a few left to me, and some I will never taste. There must be one when you hold a man beneath the water till his struggles stop and his last breath boils to the surface, for instance. There must be one when you break the trust of a wife you love deeply. Or when you can alternately abuse and succor humankind at will through the power of wealth. There must be one when, after contemplating suicide, you begin the preparations that will lead you through it. There are thrills that come with anguish, thrills when you cause profound pain to yourself or others, when you use your agency for destruction, even though it is not right. These are raw, terrible things, not for the weak of heart, but they are as much a part of us and our existence as love, compassion, humanity.

Heber watched the curdling sunset, meandering along the road, and when he spoke again it seemed to himself.

—Unmitigated desire, he said. There's an emotion I don't care for. Not at all. We are meant to be satisfied. That is happiness. The void we feel when we want something good, something worth wanting, and don't get it because of restraint and fear, I have no place for that kind of emptiness. Ah, the complexities of human relationships. Nothing is as simple as it seems.

He shook his head slowly and turned to Jack.

—And you must rebuild in order to break anew, he said. You know this. You are in the process as we speak. My soul is as misshapen and tortured as this lava flow. You let go one way of life and began another. A default. And when the default spent itself you became a dull boy on the farm. But you're only sleeping, gathering your strength for another, greater run. You say you got tired of it, that it isn't sustainable, that it's not what you really want, but you're still very young. You've got a delicious road ahead. You're climbing even if it is to fall again. Without some restraint sin holds no charm, no mystery, so you must rebuild in order to break anew. These systems are in place only to bring us to the point of departure. Even though they are not of God, God uses them to his advantage. The structure of striving for traditional righteousness feels firm and good in the beginning but breaks down under experience and becomes nothing but a slew of worn out impediments and the infinite atonement covers all. You can't do what's been asked of you, so you climb toward an obscurity that is only an illusion, and then you must fall. This is the verge, the point you must pick to move forward. You're not a common man. This is wisdom. You're a novice yet. There is so much ahead of you. And it's not about the girl. You've misjudged her, and you'll find that out soon enough. You'll become wiser than you have been. Those breasts have bled milk.

—You broke down son of a bitch, said Jack.

—You've been a fool, said Heber. But I warned you against that. She was a mystery, that one. But it's been discovered. God, it's been discovered. As the virtue of our women goes, so goes our nation. We're already in our motion downward, all of us. The Son of Man cometh, the great and terrible day. It can't be stopped. It's all coming down.

Heber fell silent and drove on. He kept the Bronco in a low gear and let it make its slow way over the winding dirt path, up and down the swells of land with sagebrush whispering against the sides. The evening dimmed farther. Ahead of them about a mile stood an unfamiliar structure. As they neared it took the form of an old cabin with a broken corral next to it. Its windows were empty and black and the whole thing leaned to the east. It was made of wood with interlocking corners and its roof was breached in several places. Its door lay open and crooked with the top hinge broken. Heber took the track that led to it and parked the Bronco some thirty yards away. Both men got out and faced opposite directions as they urinated on the wet ground. Heber rummaged in the back of the Bronco and produced a bottle of whiskey. He unscrewed the cap and upended it and grimaced afterward. He held the bottle out to Jack, who drank and wiped his mouth.

—Old Eli's place, said Heber. He lit a cigarette and pulled from the rear of the Bronco a jug of gasoline stoppered with a blue shop towel. The jug lay heavy against his leg as he walked toward the cabin and into it, and then he began to douse the inner walls. He made it around the outside a time and a half before the gas was gone. He threw the empty jug inside with a hollow thump. Casting a sidelong glance at Jack, he drew on his cigarette and took it from his mouth and flicked it toward the cabin. The cigarette hit the wall with a small burst of sparks but the gas did not light. Heber cursed and dug in his pocket. He crouched at the doorway and in a moment leapt back as blue flames raced across the floor and up the walls and the whole thing turned from dim to bright in an instant. He staggered backward at the sudden heat. He stood next to Jack and looked at what he had done. They got into the Bronco and drove farther north and within five minutes were positioned on a higher piece of land about a half mile from the burning cabin. It blazed furiously in the falling night. The desert was dark now with the low sky in the west paling. Heber drank whiskey and watched the structure burn, a single thrust of light in the darkness, illuminating the earth around it. He let the Bronco idle beneath them, the vents pushing heat to combat the cold drafts. He passed the bottle to Jack. They drank in silence and watched the strange fire below them. Flame of lust, flame of progress.

—So do you think there's anything left after her daddy got through with her? said Heber.

—Whatever happened there is nobody's fault but his, the sick bastard.

—It happened though. How does that fit into your hopes and dreams?

Heber appeared to muse on something and took his time before speaking.

—That girl, he muttered. That girl.

They sat there, passing the bottle back and forth, watching the blaze, saying nothing. Heber took a long drink, sighed, then drew a breath. When he let it out his whole body deflated and seemed to collapse. He turned himself toward Jack and leaned back against his door while below them the cabin burned like an offering, missing only its ring of worshippers.

When he spoke his voice was subdued but strong.

—I want to be understood now, he said. What I'm trying to impart is one of the singular truths of my life. It is not the girl as much as your anticipation of the girl. Your anxiety to discover her mysteries, her enchantment. But these things must eventually be realized in something as firm as flesh and as graspable. And then you'll be amazed how it flees. The spell will be broken and you'll find yourself in search of it somewhere else. This search, this is life. We rise only to fall and do this time and time again, greater and bigger than the time before until we regress, being spent, or until death takes us. This is my discipleship. Treading where you've never tread, breaking things that have been carefully kept whole in order to fill the measures of their creation. What power we hold. What power. The very act of love, on all planes, brings a man closer to God. I know you believe this.

Jack did come to believe, for a moment. This bastardized religion Heber subscribed to, something self-made, something idolatrous and blood sacrificial, seemed almost sacramental, godly, for an instant. It appealed to something necessary and irreducible within him. It resonated with his spirit. It was along the natural course of things and effortless, a river seeking the lowest ground always and always moving, changing, the antithesis to what so much of his life had been, the converse of his labor, and a comforting promise of realms he had only envisioned. Some kind of truth. He had never understood these powers, but they seemed to move about him always, these powers that sustained Heber's existence and led him all the while downward into sweet perdition, as though that were the only true course, the course men were destined to follow. He felt the tuggings of some converting power upon him, a touch of euphoria—like glimpsing something fantastic only once, briefly, through a wood—and then it was gone.

Heber's eyes became raw and wet. His tone grew resigned like a prophet at the end of his ministry, meting out still the redundant truth against the resistance of its hearers.

—Love her, he said. Love her with violence and passion, and together you will drink the dregs of the cup of trembling wrung out.

Jack burst out in laughter.

—You've gone crazy, he said. You need to come back. Where's the old boy at? Where is he? Gone for good? Just because you sprinkle your ideas with scripture, you crazy fuck, doesn't make them worth a damn.

—That hurts me.

—You've lied from the beginning, said Jack. And that hurts me.

—I'm not lying now, said Heber. I'm in love with her too, you see. We all are.

He gave a strained smile and put the Bronco in reverse. He took them away from the fire, solitary and bright in the blackness of the desert, and they came back to town on a different track. They didn't speak again and as Jack left him at his trailer and walked across the balding scratch of lawn, and then across the wet field, a mild despondence settled on him. He felt better moving away, and he knew if he looked back he would see Heber's tortured face in the window, watching him go.

On one of the first fully warm days of the new season, the ground soaking wet with draining snowmelt and the birds trilling in the trees, a day too suddenly fine to organize any meaningful work around it, he found her in an old chicken coop behind her grand-father's house, breaking up the years-old dung with a pitchfork and throwing it into a metal wheelbarrow worn paintless from use. He heard her grunting through the open door before he entered. She sweated and wiped her brow when she saw him and this scene pleased him in an unexpected way, to see her at a man's work. He had a vision of her on the farm driving the big tractors, building fence, even milking cows daily, and he nearly asked her if she wanted to learn those ways. She leaned the pitchfork against the wall to rest and he took it and broke up more of the floor. Layers of chicken dung and old straw came up feculent, in some places moist like the layers of some master's painting decades old and drying still. She stopped him before the wheelbarrow was full. He went to take the handles and she pushed him away and grabbed them herself and grunted as she lifted. The edge of her pink tongue stuck out from her lips. She wheeled the dung out the door toward the bare garden.

He took her to the barnyard and they walked the long fence-line between the barn and the farmhouse. When the fence proved sound he opened the gate for the largest heifers at the house and left them to discover their freedom. As he walked with her toward the farmhouse she told him that Heber had sent her a letter.

—Did he mail it or drop it off? he said.

—He stamped it and mailed it through the post office, she

said. Kind of funny.

—What'd it say?

—It was sweet. He apologized. I know he didn't mean what he said. He reminded me of how my dad could get. The meanness and the wrath. I worry about him.

—I want you to stay away from him, said Jack. He's not right these days.

—What's wrong?

—Just stay away from him.

—He needs us. He doesn't have anything else.

—Rebekah, he said.

She was silent as he led her through a broken door and into the shed where they sometimes raised pigs and walked to the box on the wall that ran the electric fence. He plugged it in and electricity went out in pulses. The box ticking, he threw himself onto the pile of burlap gunnysacks in the far corner and pulled her down to him with only her laugh as resistance. The shed was void of livestock but smelled faintly of old manure. The windows were opaque with dust and the shed warm with trapped sun. She seemed from another world, one not unlike this world but ruled by a more generous god. When they kissed it seemed clear she wished to be with him. He kissed her through the darkness of his soul, through the shadow, and when they were loose and besotted with it they rested.

—Are you leaving? he said.

—I might be.

—College?

—Among other things.

—For good?

—Most likely.

He lay with his head in her lap and she ran her fingers through his hair.

—Will you marry me? he said.

She laughed.

—It's not funny, he said.

—I know it's not.

She paused, then looked toward the far corner and said, I need a good man, Jack. There's no chance for a child in this world without a good mother and father.

—Damn it, he said softly. I'm a good man.

He closed his eyes and she dragged her fingers around his neck and over his chest and ran them through his hair. He thought she would leave him there, but then she bent over him and her hair fell on his face. He opened his eyes and she smiled. She bent farther and he kissed her lissome mouth once.

—You've got a good heart, she whispered.

Before long he was asleep and when he woke she was gone. He felt as a child must feel when his mother has put him to sleep and he wakes to find her gone and the room dark, for she was gone and the shed grown dim and cold.

15

T HE NEXT DAY WAS RAW WITH WIND. THE WIND TOOK the heat from the sunshine. It chilled his fingers and the tip of his nose. As it did with earth and stone it wore him away. The wind was friction on the earth. It could change the speed at which the earth spun, hurrying the setting of the sun or delaying the dawn. There were winds that spanned continents and oceans, and this wind was wearing him down now as he built a set of new pens for spring calving with baling twine and sections of pig wire.

Blair shuffled through the gravel toward him from the milking barn, hands in pockets like a man carefree and at peace with himself.

—I want you to run over to Larry Frick's place and ask him what kind of water agreement he wants to work out this spring, he said. See does he want to run it the same way or what.

—Why don't you send Elmer, said Jack. I got real work to do.

—He don't feel good today. He's in the house still.

—It's an easy job. Drive over and talk.

—He don't feel good enough.

—Not good enough to drive over and talk to a man?

—Guess not.

—What's he got this time?

—You little pecker, said Blair. You got your health and you better thank Almighty God for it. That man runs out of energy. He runs right out. You know what that's like? How'd you like a stomachache all the time. Shitting liquid a dozen times a day. How'd that be? You come find me every hour, I'll slug you in the stomach, give you a feel of what he's living with any day of the week.

—I already got plans, said Jack. So tell him to do it or do it yourself.

—Now damn it, you know how this has to go. Don't argue with me.

—There is no way this has to go, said Jack.

Blair looked at him.

—To hell with it, said Jack, dropping the panel and walking past Blair. Rig up these damn pens yourself then.

He drove to the co-op and Seth's mother approached him at the drink cooler. She was a small blazing woman with piercing eyes and a falcon's scowl, neat and religious. A woman who appeared to be in control of what mattered in all matters save that of her son. He thanked her for the casseroles she had brought over and she asked about several of her dishes. Then she asked if he was living with Seth.

—More or less, he said.

—Is he okay? He won't call me and I don't want to make things worse by going over there. Is he working?

—He's working masonry with Heber.

—How does he get to work? Does he need a car?

—Heber takes him.

—Do you think he's okay for Seth?

—What do you mean?

—Is he teaching him bad habits?

—Your guess is as good as mine.

—I know I'm putting you in a tough spot, but please tell me

the truth. I don't have anything else to go by. I'm terribly worried about him. You probably know what I found in his pockets. Since he doesn't work for his father anymore I never see him.

Her scowl had softened into something more desperate and her eyes had changed from fierce to supplicating. For a moment he thought she would cry. It seemed that even within the geographic boundaries of this town the distance between a mother and son could not be traversed.

—Do you think that Rafuse boy has influence over him?

—Not much. Seth'll work through it. He's still a good kid.

—Oh dear, she said.

One nervous finger curled at her mouth and she bit it.

—Thank you for being good to him.

He nodded and wished her a good day and pulled a Pepsi out of the cooler and walked to the front. As he stood there waiting for Noreen he watched Seth's mother drive off in her car.

—There's a worried mother, said Noreen.

—Worried or half crazy? said Jack.

—Half crazy because she's worried, said Noreen.

The evening after he and Seth had moved in he had entered the basement and heard a voice from the bedroom. Through the open door he'd seen Maria's smooth bare back arched, the sheet tousled around her curved hips, her long black hair spilling down like water, and Seth's skinny hands on her plump waist. They were laboring together slowly, teacher and student. Seth was feasting, Jack supposed. He doubted his mother could imagine it. He understood her fears and worries, for they were fears and worries he had for himself and for others, including Seth McQuarters. But the origin of these fears and worries and what to do with them he did not know and was uncertain whether anyone did.

In the evening he sat outside the apartment on the yellow grass in a lawn chair and observed the raw weather around him. Clouds built as they passed to the north and the highest peaks of the mountains were gone. To the northwest towering cumulus caught the sun and displayed many shades of heaven as they moved in single form. Storms of spring. He believed he sat in the same chair his grandmother had used her last summer. As he watched the little town around him he saw a red car rolling down the street, and from the direction of the park he heard a child call out. He was seized with a spell of déjà vu, a sense that some catastrophe was imminent. Then the feeling passed.

Seth came home and they drove to the barnyard. As they walked around to the side door of the barn to get the bull records it was nearly dark, a pulse of light still brooding in the west. Dark droplets dotted first the gravel and then the concrete pad outside the door. They trailed off in the direction of the east field and the riverbottoms beyond. On the old concrete near the door the drops had run on top of one another. Jack reached down and touched them with his fingers and they came up wet.

—Blood? said Seth.

Jack first thought of the boy, Edward Elmer, and a succession of death.

The door had been left slightly open and the trail led into the barn. When they walked inside the dark interior a low sound echoed through the empty space, a growling whine that made the hair on the back of Jack's neck rise. He stepped over and turned on the lights. The drops led through the open door and into the office. Halfway there they were smudged—not clear splattered circles, but a red smear across the floor. The low whine sounded again. He told Seth to wait and walked down the parlor and grabbed the new axe handle from the stairs and a metal weight off the lower pipes. He handed the weight to Seth and walked toward the office. He flipped the light on and swung the door back against the file cabinet and as it bounced off with a clang there came a hiss from beneath the desk.

Seth pulled the chair out and bent down to see. He jumped back and swore and said, It's a cat. A big one. Biggest cat I ever saw.

—What's wrong with it?

—Its guts is hanging out. It's bleeding all over the floor.

Jack bent down to look and the cat was huge, its pupils wide and fearsome under the desk, its black-tipped ears lain back and its fangs bared. It hissed at him and a purring growl cycled perpetually from deep inside it.

—That ain't a barn cat, he said. It's a damn bobcat. Look at its ears.

The blood in the barn reminded him of Roydn Woolums. He looked down at his fingers.

—Got to put it out of its misery, he said. How should we do it?

They deliberated for a minute and Seth stepped into the office and kicked the chair away against the fridge and the cat's whine pitched upward. He positioned himself on the far side of the desk because he was right-handed and threw the weight underneath. It clunked against the wall and clattered on the floor and Jack knew he had missed. The cat hissed and spat. When Jack looked again from the side he could see its gray guts trailing out of its torn stomach and blood soaked into its fur.

—Give me that axe handle, said Seth.

—That'll be a tough job.

—To get the weight back.

Seth stuck the handle beneath the desk and the cat went wild. He dropped it and tried to get out of the office, pushing Jack ahead of him and laughing.

—Ripped it damn near right out of my hand, he said.

—There's another weight. Make this one count.

Seth took the second weight and threw again and there was a dense thud and wild yowls from the cat and a violent thrashing under the desk. The animal's cries rang off the walls outside the office. The desk thumped and a pen rolled off and hit the floor with a thin sound.

—Got it in the head, said Seth.

Jack looked beneath the desk. The cat was tossing about on the floor.

—Hit it again, he said. It's still alive.

Seth grabbed at the axe handle and retrieved the weight and threw it again, and again connected. He dragged the flailing cat out with the handle and brought it backward with a series of pulls. Its long black claws grew and retracted. He brought it still moving and crying in its death spasms into its last starry night and lifted a heavy work boot and brought it down.

—Cats don't die good, he said.

Three times with the heel and it was hard to tell because the cat was still moving. Jack went for a shovel and when he returned Seth stood over the dead animal looking down. Jack scooped it onto the shovel blade, its body hanging limply over each side, and laid it next to the barn wall. He guessed it weighed as much as thirty pounds and said so. In the barn he washed his hands and rubbed the blood off his fingertips and squirted the floor down.

—I feel like I need something after that, said Seth. I could use a chew.

—Could give you a shot of apple vinegar.

Seth went into the office and opened the fridge.

—You're kidding me, said Jack.

—I ain't kidding you.

Seth rummaged among the sodas and bottles of medicine, digging in the back where single plugs of tobacco were stacked for treating sick cows.

—Consider it pay for removing a wild bobcat from your barn, he said.

He unwrapped the plug and held it in his hand, where it looked like a compact rectangular turd.

—Days O'Work, he said, reading the label. Want half?

He tore the plug in half and put one piece in his mouth and worked the large chunk hard with his jaw until it was in the side of his cheek, but he couldn't mold it to fit. He chewed on it to break it down and brown juice flowed over his lip and down his chin. He wiped at his mouth with his hand and his eyes began to water and he coughed and gagged and the plug came out and hit the concrete with a wet slap. He hacked on and pushed past Jack for the hose. When he had cleaned his mouth and had a drink he said, A smaller piece, maybe.

Jack grabbed the bull files and shut the lights off and wondered whether they would be kept from harm that night. They stopped at Rebekah's house to pick her up. Martha answered the door, and when she said she had taken her to Heber's house already Jack swayed a little on the step.

—Is something wrong? said Martha.

He pushed his truck four barrels open down the road not hearing Seth's questions and roared through the town square, his mufflers echoing off the dilapidated storefronts and his rubber crying out around the final corner to Heber's trailer and its empty driveway. Rebekah was sprawled on the couch. She lay on her back, her shirt twisted around her torso, one breast in stark relief against its pull. He moved toward her and stood over her, saying her name, and she would not respond. He knelt and smelled urine. Seth uttered soft and inquisitive curses behind him. She was warm. The flesh of her close hip showed some, her waistline too low. Jack moved slowly, doing things that needed to be done. He knew the task before him as clearly as he had ever known any task. It was something that required his attention and he would give it his attention until it was complete. He could not keep his eyes from the triangle of white in front, exposed and blasphemed as it was. He did not touch her underwear to straighten it out where it had bunched together over the edge of her pants, but tugged the waistline up. Her body moved limply with his effort. He pulled her zipper up with shaking hands and snapped together the button that his knuckles pressed against the warm flesh of her belly. A car pulled into the driveway and he stopped with his finger a clear line of drool creeping from her open mouth. Seth called out a warning. Jack was still kneeling by the couch when Martha tore him away with tremendous strength and looked down at her daughter. Wiped her hand savagely at the darkened crotch and looked at her fingers. Sniffed them.

Martha struggled and failed to lift the girl and set her wild eyes upon him in fierce entreaty. As he carried Rebekah to the car her body was heavy in his arms. He carried her as he had the slick dead bull calf on a better day. Martha's taillights flashed once at the corner and were gone.

Sometime later, after he had gone by the bridge, Jack drove alone through the desert, an illumined patch of dirt, grass, and sage the only unwinding before him, and when he returned hours later to her house on the lane he caught those intimate scents on the air that were the boundless issue of the Selvedge Dairy. The full odor of the damp soil, the clean richness of manure breaking down in the fields, and from farther away, presiding over them all, the raw scent of the cows they kept. He approached her house and low lights haunted the windows. He stopped to tilt his head back to look at the black sky where the stars turned in their indifferent mass, and couldn't go on. He craned his neck and took in the sky, every star, and couldn't go on.

Beneath the trees, another time. Seth was speaking. The darkness around them was complete, and they could hardly see each other but for the flick of flame to start their tobacco burning. He said the girl was a friend of his little sister's. She was left behind at the house after a falling out while the rest went out to roam the countryside under a bright moon. He said he knew this girl. He was seventeen and she was fourteen. She was emotional from the girls leaving her. He used the word *vulnerable*. He got close with her and kissed her and went about feeling her up even though she said she had never let any boy do that before and she wasn't sure she wanted to now. Heber asked about her physical development and Seth said that she was getting the body of a woman. Heber asked if that was it and Seth said she had cried afterward, and that he wasn't seventeen but that he'd been eighteen for three days, if that mattered at all. Heber said it did, and his face came out of the darkness as he lit a cigarette.

Jack told of one hot afternoon when he had taken Elmer's son out to move a line of sprinkler pipe in a distant field below the McKellar house. The boy had been sick and his mother thought being outside might help his convalescence. Jack dropped him off at the riser, rode on the three-wheeler to the end of the field where they would finish, and walked back. He sweated hard in the sun and mosquitoes in the hot humid field. He moved the line while the boy walked alongside with two feeble hands on the end of the pipe Jack carried from the middle, the boy's presence and assistance no help at all but instead a hindrance. Jack lost his temper halfway down the line. He threw the pipe down, cursed foully while slapping at himself for mosquitoes, and told the boy to keep his hands off the pipe. When they reached the end he explained his hand signals and how to turn the riser on slowly and sent the boy to walk back some half mile to the beginning of the line instead of taking him on the three-wheeler as he might have done. The boy did fine turning the water on. Jack went back up the dirt road that edged the field. Some cruelness rose in him. He could see the boy walking toward him from the riser, small, sickly, his shirt sticking to his bony torso for sweat, but instead of cutting over to pick him up he continued along the road. He looked behind once and saw the boy stopped, his hand to his brow to shade his face, a posture of confusion, watching Jack leave him behind. He wondered if the boy even knew his way back, were he to have to walk it. He rode up near the McKellar house and into the shade of the trees behind it and looked down to the field where the sprinklers turned and the boy stood in his chore boots, his corduroy pants, a dirty white T-shirt too long for him, slapping once in a while at the mosquitoes that were eating him. He said he watched him wander in the general direction of the lane for some time until the boy finally made his way to the dirt road, and then to the main road and across it onto the lane. He waited for him to come up the hill before riding out. The boy looked wretched, infirm, his thin chest rising and falling deeply to get air. The red swelling bites on his arms and face couldn't be counted. Jack dropped him off at his house and went to find water. Heber said that was very cruel and that it spoke to the darkness in his soul, and Jack nodded, though no one could see him.

Seth said he hadn't told all of it. He didn't just feel the girl up. She protested as he took off her pants, vocally, and without much conviction. There was hardly time for a second thought. It seemed so easy he wasn't even sure it had happened. He left her stunned on the couch and went for a drink of water to slake a sudden thirst. When he returned he put a movie on and sat at the opposite end of the couch from her and after a while fell asleep. She woke him up in tears. Seth said he knew what this was. He'd never seen it happen before or even heard about it but he knew what it was just like he'd known what to do before. He thought he knew the antidote. He told her to get some scriptures and read them, and she lifted the family set from where it sat next to her on the couch, open, to show him that she had been reading them, amateur makeup running down her cheeks, swollen eyes. He told her to pray, kissed her on the cheek, and made his way to his bedroom to sleep. He said it was funny he didn't feel the same thing, the same loss. It had been the first for both of them. But there she was, God's virtue gone out of her. It was irretrievable and he believed they both knew that. It didn't matter how much scripture she read or how much she prayed, it wasn't coming back. He said he remembered every detail about that experience. He saw her next in the hallway of the church house and as they passed each other he tried not to look at her and never said a word to her again. Then she left town, relieving him of that huge burden and leaving him in some tin version of peace.

They heard the sound of Seth's finger slapping a can of chew and saw the flash of his white hand. He put the can away and Heber handed him a cigarette, then reached over and lit it for him. In the flame's light shame burned his face.

—How many others before Penelope? said Heber.

—None, said Seth. That was it. I never counted it.

Heber shook his head and lit his own smoke.

—Well you should have, he said. They smoked. I've got nothing on you two boys, said Heber. I'd like to put something up that could match you, but I've been thinking hard and can't come up with it.

—You've got the worst history among us, said Seth.

—Tell me what it is, said Heber. If you know it tell it, because I don't. It's not a judgment when I say I have never done the likes of what you've both told. He drew on his cigarette and the coal streaked down into his lap. All right, he said. I used to steal from Wriglesworth's. He paused frankly, as if the other two would not believe him. Yes, he said. I'd go in there on a regular basis, buy a soda pop and a candy bar, but goddamn if my pockets weren't full of batteries, gum, candy bars, fingernail clippers, earrings for my mother—if that old woman sold it I took it at one time or another. Maybe that's not much of anything. Maybe it is. I took a lot of stuff. Sometimes I wonder if I was the reason they closed up. One day I took something right under her nose. She rang up my purchase and I gave her a dollar. My pockets were full of plunder. She put the purchase in a brown paper bag and pushed it across the counter. Then I stood back with her looking straight at me and took another candy bar from the shelves below the counter. I turned and walked out of the store. It was like she refused to believe I could do it, even when her eyes told her otherwise. I robbed them blind for three years until they finally closed.

—You're both liars, said Seth. Those aren't your worst things.

—Well fuck, said Heber. I took them under.

They sat for a while beneath the tree, listening to the night.

—You want something else? said Heber. All right. Consider on what I'm about to tell you. When I was a boy I found a kitten in the neighbor's haystack around back. It was young enough that its eyes weren't opened yet. I took it from the haystack to our barn's concrete landing and played with it awhile next to the barn, petting it and holding it and watching it crawl around without any sight, its head so damned big for its little body. After a bit of that, I picked it up and I threw it into the air and let it come down on the concrete. Seth froze, his hand halfway from can to mouth, his fingers pinching fine moist tobacco. Heber used his hands to articulate. I did it again and again. I must've done it a dozen times, throwing it way up there and watching it fall on the concrete, hearing it hit with a smack. I talked real sweet to it all along and it crying the whole time. I can't explain why, even now. Good God. It was some sick fix for an urge I never knew I had, but as soon as I tasted it, it was impossible to stop. I was entranced. Captivated. What evil was this? And how was it in me? Finally I took it up in my hands, its small broken body, still alive and whimpering a little, and I took it to the haystack and put it back where I found it with some absurd idea that the mother would know what to do, like I could undo what I had done.

The other two searched out his face in the darkness and both swore rare oaths barely audible. Heber's eyes caught some faraway light and he looked back at them. He said being from the shared lineage of humankind meant each of them had it in him to do the same, that a man needed only to look deep enough to find those impulses.

—I should not be absolved from the act, he said. But neither should you be quick to feign astonishment until you've reckoned with the same inside yourself.

The eyes of the other two were large and dark in the night.

—I shouldn't have told it, said Heber. You should never tell something like that. I know you fools didn't tell your worst thing.

Jack dreamt of many things, some of them terrible, all of them replete with emotions heightened like nothing known in waking life. In one dream he stood in the frosty river grass, the sunlight sparkling in the frost crystals, prismatic color winking across the landscape. His breath clouded the air more than was possible, the sunlight too deep and rich for this earth. He felt peace as he looked at the river. In another predawn hallucination he dreamt of this Almighty God he had never rid himself of, the testimony of whom he had never fully dismantled but which had stayed with him in subtle and constant torment like a pebble in his boot or like a cyst that forms around a sliver. He was afraid, as all men in holy writ are when they encounter angels or gods. Everything was infused with the light, but there was a darkness brooding at the center of the light like a spot on the sun and as unviewable, as abstruse. The dream faded, but the memory of how the light lifted him remained, and the memory of the darkness within, and the impression that the darkness was something—knowledge? indifference? compassion? capacity?—something of such profundity that it had made his bowels tremble to near it. This was God's darkness. When he woke, he felt a great loss at reacquainting with reality and found his tongue inadequate for description. He felt a brooding warmth for several minutes afterward, and he remembered the pure desire to go forward in the dream, one desire out of the many he had ever felt, and one only.

The leavings of this dream stained the days that came after, its mood staying with him and rendering his manner deferential and contrite. He understood the girl possessed a great void and he knew that he could not comprehend the significance and depth of her irreducible existence, nor his own, nor what they might mean intertwined. She was a singularity, a necessary being made of strange lovely flesh, tremulous flesh of dust and earth that he had touched and tasted, that housed a tremendous spirit and energy. Her flesh possessed the proper dimensions and the correct proportions in good form enough to drive a mortal man mad beyond his ability to reckon with and restrain what was in him. To account for her individual existence in the spangled universe was something akin to loving her, but it fell short of plumbing her emotionally, of delving into her physically. He could bring her milk. He could walk with her. He could help her take dung from the coop. And though he could not have her, these delegate elements seemed deeply important, as if they were extraordinary, unrepeatable, or coupled with weighty discourse. How often he remembered the way she fastened him with the ever-changing light of her eyes, those pellucid puddles of sun at times, at others those dark stars.

16

H E WORKED, THE ONLY TRUE SALVATION HE'D EVER known. He fed his grief with wrath and labor. Work was a balm, work was an opiate, and he fabricated tasks out of nothing to keep himself lost within the only boundaries he felt comfortable. He worked until his hardened hands ached and curled into themselves stiffly, growing sheets of new callus. His skin took the warming sun until it was hard brown. He pushed the tractors forward, raking the earth behind him or flipping fibrous dung to the ground. He gathered cows to the barn each morning in the darkness, his hands gentle and firm and experienced, hands that touched and guided as second nature, that pulled on the wet legs of calves as they squeezed from the laboring wombs of their mothers, and when he split a knuckle on the engine of a tractor or tore flesh stretching barbwire he regarded the quick bright blood as he would the first drop of rain. Unknown to anyone but the buyers he troubled the bulls, separating and selling to the beef market, working the herd down to lines of young muscle and hostility. He threw haybales against the concrete wall of the manger like things killed and dragged two at a time when unhurried, worked from predawn to post dusk steadily, calmly, and deftly, and once when a cow fell into the manure pit and with her thrashings began to liquefy the semi-solid mass around her until she sank her great self and only her nose, mouth, and tongue could be seen pulling in what would be her last breaths of air, he threw down a piece of old sheetwood and leapt onto it and stuck his arm shoulder deep in shit to hook a chain around her neck so that she could be lifted out with the bucket of the tractor. He worked that his body did not heal at night, woke before the sun only to find that he had not rested from the day prior. He worked ungovernable to the stoic awe of Blair and to the unease of Elmer, who had never seen such demonstration.

He was glad she'd left town with her mother, but it rendered him crippled, the only relief being something he couldn't get with her gone. Seth went back to work for his father and evenings they turned to what bulls were left. Seth rode them like an addict and Jack kept him safe. They did it alone, as they were at first. They leaned on the fence railing one evening after work and watched the animals. Seth carried a pouch of Redman and Jack took a leafy mess of it in his fingers and stuffed it into his mouth. He worked it with his jaw into a ball and it bulged his cheek and burned his gums and leaked its rank juice into his mouth until his tongue gathered the juice and sent it out in a long silent stream. They chewed the tobacco and spat on the ground. Seth threw glances toward his house once in a while, as though he expected something to come from there.

—Well let's get it over with, said Jack. He's right there in the pen, and he has killed a man.

—You want me to ride him now?

Jack stared at him.

—Wild bastard, though rusty, said Seth. Probly.

—You ready?

—Be damned, I am.

The two worked the small herd until they had the bull in the chute and Seth put his gear on and readied himself on the platform.

—Hell, I'm getting good at this, he said, shaking himself loose. I feel good on these bulls. I ain't as scared as I once was. I still have a healthy respect, you understand. But it ain't no longer a fear.

—And I admire you for that. I am still scared of um. Specially this one.

—Member that time Woolums rode? said Seth. He broke out laughing as he pulled the leather glove on his left hand. Giddyup, he said. Let's get this rope on.

When the rope was around he lowered himself down. He looked comfortable on the bull's back, like a mechanic reaching into the guts of a car or like a feller with his hand on the saw. Jack felt sure this needed to be done. He'd seen a man wrap the wet scrotum of a bull around the gear shifter of his truck until it dried there stiffly and tightened and seemed born of the truck itself. He held the pull rope and waited.

—Say when, McQuarters.

Seth pushed his hat down tighter and raised his right hand above his head.

—When, he said.

The white bull bucked well for its age, all four hooves leaving the ground in a series of leaping twists and kicks and its descending weight shaking the earth. Seth couldn't find a rhythm. The bull bucked violently and scooped and threw the air with its head as though shoveling dirt from a grave. It broke pace and kicked its hind legs up into the air that its great back was vertical, and Seth was thrown forward. His free hand came down to break his fall against the bull's massive head as it rose, and he collapsed onto it. The bull tossed him three times his height, his limp body turning like a thing made of straw before hitting the dirt heavily. Then the bull was on him. Jack had no time to anticipate the aggression and so had no time to fear. He rushed in over Seth and waved and slapped at the bull's face. The bull tossed Seth forward through the dirt with quick head thrusts, rolling him like the beetle rolls dung.

Jack yelled, gripping a huge, grainy horn before it was torn from his hand, and the bull swung its massive head and he was thrown backward to the dirt. He went in again and the bull turned on him. Before he could reach the fence at a sprint and vault onto it he felt himself picked up as gentle as a baby in its mother's arms and thrown upward and forward, well over the fence, the world turned upside down as he rotated backward. He completed a somersault and landed upright but his legs buckled and he fell onto his knees and hands. The bull trotted around the pen, its tantrum over, its muzzle dripping and its eye holding a gleam of aggression. Jack went in and shook Seth and called his name.

—Haystack, muttered Seth. He's in the haystack.

He curled up on the ground with his eyes closed. He opened his eyes and scowled and raised himself on an elbow and looked around.

—Where is he?

—You all right?

—What'd I do, get knocked out?

—He threw you onto his head.

—Yeah, I remember that.

Jack helped him get to his feet and Seth looked around for his hat.

—He was on me, wasn't he.

—He was on you, said Jack, his voice surging with excitement. We nearly got killed. He was rolling you with his horns and I got in front of him and then he turned on me and chased me and threw me clear over the fence. I somersaulted backward and almost landed on my feet. I tell you, he threw me. A younger bull wouldn't of let up. Would of killed us both. Lucky you didn't get ran through with a horn, the way he was going. I was sure you had.

—Wished I could of seen that, said Seth. Hold on, I'm dizzy.

—Look, said Jack, stepping toward the fence. I was about to here and he caught me. Threw me clear over the fence. What's that, twenty feet?

—I've seen it done. Sometimes you get lucky. Let's get that strap off, I guess. I guess I'm done for the night.

Jack herded the bull into the chute, took the strap off, and turned the bull in with the others. He heard Seth laughing from the middle of the pen, his hat in his hands, trying to restore its form. Then they were both laughing and walking toward each other. When they met they grasped hands in a shake and threw their arms around each other's shoulders and laughed and swore. They cursed the bull and praised the bull.

—You got a bump, said Jack. Holy hell, do you got a bump.

Seth's hand went to the spot on his forehead.

—Must of knocked it good. Headbutted the sumbitch. Thought I was a dead man.

—Thought you were too.

—I think I can remember it. In my subconscious I felt the sumbitch's horns on me and kept expecting um to go in me.

Seth laughed and the knot on his forehead grew larger, his own horn about to sprout.

—Wished somebody'd been here to see the whole thing, he said. His fingers moved to the spot tenderly and felt it as they would a fragile pheasant's egg.

—Does it hurt? said Jack.

—Yes it does, said Seth. It does.

—It's getting bigger.

—I'll take it, said Seth. Headbutted the sumbitch. Cheated death.

They made their way over to pick up the bull rope and bell.

—Ruined my hat though, said Seth.

Jack felt so good he told Seth they needed to go into town. They cleaned up and rode in to a pizza parlor, grinning for no reason and laughing without provocation. Seth set his crushed hat near him in the wooden booth and beamed at the waitress every time her eyes went to the lump on his forehead.

—Just tell her what did it, said Jack.

The good feeling stayed with him that night and part of the next morning before it wore off to the darkness that had beset him before. There was no more solace to be had. The black dreams the mind can construct, the torment of the unfettered imagination. The mad lust-crazed fool had done something that could not be undone and Jack imagined her changed, as if the inviolability and virtue she carried had been her power, the core of her essence.

Nights when his blood was hot and hammering through his body he felt the need to walk the river. He followed its curves for miles. More than once he found himself below the barn, and once in his midnight delirium he stumbled upon the temple that was the duckblind. He built a fire and sat within its strange narrow confines, away from the heavens and the distant eternity that were all around him. He thought of that night when he had brought her there. He wished he had carried gasoline with him so that he could burn the thing to the ground and see it blaze in the night and consider its orange reflection in the river. He tried for half an hour to light its foundation but the wood was too wet. It would not burn.

One evening he and Seth sat on the curb in front of the co-op and watched night descend on the countryside. Seth said, How is she?

—God only knows.

—You talk to her lately?

—I ain't yet.

—You ain't talked to her at all?

Jack shrugged.

— A little.

—I know you ain't talked to her yet.

—All right. I ain't then.

—I won't say what I want to say.

—Say it.

—I won't, I said.

Jack stared at the pebbles on the asphalt.

—You need to get back on that, said Seth. You need to be a man here.

—Do you know what the hell you're even talking about? said Jack.

—Does it got to change things like that?

—It ain't whether it's got to change things or not, it's what is. Seth spat thoughtfully onto the pavement.

—It don't got to change things at all.

Jack said nothing.

—Does it?

—It ain't whether it's got to, said Jack. It's what is.

—So what is it?

—I'm telling you, McQuarters, I don't know. I don't even know where she is.

—Is she coming back?

Jack looked at him.

—If you were her would you come back?

A letter came a week later postmarked from Rock Springs, Wyoming. In the upper left corner for a return address were only the chickenscratched letters H. E. R. He carried it with him half a day of work before walking to the far side of the west hayshed and dropping down against a support, exhausted from his labor and from broken sleep. He opened it with his little finger and unfolded it. Before reading, he looked over the field. His eyes lost focus and he sat that way awhile. Below was the unmarked grave of his dog and below that the river. The yellow paper shook a little as he read.

John

I will never know if your eyes see this letter. It may be that it was written for me, never to be read by anyone else. Regardless, I consider its purpose fulfilled in writing it. And yet it seems there are some events that have no use for explanations. It is true that in my life I have harvested phantom crops and lunged at shadows, but in my burning and vile plunder of the girl I have delivered and have been delivered.

You must have known that she could not belong to you alone. It is part of the Great Design. You understand the turbulence that stirs beneath, the unseen things that trouble the surface of this water, the hot hell that burns within, for this is the balance of humanity. I am the town. You are the town. You also understand the power that is the agency of man, the destruction he is capable of doing to himself. Give a man agency and watch him tear himself apart brick by brick. It is an astonishing thing. What kind of god gives a man this power? Yet this is God's power in its purest essence—a thing valued by God above all else. Why else play such a dangerous and serious game? Verily, a true thing. An absolute thing. Dear God above. I have entered realms I never knew existed and found some of them barren, some of them rife, and I will finish here, for there is no return that I can envision, nor will I retreat. My life, it must be said, has been complete. I have lacked nothing.

I've never ceased to wonder about my father. Among other things I've wondered why he took his life. It's not the lack of reasons that troubles me, but the abundance of them. I've lived a lifetime these thirty years. What do I have left? I have lived my life, and I have failed to understand God. I have gazed into the abyss too long. Perhaps the old man ushered himself through those doors the sooner in order to see what was beyond them, to have done with the mystery, to meet the Great Incognitum and see what it is, and to demand an explanation. But those on the other side might be just as confused as we are. God may be just as elusive there. I intend to search him out. I must find out if I exist.

I grow tired. My virtue was wearied till it tore. I know why ascetics move to the desert, I do. It is not only to escape the sensual (they may be the worst among us), and it is not to think, which leads men to doubt, but it is to fill their heads with the roar of emptiness in order to ward off the terrible questions that lead to true despair. This emptiness becomes their thought and they move forever on toward the manifestations of their imaginations. Do men wrestle their entire lives? Lord, how is it done. It always was a tremendous weight before me, and so shouldn't I have buckled at its feet? I threw myself against it to break it, and instead I was the one broken.

And yet you must hate me the more when I tell you that I love the girl. I love her deeply. I can't get her taste out of my mouth. I can't divest myself of what is innate within me, and here the physical and the spiritual have merged.

I love her and yet I have done what I have done.

I have done what I have done because I love her.

I love her because I have done what I have done.

Please do not simplify in order to produce an answer you can understand. That is cheating and will yield nothing of substance. Simplicity is for the ignorant and feeble minded. To say that this is merely evidence of the Great Impossibility is to undermine its full accomplishment. Some will tell us to have faith and to let it lead us to hope and good works, but what is faith? Is it the ability to ignore reason and sense? Is it some enabling power selectively dispensed? If it is power then we have not been given sufficient with which to perform the task. I hope. I do hope. It is all I have. I would never pretend that the pain I feel is significant, nor my plight pitiable, but there is one step

I can take for my own reparation, and I expect it to be at once bitter and delicious. Do you believe me when I say that everything I did was for you? I am undone. God be with you till we meet again, my dear, dear friend.

Yours,
Heber Edgar Rafuse
John 5:19
Ether 12:4

Jack read it again. A third time. He understood the words and they were now a part of him. He tore the letter slowly to pieces and watched the wind play with them behind the hayshed.

He felt the turn of the season wrenching inside him. Nature changed too fast to take notice of it all. Trees bare one day were suddenly green with buds the next, and he had not seen the buds creep out. He breathed in the change in the atmosphere and felt a new pressure to make something happen, that his life should be his to manipulate, to bend, to fashion and create, and that it had always been this way. This is where those lazy years had carried him. A man's will, if it seeks the course of least resistance, will as water always lead him downward, until it settles him in puddle or ocean. He wondered if he would take the money he had saved and travel to the Karakoram. Or to deserts vaster and crueler than his own. He thought he did not want to see another winter at the Selvedge Dairy. Black smears encroached his vision of the world like the edges in old film. The sun produced warmth and color, but rather than inspiring him as it had every spring of his life its heft was oppressive and steadfast in the face of the winds and moving storms and he only looked forward again to autumn.

He had worked all day and then driven the desert and was late coming back. When he got to the basement apartment Seth was sitting at the kitchen table with a backpack and duffel bag beside him.

Seth shook his head.

—I got to leave, old buddy. It's time to go. If you want to come with me then come. There's nothing here for you no more.

—It ain't that easy.

—I got to go. I don't know when the bus leaves. Let's talk about it on the way.

Seth picked up his bags and walked out the door. Jack followed him outside into the cold April night. When they were in the truck driving away Seth said, Should be in Amarillo in two days. He smiled. Amarillo by *two* mornings.

—You got money?

—Some. Things've turned sour around here.

—And now you're leaving.

—Come with me.

Jack ignored him and in a few minutes they began to talk of recent times like they were old times.

—Member old Woolums? said Seth. He sure was a good kid. He sure was a dumbshit.

He looked over and they both started laughing, and they laughed harder. They broke down to titters and then started over again. Seth wiped a tear away.

—And those bulls were great, he said. I feel like we had some real good times. We had some great times growing up here.

—We did, said Jack.

They rolled through the night and into Willow Valley and pulled up to the empty bus station. They had stopped talking when they reached the city limits and now Seth stared straight ahead through the windshield across the parking lot to a closed grocery store. His eyes stirred with the same anticipation as the time he rode the first bull, and Jack wondered if life unfolded that way for some people.

—It's getting warmer ain't it? said Seth.

—May's coming, and that's a good month.

—What'll happen to the bulls?

—Don't know. I guess Elmer'll probly sell um when he gets the farm. He won't want to bother with that again. And there's no reason to keep um otherwise.

—They won't give um to you?

—What would I do with um?

—Well shoot. If you could get those bulls, and you'd let me buy in with you, we could put um in the circuit again.

—Nah.

—You don't think?

—That's a pipe dream. We might as well be honest. Even what's left in that pen has sat too long. They're meat in the grocery store, they just don't know it. It's the one senseless extravagance I can't explain on the farm, but I'm glad it's there. It's not like those two frugal bastards to keep animals for no reason. It's like they've forgotten about um, or that I'm feeding um every week.

—We could buy up more. You don't think we could put um back in the circuit? Get some new mean ones in there and build a good herd? It'd be a good hobby, no?

—It'd take a lot of work. And money. I wouldn't even know where to start.

Seth fell silent, then said, Ah forget it. I got to get out of here. I feel it calling me.

—I know the feeling. I just never know where the call is coming from. But who knows about them bulls.

—Forget it.

—Well, maybe. Maybe we could do it. We could do something with those bulls. Just got to figger it out.

—You been a great friend, said Seth. A damn great friend. I'm going to miss the hell out of yuh.

—Come back and visit.

Seth opened the door and grabbed his backpack.

—I love yuh, brother, he said.

Jack watched him walk into the waiting station. The ticket windows were all closed. He honked and waved him back.

—Why don't you set in the truck awhile, he said. This place won't be open for a bit.

Seth climbed in the warm truck and they dozed to the rumble of the engine and the push of the heater until Jack had to get back to the barn for milking.

Under a blue sky he rattled down a driveway toward a lone trailer on the edge of the desert. He parked near the big mudding tires of a tall pickup truck and saw the reflection of its beat up ancestor in the rims. There were old straw bales left around the base of the singlewide for insulation against the winter past and would probably remain for the winter that would come. A satellite dish had been tacked on the corner of the roof. A Rottweiler mix chained to a gnawed doghouse was barking and when Jack got out and began to make his way toward the trailer its barking intensified. It reached the end of the chain and strained against it. He made a wide arc and it snarled and barked, pulling the doghouse with it. He swore at it harshly and backpedaled toward his truck. He looked for a good rock near the driveway but found only gravel.

—Balls, he called. Hey, Balls.

The front door opened and Balls Murphy stood in the doorway in a flannel shirt and long-john underwear with a mug in his hand. His shock of stiff red hair was matted and misshapen and his loose socks flopped like tongues over the threshold to his home.

—William the Bastard! he yelled.

The dog turned and lifted its ears.

—Get back, come on. How many times do I got to tell you not to drag that house? Come on, get back. Hey, Selvedge, you mind dragging that house back where it was? I don't have my boots on.

Jack stepped toward the dog and it came at him, snapping the chain taut and jerking the heavy doghouse a full foot. He jumped back and looked at Balls.

—Hold on a minute, said Balls.

He returned wearing untied tall-heeled roping boots on his feet. His spindly legs looked like knobby twigs as he wrestled with the doghouse until it sat against the straw bales again. Jack walked up the steps and let himself in the door and Balls came in behind him breathing heavily.

—Crazy sumbitch. He's getting too big now. Used to not be able to drag that house anywhere. Now if he gets a mind to he could go clean up to Idaho. Caught him halfway through the field the other day when a herd of deer came through.

—Good guard dog, though.

—Good guard dog. He tore Claude's boot clean off his foot the other day and wouldn't give it back. I told him not to mess with him but he thought he could. Lucky he didn't lose his foot with it.

Balls signaled Jack to sit down on a battered yellow love seat covered in anonymous filth and sown with dog hair, and Balls himself fell into a broken recliner. He looked at Jack across the narrow room.

—Well, he said. Let me put some pants on and we can go.

They climbed into the high cab of Balls' truck and as they moved down the driveway the road became smoother.

—This is my runway, said Balls. Long as I can take off before it ends back there by the house I get out all right.

The scent of an air freshener filled the cab. It was a photograph dangling from the mirror of a beautiful woman, topless in a cowboy hat, tanned and oiled breasts, one gaudy cowboy boot propped on a saddle and her smooth thigh bared.

A large Quonset shed stood ahead of them. Balls parked to one side and got out and unlocked the entry door and Jack was drawn to an old truck bed camper sitting next to the shed.

—You still use this? he said.

—Haven't in a while, said Balls. But most everything works, last time I checked. I'll sell it to you for a hunnerd bucks.

—I'll give you fifty.

—Done, said Balls.

Jack reached in his wallet and found two twenties and some ones.

—How does forty-three sound?

—Give it here, said Balls, and took the money. Now get your ugly camper off my property.

He flipped a few switches inside and there was a buzzing overhead but no light. He stood close and breathed loudly and the smell of old cigarettes and coffee came from him, mingled with the faint mask of Stetson cologne.

—Take a minute to warm them lights up, he said.

He walked toward the bay door and a vertical shaft of white light pierced the darkness. It shone straight through to the red airplane in the middle of the floor. The shed was a clean open place, an exact opposite of the trailer house, and their footsteps echoed as they walked.

—Here she is, he said, setting his hand on the lower wing of the plane. She's a Boeing something or other, used in World War II. Now she's used here in the Scrag to dust fields.

It sat like a marvelous toy. It had two seats, one behind the other, and no windshield.

—Needs a paint job, he said. And probly a few new parts, but she flies all right. I think I'd feel good about both sides for the price I told you. You want to go up?

—No.

—You want to sit in the seats, feel her out?

Jack climbed in the tight cockpit and studied the instrument panel. Balls reached into the cockpit behind him and pulled out a long scarf.

—Maria gave me this, he said. She made it herself. I'll bet you didn't know she had a knitting talent.

—I didn't, said Jack.

—And that ain't all, said Balls. She's a smart girl. Saving up for school. I'll bet she can be almost anything she wants. She's got that kind of savvy and ambition. God knows she deserves better than me, and maybe she'll get it. But I love her.

Balls looked at Jack for a moment. He put his hand on the plane.

—Just a machine, he said. Not much differnt than a tractor. Just a engine that turns the propeller. The shapes of the wings do everything else.

He walked around the craft, eyeing it like he was the one considering purchase.

—I had to crash land this whore once already, he said. Out on Eli Warren's sheep ranch two summers ago. Missed the start of his old runway by about fifty feet.

—That must of been a great time for you, said Jack.

—No. No, it wasn't. I broke the left wheel clean off and bent the support bars. Well, if you don't want to go up, I got a brochure at the house I want you to see.

Jack began to climb out.

—Is it like the brochure you stuck under the seat of my truck, you sly son of a bitch?

—Oh you found it, did you? I thought I'd wasted it. Or that you were too busy with it to say anything.

—I didn't find it. Rebekah did.

—What'd you think of page number thirty? That's why I give it to yuh. That girl looks like her. That's prime, I tell yuh. Prime.

—I got to get back for work, so let's go.

—Can I get that magazine back? said Balls.

Balls had to hold the dog again so Jack could get past him. Inside he handed over the brochure, a full color spread of planes complete with specs. The pages had coffee rings on them and were soiled from food grease, planes Balls had looked at long but would never buy. They sat down at the kitchen table and Balls poured himself a cup of coffee. They talked about planes and crop dusting and money and when they were through Balls rolled up the brochure and handed it over.

—Good luck, buddy. Get in touch with me if you want to buy her. Otherwise I might just sell her to anybody. Or I might just keep her here. If I'm gone you know where it'll be to, and you can get me there.

Jack gripped his outstretched hand in a firm shake and they locked eyes. Balls' gaze was steady and intent, his pale blue eyes communicating nothing more than brotherhood and humanity, an acknowledgement that life was what it was and all a man could do was his best. Jack stepped to the door. As he looked down the steps he said, What about the dog?

—Is he looking at you?

—He's around the corner.

—Then run.

He harrowed the earth that afternoon, dragging dull teeth over hay stubble, until the tractor broke down. The muffler had worked free from its base inside the engine. It made a huge racket and he was forced to kill the throttle. He climbed down from his seat and looked inside the engine and then sat in the open sun against the rear tire, facing away from the lane and waiting for the metal to cool. The field sloped gently down below him, and beyond that lay more fields, a few houses, and eventually the riverbottoms. Upslope stood the tall pines that guarded Rebekah's house. He heard the crunching and popping of stubble and he tilted his hat up and leaned over to see Martha's car approaching across the field. She was alone. She rolled up to the tractor and parked.

—Caught you slacking on the job, she said as she climbed out.

But I won't tell your grandpa.

She smiled and it was Rebekah's smile aged.

—The tractor broke down, he said. You can tell him that if you want. Tell him I'm tired of wiring his damn muffler in forty different places.

She lowered herself next to him and they sat in silence for a while.

—When we left this town we had such great hopes for our family, the three of us, she said. That was back when my husband was wonderful and strong and Rebekah was young. Somewhere things went wrong.

—Why did you leave?

—It's hard to say. I felt it was more for Rebekah than anything.

—Why did you bring her back?

—We came back because we were trying to get away from trouble there.

He stared across the field to the barbwire fence he had built.

—It's difficult to talk about, she said.

She made several false starts before settling on something she could make known.

—Rebekah doesn't know I'm talking with you. She's afraid to call you. We went to see a doctor in Salt Lake and the news was better than I'd hoped. He was either gentle or he was…small. He used an animal tranquilizer on her that limited her resistance, and she says she doesn't remember much. She is uncommonly strong, Jack, but it would be good for her to see you. She's still trying to settle it all and it will take her a while to mend.

—How long've you been back?

—A few days.

—Have they found him yet?

—No.

—Am I the last option?

—Please.

—You're late in your opinion about me, he said.

They sat side by side against the wheel of the tractor and looked across the field. She reached for his hand. He allowed it and felt emotion well up in him like a bucket filling with water and his shoulders heaved once and he made a strange sound. Two fast tears ran down his cheeks and dropped into his lap and that was all. He turned his face away. After a while she let go his hand and got up without a word and left, and his hand was newly cold where it had been held.

17

THE HARD WINTER MADE FOR A MORE BEAUTIFUL spring and people emerged from their homes to feel the air and smell the earth. Farmers took wholly to their drying fields as if returning to lost lovers. It had been a kind spring. The snow melted and the ground dried and the rain stalled to allow for planting seed. Jack sat with Blair in the living room after work as rain patterned the gray window in rivulets down to the sill. The back door opened and the family of three appeared in the room like some peace contingent, the pale thin boy following so close to his mother Jack would have counted only two had he not known better.

—Well hullo, Eddie, said Blair loudly. What do yuh know?

The boy peeped out from behind his mother's legs and then hid again.

—Good to see you out, said Blair. How's he doing?

—Oh, he's getting better, said Carrie. Aren't you, Edward. It's been just too cold to play outside, hasn't it. She turned to Blair. It's been a blessing in disguise.

Elmer walked to the couch and fell onto it and Carrie and Edward Elmer followed. Carrie wore one of her knitted hats and it sat crooked on her head. Her sparse tawny hair came out in wisps beneath it. She carried a large paper sack with something heavy inside and set it on the carpet at her feet.

—Well, Dad, you got the planting in, she said. That's good.

—Yes, said Blair. Turned that fallow west field into hay. Too early yet for corn.

—And this rain is good, she said.

—The rain is good.

—It's a blessing in disguise.

—Yes, said Blair. Not even in disguise.

—How's that girl doing? said Carrie. Does anyone know? We saw her walking the lane just now. Well you just don't know what kind of effect something like that can have on a girl. I was watching a talk show the other day, and there were four women on—

—Three, said Elmer, patting Carrie's leg. It was only three of um.

—Well, three women were on who'd been taken advantage of and they talked about how they were putting their lives back together. They were saying it usually happens with someone you know, funny enough.

—It's a terrible thing, said Blair.

—It is, said Carrie, her tone thick with sympathy.

—Not funny at all, said Blair.

The boy sat between his parents. Once Jack caught his darting eyes the boy kept looking back, frightened by the attention, and each time Jack was waiting.

—Now what about that man, said Carrie. Ed Rafuse's boy. Do they know what's happened to him?

—I don't know what's happened to him, said Blair.

—No one seems to know, said Carrie. Weren't you friends with him, Jack? He's up and vanished about as far as anyone can tell.

—Maybe he's in a haystack somewhere, offered Elmer soberly. Has anyone checked haystacks?

—It's a terrible thing, said Blair.

—It's been a long time since something like this happened, said Carrie. That little Andersson girl kept in the basement half-starved, wasn't it? How long ago was that?

—Some years back, said Blair.

—About ten years back, if I remember, said Carrie. And that was some vagabond family. Not one of our own, grown and raised.

—Now Dad, said Elmer. How are you doing?

—I'm fine, I'm fine, said Blair. Jack here keeps me out a trouble, don't you Jack.

—If by keeping you out of trouble you mean applying your ass creams, then yes, said Jack.

Carrie cleared her throat and blushed.

—Jack's a good boy, she said.

Blair said, Mother Nature with her seasons and natural destruction brings renewal and continuation. I'll see her again.

No one responded. The boy had crept away from the couch and was now fingering a glass dove where it sat on top of the old wooden stereo system.

Blair said, Well hullo, Eddie. What do yuh know?

The boy shriveled under the combined gaze of the four of them and sidled back to the couch.

—Tell him you're doing good, Edward, said Carrie. Tell him you're excited to play outside again. Maybe you and Grandpa can go on a ride to the mountains soon. What do you think?

The boy turned his face and buried it in a grease-shined couch pillow.

—Don't want to talk, Eddie? said Elmer. That's okay.

—Well, said Carrie. I've been working on some things for you to hang on your walls here. I know you have some things already that dear Addie made with her very own hands, but you can never have too much of this kind of thing in the home.

She pulled a stack of frames from the paper sack at her feet and displayed one at a time. It was all cross-stitched scripture and homespun sayings of goodness. Jack read them as she held each one, her face beaming overtop.

A Family that Prays Together Stays Together, read one. *Charity Never Faileth*, read another. *Home is Where the Heart is. Blessed Are the Meek. Faith, Hope, and Charity. Live, Laugh, Love.*

—Jesus wept, muttered Jack.

She went through them all again, talking about how she made each one by hand and at which church event she had learned to do such and such and the times when she and Adelaide, before her illness kept her from it, had spun the craft together. She went on and her soporific voice was mellow and soothing in the low-lit room. Jack felt drowsy and comfortable while the rain fell outside. Meanwhile the boy sat pallid and silent at his mother's side, his bruised lids sliding down over his eyes from time to time and then pulling back up, fighting sleep or lingering sickness, it was hard to say.

Jack got up to leave and no one seemed to notice. He climbed the stairs and lay in his bed thinking about Heber. His thoughts turned to Rebekah as they did most of the time anymore. Disregarding the recent blackness that took him when alone in his room he had always been able to sleep anytime he wanted, as though it followed behind him like a shy and admiring friend, always waiting for him to notice it. When he did remember dreams many of them contained water and most of those were of clear fast-moving rivers or wide clean lakes. His dreams were often vivid, if incomplete and bizarre, and filled with strange moods and passions. As he edged toward sleep he began to think of the river below the house. His thoughts segued to dream, and the world became dim as it is in dreams. He seemed to be watching from above, following the checked flannel jacket of Heber Rafuse as the recreant walked along the riverbank. Heber turned his face up to him often as if he could see him. He stopped and spoke, but his words were gib-berish, garbled like language under water. Now Jack became the river walker and he stopped where a stark white dead tree, grown sideways from the eroding bank, reached into the water. He saw an animal at its edge that he didn't recognize, growling and muttering anxiously, digging in the sand. Then he knew it was a wolverine, which didn't exist in that region. He growled at it and the animal turned and attacked him. He called for a knife—the long serrated folding knife he kept in the glovebox of his truck—and flicking it open with his wrist he severed the head of the animal in a sawing motion, and it felt good to kill it, to come off superior. He woke and was surprised to see it was nearly four. He walked downstairs and dressed and sat at the kitchen table. He waited for Blair to appear and thought about the dream and savored the bare emotions as if with his tongue at a phantom taste.

After milking the morning light blazed up their table as they ate. Blair filled himself with an air of business and said, Elmer's biggest question is whether he needs to start looking for hired help, or whether you're going to stick around.

—It ain't the best option I got, said Jack.

—What's another?

—Is that how you see it?

Blair looked at him.

—You know, said Jack, I've been underpaid my entire life. I'm twenty-one years old and getting paid like I'm twelve.

—You got room and board. Don't forget that.

—I'm getting paid like I'm twelve and I'm twenty-one years old. You said things in the past that led me to believe this'd turn out different.

—Things change, said Blair. A man can't always make good on his word. I always stopped short from giving you my word for that reason.

—You were deceitful. You manipulated me.

—Now wait just a minute—

—If my father was still alive things might be different, but he's not. I thought I had a greater stake in this farm than what you've given me, and this situation has reached its breaking point.

—You got land. And we offered you a salary.

—You know what land you gave me.

—That mountain's a sizable piece.

—I was misled.

—You know how things work on a farm. This ain't no certain profession. We can't sugarcoat it for you.

—I want the titles to that land drawn up.

—And you'll get um.

—I don't understand why it went down this way.

—God's disappointed, said Blair. Why should you be any different?

He looked from Jack to the table and back to Jack.

—I don't know what's going to come of it, he said.

—Is the farm going to fail?

—I hope not. It's in the hands of the Lord now. Or is it the hands of the bank.

—How'd this happen?

—Profit slowed and bills grew. I've come close more times than I can count over the years.

Blair looked at him soberly and leaned forward, his face and posture so sincere it seemed he was about to take Jack into some deep confidence.

—And besides, he said. It's Carrie. He straightened back up and shook his head slowly. Damn it, she threatened to leave him if the farm don't fall their way. What am I supposed to do? If she leaves him his days are numbered and you know it. Have some compassion.

Jack studied him. He watched the old eyes, pale and watery.

—Is this true?

—God, the woman's shrewd!

—She's trying to edge in like that?

Blair nodded, his eyes wide and full of feigned shock and disbelief.

—I don't even know if I believe you, said Jack. You were given apt initials old man, you know that?

—Oh hell, said Blair. Why don't you just get up and leave then.

Jack rose.

—You don't understand the position I'm in, said Blair.

—I understand mine. It's getting clearer all the while. Even if the bank comes through you might live just long enough to see it disappear, sold off, broken down and deserted like all the rest. What would you of done if my dad was still alive?

Blair swung his head around.

—Your daddy left this farm, he said. He broke with us and left us to it, and we've carried on since. He lost his inheritance the day he walked away.

—But I ain't him.

—This thing took on momentum. I couldn't change its direction just cause you fell into the mix. I should of managed the place better, not been content with its holdings, been more aggressive in buying up land when other farms failed. I didn't do it cause I didn't want to be that man. But it's a game of survival, not a game of manners. I played it the wrong way.

He fell quiet and looked out the window. Then he turned back to the table and picked up the last piece of burnt toast from the plate and took a bite.

—You say you got options, do you?

—Yes. I do.

—The dear angel, muttered Blair. Have you been able to get past the difficulties?

Jack left him there where he concentrated on buttering the toast with the same focus he used when cleaning his fingernails with the stoneworn blade of his pocketknife.

That evening between fast-moving rainstorms, when the clouds moved like great barges above him in the fresh torn sky and breathing was like some rare pleasure, he pulled a sprayer through the hayfield beneath her house. He did not need to be there, the field did not need spraying, but he had come anyway and rode along with the tractor in high gear and the solution sloshing in the tank behind him. On every other pass he watched the vernal mountains, their high slopes clean and magnified in this air and studded with huge stone. He saw her standing on his side of the trees across the field and made his way back up the long slope toward her. When he neared and killed the throttle the silence screamed in his ears and his hands tingled from the vibrations of the steering wheel. He climbed from his seat and down the steps and walked toward her at the edge of the field. She diverted her eyes and bit and released her lower lip. Then she did look at him. She folded an arm over her stomach in a certain way and touched her neck with her other hand.

—No, he said.

The sun caught in her eyes and lightened their dark color like a wet stone drying. His hand went to his brow.

—Oh, Lord, he said.

His eyesight dimmed with blood.

—Oh, Lord.

Her eyes were two wet wounds that bled pain. She wept. Large tears fell quickly, skipped off her cheeks and disappeared. He took her hands and pulled her in and she clutched at him. He kissed her head and stroked her hair, and her shuddering body shook him also.

He went behind the west hayshed in the morning after chores and sat on the same bale of hay. The land was weatherscrubbed and raw. He looked over the field and up to the mountains. When he was done he walked back around the hayshed and stopped to watch a huge flock of sparrows move in and around the barnyard. Hundreds of them. They swept the air clean with small wings and fed on fallen seed, landed on cow stalls, haysheds, power poles and lines. The flock lifted. It expanded and contracted, turned and flashed. They moved in a rippling wave and in a multitude such as a plague, as if a rubber string connected each to each, one fluid movement from the many. They threshed the air and made a great collective rush. The edge of the flock reached him, the whole community trying to alight on the ground, and he was surrounded by the furious beating of their wings. The air moved in small turbulence and he felt weightless and giddy as though he would be picked up and carried away. They did not alight but rose from around him and the whole host moved away across the field where it weighted the telephone wires the entire length of the lane.

He filled the tin pitcher with milk and took it to her. When she opened the door there was a fresh beauty on her face from the early hour. She put the milk away and they walked out to the little bench near the lane where the sunlight was rich and warm.

—If the doctors hadn't confirmed it I might question what exactly happened, she said. Or if I didn't have this new proof I might be able to deny it.

—You would know.

—Would I?

—Yes. You would know.

—I don't know that I would.

—You would, he said. What are you going to do?

—I don't know.

—It's a hell of a fix, he said. I'm very sorry.

—But you don't dream about it, she said.

—My dreams are a whole reality apart from this world.

—It has changed things.

—How can you not know what you're going to do? he said. When she didn't answer he said, It's a hell of a fix.

He took her hand and studied it in his lap. Clean nails. Delicate fingers.

He left her to work in the fields. Everything they did in the spring was to cause the fields to grow. They worked long hours to place seeds in the womb of the earth with the force of the disc and to get them to swell and break through the crust of soil. Water share meetings were held in a small shed near the town proper for the inevitable time when the moisture from winter and spring would dry up and the ditches would flow with irrigation water and it would be on again with the midnight water changes and the ceaseless worrying about the dams and ditches. Once in the evening he picked her up in his truck and drove into farther mountains on slanting, rut-riven logging roads to high basins still white and they watched the snow pull back from the meadows and herds of deer come to feed at dusk. Their time together was underlain with tragedy. There were moments when he was covered with a dark fear and the urge to see her gripped him like a revelation. He needed to prove she was there, down the lane, to see her face and absorb her spirit like the heat of the sun, to feel her warm body alive under his hand, and no matter how hard he broke those old tractors across the potholes and washboards of the lane, dragging the clattering implements behind him, or how he made the gravel roar beneath his truck, billowing huge dust in his wake, he could not get there fast enough.

She spent evenings reading to a half-blind fellow three blocks from Heber's house who had retired from teaching at the university, the only professor emeritus or otherwise in town. She read him the newspaper and Louis L'amour. He gave her twenty dollars when they were through each time and each time she left the money on his kitchen table for his wife to find. Her breasts grew ample and full. The weather turned warm for good and even without the visible swelling of her tummy she often placed a curious hand there. Her thighs filled farther into their curvature and her neck softened.

She told him one afternoon that she would carry it and give it up when it was born. At first he refused to believe her, and then she made him believe. But he swathed and baled and hauled hay and irrigated the crops with channeled water. He'd heard people say that man's travail is God's opportunity, but such a notion seemed hard to believe in those moments most relevant to the afflicted. Nevertheless he began to pray again on his knees on the thin carpet beside his bed, each prayer centered on his wish for some undoing.

18

H
E SAT WITH HER ON THE TAILGATE OF HIS TRUCK
in front of her house on the longest evening of the
year, the molten sun just above the plain. He drew her
to him and felt the old darkness like an eclipse of the
bald sun. While her body next to him was real and he could kiss her
and evoke sounds and words from her mouth that blessed his ears,
his pleasure was leavened with apprehension. This girl next to him
did not ward it off as she should have.

—It's showing, she said.

He looked down and shook his head. She took his hand and
put it there and he told her he couldn't feel anything. She lifted her
shirt and pressed his hand against her flesh. She pushed downward
until his hand was where she wanted it and his little finger lay along
the waistline of her jeans. Her belly was soft and warm.

—Do you feel that? she said.

Her hand grew moist on top of his. Then he did feel it, a swell,
hard beneath the softness, something growing and something a
part of her, and he jerked his hand away in surprise. She turned
away. She sniffed and the light pat of a teardrop hit the metal tailgate between her legs. He held her and kissed her flushed lips and
face and her hands and her head and murmured into her ear until

she stopped, and they looked west to where the sun had dropped and spread above the flat earth like a reddened yolk in a pan.

—My mom bought a bunch of seeds and things, she said. For the greenhouse. She wants me to pick up where Granddad left off. Do you want to see it?

—Not now, he said. Let's stay here.

—You don't have to have a part in this, she said.

—What do you mean? he said.

—I'm not asking for anything, she said.

He watched the low western sky and said nothing, and the small destroyer grew in her belly like an event foretold. When they sat together this way it was the three of them, and to him the presence of the third was greater than the presence of the other two combined. For how could he crawl up between her full legs before the looming thing like an insurmountable hill? How could he hold her without the press of its ill-boding wedge between them? It was the same body he would move toward, the same skin he would savor, but altered and growing with dark tumor. Had the thing been taken quickly it might have become as if it had never been. But now her body would be changed for its growth and passage and she would spread her legs and its domed head would open her womb. When he thought forward to some possible recompense afterward his mind seized up and he could not go there.

The season moved on. She colored lovely midsummer and word spread that she would carry the child. Her face took on new tones of vitality. She was a saint in the community. Such a scandal joined the ranks of the most memorable and such nobility had scarcely been heard of. When they arrived at the celebration on the twenty-fourth of July he was gently elbowed away from her until he stood outside a circle of backs. Women wanted to feel her swelling stomach, where her companion grew, and hard simple men tried to gather the innocence to touch her arm or her shoulder. She found him and held his eyes for a moment, a natural blush on her face, her thick dark hair falling about her shoulders. Some approached him and said that it was a fine thing he was doing, and he wanted to ask them what they thought he was doing.

He drove to the co-op one morning and passed a black BMW with tinted windows and wide tires, sleek and handsome. It sat at the curb of the park. He thought back to when he had seen such a car parked anywhere in Juniper Scrag and could not think of a time. When he returned with the bed full of rolled barley it was gone. He did not want to go back to the farm yet, so he swung around and parked in front of Wriglesworth's in the square and rolled down his window. The vacant square was haunted even in plain daylight. It murmured louder when no one passed through, its ghosts more agitated under the oppression of the sun than at night when the square lay in darkness. All windows opaque with dust or paint, many panes gone to cardboard or boarded up altogether. Wriglesworth's had its windows still, no deviant youth left to stone them out. A breeze came through and rolled small briar weeds ahead of it and pushed aluminum cans in a hollow rattle. The trees soughed and subdued him. When the breeze died the murmuring of the square grew louder until he was driven out, back to his day of work.

The black car was parked in the driveway of Rebekah's house. He had only a few minutes to consider what this meant and to feel sick in his stomach, because when he pulled into the barnyard Rebekah stepped out of the double barn doors. Her eyes were red and swollen. He leaned over and threw the door open for her and she climbed in.

They drove down the lane. This wasn't fear, but in earlier days he had confused it with fear, so similar was its composition. He felt that old feeling like when he used to fight commonly, that lead in his stomach born from the swirling surge of adrenaline before the first hit. The black car was no longer in the driveway. Rebekah went inside and returned a few minutes later. She asked if he would take her somewhere so he unloaded the feed at the farmhouse and drove back to the park and they got out and walked to the rusting merry-go-round. She sat down and he took hold of one of the bars and pushed it, causing the ancient toy to spin on its axis with a loud groan. Rebekah moved farther away, reached the apogee of the circle, and then came back to him. The toy's groaning grew quieter with each revolution until it was barely a thin cry. He gripped the bars with both hands and pushed again and she began to talk, her words clear and coherent when she was near but depleting as her back turned to him. He spun her around slowly and she talked about her father. The swings where he had seen her for the first time stood behind them. The park sat unused, the grass mowed, the flag-pole ready, but no children to use the place built for them because there were no children. He tried to count them, starting with his cousin, Edward Elmer, and got to five before he was stymied. There was a girl here going round in a circle, not unlike a child. She had a child in her belly.

What followed seemed unreal, disjointed, defiant toward the order of things in the world. The black car rolled into view from the direction of the square and parked next to Jack's truck. When her father stepped out he was bigger than Jack remembered. Nor did he look soft from city life. He wore khaki slacks and a light blue dress shirt untucked and the sleeves rolled up over large, hairy forearms. He was tall, tanned, and handsome. He walked the forty yards between them and stood at a short distance.

—Hi Jack, he said. That yours? He lifted his chin toward Rebekah where she sat with her round stomach in her lap. Nobody will tell me a thing about it, but it seems somebody's knocked up my daughter.

—She don't want you here, said Jack.

Rebekah shook her head and stared at the ground. She tried to say something, but her voice was gravid with emotion and her throat stoppered. Her father stepped forward when she sniffed but hesitated as Jack moved closer to her. Jack believed this man could knock him down and out and take Rebekah away. Rebekah leaned over her belly and hugged her thighs.

—Rebekah, said her father.

—The best thing for you to do is leave, said Jack.

—Can the girl speak for herself? said her father with a thin smile. Rebekah. Let me take you home, back to your mother's. We'll talk it through.

—Damn it, old man, if you want to take her you'll have to go through me.

She began to rock back and forth, her hair brushing the bare ground where the soles of past children had worn a circular trough. The tattoo on the back of her neck showed starkly. Her father stepped closer and Jack tensed. He felt disoriented, confused, like he had just woken from a strange dream and couldn't sort out reality.

The sound of familiar gurgling mufflers floated across the park, causing him to turn his head. Heber's old Bronco appeared on Main Street and floated by them like a rough beast in a dream. Jack watched it, turned his neck, turned his body until it disappeared behind the church, reappeared, and Rebekah's father watched it as well. Rebekah hadn't seen it. At the silence from the other two she lifted her head and followed their gazes and drew a sharp breath. No one spoke as the Bronco made its way along the road behind the church. It turned again into the parking lot and disappeared beyond the pavilion and the pine trees and then reappeared past the basketball hoops and turned again, one block from completing a full square. They watched it come toward them and park at the curb.

The revenant stepped out of the Bronco in a ragged shirt and pants that looked filthy even from that distance. He looked homeless and a mendicant. When he shut his door Rebekah's father turned back toward his daughter and said, Who's this?

Heber walked up with his hands in his pockets and stopped a

short distance away. He stood regarding them all as though someone had called for him.

—Rafuse, said her father. Ed Rafuse's boy.

—The great Ed Rafuse, said Heber. Looked like trouble from the road. Is there some trouble here?

He looked long at Rebekah.

—You do this to her? said her father. Is that your baby she's carrying?

—It is, said Heber. Yes, it is.

—What's going on here? said her father. Is there not enough to go around?

—You might take one of us alone, said Heber. But there'll be more than enough to go around with the both of us. Do you want to test a man who's got nothing to lose?

—Are you drunk, Rafuse? said her father.

—Sober enough to kick your ass and feel all right about it, said Heber.

Rebekah's father called for her again and she only looked back at him, through him, as if he weren't there. She seemed disconnected from the scene, a ghost on the merry-go-round, or she was real and they were the ghosts. Heber walked close enough to issue the smell of alcohol to all of them.

—This doesn't end well for you, old man, he said. I will sink my teeth into your neck like a goddamned mink and they'll have to pry my dead jaws apart with a shovel.

—You crazy asshole, said her father. It's like some kind of living carnival, this town.

He had Heber in a full nelson before Jack could register his movement. Heber struggled, his hat knocked off, his shirt pulled up and his hairy gut hanging out, and then held still. Jack stepped toward them and her father held Heber in front of him like a shield. Rebekah looked up at her father and focus distilled in her eyes. She lifted her chin.

—Dad, she said. Let him go and leave, or you will never see me again.

A cloud of sadness passed over her father's face and threatened to break. He stared down at the back of Heber's balding head, frowning, then looked at his pregnant daughter where she sat on the worn platform. He released his grip and Heber fell forward and crawled on hands and knees toward his hat. Rebekah and her father looked at one another, and then her father turned and walked to his car.

After he was gone Jack sat down on the merry-go-round. Rebekah could have been a park statuary for her rigidness, an immemorial mother come too early for her enwombed child to play there. Heber moved to the large tree and leaned against its trunk. His hands went into his pockets and for a long time no one spoke.

—You can't be home tonight, said Jack to Rebekah. He looked at Heber.

—I'm here and gone, said Heber. Some unfinished business is all.

Jack felt the dumb blankness on his face, no clear emotion to configure it. Rebekah leaned over her stomach, her dark hair shrouding her face, her forehead resting in her hand. Jack didn't hear Heber walk away but looked up when the door to the Bronco opened and closed. The engine growled to life. He watched Heber move around the block and over to the trailer. Heber parked and got out and shuffled to his door and disappeared inside.

He took her home and delivered her to her mother and drove back to see Heber. The Bronco was gone, the door to the trailer unlocked, and no one inside. He drove around town, to the shed, to the co-op to fill his gas tank, and eventually into the desert where he wandered the dirt roads with some hope that he would find Heber there. He entered three-sided theaters, small box canyons replete with shot up appliances, vehicles, and sundry metal refuse. The desert was empty and this sharpened the need he felt to find Heber until the need took the feel of a spiritual impression and was impossible to think beyond. He didn't believe Heber had come and gone so quickly, gone again to wherever he'd come from. He mazed through the hard landscape until it was no longer a search, and evening found him this way, burning gas, rumbling between heaves of hardened lava and ragged brush. When dusk fell he sought his way out.

He drove to Rebekah's and no one was there. When he reached town it was dark. He parked his truck at the basement apartment and realized he had forsaken his chores. Someone would have fed the cows. The cows would not be denied their evening feed, for it was better to slaughter them all on the spot than to listen to the chorus of their hungry bellows as night fell. He went inside and called her house and sat down at the kitchen table and had nothing to do with himself.

There was a pounding on the door and Maria's voice came through the hollow wood with urgency. He got up from where he'd been sitting, freshly showered but staring yet at the blank kitchen table as though his life played out upon it. He opened the door.

—Heber's at the shed, she said.

He followed her outside under darkness and they turned to see an orange glow from the town square. The siren at the station started. It was loud and unsettling that close, and then he understood what was happening and marveled that he hadn't thought of it before. He got into the passenger side of her car. She drove through the square and they saw Wriglesworth's burning on the corner. The windows were alight from the inside. It would be a tinderbox in there and next would be the barbershop and then the bar. Maria pointed across the square to the old bicycle shop burning at the opposite corner. Flames consumed it from the rear. All four corners of the square were burning. The door at the fire station was still closed, the siren howling above it, none of the men who were the town's volunteer firefighters yet arrived.

—He won't be around here any longer, said Jack.

Maria didn't hear him. She watched the fire as they rolled between old residences, the colors of the houses and their trim bespeaking decades gone by and lit up oddly by the flames. She stopped the car and got out and he followed her as she walked back to the square. They stood at a distance and watched the corners burn, watched other buildings take through the gap of street. The fire built quickly, a steady breeze fanning it and sending it out in what would become a perfect square of flame. Glass broke and tinkled and a dull roar sounded from everywhere. A few had come from their houses on the other side of the street to cry out and watch. In a minute he and Maria stepped back, the heat too great and becoming greater.

—I want to go in there, she said.

She was already walking. Soon she was running parallel with the north side of the square along a back alley, seeking the unburned middle. More people emerged from their homes and stood in the firelight and watched their town burn. Men with houses nearby scrambled to unroll hoses and some were already spraying water on their roofs and hinter buildings.

He caught her when she reached the backside of the square because the fire was too hot and she could go no farther. They returned to the car and drove down the street.

—He's still there, she hissed.

His old beaten vehicle sat unevenly on its wheels ahead of them. When they opened the door and flipped the light on the shed was empty, the restored version of the wreck outside gone.

—The bridge, said Jack.

They took the back way to avoid the square and drove down the dark road. They passed an old Wagoneer racing toward town. He recognized it as Chuck Spackle's, the custodian of the church house and the oldest firefighter on the crew. So that was part of it. But he hadn't even had a chance to try like his father had.

They came to the Bronco parked near the iron bridge. The vehicle was nearly finished, a serene glint of stars on its glass, its vintage appearance throwing them back thirty years. A ruddy moon rose over the mountain and emblazoned upon its dark seas were the shapes of the sparse pines along the ridge. They got out and there was no sound but the breeze. The fire siren did not carry this far.

Maria began to speak but he stopped her with a finger to his lips and pointed out over the dark river. They searched the water. The river was the color of night, the water seeming not to move until detritus or foam floated by, and then slowly. He walked up and down the bridge. He leaned out through the supports and strained his eyes into the darkness. There was movement all over, trees moving in the wind, single-minded creatures in the genesis of their nocturnal prowls. At the bend of the river a dark shape broke the surface of the water. It could have been a bobbing head that emerged or it could have been a river animal, or nothing at all. The shape drifted toward the riverbank where trees grew thickly and a sound like a pleading voice carried across the water, or it could have been laughter. Or it could have been the voice of the river, the tittering water as it eddied and swirled. Maria reached out and touched his arm and he started. Her face was full and calm and her black eyes fixed on him. She looked at him with something like seduction and she was beautiful in the pale light. It seemed impossible not to love Heber anymore, impossible to lose him. The heavens were reflected in the river like an inverse sky, and what was it that made a man want to leap into it, as if he stood on a precipice and instead of the earth below him it was the dark sky with no ground to stop his fall. In the daylight its appeal was innocent, but at night it was a different urge. Above them on the hill he could see the glare of the pole light by which he fed the heifers winter evenings.

—Did you tell anyone else he was back? he said.

She shook her head slowly, her face still tender, her expression transcendent. He had never seen an emotion like the one on her face, and he had no name for it.

He searched the hillside and listened for any sound and heard the wind. The distant growling of an engine somewhere. Downstream something splashed heavily and he broke from Maria and leapt over the gate and sprinted down the path that ran along the river. He ran for a minute and his wind began to fail. He passed through a shroud of trees and into the clearing where they had fished. There were three men standing by the blackened pit and he recognized none of them and kept running. Small hums and whimpers broke from his throat, and his pace slowed. When he rounded the bend he continued past it and leapt off the bank and landed in water. He pressed forward on a submerged sandbar until it fell away from his feet and the cold black current of the river carried him. He swam for the first time in this water and swam heavily for his boots. He strove for a dark shape and when he reached it he grasped at the wet jacket. They went under. They surfaced, their arms on each other and any sounds between them garbled and wet, and together they couldn't float but sank and fought to the surface in bizarre allegory. He found him and lost him, caught him again and they struggled and went under and he choked on water and came up coughing and gagging. His teeth ground dirt. He grabbed at the bulk again but couldn't swim with his boots, or it was the undertow, something pulling him down. The river pulled him under and his world was black and silent and cold, and as he reached and trod through the sluggish dark his arm struck some moveable weight and he broke the surface and gasped for breath. He went down and pulled at his boots until they were off and lunged for the surface again, carried by the water downriver like a dancing bottle all the while. Water filled his mouth and nose. He coughed and struggled, sank beneath and resurfaced. He brawled to stay afloat, and when he could take a great gulp of air with his exhausted strength he rested and let himself go under and everything was blacker than the sky and as soundless. He couldn't find the surface, but shot his limbs out only into the river. It was deep here, the water colder. He was afraid of touching bottom, more afraid of not ever touching bottom. His lungs seizured for air and he believed he would drown. When he had consumed the river and consigned himself to fate a great hand cradled him, lifted him. The branches of a tree held him against the force of the river and he broke the surface and retched the river back into itself. The water pushed against him with a steady weight but he was held sure. He felt hands on him, lifting him up, carrying him to the shore where he was lain on pillows of dry grass. The water drained off him and above him the stars turned slowly.

In some half-consciousness he spoke with Heber and Heber said, She didn't bleed. What do you think of that? She didn't bleed, and then Maria knelt over him. He felt the weight of the river pushing against him still and saw the dead tree, its white branches reaching out into the water, collecting what they could.

—He's drowned, he said.

She said nothing but put her hands on his forehead and his chest like warm stones.

—He's drowned, he said.

She shushed him gently.

—I lost my boots, he said.

She helped him up and they walked back down the path. They reached her car and she took a blanket out of the trunk.

She helped him remove his shirt and she toweled his body and rubbed his head dry. She wrung his shirt out and gave it back to him and he pulled it on. She wrapped the blanket around him again and stood in front of him and he let her into his arms and wrapped the blanket around them both as she wept against his chest and his hand moved over her dark hair. Her tears soaked through his shirt and he felt their warmth on his skin. The wind that came to them was sown with the smell of smoke. The first ashes began to fall.

They saw the light of the flames as soon as they gained the upper road. In town the bulk of the population stood in the streets and watched the fire like a midnight pageant. They had gathered in the light of an unnatural day, their faces bathed in an ocher glow and their countenances full of rapture. Few turned from the blaze to see the two making a slow circle around the side streets in Maria's car. The BMW was parked near an old garage, the flames of the town square reflected on its hood, and Rebekah's father stood alone in what shadow he could find, his face turned upward to the inferno. He wore a tranquil look. Rex Marchant, the town mayor and manager of the co-op, also stood alone watching the fire. They rolled past. They had arrived for the culmination. The flames reached some hundred feet into an orange-lit sky, sending light to the heavens. Fire trucks cluttered the square, shooting water toward the four flaming walls that seemed to entrap them. Departments had come from all over: Hansel, Willow Valley, Clark, Richland and others. Some lined the outer streets and doused the houses with water. An old man Jack had never seen before stood on his front porch in striped pajamas, complete with a night cap and bobble, his whole person lit up by the holocaust of his town.

This was Heber's flame. Flame of Heber himself. It seemed to him then that the town its inanimate self had resisted any hope harbored in the hearts of its people for revival. It had pressed toward a change, giving in to whatever fate of evolution had suaded it in that direction. It had been set for demise the moment it was built and now realized its demise in its consumption, and would now be reborn an altered thing. It had reached a zenith in its immolation, for now it was flames, now it would be ashes, and like a corpse turns to dust so would turn its ashes.

Midsummer. Work had outlasted the daylight and they were tired as they ate hamburger and potatoes. On the television a woman predicted clear skies with no promise of rain for the next ten days. Blair drank his milk from a large plastic cup. He watched the weatherwoman.

—Pond's getting low, he said. We might have enough for the corn if we stop watering other places. And the price of milk is dropped.

—How low? said Jack.

—I've seen it lower. Lyle Tyson is hurting. Told him to come load up his trailer with hay, take it from the east stack. So don't run him off.

—So the bank came through?

—I expect they will, but either way I ain't about to turn away a man in a worse spot than us.

—Is he selling?

—Not yet. He's setting back and waiting for the right price.

Jack grunted.

—When you see farmers waiting to give up their land to anyone but another farmer, you know times is changing, said Blair.

They sat in silence, chewing hamburger and drinking milk. Blair fixed his pale eyes on some faraway place out the window. In the fading light the wrinkles and blemishes on his face were vivid, each whisker like steel and the hair curling from his long red nostrils like the earth turned back to wild. His jaw quivered as he chewed on some small thing he had found with his tongue. He operated like a tired machine anymore, handling the cows he had pulled from the wombs of generations of cows he had outlived, hundreds of them over the years, and how many teats tugged and how many gallons of milk gathered and sold. This dream he had built with Adelaide had become a solid thing even if it was precarious. It was a fixture of the landscape now and it had been built slowly, for in those days dreams were built slowly and firmly and well, and the emotions they spawned were true and pure. Jack had heard it said that when a man is young he looks forward and when he is old he looks back, yet Blair seemed to be still looking forward, beyond the shroud of death. He talked more of seeing her again than he did of their life, bound together as they were by a power not of this earth. But at the table both men were content in the moment, as if they reckoned that what they did out there on the farm was all there was to life. Jack's thoughts moved down the road a half mile while Blair's might have been probing the veil between two worlds for the distance reflected in that gaze.

—Who's buying?

—Hard to tell. For every one who wants to regulate this coming land grab there's two that want to sell out, no questions asked. Folks around here ain't used to money being thrown at um like that. Money's come sniffing around. Don't know yet whose.

—Any for you?

—Not yet. Times was I knew twenty dairy farmers. Knew every one of um and knew their wives and their children. Today I know three others. The cows are gone but people still get their milk. We milk about a hunnerd fifteen at full capacity, these new farms milk thousands. They milk around the clock, never stop. Can you imagine it? Is that farming?

Neither man spoke, and then Blair said, You going?

Jack shook his head.

—Well I suppose I will. For social purposes.

He got up and took his plate to the sink and went into his bedroom. The news anchor on the television was reporting on the aftermath of the Juniper Scrag fire. The channel showed shots taken earlier that day of the ruins still smoking, then switched to a streetside interview with Barb Merrill, a woman who lived a block from the square. She looked bewildered as she answered questions from the anchor. Blair came out with a white shirt on and in suit pants worn shiny on the knees and thighs. He carried his jacket and a tie.

—Help me with this?

Jack rose and took the tie in his hands and stood behind the old man.

—I don't know how these things go, he said.

—Well do something with it. I can't get my fingers to work that way.

Jack messed with the tie, looping it a few times around itself then bringing it through one of the loops. He pulled it tight and it looked like a child's attempt.

Blair left.

There was a time after the reconciliation at his house that Heber had found Rebekah and Jack at the swings when he came out for his nightly sit. Their thick winter blood told them it was warm and Jack was in shirt sleeves and she in a hooded sweatshirt. She sat in the swing and Heber appeared from the trees, wearing a shade of embarrassment on his face at his interruption, but coming forward anyway.

—Small town, he said.

Rebekah rocked back and forth and played her toes in the patch of dirt beneath the swing. The two men stood watching her on either side. She stared at her pivoting toes. Jack leaned back to see the stars. Soon she was swinging and soon she was rushing past him, creating a wind that lifted his hair and brought her smell to him in pulses. For some reason she began to laugh, unrestrained peals of it so clear and bright that he battled to keep from laughing himself. He watched her, and when he heard the slosh of liquid against glass he turned to see Heber slouching there with too many layers of clothing on, a bottle gripped by the neck between his large-knuckled hands, and he had seemed misplaced. They had watched each other between the back and forth flash of the girl.

Heber had remarked once how women bleed in different ways. He said blood from the womb—menstrual blood, virginal blood—was sacrificial. He said blood must be spilt in this way, that this was the way it must be. He had said so much about the river.

Rebekah had rivers inside her.

Jack got up from the table and put his boots on and walked

through the field to the fence where the hill dropped down to the river. The soil was dry and cracked beneath him. The serenity of the river was the serenity of Rebekah. He spread the wires and ducked through the fence and made his way down among the trees. The light inside her poured out like water, as if by carrying this blunder in her belly, by giving it a chance at life, she was elevated to some higher plain of virtue, that her spiritual beauty was not only restored but heightened. Could you have saved him? she said. Did I want to? he said. I don't think I could of even if I wanted to. But did I want to? If I could of, would I of saved him? I don't know, I don't know. I don't know the answer to that. He walked along the river and knew the spot where they had pulled him out, a good distance from the dead tree. How long does a drowned body float before it sinks. The slow current had brought him to this point and here it had left him. Waterlogged, swollen, leaking river and mud from his ears and nose and beard, he had been pulled from the river still wearing his red checked jacket. Jack had watched from the hillside. His old friend, dead, drowned. Dead. Strange raw feelings came with the drowning of that man here at this place, and how long did the river alone carry him. Did he try to swim longer, thinking it through, extending his final moments, or did he try to sink. In the end was it the river or was it him. They had pulled his father out closer to the bridge. He had not made it this far.

19

S HE GREW HEAVY LIKE THE CORN, AND IN THE ARID HEAT of a waning summer, with the breeze pulling at her white skirt and tossing her long dark hair, she walked tenderly in bare feet through the hay field below her house and he walked beside her. He did not carry the baby within him, did not feel it shift itself nor move its limbs. He did not feel its strange clamorings for food nor the satisfaction of quelling them. And from the way she talked about it, not the event nor the circumstance, never those things, only the baby as some entity, some life sharing her body and taking life and sustenance from her, he learned something he wasn't sure she knew herself: she had become more than a carrier, a temporary steward, a harbinger of human life—she had become its mother. And he could not say he understood. Like a woman does not mind the smell of her own excrement she would birth this creation with acceptance and with what tenderness.

She said to him, dangling her sandals from one hand, beautiful in the soft dusk, I feel like you're giving me something I can't equal.

—What do you mean?

—Your support. I don't know what I'm giving back.

—Do you love this baby?

She turned and looked at him.

—What do you expect me to say to that?

—I want to know.

He waited and she said nothing.

—What are you going to do with it once it's out? he said.

—I told you.

—Have you changed your mind?

She kept her head straight forward as she walked and said, I don't know. If I knew it would get a good family it might be easier.

—They find good families for these things.

—Who's going to want a child conceived the way this one was? It would end up in an orphanage. That's not any kind of life.

—Just send it off. Give it to the adoption. They know what to do, and nobody has to know how it happened.

—But they do. They know everything. I could do so much better. It doesn't have to know what it is.

—But you would know, he said.

It was the soft evening light that illuminates the shadows and dims the world like a lamplit room. The golden sun filled the clouds in the west and pushed through in long searching beams. The breeze picked up in gusts. Distant trees waved their great arms and the hay was pushed and sprang back. She stopped suddenly and pulled in breath between her teeth and raised her foot to look at its underside. She cursed, and the word, its literal meaning a thing ubiquitous on the farm and a substance that nurtured this green crop they walked in, a foul matter that marked a man with stain and odor and ultimately an identity in this world, was sweet on her mouth. She raised a hand quickly to her lips as though she could still stop it.

—I stepped on a thistle, she said.

She grimaced and looked at him, her hair lifting and settling on her shoulders. She put her foot down tenderly and the wind pulled her clothes to her body. His eyes traced the shapes of her thighs, the curve of her hips, the shapes of her breasts that pushed against the fabric of her shirt, and the gentle bulge of her stomach.

—Sit down, he said.

She sat in the plush hay and when he lowered himself next to her their heads were just above its swaying crown. The blossoms shone in the sun and he was reminded that this hay should have been cut already. He took her foot in his hands and when she leaned back on her arms and straightened her leg out her skirt flashed up and she laughed and righted it chastely around her legs. He had never seen anything so lovely as this girl blushing from the unintentional compromise of her modesty. He examined her foot, her ankle, her shin and calf, and said, Have you ever broken any bones?

—Never.

Her legs held no bruises, no blemishes. The skin was young and seamless, faint tracks of eczema on its surface like the seas of the moon. With his fingers he picked the thistles from her foot and got all but one. It had gone straight in and broken off flush. He lifted her foot and put it to his mouth and tasted the paste of soil and the green of alfalfa. With his tongue he learned the thistle's location and felt its diminutiveness between his teeth and pulled it out. Wiping his saliva away he held her foot still while she leaned back on her arms, her breasts tilted up, her chin down and her eyes grown intense. He bent and pressed his mouth into the delicate arch of her foot and it fit the bottom of his face. He scratched it with his beard stubble and kissed it and bit the calluses. She giggled. He kissed the plump cushions of her toes. He kissed the slight ball of her ankle, feeling with his lips the thin skin over bone. She pulled her leg back shyly and smiled. Holding her leg in his hands he kissed up the side of her calf, and when he reached the corpulent flesh behind her knee and dared to press his tongue to taste the sweat and oil from the fine wrinkles there her skirt had fallen against her waist and her full thigh caught the light of the sun. He met her clear gaze and some murmur of blood ran through his hands where they held her leg and made his palms and fingers buzz. He took one more kiss from the lowest extremity of her thigh and the summer drew on in a rush.

The wild grass of the mountains whispered loudly and breathed with desert winds. The skies filled with smoke and dusk was a gash of blood in the west. The sun could be watched directly as it lowered, a glowing sphere, almost translucent, into the earth. To look to the mountains at night at the right time was to wonder what pale red monolith was being raised to what primitive demigod, what ruddy horn borne forth from the highest ridge as the cusp of red moon was heaved into the sky. They braced for the dry end of season and watched the pond shrink and the corn slow in growth and fourth crop alfalfa stay low, sere and withered in the sun.

In the morning he pulled the bale wagon into a field that was studded with what would likely be their last crop of hay—third in a place where a fourth was expected—and went among the small rectangular bales to gather them. He ran through the field in high gear, working the lever that was mounted to the wheel well of the tractor and guiding the receptacle around each bale. The teeth took them up and a series of hydraulic tables organized them and stacked them in the hold behind him. When the wagon was full he returned to the barnyard and backed into the hayshed and lifted the stack upright and propped it there with long boards. They had long since placed stacks of hay over the spot of Roydn Woolums's demise.

Returning to the field he watched swallows cruise over the ground erratically and swiftly like day bats. They flew a foot or two above the stubble. When the field was cut they hunted displaced grasshoppers. They navigated the bales deftly, changing their pattern suddenly and with fluid agility. He watched these quiet nimrods fly low over the field, his unacknowledged companions.

The afternoon grew sweltering and still and Blair and Elmer intercepted him and took him along to the cornfield. He walked deep into the crop between the rows and stopped to feel the bulk of the ears or to peel the husks back and look through the silken strands to the crown. Dust burst from beneath the soles of his boots with every footstep. The corn was well taller than he was but should have been taller. Blair had sent him into the corn saying sagely, Go find out. God's way is to squeeze men's souls, crush them to humility and return them to the dust. He can do it easier here in this land, and he does.

A quilted sky formed over the desert in the southwest and moved toward them, over them, but they'd seen this before and gotten nothing but heat from it. Lately he had looked across the desert to see virga falling in purple trails, the moisture evaporating before it touched the ground, and nothing fell on Selvedge land. He was ready to tell Blair to harvest now while the corn still held some green life in its stalks because it wouldn't for long. September rain be damned, he would tell him, if it comes at all. Cut now. Salvage what crop you can. He would tell him this even though they would have already made their decision by the time he returned and would listen to his own verdict only as a considerate formality. The dry corn blades rasped among one another in a building breeze and gossiped about the coming clouds. As he turned to make his long way out something tapped a leaf. He paused and heard more taps around him. A raindrop splashed against the back of his sunburned neck. The dusty leaves began to dance and the sound was the murmur of growth. It rained slowly and steadily through the day and into the night. It rained on the crops and the desert, on the just and the unjust. It rained on the black skeletal ruins of the town square, and the sound of the rain on the earth was also the sound of the communal blessing of relief and gratitude gone up from the toiling men and women who had prayed it there.

Balls Murphy met him at the loading dock. When they had loaded the truck with rolled barley they leaned against the bed and Jack asked him why he wasn't in Amarillo yet. Balls told him he was getting things together. Balls asked if he'd heard from Seth and Jack told him he hadn't.

—Must be getting lonely down there for the little shit, said Jack.

—Oh, he'll be fine. It's the number one state for girls.

—So I've heard.

—When does she have it?

—Supposed to be a couple days before the end of December. But she thinks it'll come early.

—What makes her think that?

—Nothing. She really has no idea. She thinks it's some kind of intuition. She's getting into it, I tell yuh.

—What's she going to do with it?

—I don't know. Was going to give it up for adoption at one point, but we'll see.

—That's a good thing. Though not a soul would of blamed her for the other way. But it's nobler, doing it this way, if you can stand it. It's quite a thing. Got to admire that in another human being. Too much dark business in the world. It's something to see somebody turn it around like that. Made me cry when I heard about it. I truly wept.

Jack looked at the ground and spat.

—Yes, he said. It's quite a thing.

—Makes you wonder what the kid'll be like, don't it?

—It does.

—You ever wonder how a thing that big comes out a hole that small?

—Well, you ever seen a calf come out? That's a lot bigger than a baby.

—But the cow is bigger too.

—That stuff must stretch.

—It must. It's got to. Take a look at the size of a man's pecker, which seems to fit just right, and take a look at the head of a baby. That's why they have to cut um.

—They what? said Jack.

—They'll take a razor blade and cut it bigger.

—Is that right?

—Slit um from hole to hole if they have to. But then the doctor, he stitches her right back up. I think when my woman has a baby I'll have him put a couple extra stitches in there, just for me. Is the thing healthy?

—Well, said Jack, it seems to be, but what can you really tell? Had something with its kidneys once, but that cleared up. It's the way it goes with these things. Anything could go wrong.

—Miracle of life, said Balls. You get lucky if the thing comes out with one clear sex.

—Very lucky.

—What is it? Boy or girl?

—She don't want to find out.

—That son of a whore, said Balls, suddenly wrathful. I wished we could of gotten to him sooner, buddy. Would of saved a number of things, the least of which ain't the town proper itself. I am awful sorry about what happened.

Jack looked up and Balls stared back at him with a wild look. His eyes smoldered in their sockets, searching Jack's own and darting back and forth between them.

—Tell me what you know, said Jack.

—Knowledge is a funny thing, said Balls. Once you know something you can't unknow it. Sometimes it's best to stay ignorant. Sometimes. But I'll tell you one thing. I had to lick Maria's wounds. That girl had bruises and bite marks all over that full body of hers. A hunnerd of um at least. Crazy bastard tried to eat her alive. I wished we could of gotten to him. But God himself has a way of working these things out, don't he. He was just a tad late with this one.

Jack watched him carefully. He had a vision of Heber, naked, moving over Maria's plump body, also naked, like a storm of flesh, taking bites where his mouth led him like lightning striking.

—Speaking of which, said Balls. You seen her old man around?

—No, but I heard he was around again.

—Hard to miss that car.

—You seen him?

—He come by the co-op twice on different occasions. You ever need help with that problem, you let me know. Or if I'm gone Dirt and Wrink are good for it. Couple of good old boys, them two.

—Appreciate it, said Jack.

—And come get your damn camper, said Balls. I'm sick of looking at it.

Jack drove back through the square and pulled over in front of what had been Wriglesworth's and got out. The front of the store had collapsed to reveal a charred interior, fire-gutted and strewn with blackened detritus. The wooden structure had been burned away cleanly and this left three brick walls and a chimney standing, but they were the only things standing, weirdly thin and articulating the inscrutable nature of the ruin. The buildings around him were in various stages of destruction but the fire crews had not saved anything. Some leaned their charred walls against others and some had collapsed entirely and burned like the pile of dry tinder they were. The square had smoked for nearly two weeks, fire trucks lingering about, spraying water, and once everything was cool a bulldozer was brought in. It had pushed the rubble around a little here and there, made a few piles, but sat now in the center of the square on grass dead from the heat that night, waiting for dump trucks and trackhoes to prove their interest. He'd heard that the county would bring in a demolition crew and then subdivide the square for houses, though who would buy the lots or build on them no one could say.

When he got back to the barn Scab Oswald was there. His

truck was brand new, a four-door Dodge dually long as a limousine, and its high-end diesel engine growled through the tailpipes. Blair leaned against the truck with his arms folded over the open window and talked with Scab. Neither man acknowledged Jack as he walked past, and Jack watched his distorted image pass in the shine of the body.

He came upon Elmer sitting on a bale of hay with a heat-red face, sweating and rapidly chewing a piece of hay to mush. Elmer looked up at him with some form of compatriotism that seemed the most earnest glance Jack had ever received from the man.

—What's up, Elmer?

—It's muh heart. Muh heart's acting up. I just had to set down for a minute.

—Well shit. Let's get you in the barn where it's cool. Get you a drink of water.

Jack helped him up and led the way to the barn. Inside he turned the hose on and brought it to where Elmer sat on the folding chair Blair had claimed his by way of adverse possession during his late sedentary months in the barn.

—Drink some water, said Jack. Just set there for a bit. I'll take care of the work.

Elmer bent over and took a drink from the hose, and gasping a little, said, He still here?

—Who?

—Scab.

—He's outside.

Elmer's skin was now mottled pink and white. His pupils had dilated and he took a minute.

—I think you got sunstroke or something, said Jack. You better get in your house. You want me to go get Carrie?

—It ain't that. Oh boy, Jack. He's really done it now.

—What's he done?

—He's sold the farm to Scab.

—Scab Oswald? He's sold the farm to Scab Oswald?

Elmer nodded and set small bewildered eyes on him.

—When did this happen?

—It's done. He told me he was going to set on it awhile cause I wasn't behind it. But then he's just gone and done something in town this morning. Went in to the lawyer's. Oh boy, Jack. Oh boy! Carrie's going to leave me.

—Why in the hell would Scab want it?

The side door opened and they were blasted with sunlight. Blair's worn but sturdy figure filled the frame coronal. When the door closed a slight pulse of headache spread from the rear of Jack's eyeballs through his head. Blair came out of the gloom wearing a grim smile on his face, his head lowered on his thick neck like a bull coming into the chute. He stood before them both and said nothing.

—What have you done? said Jack. Have you sold it outright?

—Oh hell, said Blair. I tell yuh what.

—Oh, Pa, said Elmer. I thought you was going to wait on me for it. Why'd you go and do it this way?

Blair grinned like he'd just eaten manure and enjoyed it. He smiled down on them in tin benevolence.

—The Milky Way, he said. How'd that be? Said it should be called The Milky Way.

—Good Lord, Blair, you've damn near killed your son here.

—Cool it, both of you. You let the king chicken run the show. I got us this far and I'll get us farther. I ain't done nothing that wasn't in the best interest of all parties concerned. I've been in to the lawyer's to see about things. Even deeded the house over right there on the spot. Old Scab thought he might buy the place, sure. Who wouldn't want to? It's a fine farm. But I told him it ain't for sale. So he asked about some land and I sold him the highway piece. Said he thought he'd hold onto it for development someday, let us lease it for crops in the meantime. First year free as part of the deal. He paid cash. You've both gone and got yourselves worked up over nothing now. I aim to give you what I told you I'd give. To Jack Selvedge goes the north field and the mountain and to Elmer Selvedge the remains.

—What about the farmhouse? said Jack.

—Well it's Elmer's on paper, as of this morning. But I don't foresee it being a problem that we stay there. Right, Elmer? Beat the tax man this way, I tell yuh what.

He beamed at the other two.

—The Milky Way, he said. How about that.

He shook his head and grinned. Then he turned and walked out of the barn.

It wasn't a month later and the weather turning cold that Jack came home and found the old man scrubbed cleaner than he'd ever seen him and smelling of some fetid cologne fermented in a dim bottle for untold decades. His gray hair slicked down pat but for the sprung rooster tail in back. He stood at the calendar with a glass of milk in his hand and two old suitcases on the floor beside him.

—The hell you going? said Jack.

Blair took a drink and smacked his lips.

—I'm taking a little trip to the southern part of the state to see about some ancestry. Your grandmother, you know how she loved genealogy in her better days. She wanted me to do this for her before she passed on, but I never did get around to it.

—Who's milking mornings with me?

—Well, I believe Carrie is. But I'm not sure. See, I'm retired now.

—Is that right. Just like that.

—Just like that.

—What are you going to do with yourself?

—You're looking at it.

—Things've turned around that quick?

—I believe they will, said Blair. Sold that land…

He trailed off.

Jack did milk with Carrie the next morning, and every morning after. Elmer stayed in the house recovering from a kidney infection and the next Jack heard from Blair was through a postcard a month after the old man's departure. On the front a smattering of dark-skinned children in school uniforms of green gingham smiling, their white teeth a blatant contrast to their pigment. In the lower right corner it said: Jamaica. Jack sat down at the kitchen table. He turned the card over and read in Blair's ancient hand: Your grandmother would have loved it here. It was signed: Grandpa. Jack checked the postage stamp to confirm its origin. He swore aloud.

20

NOVEMBER. IT HAD NOT STOPPED SNOWING SINCE starting the evening before. After milking nearly four hours alone because Carrie had had enough he took the old snow machine in a warbling racket over the roads and through the middle of the half-gutted crumble of black bones that was the town square. He parked at the gate of the cemetery and broke snow among the silent hills and cold gravestones, under bare winter branches that held thin piles of snow. Six stabs of color drew his eye. He approached the tandem graves of his parents, different dates of birth, same date of expiration, and looked at the bright flowers gathering snow. He reached a warm hand out to brush the snow from the tops of the gravestones. The stone stung his fingertips. Snowflakes fell on his coat sleeve and held their intricate patterns of perfection before vanishing. There was Adelaide's grave beside them, also with flowers. Roydn's grave was not far off and had flowers. He walked over to find that the last two were Tom and Elizabeth McKellar. Footprints led between all these graves and off into an area he couldn't see. The dead lay around him and his toes grew cold. He recalled the image of Blair standing over his wife's body as he let the weight of her death settle upon him, no doubt seeing more in the coffin than others. The smooth full lips of his young bride wrinkled and depleted. The deep lovely hair turned coarse and thin and dead. The smooth clear brow turned pasty, lined, and gray. The ears he had tugged on gently and whispered dreams and promises into loose and hung like deflated flesh balloons. She had been a dream of his, and the farm had been their dream together. And all of his late cunning and foolishness cast the whole thing in a farcical light.

He followed the footprints through a swath of chipped and tilted gravestones. Some years before a drunken man recently bereaved of his wife had driven his pickup through with a heavy, homewelded push bar on front, obliterating gravestones and desecrating the dead until his truck came to rest on a truncated monument. The demolished gravestones had been replaced, but some of those chipped or knocked over had been merely righted according to the wishes and budgets of the survived. As he rounded the curve of the cemetery he saw a lone dot of color behind the falling white. The footprints stopped at this simple stone in the corner lot and then fell away in the direction of the entrance. The flowers were quickly dying at the base of the marker. They shocked the place, broke the serenity, startled the dead. He looked at the footsteps as if he needed to judge the weight, hour, and gender of the visitor.

He followed her tracks to the entrance where the machine sat with snow like thick dust on its seat. He brushed it off with the knuckles of his hand and the snow stopped falling. The racket of the machine broke out over the landscape and he went down the cemetery road, following the footsteps that continued a quarter mile to the highway.

Thanksgiving dinner at the Selvedge's. The smell of the barnyard partly stanched by virtue of the frozen earth and the four of them gathered round a small table. An overcooked turkey lying mis-carved by Elmer's simple hand and the sallow boy resting his chin on the table near a boat of botched gravy. The day overlain by low milk prices and high diesel prices and broken down equipment that could only be fixed on credit they didn't have. Who should come through the door bearing foolish gifts and tin smiles but the great patriarch of the family. That derelict geezer nearly a month gone, that newfound sybarite speaking in an odious counterfeit accent and finding no seat and no plate set for him at the table. Hollering and hooting as if an aged old fool can find rejuvenation in impetuous flight and lingering affection upon his sudden return.

—Couldn't understand a damn thing anybody said, he said. Couldn't find one Holstein on the whole damn island. Couldn't sleep past four in the morning. If I'm up at four I might as well be pulling teat.

Finding that night the farmhouse rented to transient strangers and nowhere to lay his travel-weary head.

They sat at the breakfast table with the television on a few days after Thanksgiving. Blair pushed his plate away and left the table and returned with a sealed envelope and handed it to Jack.

—Where's the other one? said Jack.

Blair sat down, his face somber.

—Can't, he said. I'm very sorry. I can't do it. I'm in terrible pains about it. Some realtors have got a hold of me. There's been interest in that mountain by a company that builds ski hills. They've offered me a sum I can't turn down, and it's the only way to secure the farm against the future. So I'm thinking about another piece for you. Ain't figgered it out yet.

He seemed braced for an explosion. Jack looked down at the deed in his hands, and then he looked out the window.

—I see, he said.

He rose from the table and folded the deed. He tucked it back into the envelope and pressed the flap down. The two exchanged a glance and Jack saw a lifetime of uncertainty in those pale eyes. He nodded to his grandfather and left the room.

On the last day of the month he walked to his truck carrying a sleeping bag and a canvas sack full of clothes, toiletries, and other liveables. He was showered clean from his chores that morning and on his way out of town he understood that seeing her would simply not work, how it was not something he could do. On his way out of town he swung by Balls Murphy's and backed his truck beneath the camper he had purchased and secured it to the bed. He had with him a roll of cash he had taken from the inside of his dusty Sunday shoe, and now he wandered mapless through solitary roads he'd never seen, south and west across the open desert. He was alone on these roads and therefore alone on the earth. His first fill-up had been to get him back, but it had taken him forward.

He passed the northern reaches of the Great Salt Lake twenty miles to his left. He passed loose groups of white cattle and fields of wasted crops, and once a flock of sheep with a lone donkey in their midst as shepherd. When he found himself beyond sight of any house or structure he stopped the truck and got out and walked north toward a mountain range that seemed closer than it was. He walked for what he reckoned was an hour and when it seemed that he had made no progress he turned and walked back. He left pavement and the land he came to lay hammocked between rugged deadlooking mountains beaten by the elements and still wearing under them all these millions of years, filling their own basins with their sloughing. Thin patches of snow on the floor like blown tarps. He drove from range through basin to range and on, always finding another range farther, all of them staggered like a movement of giant slugs across the land. There was nothing but this desert, these solitary mountain ranges, and the occasional despondent ranch.

When night fell he drove into a curtain of darkness. He could see the mountains against the stars like shapes of cut felt and no

light within them. He built a fire and sat near it. There was no working heat in the camper and he had the warmth only of his sleeping
bag as he slept—an old down army-issue that had belonged to his
father. In the night the wind picked up and rocked the camper. He
woke in the darkness and climbed down and out of the camper into
the bitter cold to urinate. As he did he looked across the desert to a
glow above the east mountains like a counterfeit dawn and guessed
it to be Salt Lake City or the vast conurbation to the north and
south of it. He slept in the small area above the cab of his truck and
when he woke from his dreams at dawn to see his breath clouding
against the ceiling he momentarily forgot where he was until he
placed the smell of the camper. He went outside and discovered
the strange world he had wandered into in the darkness, a thick
forest of cedars and a groundwork of sage. Standing next to the
cold fire ring, salted by smoke, dust, and desire, he beheld a silence
so complete that he strained his ears to hear it and heard nothing
but the roar of utter tranquility.

He drove on all that day and into the evening and at night
he lost his sense of direction. He did not know he had passed into
Nevada until he saw a strange little town lit up garishly among dark
stone mountains and a great void beyond. He entered Wendover
and drove between the smattering of casinos and watched loose
gaggles of winter gamblers on the sidewalks. Some turned to see
his truck with the hulking camper in its bed, and when he met their
vacuous stares he felt like some species of wildlife wandered in off
the desert, baffled by the lights and the people, though the people
were few and the place seemed deviant and lonely. He drove south
and rose in elevation and the neon town soon fit into his side mir-
rors. It lay alone in the black night, small and brilliant and hemmed
in on all sides by darkness. When he looked to his mirror again it
had been swallowed by darkness.

He left pavement and after an hour of dirt road he passed
through an empty collection of homes and buildings. This town

had been a settlement of thousands at some point. There was some kind of mill above town, a lone and crumbling yellowbrick building, and an old town proper that spoke to bygone affluence and commerce. One dirt road leading in, two leading out. Empty houses and buildings settled among the hills. He camped near the stone ruins of a pony express station and ate canned stew heated in the fire and took from a loaf of bread. In the morning he had a breakfast of hard beef jerky he found in one of Balls' cupboards and chipped a tooth on it. He drove through the hills and when he reached a portion of the road where a ravine had reclaimed its path in an earlier flood and the road disappeared into a ten-foot wash as if cut with a saw he turned back and found a new way around the hills. As he rounded the eastern edge a vast plain lay to his left, white salt flats stretching some fifty miles to the next mountain that rose like the cataphracted back of a prehistoric monster buried and fossilized in the dirt. He drove a little farther and got out. The sky was turbulent and restless with small storms. As soon as he stepped from his truck he seemed to shed the anxieties that plagued him, the clamor of his thoughts. He stepped from the world inside his truck into a sanctuary of strange color and quietude—the dry yellow of the grass, the gray-green sage, the deep green, almost black, of the junipers, the sound of the breeze. He climbed a nearby hill. When he reached the top he scrambled up a rock formation and sat and sucked on a piece of beef jerky to soften it and looked across the unfinished landscape, its vast clean lines, ranges rising broken through the pan. Again the humming silence, paste colors among the groundwork he had never seen. He could hear the wind move through the grass and the junipers, his own movements when he changed position, and nothing else. He was sickeningly lonely, an abyss inside him, and he drank this emotion like liquor. She had disturbed the landscape of his life in the way he saw the land below him disturbed, had pulled plates apart and cast up rugged stone mountains, and his landscape would be altered now for the eons it took the mountains to crumble and spread their remains to the floors of their valleys, for the land to become smooth and feature-less again. Would the cause of alteration provide the meaning and substance it had promised, or would he be left in a landscape bereft of the agent that changed it, to continue his wanderings as he had before, only now with anguish and knowledge for company? Could he learn to be comfortable in the bleak, barren world that had come to him, or would he despair?

—If nothing fills the land, he said aloud, he must needs despair. Despair.

Then he was in shadow. He looked up to see heavy clouds coming over the mountain separately like a herd of giant white cows, their udders bruised and swollen. He lay backward and watched the purple mass move over him. The storms moved across the basin below and it seemed a private display meant for him alone. The distant mountains turned indigo, the desert floor shaded in a thousand hues of broad color, variations of blues, purples, reds, yellows, ochers, and browns. At some distance across the valley a single cloud dropped her underside to the ground in a vast white pillar and he wondered if the God of All Creation could be in there, if he, John Blair Selvedge, had seen any or the least of these, seen God moving in his majesty and power. And what failed prophet parched and delirious and also within was being revived?

The clouds moved across the land, dropping their undersides and giving to the desert in random selection. He felt a cold drop and looked up to see a wispy pillar descending on him, the cloud above him lowering her great teats. He leaned his head back and opened his mouth and felt the rain, cold, on his face and tongue. It passed and he was in late sunlight, the land below him still in the shadow of storm. He looked over the blue basin beyond the sun-light, rifted with solitary blue mountains. The smell of the sage after the rain was so sharp it stung his nostrils. No more storms came.

He walked stiffly down the slope to his truck and by the

time he reached it the shadow from the mountain covered him and moved across the valley floor. He was very cold. He drove into the mountain a few miles to where he would camp for the night. He changed his clothes and carried his sleeping bag and blankets down into a small draw where he could see the dim basin below. He gathered juniper and sage wood and built a ring of stones. He broke sticks over his knee to size and made fire. The sage wood was pungent and smelled faintly like dung, a pleasant smell. It pleased him to have this small fire in the otherwise consummate dark, to have its warmth in the stinging cold. He raised his head and was surprised to see the stars so bold and infinite. When he got up to climb the hillside to better see them he turned and watched his fire yaw back and forth amid the dark hills, and that pleased him. He reeled like a drunken man under the spectacle above him. Here was a desert not made a garden, a waste place not comforted. Here was a solitary place left alone.

He stayed until he could not stand the cold and then returned and built his fire up again and watched the tiny devils rise and dance into the darkness. A leaning juniper stood nearby and he examined its trunk in the firelight. He remembered that a juniper could live over two thousand years. This one was young and spare. He considered the ordered chaos of the juniper's bark, its purposeful entropy and dishevelment. Shaggy thing. Lovely thing. The tree was wrapped in stringy paper, so unafraid to show its essence that it was disrobing itself.

From across the desert a bright light flashed. He waited and in a moment saw it again, a flash at ground level as bright as lightning. It was impossible to tell how far it was, but he guessed it to be at the foot of that faraway range some thirty miles to the east. In a moment it flashed again, followed by a series of smaller flashes from other lights around it. They ran in a rapid and complex sequence, maybe a dozen lights in all, all flashing in under a second. He watched for them again and saw the brightest light flash once.

At that distance he wondered what kind of light could show that brightly. Once more he saw the sequence and then it fell as dark as the desert around it. He waited and the lights did not flash again. The fire was gone and he was shivering. He listened to a new wind that moved selectively among the junipers, leaving one tree and passing to another, possessing them one at a time like a lone spirit.

In the cold morning he looked across the desert and could see nothing but the open land turned gray. Light snowflakes began to fall around his shoulders and melt on his neck as he sat by his fire. He stayed until the fire was gone and then got in the truck hungry and drove down onto the floor. He joined the road there and went south, passing below a bearded man who sat alone next to a fire on the white bone dust of the mountain, the mouth of a stone canyon yawning behind him. Jack lifted a hand and the man lifted his in return.

He came to a collection of non-native trees and a string of dilapidated homes, most abandoned. Water here, then. Several old wood cabins gaunt and empty-windowed and collapsing. A corral of horses and a few early model camp trailers. Smoke twisted from the chimney of a small clapboard house and he walked through the falling snow to the door and asked a grim-faced, wide-hipped woman in boots and jeans if he could buy some food. She told him to come in and left him standing near the door while she disappeared. The house was clean, rawkept and warm, dim inside for the pulled curtains. A rifle with a scope stood against a log-hewn chair and a fire burned in the hearth. A dwarf of indeterminate age sat in a chair near the fire in a filthy and frayed tuxedo. Were it not for his loud breathing Jack might have thought him a ragged puppet brought in from the corn for the season. The man stared in two directions, one eye staring straight ahead and the other wandering severely to the side. Jack nodded to him and got no response. The beard on his face climbed nearly to his eyes and disappeared in a constant growth down his neck and into his collar. A solid line of drool ran from his mouth, descending down his beard to his jacket where the cloth was crusty white from the habit, and it glistened in the firelight. He had his bare feet tucked under him on the chair, a blackened webbing spread between the toes. Behind his feet a piece of pink skin showed, this his hairless scrotum where it poked through a breach in his pants. The woman came back with a scandal bag filled with canned goods, a grip of twisted meat, some brown eggs, and when he offered her money she held a hand up. He asked her what they did in that town and she said that some of them had been ranchers and some of them hunters, one was a hermit who took wild horses from the desert and one was a shepherd, but the shepherd hadn't been seen since spring when he'd taken his flock into the Deep Creek range, so that made five total left in town and most of those seasonal, meaning the other three. He asked her about the lights he'd seen the night before and she said there were always lights out in the desert but there were no buildings. He looked at the dressed up malkin in the chair and she followed his gaze.

—That's the king, she said.

—The king?

—The king of This Place. He's seen better days.

—Is he all right?

—He likes it there by the fire.

As they watched him the small man began to lean and in a moment he fell from his chair and sprawled out on the floor with a grunt. His hairy backside showed through the eaten rear of his pants and his nates were smeared with feces. The woman went to his side and struggled to right him. She called for Jack's help. As Jack neared the man the smell shocked him and he reeled backwards. The man's breathing became more labored as they lifted him back into his soiled chair. He was heavy as lead. Small groans came from his throat and his wandering eyes held a wild look they had not a minute before.

—Can he walk? said Jack, looking closer now at the webbed

feet, the skin between the toes like that between the thumb and the index finger.

—Not too good. He's got his walking crutches.

She nodded to another corner where miniature steel crutches with arm braces stood.

—He's done shit his pants again, she said. He's in the need of a cleaning. She gave Jack a look of gravity. He was better back before they was all called.

—Who?

—You must of seen all them empty houses around.

—What do you mean, called?

—Have you ever heard of the city of Enoch?

He told her he needed to be on his way and she said it was too cold to be out there without a home. She offered him to stay with her, and when he declined she advised him to take the road south and head for pavement and warmer weather. He did so and made his way parallel to the mountain range on his right, it growing taller until he saw its noble crown rising seven-thousand feet above the desert floor.

At evening he saw smoke rising off the desert pan. He took a dirt track toward it and when he could drive no farther he got out and walked. He came to a series of thermal springs issuing steam into the cold air. An abandoned school bus sat cockeyed, misplaced, and without tires beyond them, its decay proof that all things will return to the elements that formed them. He bent over to feel the temperature, and when he tasted his finger it was salty. He shed his clothes and stepped into the water and sent tiny creatures scuttling along the muddy bottom before him. He shivered as he made for the center where the water rose in gentle swells. There was something sinister about the place the water came from and he distrusted that breach in the earth's crust. The water became too hot and he changed his direction. When he was mid-thigh he crouched and sunk to his shoulders. He let his feet come up and floated. As he wallowed and turned he thought he might gather rocks and dig out a pool, one where he would allow the hot water to mix with the cooler to regulate the temperature. Night fell as he relaxed in the spring and the myriad stars arced in the black dome above him. He thought of her body babyless, trig and firm and unburdened. She would look beautiful in this steam, his new religion, his full investment. He would study the ribbed pink roof of her mouth as she gasped at the stars, suck the warm tongue from her mouth. Her skin fresh and gleaming, he would lick the salt from her pores.

He drove until he crossed a paved highway and continued south on gravel. He was several days wandering dirt roads and visiting ranges and canyons and twice he had to buy gas from desert ranchers in whatever broken settlements he came to. The first rancher was old and friendly. They talked gospel and crops. The rancher told him he had four daughters, three in college and one married with a child. The other rancher was likewise old, and there was a girl came out of a house lined with asbestos tile, twentyish, with a red baby on her hip. It was a mild day for the season and the sun was out. The girl wore bib overalls and a thin shirt too short to reach her waist, and she seemed to have nothing but underwear on beneath them. As she walked up Jack's thoughts drifted from what the rancher was saying about his methods of procuring petrol in such a place to this girl, his apparent daughter. He could see full muscular hips curve and disappear in the denim overalls, though the material moved and shifted with her and farther revealed defined lines where the parts of her went together—leg to hip, abdomen to loins—clear soft skin there, and her breasts were full also, round with milk and spilling from their restraints. The man commanded her to fill the two cans Jack had set on the ground. The girl handed the baby to the man, who took it in his rough hands as he would anything that was not feasible to set down immediately. The girl averted her eyes as she came forward for the cans and took them fifteen yards away to a free-standing tank with a faded smiley face painted on its end. As she leaned over to fill the can her bib pouched out and her breasts hung down like an udder, her ragged brassiere not sized to hold the ample flesh that strained it. Jack let her lug the cans back to his feet, paid the man in cash, and drove away.

He kept his direction by the north-south lay of the mountains but could only go where the dirt roads took him. When he reached pavement again and saw the glow of a city to the southeast he made for it, and when he read the name of the city he was surprised to be only at the bottom of the state. He fueled his truck and ate at a diner before crossing the interstate and driving on.

When he woke in the morning he followed any road that promised to take him south and east. Without a map he zigzagged across state lines and at times found himself going north again, and once west, but then he crossed into New Mexico and saw the first sign for Amarillo. Outside the city he picked up a country station that played the old stuff that every song seemed to speak to him, its words trenchant poetry and its sentiments his own.

He arrived in the city and didn't know what to do. He drove his truck and camper up and down the streets, taking in the stores, restaurants, houses, people. He ate dinner at a steakhouse and ordered the largest steak they had with mashed potatoes and gravy and steamed vegetables and imagined that Seth and Balls could be with him at the table with good conversation and companionship. When he was finished he sat back in his chair and watched the people around him. His waitress could have been in her early thirties. She wore a miniskirt and her sturdy, smooth legs, youthful and of lovely complexion, disappeared into beautiful cowboy boots. He found her slight accent attractive. When she brought him the bill he asked if there were any rodeos in town. She asked if he was a cowboy. He told her his friend was and said where they were from and asked if she knew where he might find him. She laughed and told him there were a hundred thousand people in that town.

—What do you do when you're not coming to Texas to look for your friend? she said.

—I farm.

—Mmm, she said. Her eyes rolled back and her eyelashes fluttered. That's romantic. The warm soil between your toes and God's earth on your hands.

—Everything is done with machines, said Jack. The disc feels the soil, not my hands. And I've never seen a farmer standing in his field with his boots off. Maybe it was like that once, but it ain't like that anymore.

—Maybe we should take our shoes off more often.

—And you'd be the pretty little dairymaid, sitting on a three-legged stool, milking her cow in a pasture. Is that it?

—I could do that.

—Lord, how she must smell.

—What does your friend look like, honey?

Jack gave a description and she said, Well, that looks like him right over there. She nodded to a young man sitting at a table with a woman and a child. Or is he one of those two strangers? She lifted her chin in the direction of two young men who were standing to put their coats on. She smiled.

—You're a long way from home, honey. Don't forget your receipt.

She reached for Jack's face and laid her hand a moment on his whiskered cheek before taking it away in a light touch. She left, and when he looked at his receipt he saw her name and number written at the bottom.

He was there three days before he gave up, uttered dark and opprobrious curses on both Seth and Balls, and wondered at the ignorance of all three of them, their assumption that a man could simply be found in such a city. He purchased food and water and filled his fuel cans and the tanks in his truck and wandered back into New Mexico. He moved due west and planned to enter

Arizona and then go on to California to see the Pacific Ocean, but one evening he was drawn off the highway by the sight of low indigo mountains to the northwest. Their shape against the paling sky was like the edge of a rust-eaten plow disc buried in the soil. He drove toward them until they faded into the darkness and then he pulled over and cooked dinner. With his new supplies he had a frying pan and a sauce pan. He had ice in the icebox and white packaged beef. He had eggs and cheese and salsa. He ate well and did not cease to think about her, pulchritudinous and calm, her beauty fresh as one of these desert dawns.

In the morning he drove toward the mountains, gray now in the rising sun and hazy in the distance. It took him half the day to reach them, rough as the road was, and they grew to be far larger than he had first judged. As he drove he spoke to himself, pausing between thoughts and allowing the next to form.

—I am happy with my life up to this point, he said. It's a strange thing to realize. I keep looking for something I believe I should have and don't, but I don't need it. It's an illusion. I feel it is time for a change. This way can't keep going. But up till now things have been good. I don't know if it's a lasting good, but what is? I have enjoyed it for the good. I am comfortable with who I am and I am hopeful for things. I need her, but I don't need anything else. I've lived a goddamn good life.

He drove around the foothills of the mountains on winding roads and canyon offshoots, through cedar and juniper forests, sage and cacti, for two days, stopping to see about certain rock forma-tions, stooping through sagebrush on spoor he didn't recognize, examining canyons to their ends, the eldritch moon following in parallax as he veered back and forth at night and camped wherever he happened to be.

A fortnight since he had left his home, alone in the desert and growing thin from food rationing. No radio station carried this far. He read scripture he had brought and learned that the words were not yet dead. He sang at night by the fire until he had no songs left and hadn't the heart to start again. His desire for her was enough that he spoke to her aloud, and in his solitude his ravings nearly took the form of prayers to her. He came to better see truth from error and reached the true bottom of things, and these verities settled into his ultimate awareness. His soul was opened to her fully, nothing held back.

In driving he came to a large canyon and climbed upward until the road ended, and there he parked his truck. He hiked up the dry slope with his sleeping bag and reached a high ridgetop at evening where he sat atop a cliff band and watched the sun drizzle and melt into the orange horizon and the desert cool and darken. How far could he see. A hundred miles. Two hundred. This earth that had just been made for all that it was unmolested and pristine. The voice of his father spoke to him as he had spoken in life and Jack spoke back, long dialogue, justification for his actions, explanations of things he did not understand, the working out of complex matters. He spoke to Heber, Heber who had sown and reaped, who had wondered, asking questions and providing the answers Heber would have given. He was consumed by the state of his faith, what it had been, what it was now, and the obscurity of the path between. He looked for things that had been there and was startled to find them gone. Like losing anything, he could remember a time when he had it, but he could not remember the moment he lost it, nor where it was now. If the milestones of his unbelief had ever been definite, they were no longer. Some beliefs had unraveled under honest scrutiny, but it seemed that the beliefs he had not seen fall away were victims of interdependency, where when one falls, more fall by virtue of their connection to the one, and the crumbling goes quickly. And there was nothing he could do to retrieve them. He could not will himself to believe. And while he would not trade his current understanding for ignorant belief, he was saddened to know this reality.

Atop the cliff band he faced the east and watched the stars appear. He felt what he had always known to be true, that only alone could a man clearly reflect on and reckon with who and what he was. Only in isolation, apart from the influence of humankind, could he understand his place and purpose on the earth, his place among a forsaken community. If he could not stand his own thoughts, his own company, or his conscience, which grew clearer and more poignant with seclusion, then he could not live generously among his fellow men. In these mountains he felt the teasings of some immemorial knowledge of the creation of the land, felt privy to a secret he could nearly remember but which ultimately escaped him. *Who hath measured the waters in the hollow of his hand, and meted out heaven with the span, and comprehended the dust of the earth in measure, and weighed the mountains in scales, and the hills in a balance?*

Who?

The threnody of wind carried auguries to his ears and moods to his heart. The mountain around him was visible from lesser suns. Within the new expansion of his soul he missed nearly everyone he had ever known and longed for them each in turn. He leaned back and regarded the Milky Way where it stretched from horizon to horizon like the ruinous wake of a universe long passed by. What was man in the scope of all this? The earth had been here before, and it would remain after. He hunched down into his coat and stayed on the cliff top watching the sky. Far out in the distance he saw a twinkling light on the ground moving north to south, the only human evidence to confirm that he was not some Eveless antipode to Adam in a more desolate Eden. Meteors streaked above him sporadically and within the hour there were so many he couldn't keep his head still. He watched their long trails of burning matter as they stayed lit for full seconds, ephemeral as a man or woman, as a man and woman together, and made simple wishes that he knew could not be granted.

When the sky turned a sudden blue and the entire mountain became like day he thought it was an angel come to visit and was shaken off his perch. From a prone position he looked up to see a streak of light tearing through the atmosphere. It flashed brighter in its fall and seemed to burst, and then it was gone. The sky cracked like thunder and the sound rolled away in a broken rumble. He heard a high whistle which grew louder and changed pitch. Something crashed through a copse of pines below and thumped the ground not three hundred yards from where he lay, and the earth resounded like a drum. A ricochet of the distorted sound came from some unseen stone wall above him. His heart beat hard and fast in his chest. He felt his adrenaline ebb away. He kept his head turned toward where the thing had crashed, his eyes wide, as if something might emerge. When he moved he moved carefully, picking his way slowly along the ridge. He came to the meteorite where it lay in its new crater. It was roughly two feet across at its top and had hit the mountainside dead on and had not skidded nor furrowed the ground but sat cradled in the dirt, parts of it melted from its friction with the atmosphere, the whole thing misshapen and warm and ticking. He took his knife from his belt and poked at its crust to see if it was molten as it looked. The stone popped and he drew his hand back quickly and dropped the knife, but the blade stuck to the stone by some magnetism and did not fall to the ground. He left it there and stood back. Wormwood. He went for his sleeping bag and smoothed out a place next to the stone and fell asleep with its fading warmth on his face.

It took him two days and no end of improvised ingenuity to get the meteorite down the mountain. He had no tools to work with but a small foldable handpick-spade, a tow strap, and an axe. He dug the crater away on the downhill side. He searched the mountainside for a sturdy stick and, cutting one from a tree, used it as a lever to dislodge the stone. When he came to a slope steep enough he tried to pull it like a human mule with the tow strap around his waist. Where the mountain was steeper he started it rolling with the stick, end over lopsided end, until it took off on its own, tumbling roughly through trees and bushes, breaking some trees and smashing lesser stones to pieces, and once taking short flight before truncating a pinyon twelve inches in diameter. By the time it came to rest at the bottom of the canyon he had forgotten which day it was.

The sun was just warm and the nights were very cold. All the mountain was quiet and empty. He negotiated stones, trees, and sagebrush and backed his truck up to the rock and pulled it with the tow strap hooked to the hitch, digging a furrow behind him, to the valley floor. From there he dragged it along the dirt road like a stubborn pet and contrived ways to get it into the back of the camper. The tow strap broke on the first afternoon, and though he tried to tie its frayed ends together, it proved unusable.

He began to ration his water. By morning he struggled with the stone to no avail and by evening he ate his scant dinner and studied the stone from where he sat in the doorway of his camper.

If he were to perish out here, no matter, he carried the center of the universe with him. He was the center.

He gathered other stones from the sides of the road and carried them toward the meteorite until he could lift them above his head and drop them in hopes of breaking it open, but the meteorite only rang like a church bell each time it was hit. It had been at least three days since the strap broke and still he didn't move his truck from that spot. He ran out of food the next day and didn't realize it until that night, and when he did it seemed of little consequence. At the end of the day following he was weak and his water was gone. He lay by the meteorite in the road and stared at it sideways. He was uncertain how long he lay there, but night came on dark and too soon. He must have slept because he dreamt he was being strangled by unseen hands and he woke tearing at the collar of his coat. When he rose stiff and cold and entered his camper dizzy and disheveled he believed without having any way to tell that it was the twenty-first of December, and he retired to his bed and slept until he woke curled up in hunger pains and could not get back to sleep. He dressed and shuffled through the gravel of the road toward the dark shape.

The stone blocked the way he had come. His Ebenezer. Heaven's pale, trembling gaze upon it. He sat on the stone and tried to purge himself by weeping, like a man trying without success to vomit. When he could not weep he sat in his coat and shook with cold. Dawn spread pale blue over the cold eastern rim with a water-fresh beauty. The stars were disappearing across the expanse, the firmament held between two worlds, one that would become near, flat, and blue within minutes, and the other always endless and only seen when the sun was gone. He shivered in his coat. He walked away from the stone until his boots stood on dirt that cracked and crumbled to dust beneath his heels. He walked out and picked his way around desert brush until the ground declined slightly in a shallow ravine, then crossed and climbed the other side. There was sage here but it was sparse and small. Patches of bunchgrass and thorned bushes scattered over the rolling land.

Beneath him the earth spun, and behind him the sun rushed unseen toward its emergence. He stood in the middle of a large patch of bare dirt and breathed deeply the cold air of the desert. His mouth was dry. His ears burned. His hands stung when he left them out of his pockets. He closed his eyes for a moment and the heavy lids stayed down. He felt that any minute he could be touched by warmth and stop shivering. He remembered the time he saw her in that first fey vision and he'd felt his soul tremble. He thought of her darkness and her eyes full of pain. He thought of the ruin of her, the renewal of her.

When he opened his eyes he faced the dim northwest, the direction from which he had come in the beginning, and where home lay, and the whole landscape was bathed in red. He turned to face the east and the sun was like blood spilling through milk. The last stars departed to dawn and the world diminished all around him. It didn't feel right to leave this rock. It hadn't felt right to stay in Juniper Scrag. The edge of the sun broke over the low distant mountains and the shadows of pebbles and bunchgrass stretched across the dirt far taller than they were in truth. True light touched the tops of the near hills. He had rarely had occasion to watch the sun rise, though he'd been awake for the better part of them throughout his life, held inside the barn in deferential supplication to the udders as the sun came to do its own daily work. Blair would be milking, even at that moment.

He got off the rock and made his way to his truck and camper. He wouldn't know what day it was until he could find a town, but he believed the child had been born. He regarded one last time the serpentine trench made by the dragged stone and then the stone itself. He touched it and then he climbed in his truck and wandered out on dirt roads directionless, the sun a weldflame in the cobalt sky. It arced south on its short route and had begun to curve around to the west when he came to pavement. He climbed onto the highway and its smoothness seemed strange, the rumble of gravel under his wheels a missing sound.

When night fell he found a town built lengthwise along the highway and stopped at a gas station where lighted tractor trailers sat in the parking lot rumbling side by side. He walked inside slovenbearded and bewildered by the people who seemed to be living their lives as they always had. He found a booth at the end of the diner and sat large-eyed and starving, unsure whether he should approach the waitress or whether she would come to him. She brought him a menu and he ordered steak and potatoes without opening it. When she came back with his food he asked her what day it was and she told him and he realized he had misjudged the time and was late. He ate his food as slowly as he could given his hunger and could eat only a third of it. When he paid he asked for change in quarters. He walked to a row of payphones and huddled in front of one and dropped coins in. Martha's voice came on the answering machine. He deposited other coins and dialed again and let the phone in the barn ring a long time before Blair's gruff voice came curious on the line.

—It's me, he said. His breath clouded as he spoke.

Blair held forth and then said in a quiet voice, Well I'll be damned, you dumb restless son of a bitch. Where in the name of hell are yuh?

—I don't know.

—Boy, you've no idea what you've done.

He could hear the workings of the barn through the receiver, the faint whine of country music coming from the radio.

—You've broke that poor girl's heart, said Blair, and you'll never find anothern better.

—Did she have it yet?

Blair didn't answer.

—Did she?

—Your dad'd be ashamed of what you done.

—Get me the number to the hospital.

—Well I ain't got it. What do you think, I got the yellow pages right here in front of me?

—There's a phonebook in the office. Bottom drawer on the left.

Blair cursed. The phone dropped and tapped against the block wall and Jack identified the song playing over the distance.

Blair came back and gave the number and Jack hung up. He stood and waited, shivering, his tired body resting against the booth as truckers walked around him to their light-lined rigs and climbed them to sleep for the night. His truck and camper on the far edge of the lot looked absurd this far from home. It seemed there was nowhere on earth he could be. Curious how he missed the farm even now, how he longed for its familiar feel and worn routine. For the first time in his memory he could not smell the barn on him. He was clean. He smelled instead of cold dust and smoke, the scent of his new occupation as desert wanderer.

After being routed through the hospital the phone was on its final set of rings. His blood beat a hot tattoo against his skin. She picked up and spoke in a sleep-filled voice.

—Where are you? she said.

—New Mexico, I think.

There was a long silence.

—It's a girl, she said. She has dark hair and big dark eyes.

—So she looks like you.

—That's what everyone says.

—Of course.

He waited and listened to her breathing and to what she did not have to say but what he felt from her as if they were next to each other. So it was Abigail then. There had been no name if it were a boy. He was sure it was going to be a boy, but it was a girl and the girl's mother was crying.

—I'm coming back, he said.

He watched people move around him, watched the long trucks like sleeping caterpillars in rows. The ensuing silence was filled with a new mother's grief. The baby had emerged frank breech, late, she said, with a grotesque snake wrapped around her neck three times. As she dropped the snake tightened. The baby was dying. She told him her father had been there and that he would be back.

He bought a map from inside. He asked a passing stranger where he was and traced what looked like the straightest route home. He drove all night sleep deprived and delirious. He slapped himself and rolled down the window for the freezing air. The distance seemed too great, the mantle he had built for himself of the great stretch of north-south Utah with its strange desert highways too much to shoulder. He thought of the child as he drove and he felt a startling warmth at its birth, its fragile life.

It was unclear whether his father's journaled questions pre-saged his own wrestle with them as mere antecedent, or whether they were cause for his inheritance, but he was now set adrift. While living, his father had maintained that this mortal battle of good and evil was terribly real, that its stakes were more dire and truer than realized. That this was a terrible contest, the outcome of which was not at all certain. It is possible, he said, for God to lose this battle. And in some ways he's already lost it. Despite his father's careful study of holy writ, the theology of his professed religion and others, and the world around him, he had never claimed to know God, had never justified the ways of God to man to his satisfaction. He was set free to his own devices, self-governing, for he saw in himself sufficient for his needs. A manipulated reliance on God did not suit him. An independent man, he had withheld obedience to any authority incongruent with his own conscience and had distrusted anyone who sought place between him and God, querying: Of what use is a hierarchy of authority if a man has a conscience and the sense to use it?

As he drove Jack reasoned that if the Lord was in control the way many claimed then he was necessarily in the evil of the world—the evil actions of men and women, physical and mental deformity, natural disasters that swept hoards of his living creations from this earth in pure senseless fashion. He was in violence, meanness, cru-elty, in destruction, injustice, and inequality. He was the cause of utter sorrow and despair, as if these things would work somehow to his name's glory. He was in the hand that tied the knots that kept the little girl bound in her basement for a year and a half on oatmeal and water, bone-gaunt, her skin like an empty tent and she vacant-eyed and ruined. He was in the grown hand that fondled the child's genitals. He was in the wind that blew the barn over and crushed the father of three. He was in that tremendous scene when the baler's son came to spell his father for the evening and found Him, his other Father, instead. But if he were less orchestrator and more limited and anxious observer then a man was to understand that the events of the world were not his doing but were the product and consequence of a creation set loose. His method was one of mere persuasion this way, not coercion, and this method by its nature was limited in its efficacy. He wasn't in the baler nor his the hand that took the old man by the scruff of his shirt and twisted until he couldn't breathe, until he must have thought—By God, this is the way it will be then. By God! and grinned in terrific death as his face turned blue. This was God as troubled creator, divine though imperfect, this afflicted sphere of curious workmanship and intricacy the best glory he could muster. And when his fingers did not loosen the cord of life as it tightened around the infant's neck it was not in restraint, to answer the prayer of his son at the cost of failing to honor the prayer of his daughter, and it was no more a dearth of his love than was the mother's inability to birth the child whole. And whom could the child worship otherwise?

He reached her hospital room the next morning. She was dressed in regular clothes and the television was on, though she wasn't watching it, and she looked ready to leave with the bundle she carried. She began fresh weeping when he entered and he didn't touch her. She told him they had let her hold the baby. It was no one's fault, she said. He sat beside her in silence and waited with her. She whispered things to the bundle. She rocked it in her arms. She told him that the baby had cried only once, a small cry, an unexpected cry, and had surprised them all. She gave a strange smile and her eyes flashed at him through large tears that dropped quickly and abundantly. Her dark hair curtained the infant, her tears the first true moisture it had encountered since being delivered from the womb in a marred advent, this primordial symbol, an emblem of the meridian of time, mother and infant, its form corrupted here but nonetheless holy, a marvel seemingly common only for its abundance and generosity. It was a seed misplanted, missown, and that this small thing should come from it was a wonder. It had stopped her blood and would not drink her milk, *and so who would drink her milk, would he?* She held it and wept, rocked it and wept, how long after it had turned to dust in her arms.

Epilogue

HIS TRUCK WAS STILL DUSTY AND HAGGARD WHEN they climbed into it, the camper in the bed like the veteran shell of a desert insect. The plan they had laid out with Martha was not to Martha's liking, but the nerve-ragged and spent woman realized she had no choice. He would drive Rebekah to Arizona where she had relatives that had offered her to stay with them, she would enroll in the university there and finish her studies, but what would become of him after he delivered her no one knew, not even he. His hope in this, as in so many other things, lay in uncertainty.

His hope was different from belief, from faith. He hoped things were true, or would be, but that was different from believing they were or would be. Hope was an element more enduring, and it alone could remain. He hoped and nothing more. Perhaps this was all the disenfranchised had, this hope. They no longer claimed belief with assurance—they couldn't. And did this make them any less worthy of a good life and of truth? Hope was his faith, his religion. It was the consequential vestige of maturity, of knowledge, a remnant product of adult sin. In the end they had nothing more than a hope commensurate with their fear, and in this way they were purified and set free. They drove past the deflagrated ruins of the town square. Three small children stood from the black waste and watched them go with solemn eyes, charcoal smears on their fair cheeks. He didn't recognize them. He drove south, out of town, into the open desert, and she buried her face in his neck, the cold point of her nose pressing into his skin. She wept slowly and silently. In the aftermath of the birth, its issue demised, she seemed incomplete, not whole, and he was amazed to realize it. The dashboard held a thick layer of dust it had collected from weeks in the desert, the dust he had gone out to get and had carried back with him. Her face over the past few days had been ever tired, ever beautiful, but it was now hidden on his flannel shoulder and her soundless weeping was like wide water without sound, like the wide land without sound, and he didn't know how long it went on. Sometime later she pulled upright and brushed her hair back with her fingers and gathered herself. When she looked at him her eyes were sad and lovely and deep.

Early evening they stopped and he leaned on the truck and watched the sun fill the clouds that built in the west above the mountains. They were alone. She emerged from a small restroom and came toward him. The sun fell through broken clouds and colored her in gold. She took the wheel and they drove on. He woke later with a jolt, in the midst of some dream where she was not with him. She had said something to him. They had come into a land of red stone. Red dirt and red stone the reddest he'd ever seen, hard to believe he wasn't still dreaming. Huge walls of crimson ran through with black tailings. Monoliths of a war god. A land without people. She gazed past him to the west where the sun smoldered in the evening clouds, and the red desert filled her eyes. She peered into the ruddy landscape mesmerized. There was fear in the desert, fear in his soul, fear in the sinking of the sun. He turned to watch the horizon as the sun bled itself out over the ancient mountains and sent its arms through the clouds and charged the landscape with a deeper radiance. The earth glowed as though it harbored an inner fire of its own, as though it were about to be reborn. For the first time in his life he acknowledged that his own death waited somewhere, hers also, that their deaths approached them from unknown distances, coming as the beams of the sun came to them now, coming to them across the blood-red sand of the desert as they moved together toward the dim roar at the edge of the earth.

Braden Hepner

An Iowa Writers' Workshop graduate, Braden Hepner lives in Idaho with his wife and son. This is his first novel.

Torrey House Press

The economy is a wholly owned subsidiary of the environment, not the other way around.
—Senator Gaylord Nelson, founder of Earth Day

Love of the land inspires Torrey House Press and the books we publish. From literature and the environment and Western Lit to topical nonfiction about land related issues and ideas, we strive to increase appreciation for the importance of natural landscape through the power of pen and story. Through our *2% to the West* program, Torrey House Press donates two percent of sales to not-for-profit environmental organizations and funds a scholarship for up-and-coming writers at colleges throughout the West.

Visit **www.torreyhouse.com** for reading group discussion guides, author interviews, and more.